Next to You

Next to You

A Novel

Hannah Bonam-Young

DELL

NEW YORK

2024 Dell Trade Paperback Edition

Copyright © 2022 by Hannah Bonam-Young

Excerpt from *Out on a Limb* by Hannah Bonam-Young copyright © 2023 by Hannah Bonam-Young

Published in the United States by Dell, an imprint of Random House, a division of Penguin Random House LLC, New York.

DELL and the D colophon are registered trademarks of Penguin Random House LLC.

Originally self-published in the United States by the author in 2022.

Library of Congress Cataloging-in-Publication Data
Names: Bonam-Young, Hannah, author.
Title: Next to you: a novel / Hannah Bonam-Young.
Description: Dell trade paperback edition. | New York: Dell Books, 2024.
Identifiers: LCCN 2023040325 (print) | LCCN 2023040326 (ebook) |
ISBN 9780593872123 (trade paperback) | ISBN 9781778027734 (ebook)
Subjects: LCGFT: Queer fiction. | Novels.
Classification: LCC PR9199.4.B6555 N49 2024 (print) |
LCC PR9199.4.B6555 (ebook) | DDC 823/.92—dc23/eng/20230907
LC record available at https://lccn.loc.gov/2023040325
LC ebook record available at https://lccn.loc.gov/2023040326

Printed in the United States of America on acid-free paper

randomhousebooks.com

2 4 6 8 9 7 5 3 1

Book design by Jo Anne Metsch

This one is for all of us criers. For the ones who seem to feel nothing or everything all at once. For anyone who's trying to build a life where constant distraction doesn't feel so necessary.

And, for my grandmother, Lorraine, who taught me the best stories don't require an audience.

AUTHOR'S NOTE

Dear reader,

> "He who has felt the deepest grief is best able to experience supreme happiness."
>
> — *The Count of Monte Cristo* BY ALEXANDRE DUMAS

Next To You is, ultimately, about finding happiness after loss. Therefore, please be aware that grief is a constant theme throughout the book. I know that it can be difficult to read about losing a loved one when you've experienced it yourself, but it's my hope that you may find it healing, if you do choose to proceed.

Content Warnings:
- Sudden death of a parent
- Fatal car accident
- PTSD, anxiety symptoms and treatments, and descriptions of agoraphobia
- Multiple, descriptive sex scenes
- Infertility (mentioned only in epilogue)

All my love,

HANNAH BONAM-YOUNG

Next to You

PROLOGUE

ONE HOUR UNTIL I CAN LEAVE. WELL, MAYBE ONE HOUR and three minutes, so as not to appear rude. Midnight is the minimum expectation at a New Year's Eve party, after all. But the time beyond that is all mine.

Chloe's apartment throbs with the bass from a stereo that should be called "neighbor's nightmare." That's what I'd market it as. I can see the design I'd make for the ad if I shut my eyes.

The music playing is unfamiliar, but the playlist I threw together this morning was hoisted off the auxiliary cord around ten. The TV and speakers have been playing *Rockin' New Year's* something-or-other live from New York ever since—and right now, it's a DJ who's pumping up the crowd, saying we're about to have the best year *ever*.

Yeah, right.

I steal two bobby pins from Chloe and Warren's bathroom cabinet and pin my bangs out of my face. The purple hue of my hair is beginning to fade at the roots, revealing a pale brown. I canceled my hair appointment a few weeks back for the third time in a row. It always seemed too big a chore. Too far from home. The only place I want to be these days.

I'd hide out in the bathroom forever, but there's only one in the apartment, and I'm sure by now there's a line forming at the door. All the other guests are probably wondering if I'm taking a massive shit. *Nope*. That smell, dear friends, is the scent of fear.

My piles of self-help books would suggest I ought to evaluate. *Get to the root of the issue,* they'd say. But I can't be bothered. *Let the fear live,* I proclaim! It's what's kept the human species alive. Survival of the fittest, baby! Perhaps I'm a *little* drunk.

I step—and almost fall—out of the bathroom into an unexpectedly empty hallway. Chloe and Warren's friends have impressive bladders. Speaking of, when did they even acquire this many friends? There have to be twenty people crammed into the apartment Chloe, our other best friend Emily, and I used to share while in university.

Life was simpler then. When all I had to do was complete homework and assignments from the safety of my room, occasionally coming out for air and food. It's expected of university students to be shut-ins. Hermits. Recluses. Homebodies. All words that are affectionately used until you reach a certain age. Or meet a certain doctor. Then it's "agoraphobia."

Agoraphobia . . . I always thought it sounded like a fake country from a Disney movie, like *Genovia*.

"Prin*cess* of Genovia," I say to no one in particular as I reach into the fridge for another vodka cooler. My fifth, if you're counting. Which I am not.

"Pardon?" a soft, deep voice asks as I shut the door.

I turn to walk toward the loft's spiral staircase, hoping to find a private perch away from the other guests. Like a nosy owl.

"Guess not," the same low voice says from behind me, hitting me in the gut. I turn to find the source.

Familiar dude. Handsome. And we've definitely met before. I think he's Warren's friend or co-worker. Basic name . . . Steve. *No.* John. *Nope.* Kevin?

"Matt." He points to his chest, wearing a quizzical expression with one raised brow. He's got a warm, welcoming smile, like he's hearing one long joke—but not at your expense. His light brown eyes have a certain kindness to them that puts me instantly at ease. His dark beard isn't particularly tidy, but it's full and fluffy-looking. His nose is ragged, like it's been carved out of rock, and his hair is longer than mine, thrown haphazardly into a bun on top of his head.

And, *goodness me,* his lips. I could curl up on them with a good book.

"I'm Lane." I raise my bottle to him before turning to take three steps up. I fumble back onto the stairs, my palm finding the step just before my butt does. The cool metal touches bare skin a fraction below my underwear, eliciting panic that I've flashed my backside to everyone below the stairs. I reach under my bum to tuck the black fleece skirt under me and tug it farther down my thighs, keeping my knees tightly pressed together. My black turtleneck shirt is new and itchy around my throat. I have to actively fight to stop myself from adjusting it every few seconds. This outfit is cute but not conducive to settling nerves.

"I know, Lane. We've met. . . ." He smirks into the top of his beer as he takes a sip. His lips look even better that way. "Here alone?" He asks this as if he is an adult who's found a lost child. *Your mommy around, sweetie? Let's go find her.*

"Alone," I confirm. "And you, Matthew?" Surely a guy with silky black hair, full lips, and a strong dad bod is here with someone. Guys like him are *everyone's* type.

He huffs out a quick laugh. "Yeah, me too."

Ah, well, he must be deeply flawed then. *Just your type,* my inner saboteur hums. *Shut up,* I quip back. *So why is he talking to me and not someone else?*

"Is it me, or does everyone at this party seem to know everyone else at this party?" I sigh, looking down at the large group of people strewn about the apartment below.

"I'd have thought you'd know most people here, being Chloe's best friend." Matt takes another sip of his beer.

"Mmm, but you see, Matthew, I do not venture out much." *Ever.*

"Introvert?" he asks, standing at the bottom step, a firm grip on the metal railing.

I bite the skin around my thumb just once before I remember I'm no longer alone and that habit isn't the slightest bit attractive. I let out a nervous laugh, placing both hands around my cup. "No, actually. I'm an anxious extrovert. We are a rare but not extinct breed."

Matt nods, his eyes narrowing, causing happy, wavy crinkles on the outer corners. "I didn't know there were others. I've been living underground."

"Aw, well, we do like to hide." I chug my drink and stand to fetch another.

"You know what's great? Ice water," Matt adds as I sidestep him and make my way toward the fridge. "Have you had some today?" His voice is cautious, like he's approaching a street cat. "Can I get you some?"

I nod, grinning ear to ear as I look up at the curl that looks like an upside-down question mark resting on his remarkably tanned forehead. "D'you work outside, Matt?"

"I work with Warren." He takes my glass and places it on the counter, turning his back to me.

"I do not understand the mechanics of mechanics."

Matt looks at me over his shoulder, not laughing but obviously amused—a small tug at his lips and inquiry in his eye.

"I work inside the shop mostly." He uses tongs to place a few cubes of ice in my glass before pouring water from the tap. *Tap water?* My mother is somewhere clutching her pearls.

"But you're so tan . . ."

"Built-in skin tone." He hands me a full glass of water, and I take it with two hands, trusting neither to do their job alone in my inebriated state. "My mom's Samoan," he adds.

You dumbass. Why'd you ask such a stupid—

"Got any straws back there, barkeep?" I ask, hoping to swiftly move past my blunder.

With a smile and a less-than-sincere eye roll, he turns and grabs a straw off the counter and drops it into my cup.

"Thank you, Matthew." I bow slightly, trying to capture the straw with my tongue as it dodges me and spins around the rim.

"It's Mattheus." He chuckles under his breath, scratching where his cheek meets beard.

"Huh?" I turn and walk back to the stairs.

"You keep calling me Matthew . . . but Matt is short for Mattheus," he says, following close behind.

"Oh, sorry." I sit down, careful not to spill my water.

"Don't be." He gestures to the stair below mine, a question in his rich honey-colored eyes.

"Have at it." I signal to the step with a flourish.

"Is Lane your full name?" he asks, lowering in front of me. His body is so broad all over that he barely fits on the step, so he sort of hovers, balancing himself against the railing.

"Elaine," I answer. "But I've never suited *Elaine*. Maybe I should try it. New year, new identity." I push up an invisible pair of glasses up the bridge of my nose. "Hello," I say in a hoity-toity accent. "I'm Elaine . . . the third. Charmed." I hold out a limp wrist that he shakes lightly, his lips curled between his teeth.

Matt's laugh seems to burst out of him. It's deep and full and shocking. I focus on how his throat bobs while he does it and the way his lips part. *Cute.*

"Wow, uh . . . thanks," he replies, looking down between us with a subtle, pleased grin.

I said "cute" out loud, apparently. He studies me and then looks off to the crowd, glancing side to side. Still trying to find my keeper, I think.

There's an ease to him in total juxtaposition to the liquid energy that seems to be rushing through his veins. No part of his body appears to stay still for long—a knee bouncing or a foot tapping. But the smile that's yet to fully fade has a calming effect. I wish I could bottle it like a perfume. I could use a few spritzes throughout my day when my brain won't cooperate.

I'm still staring at him, with no words being said. I don't even think I'm smiling, just blankly looking at him like art in a gallery. Yet he doesn't look uncomfortable. He just looks about the room, his gaze landing nowhere in particular.

Attempting to look away from him feels like swimming against a current. I start up the conversation again so I don't have to. "Any New Year's resolutions?"

He turns back toward me slowly, his shoulders raising and tensing a little. His eyes shift from side to side for a moment, then he shrugs. "Not really. I'd like the shop to do well."

Right! This is Warren's friend who will be running the shop with him when their burly boss guy retires. That is soon, I think. "When do you and Warren take over?"

"My uncle Ram retires at the end of January, then it's all ours." His jaw tics as he throws back his beer. He blinks a few times too. He's either nervous about this takeover, or I'm far more drunk than I thought and misreading him entirely.

"You worried?" I ask.

"Little bit," he replies with a dim smile. "What about you?"

"Constantly." I blow out a breath, trilling my lips.

"I meant, any New Year's resolutions?" he asks, voice sincere.

"I—uh." *Where to begin?* "This year hasn't been my best. There's . . . a lot to improve on."

He pouts his lips but stills, waiting for me to go on.

"I'd like to start by being a better daughter," I offer plainly, but I'm not sure—even if I was sober right now—that I could stop the emotion tensing my expression. "My mom has stopped asking me for things. I'd like her to ask again."

"What sorts of things?" he asks.

"She's on a board for this charity, and they have a gala every year. I used to do the designs for it—invitations, posters, stuff like that. Now? She hires out. She doesn't want to ask me."

This change only happened about eight months ago, directly after a phone call with my sister. I mentioned, in passing, that I was going to the pharmacy to pick up my anxiety meds. Since then, it's been near silence from my mom. Fewer phone calls, texts, requests, and questions. Instead, I get care packages in the mail. Bath bombs with lavender, an oil diffuser, self-help books, a weighted blanket, Sleepytime tea . . . you get the idea. Like get-rich-quick schemes but for fixing mental illness.

Matt nods thoughtfully, slowly. It spurs me on.

"I'd also like to call my sister more. She isn't much of a texter, but she gives in because I hate talking on the phone, but that's not fair." I rub the back of my neck. "I miss her," I nearly whisper.

"That's a good one. I'm stealing that," Matt says.

"You have a sister?" I ask.

"I have five sisters." He lowers his emptied bottle from his face and watches me with a knowing smile.

"Five?" My lips part into a wide *O.* "You have *five* sisters?"

"And three brothers," he adds, grinning.

I slam my drink down beside me and bring two hands in front

of my face, raising five fingers on one hand and three on the other, then adding one for Matt. "Nine of you?" My voice is quickly approaching a pitch only audible to dogs.

"Nine."

"Your poor mother!" I laugh, and so does he. Thank god— I hoped I hadn't sounded rude. "That's a lot of phone calls," I add.

"Well, I guess I'll call my parents more, then," Matt replies. "What else is on your list?"

"I'd like to take my job more seriously. I'm . . . not the best employee. I show up late, I call in sick when I'm not. . . ." *Technically.* "I do the bare minimum."

"I'm sure that's not true."

"That's sweet—but it is. I started over a year ago, and the person I trained last spring just got a promotion to be my supervisor. It's a tech company, and people bounce around. There's lots of room for upward growth—if you're trying." I mime climbing a ladder and falling to my death, and Matt watches me with a subtle smile. I should be embarrassed, but I'm not. The alcohol is working.

The television in the living room catches my attention as the presenter begins speaking over cheering crowds. "We are just ten minutes shy of midnight, and what an incredible night it has been. . . ." My focus falls to the ice in my cup, and I stop listening, watching the ice cubes dance around one another until my brain goes quiet.

"You okay?" Matt asks, leaning into my view to catch my eyes.

"Hmm? Yeah." I smile weakly.

He sits back and looks across the room to where Chloe and Warren stand near Emily and her boyfriend, Amos. They're all laughing, except for Warren, who shakes his head and smiles into the top of his glass.

"They seem happy," Matt says, petting his beard absently.

"They do," I answer, my voice not hiding the jealousy that creates an ache in my throat.

It's not that I'm not happy for Chloe, I am—she deserves the world. All I could want for any of my friends is a guy like Warren. He worships the ground she walks on and lets her shine, unafraid of being in the shadows. Emily deserves it too. She and Amos have only been together a few months, but they make a gorgeous couple. Stylish, tall, and equally striking, they get a lot of head-turns walking down the street. I know this because I'm usually trailing behind them, cementing my third-wheel status.

"Three things . . ." Matt says, dragging my attention away from our friends. "The shop, calling my parents, and finding someone who looks at me like that." He points with the tip of his beer bottle toward the happy couples.

"Single?" I ask.

"Perpetually." He blows out a long breath.

"That's an eighteen pointer," I say before cracking an ice cube between my teeth. *A bad habit,* my mother would say.

"Eighteen?"

"Perpetually is worth at least eighteen points on a Scrabble board," I explain.

"You play a lot of Scrabble, Lane?"

"Used to. With my dad." A trapped sigh comes out. I rarely talk about my father—and when I do, it's not with people I'm attempting to flirt with. It's not just a difficult topic, it's one I still can hardly speak about—without crying, that is.

"Oh. I'm sorry," Matt says, rubbing his eyebrow as he looks down between us. I guess my face said what my words failed to.

"It's okay. Long time ago now." *Three thousand and forty-two days, to be exact.*

"I'm still sorry," Matt says, his eyes searching mine.

I look away quickly, suddenly shy. "I'm going to get another one of these. Want something?" I rattle the lone ice cube in my glass.

"Let me." Matt reaches for my cup and walks to the kitchen. From my elevated position, I watch him move about. He turns to narrowly pass through a group that's congregated near the kitchen island and makes conversation with them as he fills our cups. I can't hear what he's saying, but I hear his laugh as he sidesteps them again on his way back.

I check the time on my phone—four minutes till midnight—as he returns.

"Thanks." I take the glass of fresh water from him.

"So anything else on that list of yours?" he asks, eyes softening as they meet mine. "Or are you already seeing someone?"

I scoff. "No, the girl I was recently hooking up with called it off when she procured herself a sugar daddy." *Can't say I blame her.* "But yes, another one on the list. I'd like to be a better friend too."

"How so?"

"Well, I should probably be helping with wedding stuff? I feel like Chloe doesn't ask because . . . well—" I sigh. "She knows Emily will pick up my slack." I take a deep breath, my chest rising high.

"Right, the wedding. I keep forgetting. It's coming up fast." Matt looks toward our friends briefly. "I should probably do stuff too, right? What do groomsmen usually do?"

I shrug. "I think you get off easy until the week of the wedding."

"Right, still . . . I'll add that to my list." He clears his throat and checks his watch in quick succession. Then he raises his cup toward me, and we cheers. "To a new year, new chances, new lessons, and . . . new friends."

"To calling family and not dying alone." I raise my cup, smiling.

"To succeeding at jobs and taking charge," he responds, voice louder, as we clink glasses again.

"To you, Mattheus." I lean forward and wink.

"To you, Elaine." He matches me, and a rush of excitement has my bottom lip pressed between my teeth, biting down on a giddy smile.

As the clinking of glass sounds between us, our eyes meet and hold.

"You know, you're cute *too*," Matt says as his eyes briefly glance over my face. "Too bad." He leans back onto the curved railing behind him.

"Too bad?" I ask, voice hesitant. What does that mean? Cute but a mess? Cute but not my type? Cute but a basket case?

He freezes, as if he's said the wrong thing. His brows are furrowed in confusion, and only then does it dawn on me that I mentioned it was a *woman* who recently dumped me.

"I'm bi—" I'm cut off by every other party attendee when they begin counting down from ten. The room explodes into chaos all around us, but it blurs out of focus. I'm tunnel-visioned, looking at Matt. He's so still. Steady. His eyes hold on me in an unreadable gaze.

"Nine, eight, seven . . ." they chant.

"I'm into everyone," I say, a little too loudly and cringe at my urgency to tell him he's a possible candidate. Even though no one else can hear us from up in our little nest, I look over my shoulder, blushing.

"Oh," he says, bringing my attention back. He wipes a hand over his beard and mouth, but I can see the grin he's hiding. He drags his hand from his chin to the back of his neck and tilts forward as he rubs it like a sore muscle. All the while smiling down between us.

I can't help but smile too. The embarrassing kind where you absolutely *have* to because someone's joy is being reflected onto you.

"Three," we say in unison with the crowd. My nose twitches, and he swallows, his throat working.

"Two." His chest rises as he takes a deep breath, but I can't seem to breathe at all.

"One." The hand he has splayed across his thigh twitches, and I fight the urge to lay my palm on top.

"Happy New Year!" the crowd shouts, but not us.

The sounds of noise blowers and confetti poppers fill the room, and I turn over my shoulder to the sudden influx of sound. Couples descend upon each other's faces like wolves on the hunt. I look up toward the ceiling as confetti falls slowly.

When I look back to Matt, he's staring up at me, eyes curiously narrowed as a stray piece of silver confetti drifts between us.

"Happy New Year, Lane," he says, his smile faltering.

He looks disappointed. For some reason, I *hate* that. I make a split-second decision and throw caution to the wind. I place my cup down on the stair beside me and put two palms on his cheeks, scrunching his face together like I've done to Chloe's sweet baby girl so many times.

"Happy New Year," I say, pulling his face toward me, his lips squished and opening for a laugh as they land on mine.

A firm palm lands on the edge of my jaw, and I lean into the touch. His hand is cool from holding his drink, and the pads of his fingertips are rough on the edge of my hairline. My hands around his face soften, and as they do, his lips follow suit. I was totally right. They're lips you *could* curl up on.

A few beats pass while I'm locked into the sweetest kiss I have ever had. Time slows—as if the confetti is floating around us instead of falling, voices dropping low and drawn out, "Auld Lang Syne" stretching like a vinyl spinning at half speed.

Pulling away from Matt's lips feels like an abrupt reminder that the world is *not* so still. The party continues and—surrounded by people and noise—isn't where I want to be.

Still, as we settle back against the stairs, my pulse races and the butterflies in my stomach take off in flight like never before. I mindlessly brush my thumb over my bottom lip. It's warm and buzzing. When I notice him watching me, I play it off—using the same hand to brush hair behind my ear. He clears his throat to speak, but I'm looking for a quick escape, not more conversation.

I've been with lots of people—*kissed* lots of people, but I've never felt *shy* after. Like a part of me was exposed the moment our lips broke apart. And I don't like it. At all.

Home, my anxiety demands. *Agreed,* I reply.

I stand and raise my chin as I try to step around him without toppling.

"Heading out?" Matt looks up at me with sad-puppy-dog eyes, rising slowly as I pass him. A twinge of guilt rises, but I shove it down.

You'll see him around. You probably shouldn't go home with your friend's friend, anyway. It's hard to ghost someone you'll see at birthday parties for years to come.

"Got a new life to start, Mattheus." I shrug playfully. *Casual, unaffected, unbothered.* "No time like the present."

He nods, his polite smile masked by confusion. "Right, well, good luck."

I look over my shoulder, stealing one last look, and nod. "You too."

Goodbye, lips. I'll miss you most of all.

ONE

15 MONTHS LATER

I HAVE BEEN PROPOSITIONED FOR A THREESOME FOUR times this afternoon after being on the lovebite app for only six hours. This has to be some sort of record. People read "interested in anyone" and take it to mean *everyone* and *all at once.*

And while in college, I would have perhaps been more than happy to oblige. The difference now is that it is exclusively couples asking for *me* to join *them.* Which just about sums up my life these days.

Emily and Amos are newly engaged, and Chloe and Warren married last summer. When the five of us hang out, I'm watched over like a child, talked to like a sweet, innocent newborn on the teat of life. *Someday,* they all hum merrily into their drinks, *it'll be your turn,* patronizing me as they feed one another grapes. That last part is an exaggeration, but only slightly.

But today—the day I signed up for my first ever dating app because I admittedly may be having a hefty dry spell and a crisis about said dry spell—is my twenty-seventh birthday. The end of my "mid" twenties, and the dawning of a new era of "full adult-hood."

So, in the words of Taylor Alison Swift, this is me trying . . . to get laid (Taylor's Version).

My computer chimes with the sound of *another* message from my boss—but I ignore it while on my smoke break.

I don't actually smoke, but in the interest of equality, I take a ten-minute break every few hours, as my co-workers might.

This break has been met with an onslaught of incoming notifi-cations, and I've yet to put my phone down. Other than the three-some requests, I have a few comments on Instagram, a text from Emily about how excited she is for my surprise-it's-not-a-surprise birthday dinner, and an email from Matt.

Yes, an email. I'm insistent there was a mix-up with Matt's driv-er's license, which I *made* him show me, and they incorrectly printed his birth year as 1995 instead of 1959. He emails almost exclusively. The guy actually texts with a single finger and signs his name on each message, so, honestly, email is less painful. That he can type out on his *desktop computer* at work.

Instead of opening the email, I click on the "you have a match" notification. Ah, yes, the pretty brunette, Valerie. Twenty-nine, single, interested in women, Gemini. Her bio reads, "*here for a good time, not a long time,*" which makes me wonder if it's a *Walk to Remember* situation or if she's *that* cliché.

I message, "Stop making a fool out of me. Why don't you come on over, Valerie?" and pour one out—hypothetically, because my coffee is piping hot—for my girl Amy Winehouse. I screenshot it and send it to my group chat with Em and Chloe.

CHLOE: Make sure to ask if she has a good lawyer.
EMILY: Tell her you miss her ginger hair!

I love them.

LANE: What are you wearing tonight? How fancy do I have to be?

CHLOE: What's tonight???

EMILY: She knows.

CHLOE: What?! Dang it! Ugh . . . I'm probably going to wear my yellow dress.

Emily sends a photo of her in a fuchsia two-piece pantsuit.

LANE: Gotcha. Effort required.

CHLOE: It's your birthday, Lane. If you want to have a sweatpants party, then we can do that.

LANE: Hmm . . . Thoughts, Em?

Emily sends a GIF of a forced smile and a twitching eye.

LANE: Effort is fine. I have that vintage jumpsuit I've wanted to wear.

CHLOE: Ooh! I love that one!

LANE: I gotta get back to work. See you ladies tonight.

A few hours later, I finish my packaging design idea and send it off to my supervisor. A box that will house the newest, most rugged, most hardcore, most extreme, most badass, underwater, 360-degree, high-definition camera with a battery life longer than my will to live. I sign off and begin my grueling commute home, shutting my laptop and taking twelve steps from my dining table to the couch.

"What a day, huh, Simone?"

Simone is the rabbit I bought to replace Emily when she moved out of our place and in with Amos. I was having a vulnerable moment when I opened Marketplace, and there she was. She *and* her three siblings. I feel like the siblings are worth mentioning to reflect that I had some self-control. I only got one!

"I don't want to be rude . . . but you've yet to wish me a happy birthday." I sit up, looking at the bunny condo that cost me more than a month's rent. "Simone?"

Fuck. The cage's door is open.

"Simone!" I look around frantically. She's a little Houdini on the best of days, but she couldn't have gotten far—typically she just burrows under a blanket or laundry pile.

My phone rings, and I answer without thinking. "Hello?" I say, voice hysterical.

"Hello?" my sister responds in obvious confusion at my urgency. "Everything all right?"

"Sorry, yes . . . I thought you were someone else."

"Who?"

"Simone."

"Your rabbit?"

"No, Simone Biles! Yes, the rabbit! She's missing."

I hear a soft sigh and a shuffle that sounds like Liz moving the phone to her other ear. Shit. She's annoyed. I forgot to call her back yesterday. Or today.

"Happy birthday, Lane," she says haughtily.

"Oh! You remembered!" I tease, attempting to lighten the mood. "Happy birthday, Pudge."

"I asked you to stop calling me Pudge. We're too old for it. Especially now."

Pudge was the nickname my father gave her because she couldn't pronounce fudge. A silly little thing, but it stuck.

"Do not remind me how old we are." I stand and lift a blanket off the floor. No Simone underneath.

"Mom call you yet?" she asks.

"Yeah, this morning before work."

"Good."

I don't love that my twin sister is making sure *our* mother called me on *our* birthday to check that *she* shouldn't feel guilty for being the favorite and undoubtedly getting the same deposit into her bank account this morning. I look at the doors to each bedroom and the bathroom, all shut. Simone has to be here somewhere. Unless she could fit through the vents? Shit. Can she?

"Can rabbits do that thing cats do and fit through small spaces?" I ask.

"I don't own a cat," Liz says, matter-of-factly.

"I'm wondering if Simone escaped through the vents," I explain.

"Oh, I hope not. Your building will kick you out if the forced air starts smelling like decomposing rabbit."

"Elizabeth!" I gasp.

"What? Sorry . . ." She huffs.

"My rabbit ran away on my birthday." I slump into the chair. "I've never been lower."

"Really? Are you sure about that?" she asks flatly.

"Ow," I whisper.

Liz can't help it. She's always been . . . ~~a bitch~~ curt. My mother loved to say that we were left brain and right brain personified. Liz is the pragmatic, logical, detached one. I'm the impractical, creative, emotional one. Together we'd make one fully formed being.

I never settled into the idea of being half of anything. My brain *felt* whole—just different from Liz's. But hers is similar to my mother's, and I'm more like my father. My parents were a great team as the left and right melded together, so I know it was with endearment that my mother considered us twins the same. But when Dad died, it made the family's score uneven. Lonely on the right.

Suddenly, qualities that I had been celebrated for—spontaneity, imagination, empathy—began to make me feel alien in my own family. That, and my feverish desire to get away from my own personal haunted mansion, had me applying to arts college far from home. When I arrived here, I found creatives again. I found acceptance. I found my people.

But now they've both found *their* other halves, and I suddenly don't feel whole again.

Then there's Matt. Sweet, handsome, kind Matt who flew through the stages of *a crush* to *too risky* in the span of one brief New Year's Eve kiss.

Turns out our first real encounter, when I was drunk, complaining about my life and listing off my many failures, was *not* the sexy type of impression that would score me a date or a shag, regardless of my own intentions.

He started calling me "kid" shortly after our kiss and has even noogied me once. The universal gesture of the friend zone. It's very disappointing to Chloe and Warren, who are enthusiastically hoping we get together, but I'm glad for it.

Matt isn't the type of guy you hook up with—he's practically got "commitment" written across his forehead in permanent marker. Between his caretaking tendencies following years of helping to raise his ridiculous number of siblings and his general dad-like physique, he's begging to make someone a wife and mother. Which is the *opposite* of where my life is headed. So, a friendship is best—and it's a good one.

A few weeks after that fateful New Year's Eve, I learned that Matt grew up on Vancouver Island almost entirely off the grid. I decided to take it upon myself to introduce him to all the music, television, movie, and pop culture references he'd missed out on.

I'll be scrolling on my phone and see a reminder of some fantastic, cinematic masterpiece late one night—previous films such as *The Breakfast Club* and *The Lizzie McGuire Movie*—and I'll immediately send him a text. He'll agree the situation needs to be remedied, and, based on my level of intensity, we'll choose a time for him to come over with pizza. Often the next day.

We watch the movie with bowls of snacks, pizza boxes, or even a pillow as a buffer between us—because we do *not* need a repeat of the accidental hand brush incident of last year. Then he leaves at a respectable hour.

"Lane? You still there?" Liz asks through the phone.

Shit. "Hey! Sorry. Looking for Simone. Uh . . . what are your birthday plans?" I ask, continuing my impersonation of Elmer Fudd on the hunt for a rabbit.

"Phillip is taking me out for dinner."

Elizabeth and Phillip—never not funny. I stifle a laugh, but it comes out as a soft snort from the back of my throat.

"Don't," Elizabeth warns.

"I didn't say anything!" I protest.

"Your fascination with the British royal family is bizarre."

"Sorry . . . your majesty." I grin into the phone, lifting a chair to check under the dining table. What *the fuck,* Simone? You have a swanky bunny condo! Two stories! Why would you leave?

"Well, I'll let you go. I'm going to call you tomorrow."

"Could . . . we text?" I hesitate to ask, but damn, I'm tired of this calling every day *thing.* What started as a New Year's resolution has turned into a massive, self-inflicted pain in my ass. We don't talk about anything real, mostly bouncing between small talk and passive-aggressive remarks about each other's lifestyle. I miss her, sure, but it's not fun. And there are way better uses of our time than forcing a relationship, right?

"I guess, but I thought telling you over the phone that I was engaged would be more appropriate."

I drop the pillow I was looking under. "Pardon?" I glitch. "Who's what now?"

"Well, tonight Phillip is taking me to my favorite restaurant.

Last month he asked for my ring size, and Mom asked me to go get my nails done with her."

"Well, damn . . ." I blink rapidly. "Congrats in advance?"

"We'll probably get married in the next few months. No use waiting. It will be at his parents' estate, so late spring is ideal weather-wise." She's completely calm, her voice level, while I can't pick my jaw up off the floor.

"Few—few months? Liz, are you sure? You've been together less than a year."

"Nine months. Surely enough time to grow a new human is enough time to decide to marry one."

She's got me there. "Okay . . . yeah. You're not growing a human, though, right?"

"Not yet."

God, my mother will be unstable. A grandchild. A Hargreaves, nonetheless. The only family my mother considers richer, superior, and more well connected than her parents—who, though dead, she still tries to impress. And now my sister is marrying their eldest son. Truly, they *are* like royalty.

"All right, well, yeah, call me tomorrow then," I mumble.

"Will do. Happy birthday, Lane."

"Happy birthday, Liz." She's right. She's too old to be called Pudge now. *We're* too old.

When she hangs up, I stare at my phone until something moves in the corner of my eye, capturing my attention.

"Simone, you little asshole, get back in your cage!" I dive for her, catching her by her back foot mid-hop.

We struggle momentarily, but I manage to get hold of her without injuring either of us. "I should have gotten your sister. Betcha she wouldn't pull this crap." I stop dead in my tracks, horrified. "No . . . that was cruel. You're great. Your sister is *different* but not better. I'm sorry."

Damn. We truly do become our mothers eventually.

I nuzzle Simone as I lower her into the cage and check the time. I have a little under an hour to get ready before Emily comes to pick me up. Actually, she said she'd be picking me up *after* everyone else, but I'm not sure who *everyone* is. Chloe, Warren, Amos, and Emily for sure but . . .

LANE: Who all is hanging out tonight?

EMILY: Everyone.

LANE: Just wondering if we'll all fit in your car.

EMILY: Change of plan, Warren's driving the six of us in their van.

LANE: Cool!

EMILY: So, yes, Matt is coming ;)

LANE: Not what I was asking, but that's great!

I immediately sprint to the shower.

An hour later, I finish my makeup while practicing my affirmations and take my 75 mg of Sertraline, prescribed by a random, well-mannered doctor at the local walk-in clinic. I keep my pills in my makeup bag and my affirmations on a Post-it on my mirror.

I can always come home, but going out is fun.

I'm safe wherever I choose to be.

An environment I can't control is a memory in the making.

I added a new one, just for tonight and *not* on paper.

I will not flirt with Matt, no matter how tipsy I get. Even if he wears that gray button-up. Even if he does that thing where he flicks his wrist a few times to get his watch back in its place.

These reminders are necessary. I'm well aware of the many reasons Matt and I wouldn't work, but I'm also a raging flirt. I'll flirt with a lamppost if it flickers the right way. But with Matt, when it does slip out, there's an awkwardness afterward. Like I've stripped naked and run into a public fountain. No one dared me to, and I've made it weird. So I try my best not to flirt with him at all . . . but *shit,* does he make it difficult sometimes.

I zip myself into the tight black velvet jumpsuit and let my electric pink hair out of the rubber band I used in lieu of a hair tie this morning. With a little fluff, it actually falls quite nicely, the longest point tickling my collarbone. The good hair day is extremely lucky because I'm almost out of time to get ready.

My body is small in stature and height, but I've come to accept it in a neutral sense. I celebrate that I don't have to wear a bra if I don't want to, and being a size small makes thrift-shopping a lot easier, but often I still have to shove the cruel words of my high school classmates down when I take in my lack of hips, breasts, or ass.

*Little boy, twig, flat, skeleton—*they weren't very original, but the labels stuck.

It's probably why I always lean toward wearing baggier, darker clothing that hides me well and have a healthy splattering of patch-work style tattoos all over that are *mostly* seen by only me. But no baggy clothes this evening. Tonight, this jumpsuit is doing *wonders* for my self-esteem. I look hot.

My phone chimes with a message from Chloe that they're waiting out front. I allow myself one last glance in the mirror and give a thumbs-up to my reflection.

You can do this, I tell her. *It's going to be a great night.*

I point at her sternly. *Don't flirt with Matt.*

TWO

EMILY IS A CELEBRATOR AT HEART AND A TOTAL CHEER-
leader for her people—she also has a tendency to go overboard.
Chloe matches that energy—when she *has* the energy. Having a
toddler at home while being self-employed and in a near constant
state of flustered means that she's as thoughtful as she is forgetful.
So, powered by perhaps a bit of pity and a whole lot of enthusiasm, they've put together a *beautiful* evening.

The back room of the trendy, dimly lit bar is decorated with
silver and purple decorations surrounding a pair of black balloons
in the shapes of a *2* and a *7* that are almost as big as me. The room
has whitewashed stone walls and warm chandelier lighting, and a
large oak table in the center creates an intimate, charming atmosphere.

"Oh my god!" I say, probably for the fortieth time as I brush my
hand over the decorations. "You guys . . ." I whine, pouting my lip as
I feel tears spring loose. "This makes me feel so special. Thank you."

"You *are* special, Laney." Chloe gives me a hug, squeezing a little too tight.

"Happy birthday, babe." Emily wraps her arms around both Chloe and me and shimmies us side to side.

Warren, Amos, and Matt find our private room after parking down the street and grabbing us the first round of drinks. Warren hands Chloe a pink cocktail, kisses her cheek, then immediately pulls out his phone. Chloe gives him a teasing smirk, whispering something about trusting the babysitter and assists him in putting the phone away. Amos performs a similar exchange, except he grabs Emily's ass after handing her a martini. She looks at him with a flirtatious smile that makes *me* blush. I turn away to see Matt standing in the doorway with two drinks.

"One . . . er . . . sex on the beach." Matt extends the fruity cocktail my way with a cheeky grin.

"Thanks." I take it and only allow myself two seconds to appreciate that he *did* wear his infamous gray button-up.

"Happy birthday, kid." He raises an arm around my back, patting my shoulder with his hand. Matt's not a particularly tall guy, I'd guess five-eleven, but to my five-foot-nothing—that's huge. Everything about him is *strong*. His wide frame, his broad shoulders, his working hands with veins that must be a nurse's wet dream.

I take a sip of my drink. It's stronger than I anticipated, the alcohol burning the back of my throat on its way down. I sputter a cough. "That is *stiff*." I look up to Matt's face, wincing.

"Gimme." He takes the glass without a second thought and throws back a sip. "Damn . . . it is." He tsks. "Guys love to say women are lightweights, but I'd like to see a man drink three of those, then walk home in heels."

"Totally," I agree mindlessly, looking at the smudge his lips left behind on my glass that overlaps with my lipstick stain, just *a little*.

He chases my drink with his own, something honey-colored in

a short glass. "I watched another one of your movie suggestions last night," Matt says.

"Which one?"

His brow furrows, and then he reaches for his back pocket. He palms his drink while untucking some sort of paper from his wallet. "*Dead Poets Society,*" he reads, then lowers the paper. "It was great. Probably my favorite of your suggestions so far."

I snatch the paper from him and try to make sense of what I'm holding. Reading it over, it becomes obvious. There is a list of all the movies I've referenced or we've watched together since we became friends squished together at the top of the page. The bottom half is a chart of sorts. He's filled in the date, the title, his rating—he drew actual stars—and his favorite quote or scene.

"Matt, have you been taking notes?" I feel myself losing all sense of self-preservation. Cartoon hearts attempt to fight their way out of my eyes.

"I take my homework assignments seriously." He snatches his notes back with a wink. "I also learned how to spotify to keep all the songs in one place." He folds the paper delicately and tucks it back into his wallet.

"I sort of want assignments too," I say reflexively. Our friendship suddenly seems totally off-balance. Sure, I suggested he watch the movies and listen to the songs, but I didn't think he'd *actually* do it. Certainly not all of them, at least. Not when I didn't make him come over to watch. This is hours of dedicated time.

He pockets his wallet and crosses his arms in front of his chest before flicking his watch into place. *Striptease, why don't you.*

"What could I possibly teach you?" He laughs, a smile creasing his cheeks.

"How to build an engine," I offer, leaning to one side.

He nods with pursed lips. "Do you have a *need* for an engine?"

"Not at the moment, but you never know." I bat my eyelashes

before catching myself. "How to grow a garden?" I suggest, extending an open palm between us.

"Lane, you don't even have a balcony." He shakes his head while looking over my shoulder at the cozy room.

"True," I mumble, bringing my hand to my chin and tapping as I think.

"What about . . . books?" he asks, his attention directed back to me. "Dickens?"

I feign shock and offense. "Pardon me, *sir*? Dick-what?"

He rolls his eyes. "Austen?"

"Texas?" I shake my head internally at the stupid series of jokes I've now attempted. Still, Matt seems to find me amusing—his smile growing lopsided and sincere. "But yeah . . . I could definitely read some of your favorites. Seems more than fair. Where do I start?"

"Well, what haven't you read already?"

"I think what I *have* read would be a shorter list . . . as in, none. I read *Twilight* in high school, though. *Oh!* And *Twilight* fanfiction. *Lots* of that. There was this one where Bella gets her period and—"

"I'll bring a few over. I'll have to think about it," Matt interrupts, probably for the best.

"Not a fan of *Twilight*?" I glare playfully, baiting him.

"What? Nah, books are books. And it helps narrow down the type you may be interested in. Gothy, angsty stuff. Romance, maybe."

I want to pry as to what books that might be, but I'm interrupted by Emily grabbing my arm and hip-bumping me.

"You want to split the Brie starter?" she asks, wagging her eyebrows suggestively.

I hum my agreement. "Chloe?" I call to get her attention from across the room. "Do you have a Lactaid?"

Chloe thrusts her drink at Warren without so much as looking at him before she begins rifling through her bag. She pulls out *Sesame Street* Band-Aids, two different pill bottles, a children's thermometer, a pack of baby wipes, and a package of tissues and places them all on the table one by one before her eyes light up. "Yes!" She tosses the little packet to me with shocking accuracy.

"Let's cheese it up!" I throw back the pill and down my drink with a sputtering cough before looping my arm through Em's and walking to the bar to order together.

⁂

SOMEWHERE BETWEEN THE piece of seven-layer chocolate cake with one candle in it, the fumbling walk to the karaoke place down the street, and Amos's fierce rendition of "Somebody to Love," I've decided this is the best night of my life.

"Who's next?" Amos shouts into the microphone, sweat dripping off his chin as he uses the corner of his untucked shirt to wipe his brow, revealing the eight-pack that Emily has described *well*. She walks over with a hanky and kisses him sweetly as she dabs his face dry.

I raise an eyebrow at Warren, who's doing his best to disappear into the booth seating. His chest falls with a sigh, offering a look that says if I ask him point-blank, he'll do it. But he's begging me not to.

I contemplate how *badly* I want to hear his notorious rendition of "It's All Coming Back to Me Now" that Chloe describes as the best seven minutes of their honeymoon—much to his annoyance. I let him off easy and turn to Matt instead.

"Mattheus!" I sing out, gesturing to him with jazz hands.

He looks around enthusiastically, like he's on a game show, pointing to himself. "Me?" he mouths.

I nod like I'm Simon Cowell giving him the chance of a life-time. He stands and takes the microphone from Amos. "What's the song, birthday girl?" He smiles at me, beaming like a damn spotlight.

I scroll through the tablet's list of songs, quickly realizing that most of them are love ballads. Or at least love-adjacent. I stammer, scroll some more, and feel my brain begin to shut down. "Performer's choice." I hand him the tablet. He won't know many of them anyway.

Matt makes quick work of selecting his song, places the tablet down, and grabs the second microphone that has remained in its holster on the stage. "C'mon." He holds it out to me just as the beginning notes of "Ain't No Mountain High Enough" begin playing.

Lord have mercy.

"Listen, baby," he sings to me, taking my hand in his and spinning me around. I giggle as I'm moved about like a collection of helium balloons tied around his wrist.

We're both awful singers. He can't hold a note without losing his breath, and I can't match pitch to save my life. But it's possibly the most fun I've ever had.

With one hand on his microphone and one clasped around mine, he glides us around the small platform. He tugs me to and fro until I'm laughing so hard I'm half out of breath trying to sing. All the while, he keeps his eyes locked on me, wearing a mischievous grin.

I'm two drinks too deep to stop myself from getting lost in the moment and the giddy feelings rising in my chest.

Dangerous, my brain hums. *Live a little,* I retort.

When the song ends, we bow, and I look out to see Chloe and Warren exchanging wide-eyed, hopeful glances. I glare at them, promptly plucking my hand away from Matt's and wiping it down the seam of my thigh, as if I could remove the memory itself.

"Duets!" I exclaim. "We all must do duets!" I throw Warren a quick that's-what-you-get smirk while handing him my microphone and claiming his seat.

I curl into myself, downing the last of my drink.

Matt's not a fling type of guy, I remind myself. And god, what a guaranteed way to ruin our friendship sleeping with him would be.

I want to, though. I'm drunk and woman enough to admit it. I *really* want to.

My heart rate is approaching the speed of a hummingbird's wings, so I attempt to think of anything but Matt naked on top of me.

The smell of burning hair, feedback from a speaker, people who keep pigeons as pets, stale-coffee morning breath.

Matt, apparently unaware and entirely unaffected by our proximity, falls into the seat next to me as Chloe makes her way to the stage, joining her husband.

"You're the One That I Want" from *Grease* plays as Chloe spins circles around Warren, doing a near-perfect Sandy. I can't help but smile as Warren's grin grows wider until he's also doing his best Danny Zuko.

I feel Matt's eyes on my profile, so I break the silence. "They're so cute it's disgusting."

"I like it." He shrugs, settling back into the booth.

"Of course *you* do. You've got no shortage of romance in your life. I'm bitter."

Every once in a while, I'll do this stupid thing where I make a generalized statement about Matt's love life to see if he'll correct me. It's the least embarrassing way to bring it up, but he never dignifies it with a response. It's fucking infuriating.

"Still no luck with the apps?" he asks.

"Bit the bullet today and finally joined one. Not going well."

"No?" He leans, raising his arm to rest along the back of the booth. His hand hovers above the back of my neck, and it distracts me momentarily. "How?"

"Well, I've gotten *some* messages," I reply, looking at his wrist over my shoulder before forcing myself to look away.

"So what's the issue?" he asks.

"It's been mostly couples looking for a third."

"Ah." He brushes his nose with his knuckle, and I notice a piece of his hair has broken free from his bun and rests alongside his cheek. I resist—with *everything* in me—twirling it around my finger.

"Are you seeing anyone?" I ask boldly—and unexpectedly. I need to drink some water. Or eat some bread. Bread absorbs the alcohol in your stomach, right? I think I've read that somewhere.

If I wasn't watching him so carefully, I might not have noticed his expression fall. The happy lines on either side of his eyes soften, and the upturned corner of his lip dips too.

"Nothing serious," he says, unbothered.

As in he's sleeping around? As in he's not looking for commitment? As in . . . "And that's what you . . . prefer?" *What the fuck am I doing?*

"I'm not sure." He leans back, scratching his jaw. "If I worked less, maybe I'd look to settle down." He smiles softly, lifting his shoulders.

"You don't work *that* much. I mean, you're here right now." I point around us, as if he's unaware that he isn't elbow deep in an engine.

Chloe and Warren pass their mics to Amos and Emily, and a new song starts up. A ballad I don't recognize and can't seem to focus on.

Matt presses his lips together and tilts his head. His eyes narrow on me until I fidget in my seat.

"What?" I laugh nervously under his stare.

"I made you something," he says, voice hushed.

"For my birthday?" I ask.

That snaps the tension. He licks his lips as they transform into a smirk. "No, for Hanukkah." He laughs, then it fades to a shy sort of smile. "But yeah, for your birthday." He raises off the bench slightly, reaches into his back pocket, and pulls out a tiny wooden object. "Here." He lays it in my open palm, his fingers brushing my wrist *far* too lightly.

I look at it for a moment before my eyes translate what it is, though I'm still not *entirely* sure. A simple carving of wood in the shape of a peg doll. It's smooth as I rub my thumb over it. I glance up at him through my eyelashes.

"My dad made these for my siblings and me. They're called worry dolls. Or maybe he made that up, I don't know." He rubs the back of his neck and chuckles slowly. "It's, uh, yeah. For worrying. Or, stopping it, I guess."

"You made this for me?" I ask softly.

He nods.

"Like you carved it from wood?"

He nods again.

"So when I'm anxious . . ." My voice trails off.

"You take it out, and—well, I used to sort of fiddle with mine. Run my fingers over it, squeeze it in my palm." I mimic his instructions as he explains.

"Do you still have yours?" I ask.

"Yeah, it's on a shelf somewhere at my place."

"This is such a *you* gift." The words tumble out of me.

"Cheap? Boring? Peculiar?" He crosses one leg over his knee, which is bouncing.

"No." I find his eyes and hold his stare. "Thoughtful, careful, beautiful."

His leg stills. He blinks more than a few times, then swallows heavily. "Well, I'm glad you like it."

"Thank you." I tuck it into my bag. "I really do."

Amos and Emily finish their song. We all decide to call it a night when Chloe announces that they need to go relieve their sitter.

It's a contentedly silent car ride home, followed by a chorus of *thank-yous* and *love yous* as I exit the car and make my way upstairs. I drag my balloons behind me and place them in the center of my living room. In the middle of my empty, silent apartment.

The tears come quicker than I expected them, though they're not a surprise. I've cried on every birthday. All the ones I can remember, at least.

I'm a crier at my core. I try my best to hide it now that I'm an adult and recognize big emotions scare people off. But if I'm above a seven or below a three on the emotions scale—I'm crying. And sometimes I'm at a ten and a one all at once. Especially when drunk, as I suspect I might be as my living room whirls in and out of focus.

It could be a number of things. Relief at being home mixed with loneliness following a night of chaotic, constant company. Gratefulness makes me feel guilty about what others don't have. An awareness of another birthday passing without getting a hug from my dad. Knowing he'd still be here if I had just stayed home that night.

That last one can cause tears even on the best of days.

I strip and get into the warm shower, allowing my makeup to be washed away as the last tears evaporate with the steam.

When I get out, dry off, and find my coziest pajamas, I get into bed. My entire body hums its approval like a cat nuzzling against its owner, purring in satisfaction. A warmth in the back of my neck, a dense, heavy feeling in my bones dragging me down,

down, down. When my bed curls around me like this, when my body melts so naturally into it, I know getting out the next day will be challenging.

Anxiety creeps up in many forms, but most often, it feels like exhaustion. I'm an electric vehicle running on two AA batteries. Sure, it could run for a little while—but it's not a permanent solution.

You had a good time, I tell myself. *Quit complaining.*

I attempt to shake off the feeling and reach for my phone. I *like* the posts shared by my friends tonight and the comments on the photo I posted earlier. Me and my giant 27 balloons. It's the first time I've ever considered not including how old I am in a birthday post, but the only photos of me before I got a little sloppy feature the balloons—so *whatever*.

I don't think it's so much the age itself. Most of my friends are in their late twenties, and it doesn't look so scary when I watch them go through it. But combine being twenty-seven, working a job I don't particularly like, going without sex for over a year, living in a shitty apartment, and basically being entirely directionless . . . that's a different story. There's some shame there.

Here. There's some shame *here*.

I know what my dad would say. No direction means no limitations. A job you hate? An opportunity to find something better. A place you're not tied down to? A chance to go somewhere new. Lonely? Learn to enjoy your own company.

I'm stuck, and deep down I know I'm the only one who can do the *un-sticking*—but I feel resistant to change. Change requires effort, innovation, energy . . . which I have little of these days.

So, instead, I scroll and scroll until optimum numbness is achieved. Video after video passes, all of them fitting into neat, distinct categories. You've got your funny animal videos—that's a given. Your political hot takes and news updates that I usually watch all the way through out of a sense of obligation. Plus the professional content creators who've found their niche.

I follow a hot dude who only posts cooking videos and apparently doesn't own a top, a woman who films herself thrifting home goods and renovating her finds, a pair of friends who tap-dance to pop music in unison so precisely it makes my brain go quiet. But one video ends my scrolling and sends me into an internet research tailspin.

I spend the next hour watching videos of a couple buying, emptying, fixing, renovating, and then decorating their school bus conversion. Between the camera-lens flares of the adorable yellow bus and peppy, up-tempo music, I'm sold.

It's a bright, colorful world. It's freedom from rent and landlords. It's being on the move while also going back to your *own* space each night. A space you designed to your *exact* specifications.

They seem happy.

One Google search later, and I'm on an auction website. One click, and I'm looking at the bus I'm convinced fate has brought to me.

$27,000

2013 International 48 Passenger School Bus

- Low Mileage
- Rear Air Ride Suspensions
- 39 Foot Length makes this bus perfect for a skoolie conversion

Call Carl for details. It won't last long!

Twenty-seven thousand dollars. An obvious sign. Less obvious, the year of the bus is the year my father passed—the $50,000 he left me still sitting unused in a savings account.

My dad would've loved this idea. He'd have insisted on taking it for a test-drive. He'd tell my mother jokes until her weary, tight lips turned to a smirk, and she'd come around to the idea of her daughter living on wheels.

My sister used her inheritance to fund research at her alma mater—stating that her education had been covered by my parents' vast wealth already, and she didn't need much else since she was choosing to stay near home. But I know our dad. Knew him better than she did. He separated that money from our education funds because he wanted us to use it for something joy-giving. Something impractical. Something fun and just for us. Like he would have done.

I wouldn't be a single almost-thirty-year-old in a half-empty apartment, depressed and alone with her rabbit. I'd be an adventurous nomad, living in a home catered to her needs, experiencing a simpler way of life . . . with her rabbit.

I'm emailing the seller, Carl, as the sun begins to come up. He's two hours ahead and responds immediately. Quickly, phone numbers are exchanged, and I'm receiving a request for a video call. I keep my video off, as I'm still in bed. Once my tour is complete, I send him a deposit. He sends me the address, and then we hang up. Carl, the happy salesman. Me, the proud owner of a bright yellow, forty-eight-passenger bus.

Then, at just after six, I go to bed.

THREE

I WAKE UP MIDDAY TO THE HORRIFYING SOUND OF MY apartment's buzzer. "No," I cry into my pillow. "Leave me," I beg them. My headache is so bad I swear I can see spots.

The buzzer doesn't stop. There is an assassin at my door.

I walk to the intercom with my eyes mostly shut, my hands out in front of me. "Oh my god, what?" I say into it, pressing my forehead against the wall.

"Hey, it's me," Emily's cheery voice returns.

"Why?" I bark.

"Coffee, donuts, and medicine," she answers with a gentle laugh.

"Enter." I hit the button to unlock the lobby's door, unlock my apartment, and immediately get back into bed.

A few minutes later, Emily appears in my bedroom wearing a soft smile and tiptoeing inside. "Hi," she whispers.

I groan.

"How are you?" She perches on the end of my bed.

"I . . . I'm splitting in half."

"Hands," she commands. I present her both palms. She places a hot paper cup in one and two pills in the other.

"Thanks, Mom." I swallow.

"Okay, ew." She laughs. "I have a question for you."

I wave her off. "Yes, I'll be your maid of honor."

"Uh, no. You were Chloe's, so it's her turn. I'll be yours some-day."

I sit up and let my eyes adjust to the room slightly, taking a sip of hot goodness. "Then what?"

"Did you happen to buy a school bus last night?"

My instinct is to say no. But then I hesitate as memories come flooding back in. "Possibly." *Yes, oh I did.* "Depends on whether you're here to be mad about it." I open one eye to look at her. Her expression is filled with concern that has defensiveness rising like bile up my throat.

"I just . . . Simone was one thing, but buying a bus on im-pulse?" She tilts her head with a loving expression that makes me uneasy.

"Not on impulse—fate. And don't bring Simone into this." I lean forward and whisper, "She's already not a big fan of you."

"Lane, what are you going to do with a school bus? You don't even own a car."

"I won't need one now." I take another sip, the medicine and coffee combination already helping. "I'm gonna renovate it."

"Lane . . ." Emily says more sternly.

"There's a whole community of people who do it. Skoolie peo-ple. I'm going to fix it up and . . ." I pause. "Wait, how did you even know about the bus?"

"Group chat." Emily bites her lip, failing to stop her teasing smile.

I reach for my phone and read the messages I sent but don't remember. All of them between three and six in the morning.

LANE:
@WarrenDove how do I know if an engine is good based on a video?
@everyone Oh my goodness. Look at these dog and raccoon besties. (LINK TO VIDEO)
@ChloeDove sorry if that woke you guys up @EmilyOwusu are you awake? What color would you paint a bus?
@AmosLopez Can you ask Emily if green fabric hides stains well?
@everyone I bought a bus!!!! I'll take name suggestions please and thanks.

I study the messages and slowly lower my phone. "Well, that'll do it." I sigh. "In my defense . . . I don't appear *too* drunk in those."

"Weirdly fewer spelling mistakes than normal," Emily agrees.

"I think I bought a bus, Em." I cover my mouth with the tips of my fingers, a crazed laugh breaking through. "Holy shit," I mutter, kneading the bridge of my nose.

Why am I not freaking out more? Is this the calm before the storm, or is this my instincts telling me everything will be all right? I'm in a near constant state of panic, so why is it that I can't seem to muster any right now?

"I think you did." She pats my knee. "And green can hide stains in the right shades."

"Right." I nod. I blink, my eyes drifting to the bed beneath me. Thoughts grow like background noise at a concert as crowds filter in. I try to make sense of them all. Partially excited, mostly anxious, somewhat practical. "Do you happen to know if one requires a special license to drive a school bus?"

Em's laugh escapes through her nose with force. "No idea." She maneuvers over me and lies down at my side. "So, show me!" Her head rests on my shoulder as I pull up the images on my phone.

We spend a few hours in bed together, researching inspiration for the bus and coming up with a plan.

＊ ＊ ＊

AS SHE'D PREDICTED, Liz called me this afternoon to announce her engagement. They've set a date—in nine weeks. She's asked me to be a bridesmaid, but the maid of honor will be Phillip's sister because she's nearby. (Or so she claims.)

She also made sure to tell me multiple times I had to RSVP sooner rather than later if I'd like to bring a date. She made sure to specify that the date should be a man because Phillip's parents are "quite conservative." So, that was fun.

I did not tell her about my bus. I did not know *how* to tell her about my bus. It's impractical, impulsive, and every other adjective she'd use to describe her younger-by-ten-minutes sister, and I'm not ready for judgment yet. Not only because I don't have answers to the inevitable follow-up questions, but also because I like it being just my—and a little bit Dad's—thing right now.

The idea of taking this monstrous commercial people-mover and transforming it into a comfortable nest makes me feel warm and fuzzy—and I'm not letting that go yet.

I do know who I need to call, though. Because, as it turns out, you *do* need a commercial license to drive the school bus until it's registered privately. Matt picks up on the third ring.

"Mattheus Tilo-Jones," he answers.

"Elaine Marie Rothsford," I reply, grinning to myself.

"Lane!" he sings enthusiastically, then clears his throat. "This is a nice surprise."

I don't fight the blush that crawls up my neck. "Hey, pal." I roll my eyes at myself. "I have a question for you." *A big one.*

"Shoot."

"So, for context, I bought a school bus," I say. The line goes silent. "Mm-hmm. I'll give you a minute with that one."

"I saw you less than twenty-four hours ago," he stammers.

"Yep."

"Had you bought the bus before your party?" he asks in a tone of disbelief.

"No."

"Were you in the market for one? I would have gone—"

"Not really," I interrupt.

"Well, okay. And when you say school bus . . . ?" If Matt didn't refute technology, he'd have seen the group chat messages with several images of the bus already.

"A bright yellow school bus. Forty-eight-passenger with low mileage and something called air suspension. I'm also told it has a roof hatch."

"Right." I hear the scraping of metal against concrete, like a stool being pulled out. If he's having to sit for this conversation, I should maybe reassess some life decisions.

"So for my question . . ." I hesitate. "Do you happen to have your commercial license?" I *know* he does because I asked Warren first, and he suggested calling Matt.

"Yeah . . . Do you need me to park it somewhere for you?"

I laugh anxiously. "I, actually, and feel free to say no . . . was wondering if you'd come get it with me and drive it back to the shop."

"My shop?"

"Warren said it was okay. If—"

"No, yeah. Of course."

"I'm renovating it," I say triumphantly.

"You are?"

"Yeah."

"Alone?" he asks.

"What, like it's hard?" I laugh. "Wait, I forget, was *Legally Blonde* on that movie list?"

He laughs, and the sound is rich and deep, even over the phone. My body reacts to it with a smile I know means danger. Still, I can't help the warm breeze of comfort that washes over me when Matt laughs. Every time I solicit one from him, it feels like winning a gold medal—and he hands them out frequently. Far more often than most.

"Yeah, I watched that one. I liked it?" His voice pitches higher.

"No you didn't."

He sighs. "No, but I wish I did. Actually, I have a proposition. Did you read the email I sent yesterday?" he asks.

"Shoot, sorry, no. Want me to now?"

He laughs. "No, I can just tell you."

"Okay, what's up?"

"I was asking about hiring you to rebrand the shop. But maybe instead you could help us out with that, and I'll work with you on the bus. Labor for labor."

Ideas flick through my head like a Rolodex. "I didn't know you guys were rebranding."

"Yeah, well, Ram sold us the shop over a year ago, and we've gotten along fine since, but I think we're ready to take on some new clientele. We'd both like to see our customer base grow, and the scary biker shop vibe isn't really our thing. We've got some money in the budget for a new website, sign, paint. Maybe even some branded work gear if we're feeling fancy."

I already have ideas. "I love it. I'm in."

"Sweet."

"I'm glad, because now I feel less terrible about all the help I was inevitably going to ask you both for," I say, trying to sound *cute* instead of *entitled*.

"You wouldn't have had to ask."

"I know." I smile against the phone.

There's a lingering moment of quiet before Matt asks, "So, uh, how's your head?" I suppose I appeared more drunk than I thought last night.

"I've not had any complaints." The words slip out before I think twice. So *not* the time for a blow job joke.

He snorts. "My god, you're twelve."

"I guess that's why I bought a *school* bus. . . . Which reminds me, I *am* supposed to pick it up this weekend. You free?"

"Uh, yeah. Think so. When?"

I take a deep inhale through the nose, evoking all the confidence I can muster. "Well, it's an eleven-hour drive . . . one way. So, the whole weekend?" I wince as soon as the words leave my lips.

"Oh, okay. Uh—"

I interrupt. "I'll pay for your time! And for the hotel too. Two beds, of course. I wouldn't normally ask this last minute but—"

Matt cuts off my attempt to break the speed-talking record with a firm "Okay."

I pause.

"Right. Um . . . Okay. No, yeah, that sounds fun."

I'm *fairly* positive that was a yes. "Thank you, Matt." I tuck my phone closer. "Are you sure it's not too much trouble?"

"Yeah, of course. I do have to get back to work, though. Customers walking in."

"All right, talk later. Thanks again."

"Bye . . . Oh, wait!"

"Yeah?" I bring the phone back to my ear.

"Congratulations!"

My smile unfurls slowly, like a blooming flower. He's the first person to acknowledge it as a thing *worth* celebrating. I know I've only told a handful of people, but it still feels nice. "Thank you, Matt."

"Have a good one," he adds before hanging up.

When he does, I get back to my research.

FOUR

AMOS AND EMILY BOUGHT A FIXER-UPPER ABOUT EIGHT
months ago. Actually, it's how they got engaged too. On the day
they took possession, Amos gave her a ring instead of a key ring.
And quite the ring it was. A huge, flashy square-cut diamond set
on a simple band. Classy, like her—but also showy, like her.

Chloe, Warren, Matt, and I went by the house that evening to
have some wine and tour around before they began renovations.
Emily answered the door with her left hand in front of her face
and I honestly don't remember if we even explored the house
after all our squealing and excitement.

Emily glows in love. She's always been beautiful, but now, it's as
if her skin is silkier and her eyes are shinier. They're planning a
long engagement, prioritizing fixing up the house first—but I already know it will be an extravagant wedding. Not in a snobby
way—like Liz's will most likely be—but in a way where every detail
is taken care of for the sake of their guests. Emily and Amos are
extroverts—loved by so many—and championed by their large

families. It will be a joyous merger of two cultures—Emily's Ghanian traditions with Amos's Honduran roots.

As recent renovation experts themselves, and because Amos has a truck, I asked if they'd come to the hardware store with me for my first round of supply shopping. It's taken a dozen blogs, hours of videos, and a few emails exchanged with *@tinyhomebus _gayle* to figure out what I need. I feel equipped *enough* to begin purchasing.

Gayle, who I'm positive hates me after I asked her what a solar charge controller was instead of googling it, said that with my budget, I can probably afford to hire out the bigger jobs. Plumbing for the water supply, wiring and installation of solar panels, etcetera. I've made some calls and have gotten most of those jobs *tentatively* booked based on my schedule and Matt's availability.

That just leaves me with the *short* list of: dismantling the rows of seats, removing all siding and the current ceiling, installing insulation, replacing all the windows, framing out the bathroom, lining the ceiling with birch paneling, building custom furniture for the dining nook that turns into a guest bed, tiling the bathroom and backsplash of the kitchen, installing kitchen cabinets and countertops, purchasing appliances, installing a wood-burning stove, building a bed, decorating, and moving.

Oh, and learning *how* to do all that. With Matt's help . . . and maybe Gayle's, if she answers my messages again.

"Do we need two carts?" Emily asks, pulling one flatbed trolley free from the entrance's corral.

"I'm not sure. How much of this do we load ourselves?" I ask.

"All of it," Em and Amos answer in tandem, dejected.

"Then yeah. Let's get two."

Amos takes one to the lumber section to get the wood for

framing and the ceiling. Emily and I go straight to the fun part—appliances.

From my research and *attempt* at drawing a layout—I've decided to get an apartment-sized fridge with a low power consumption since it'll be running off stored solar energy. We also find a deep but small square sink that takes up less counter space.

"This is so much more fun to do with someone else's money." Emily beams as she turns the faucet of a few different display-model sinks. "Did you need to look at stoves?" She tilts her head, as if she's now wondering if I can even have such a thing.

"I'm going to go with a countertop dual burner and a toaster oven I can stow away," I answer. "For now."

Emily nods, and we turn the corner into the lighting aisle.

"What happens to all your stuff that can't fit on the bus?" she asks, flicking on a vanity mirror. We catch our reflections, and I pose behind her, making her laugh as she flattens her edges.

"Storage locker. I'm not ready to go full force into minimalism but, if a year from now I haven't gone there once, I'll probably donate or sell it all." I shrug. Other than a few boxes of things that I'd *never* get rid of, like my dad's collection of records and photo albums.

"I can't believe how much you've figured out in just a few days." Emily wraps her arm around me before I push the cart down the aisle. "You're killing it."

I sigh. "Thanks. Gotta make up for the impulsivity somehow, right?"

"Hmm." Emily hums, long and heavy. "You don't have to prove yourself to anyone."

"Really?" I scoff. "Because you and *everyone else*"—except for Matt, I think—"have made some sort of snide remark about it being wildly impulsive. Your concerns have been noted, and I'm making a point to prove you all wrong."

"So should I apologize for being insensitive or let this rage fester so it fuels your determination?" she asks, smiling.

"Oh, definitely do not apologize. I'm on a roll, motherf—"

"Can I help you find anything?" an older gentleman wearing a red apron asks from behind us.

I bite down on my smile as Em and I exchange that-was-close glances.

"Yes, hi! I'm looking for a composting toilet."

"Aisle forty-two. Want me to take you there?" He points with a thumb over his shoulder.

"Do you happen to have an extensive knowledge of toilets of the portable variety?"

"I do, actually."

"Then yes, please. Thank you."

⁘   ⁘   ⁘

TWO HOURS AND over six thousand dollars later, we left the store with a delivery scheduled in ten days' time and just a few bags of smaller items. Didn't need the truck after all, but I was glad to have Amos's expertise in framing lumber.

"Lunch?" Amos asks, settling into his seat. "My treat."

Emily turns over her shoulder. "All-you-can-eat sushi?" she asks me with hopeful eyes.

"Yes!" I cheer. "Amos, you a sushi guy?"

"Not really, but I'm a whatever-makes-my-wife-happy guy." He winks.

"Wife?" Emily admires her ring. "Strange, I don't see a wedding band."

"Time isn't linear. You'll be my wife soon, so you're my wife now."

"Hmm. Sounds like someone's trying to worm his way out of a

big wedding," Emily teases, brushing her hand over Amos's tight curls.

I watch as they share a suggestive glance and Amos kisses Emily's cheek. I'm happy for them, truly, but I doubt there will ever be a part of me that doesn't feel bone-deep lonely when I'm around them *or* Chloe and Warren.

I hide it well, I think. Under disingenuous teasing and throat-clearing like a mother announcing her presence when she walks in on a group of teenagers playing spin the bottle in the basement. But it hurts.

It's the moment they share an inside joke and I laugh along absently, feeling my heart squeeze. Or when we watch a movie, and they merge closer—slowly, like they can't help but twist limbs—and I become shockingly aware of my body and how cold it is.

I used to be content with casual flings and hookups. I've never slept over or even considered a future with anyone I've been with. But for the last year, it's been a near constant stirring. An undercurrent of wanting that I haven't been able to satisfy—and haven't bothered to try. It's a person out of reach when all you need is a hug.

And I hate it.

I've never been one for conventional ways of life. Dating, marriage, kids, growing old with *one* person. It was never in the cards, not since Dad's passing. But lately, when I'm watching my friends in their little bubbles of giddy love, it feels like maybe I've actually wanted it all along. Possibly so much so that I've rejected the idea to make it easier on myself. Bracing for the inevitable loneliness by giving up early. Because it can't happen. I won't let it.

Amos pulls out of the parking lot, and I'm met with a wave of anxiety. I need air. Air and space from them. From the reminder of my loneliness. "Oh . . ." I tsk. "Actually, I just remembered I can't do lunch." I swallow thickly, twiddling my thumbs. "I have to finish up some work before Matt and I leave tomorrow."

"Oh, okay." Emily turns over her shoulder, her lips twisted. "We can eat fast?"

"No, sorry." I feel my throat tighten around another excuse. "It's a big job, and I've left it to the last minute." I roll my eyes. "You know me," I say. *Silly Lane. Can't do anything right!*

"All right." Em leaves her left hand on Amos's leg as he nods and takes the next right turn, toward my place. "Rain check." She settles back into her seat.

Thankfully, I'm not forced to direct Amos home. He knows how to get there because it used to be Emily's place too.

I *really* miss her.

I focus on the buildings we pass instead of the quickened rhythm of my heart or the way I can suddenly hear it over the music, street noise, and conversation from the front seat. A cool layer of sweat forms on my palms and forehead, and I wipe it against my sleeve.

Just breathe, Lane. In, hold, and out.

It's stupid, I tell myself, *to get so worked up over your friend's happiness. So selfish.*

I lick my lips and taste salt before I realize I'm crying. No. Not here. Not in front of them. I'm already handled with kid gloves for being the single one. I don't need to add *mentally unstable* as another pin on my Girl Scout sympathy sash.

I'm so frustrated with myself that anger actually takes over as the leading emotion, ending my self-pity parade and the tears I rained down on it.

When we finally make it to my building, I kiss them both on the cheek, a playful attempt to seem unbothered. "Love you! See you soon."

"Lane, your bags." Amos points over his shoulder.

"I'll help." Em is unbuckling before I can protest.

I follow her to the back of the truck, and she opens the hatch and takes out a few of my bags. I grab the box of rust-proofing spray paint and close it with my free hand. "I can take those." I hold out my hand to her so she can slide the bags on by their handles.

"What? Babe, these are heavy. I'll help carry them up."

"No, that's okay." I shake my head and reach my hand out again.

She studies me, then her eyes fall to my hand. She slides one bag on, then the other, cautiously. "Are you okay?" she asks, voice gentle.

And though I know she doesn't mean with the weight of the bags, I answer, "Totally fine! I've been working out." And wink at her.

Emily runs up the front steps to get the door for me, and I yell my goodbye over my shoulder as I make my way across the lobby.

Once upstairs, I dump everything onto the floor and climb into bed. Before I consciously decide to, I'm on my phone, being swept away by distractions every second and a half. I won't feel all of this. Not today. Maybe never. I'm not up for the challenge, and tomorrow is a big day.

FIVE

THE NEXT MORNING, I PULL UP OUTSIDE MATT'S PLACE just after seven. I've never been inside his apartment, but I've seen him appear from and disappear into the narrow path at the side of the old brick home that leads toward his basement entrance.

He's refused my curiosity to see his home several times. I was considering for a while that he was perhaps a serial killer, but that seems considerably less likely after getting to know him. Maybe just a hoarder then. Or perhaps he has a strange, embarrassing collection—like teeth or Beanie Babies.

Even if that's the case, I still want to go in. I could figure out what shampoo he uses that gives his dark curls such shine. I'd probably look in his pantry to find out which protein powder makes him so bear-sized. I'd definitely check if his mattress is sunken in on one side and which side might need company. Out of curiosity.

"Morning boss." Matt hops into the audacious truck that should definitely be decorated with some offensive political bumper stickers or fake testicles hanging from the rear. He looks around, biting his lip and nodding like he's hearing a joke. "Nice ride."

"The rental place offered me this or a convertible, and I do not like the idea of driving something with a collapsible roof."

"No?"

"No! I mean, what do you even do if the top is down and you get into an accident and roll? Tuck and pray?"

"Go out in style, I guess." Matt chucks a backpack onto the row of seats behind us before he pulls the seat belt across his broad chest. "So, you still want to switch off every three hours?" he asks.

"I believe I said once every *Titanic*, yes." I check my blind spot and begin our eleven-hour drive. A journey that suddenly doesn't feel quite as daunting.

"Right, I looked that up. Three hours and fourteen minutes. Please don't crash us into an iceberg. *Or* anything else."

"I'll try to stay on land, but I make no promises."

He makes a show of putting a fist around the grab-handle above the door, bracing himself for impact. "One *Titanic*," he mumbles to himself as I bump a curb on a slow turn.

"Hey! I'm a good driver."

"We've been friends for a while, and I've yet to see you drive. Can't blame me for taking precautions."

"The curb was a fluke."

"Yeah, and it looked at you funny," Matt agrees, lowering his hand to his lap.

"It did," I say decidedly.

"Does this thing have a headphone guy?" Matt asks.

"Jack?" I open the middle console, revealing the wire.

"That's him," he says, plugging his phone in.

"This is so exciting! I get to hear what *you* listen to for once!"

A soft humming begins as I stop at the red light. "*Jane Eyre* by Charlotte Brontë. Chapter One," a soft British voice says from the speakers.

"An audiobook?" I press my forehead to the wheel. "It's so early."

"Okay, but we could read an *entire* book before getting to the motel."

I think of the many, many hours of movies that Matt has watched upon my suggestion, straighten my back, and smile politely. "Is it like *Twilight*?"

"The guy's name *is* Edward."

"All right then. . . . Proceed."

*   *   *

THREE HOURS AND eight minutes later, we pull off the highway into a rest stop with a few fast-food places, a gas station, and—most importantly—a bathroom.

"Do *not* pee your pants," I mutter to myself as I haphazardly park and switch off the truck.

Matt pauses our book—which I'm surprisingly into—and I toss him the keys before making a mad dash to the toilets.

Once finished, I find Matt in line for coffee. He notices me spot him but still waves me over with a beaming smile. "Thank you, good sir," I say, slipping under the rope that directs the lineup. It's a typical food-court like you'd see in a mall—probably not redecorated since the eighties and filled with people who look vaguely carsick and annoyed.

"Hey!" a dude behind us scoffs. "There's a line."

Matt puts his arm around me and turns over his shoulder with a smile I've yet to see from him. It's friendly but . . . not? No teeth; puffed out chest. I'm kinda into it.

"She's with me." *Oh, I'm definitely into it.*

I take a hesitant glance at the angry man. He's wearing a polo shirt, chinos, and a watch that I could spot as a Rolex from a hundred feet away. I know his type. I grew up around guys like this. Entitled. He has places to be and people to see who are more important than we could *ever* understand. Every other human is an obstacle in this man's way.

"Nice," the asshole responds sarcastically. "So you can *both* go to the back of the line."

"Same order as before she joined me, my man." Matt turns back around and flashes his eyes at me as if to say *yikes*. He doesn't move his arm off my shoulder until we reach the front, and I find myself wishing the staff behind the counter were a *little* slower.

"Hey, how ya doing?" Matt asks the barista, rubbing his hands together in front of his chest.

"Oh, um, good. Thanks for asking." She stands straighter, smiling. "How are you?"

"I'm great, thanks. Could we please get two large coffees? One with just a bit of cream and the other with two pumps of sugar-free sweetener and oat milk." He looks over the menu, and something catches his eye, making him do a double-take. "And . . . can we please also get two of the banana bread loaves and . . ." He turns over his shoulder, finding the rich asshole who accused us of cutting. "What'll it be?" He tilts his head toward the board.

The man is as confused as I am. "What?" he asks, looking up from his phone.

"It's on me," Matt reassures him.

He studies Matt, unsure. "Black coffee," he responds slowly.

"And a large black coffee too, please," Matt adds, turning back to the barista.

He pays for the drinks and snacks before we move to wait at the end of the counter. I look around in a daze as the asshole steps up to the counter, takes his free black coffee, nods his appreciation to Matt, and walks briskly toward the exit.

"What was that about?" I ask, nudging him with my elbow.

"He seemed like he was having a rough morning."

"Or that's just how he is," I counter.

"Yeah, maybe. Still, it can't be fun to be him." Matt shrugs as our coffees and treats are placed on the counter. "Thank you!" he calls over his shoulder as we walk to a booth by the window.

"That was nice of you. I don't ever think to do stuff like that." *Yet another reason we're not compatible.*

"My parents always told us kids that we should imagine that anyone we come across is having the worst day of their life. I suppose that stuck with me."

"That's kinda depressing."

He takes a sip and contemplates that for a beat. "Maybe. But it means I don't sweat the small stuff with strangers."

"Nothing bothers you." I smile at him skeptically.

"Well, not nothing." He swallows a bite of banana loaf.

"Okay, so what does? Tell me your pet peeves."

"Um . . . okay." He sets his food down and shakes out his hands. "For starters, I really dislike when people kill bugs outside. That's their space, ya know?"

Oh my god. Even his pet peeves are precious.

"And it really bothers me when customers at work accuse me of overcharging them. I know mechanics are infamous for that, but Warren and I have fair prices."

"Both excellent peeves." I nod, crumbs spraying out of my mouth.

"What about you?"

"You probably know mine. I'm not one to hide my annoyance."

"Tell me anyway," he says.

I reach across the table to brush his beard with the back of my hand, getting the crumbs off. His eyes dart down to my hand and up to my face, making me reel back. *That was weird of you. . . . Say something.*

"Fine. Um. Well, I don't like when people stop at the top of escalators once they get off. It's like, look around you! There are other people in the world!"

"Right, so when people aren't conscious of others." Matt throws back the last of his loaf while I nod. There are more crumbs now, but he brushes them off.

"Yeah, or similarly, when you press the elevator button and it lights up, but then someone else comes up behind you and presses it again anyway. Like, why are you the elevator god? Do you really think that's gonna make a difference now? Just wait like the rest of us."

Matt smiles, but he does his best to hide it, scratching his nose with a knuckle.

"Is that stupid?" I ask, finishing my food.

"What? No, it's just . . . you get so riled up, and it's fun to watch."

"I do not."

"You really do. You're turning red."

"I have rage," I tease.

"I can see it." Matt raises his brows. "What are you *actually* angry about?"

The question catches me off guard. "Nothing," I laugh, breathier than intended. "What?"

"I mean, what makes you mad. Not annoyed."

"I don't know." Suddenly the cafeteria feels small, and strangers' ears appear too near. "What about you?"

"I asked first." Matt takes a slow sip, one brow raised in a taunt.

"Anyone who texts and drives." The words fall out of me. "Or, just, driving dangerously," I say wearily.

"That's a good one." Matt shakes his empty cup into his mouth, getting every drop.

"People like my sister's fiancé's parents." I stand and gather our garbage.

"What sorts of people are those?" Matt follows closely behind as I throw out our trash and head toward the exit. He holds the door open for me.

I answer him as it shuts behind us. "They like to hide behind all these polite words and soft smiles in public, but in private they're . . . nasty." I open the truck's passenger door and hop inside. Matt doesn't start the car. I take it as a cue to continue.

"They've said some things to my mom and sister that upset me, that's all."

"And your sister's fiancé?"

"I haven't met him yet, but . . . I'm worried about it. I know he didn't stick up for Liz. And the other day, Liz just said this thing about her wedding—about me bringing a date."

Matt straightens. "What about that?"

"That I should make sure that if I bring a date, it's a man."

"Oh . . . shit." Matt's bottom lip juts out, and his shoulders fall. "I'm sorry."

"I know my sister doesn't care about me being bi, and my mom doesn't either, but . . . it just hurt."

"Of course it did." He rests a hand on my knee, and the sensation of comfort brings on tears.

"Ugh. Sorry." I wipe my face on my sleeve and shake my head forcibly.

"What? No . . . Lane, that is upsetting. When upsetting things happen, people cry."

I nod, brushing the tears away. When he says it, it seems so simple. A natural reaction rather than a reason for embarrassment.

I give him a weak smile. "Yeah, you're right."

"Ready?" he asks, turning the ignition. I nod, swiping the last tear away from under my eye. Matt pulls out of the parking spot, adjusts his mirror, and then merges back onto the highway.

"Can we keep listening to *Jane Eyre*?" I ask.

"Sure." He opens the center console, but then stops himself abruptly. "Sorry, I shouldn't do that while driving. Can you do it? My passcode is four, three, two, one."

I can't help but laugh. "Wow, you're going to get hacked."

"Warren just said it couldn't be one, two, three, four." He shakes his head. "I didn't even want a password."

"What?" I ask incredulously. "Then everyone could find all the dirty images on your phone!"

"My what, now?" Matt laughs, his hands scraping against the wheel as he moves them to rest on the bottom half.

"You know. . . ." I shimmy side to side. "Your *pictures*," I say in a sultry voice.

"I've never taken a dick pic, if that's what you're inferring."

I want to scream from the rush of giddiness and confusion and excitement at this conversation. It feels *distinctly* like flirting. Or, at least, flirting-adjacent. "What? C'mon!"

He laughs, and it's so joyful his smile grows impossibly wide. "I swear! Lane, you've seen me text. Do you really think I've sent naked photos of myself?"

"But you're on all the apps," I protest.

"Again, Lane, you've seen me text—why on earth do you think I'm on any sort of dating app?"

"Well, because . . ." I'm suddenly realizing that I have no *actual* reason to believe he has been. He's never confirmed a damn thing. "You told *me* to download them . . . and you go on dates all the time!"

"I told you to download them because I was tired of hearing you complain about *not* dating."

"Fair."

"And I went on dates the old-fashioned way." *Went? Past tense?*

"A letter and a dowry?" I ask.

"Little less old-fashioned than that."

"What then?"

"This weird thing called face-to-face human interaction. I'd go to a bar, or a park, or . . . one time, I even went speed dating."

"You. Did. Not."

"I did," he says defensively. "It was actually fun."

"I can't imagine that being a real thing people do."

"Well, it is."

I cross my arms and hold myself tightly. "Well, did you meet any fine young women there?"

"What's with the sudden interest in my dating life?" He turns briefly to smile at me. A taunting sort of glance that makes me feel the need to shut down this conversation.

I roll my eyes exaggeratedly in hopes he can hear it. "I'm putting the book back on now."

SIX

MATT'S PALM IS SPREAD ACROSS MY KNEE AGAIN. I COULD have sworn that I left the house this morning in a pair of jeans, but now I'm in a sundress and can see the many tattoos on my thighs. Light flares through the windshield as Fleetwood Mac plays from the radio. I look over at Matt, and his eyes are all heat and wanting and desire. He quickly switches back and forth between watching the road and my lips as they smile, granting permission. He slides his hand higher and brushes the back of his knuckles against my inner thigh, sending a rush of air up my spine as I part my legs farther for him. Just as he moves his hand up, a horn blares.

"What?" I yell.

"Just someone cutting someone else off. You can keep sleeping," Matt answers, flicking his turn signal. I look around and gather myself, wiping the drool off my chin and checking the time.

"Matt—it's almost three."

"Wow, would you look at that?" he says.

"That is more than one *Titanic*!"

Matt shrugs. "You know you talk in your sleep, right?"

"I do not." I blush. Liz used to tell me that too. "But . . . hypothetically . . . if I did. What did I say?"

Matt smiles to himself. "Can't remember."

He is perhaps as merciful as he is cruel.

"Okay, well, take the next stop for early dinner and a switch."

"There's one an hour ahead. Cool to keep going until then? After that we'll just have one more stretch to go before we get to the motel."

I check the GPS. Four hours and forty minutes left.

"If you're sure. But I feel bad—you'll be driving the bus the whole way home."

"I like driving." He smiles. "I'm sure."

I lean back into my seat and twiddle my thumbs for a second before looking out the window. There are ferocious-looking gray clouds in the distance. "Think we'll hit rain?"

"Looks like it."

I nod silently.

"You okay? You seem a little jumpy."

"I'm not a very good passenger." *And I had an inappropriate sex dream about a friend.*

Matt nods. "Can I ask you something?" he asks softly.

"Yeah, sure," I answer, turning my focus to him.

"It might be . . . it might be none of my business."

"Those are the best kinds of questions."

"And if you don't want to—"

I interrupt. "Just ask, Matt."

"How did your dad die?" he asks bluntly, as if he needed to force it out.

"Yeah . . . uh, a car accident."

His hands tense around the wheel.

"I wondered," he says. "When you mentioned texting and driving and being a nervous passenger."

"Ah. Well, good detective skills, Sherlock."

"*Sherlock Holmes,* I know that one." Matt winks, and it immediately lowers the tension.

"You know it from the books, though, don't you?" I raise a brow.

He whips his head toward me before remembering to look ahead. "Are there Sherlock movies?"

"And a show. A successful show."

"That wasn't on your list!"

"There *is* more than what I've got on my list, Matt."

"We've got to add it," he states matter-of-factly. "As soon as we get to the motel."

"Okay," I agree. "We could even watch it on my laptop."

He nods. "Done."

＊　＊　＊

WHEN WE LEAVE the second rest stop after dinner, the rain is pouring so loud that we can't hear our audiobook over it hitting the windshield. We give up and talk instead. I don't particularly mind driving in the rain, but I'm glad Matt's here. His patented calm is working on me.

"Okay . . ." Matt says slowly. "Would you rather become a vegetarian or never eat another vegetable as long as you live?"

"Can I take vitamins?"

"Yes."

"Can I make smoothies?"

"Not with any vegetable products."

"I'd rather not eat another vegetable," I answer. "I'm really thinking about fried chicken."

"Fair."

Lightning cracks in the distance, and I jump a little. "Uh, okay. My turn." I readjust in my seat. "Would you rather be invisible for twenty-four hours or be able to fly for one hour?"

"Fly. No hesitation."

"Okay, that one was too easy. Let me go again." I tap my finger against the wheel and turn up the windshield wipers slightly. "Would you rather be able to control the weather for the rest of your life *or—*"

"That one."

"Wait! Or," I say again, "have ten questions answered with 100 percent truthfulness by anyone of your choice."

"Huh." Matt tugs on his beard. "Well, that's a good one."

"See, I told you to wait."

"Still the weather," he says firmly. "My turn?"

"Hmm, maybe a different game? I'm starting to think about the rain a little too much."

"Want me to drive?"

"No, I'm okay."

"Okay, not a different game but . . . a question. If you could have a dinner party with any five guests—dead or alive—who'd it be?"

"They've got to be real people?" I ask.

"They either all have to be real, or they all have to be characters."

"All right . . ." I sigh. "Well, the first one's my dad, obviously."

Matt nods but continues looking at his feet.

"Then, because I couldn't have my dad back from the dead and *not* invite them, my mom and my sister." *Uh-oh. Here it comes. Big feelings. Loud feelings. Embarrassing ones.*

"Right." Matt's voice cracks. "So, two more?"

"Yeah." I force it out. I check my blind spots and mirrors before pulling off onto the highway's shoulder.

"Lane?" Matt looks nervously between me and the dashboard.

"Sorry. One second," I say through a trembling breath. I feel tears rush down my cheeks and shut my eyes tight in an effort to stop them. I press my forehead to the steering wheel.

"No, *I'm* sorry. I shouldn't have asked about that. Obviously you'd want to see your dad, and that's not something you need to think about right now. I'm—"

"No, I'm—" I interrupt but fail to speak until I take a deep breath. "God, I can't believe I've cried in front of you *twice* today. This is so embarrassing."

"Please don't be embarrassed. Please." Matt takes my hand in his and pulls it toward him until his other hand holds it too. "It's my fault."

I can't help but look at our hands and then his face. "I just thought . . . Well, I thought I should invite Liz's fiancé Phillip too. Because he never got to meet Dad, right? And maybe, if he isn't right for her, she'd listen to him." I brush tears away with my free hand. "Then I thought that I'd want *my* person there too. But . . ." I sniffle. "The chair was empty. Ya know?"

Matt sighs, his upper body hunching in on itself. He lowers our hands to his lap and then releases mine. "Can I come?" He looks up at me through heavy brows.

I suck in a breath. "What?" I ask, trying to find a napkin or anything other than my sleeve.

"To your dinner party. I'd like to meet your dad." His lips twitch into a dim smile. "I know I'm not your *person*, but it would be nice to meet your family."

I nod, my tears turning into soft laughter at his sweetness. "Yeah, okay."

"Do you want to sit here for a while?"

"Could you . . . could you take over?" I ask.

"Of course. You all right?"

I shrug. "I don't really know."

"Long day." Matt nods. "Just one more hour."

"Yeah." I wipe the last of my tears. "I really am sorry for crying so much today. I've asked you for this massive favor, and now I'm treating you like my therapist or something."

Matt laughs. "You're not, and even if you were—I'm used to it."

I narrow my eyes, waiting for an explanation of whatever *that* means.

"I'm the middle of nine kids, Lane," he says pointedly. "You know what role that puts me in?"

I shake my head.

"Mediator. Middleman. If my siblings were the United Nations, I was Switzerland."

That makes me laugh. "What sorts of disagreements did you settle?"

"Let's switch seats, then I'll tell you."

I nod, and we both unbuckle and open our doors, the rain pelting us until we run around and make it safely back inside.

Matt whoops, slamming the door shut. "That was the wake-up I needed!"

Even in a thunderstorm, he's finding the sunny side.

Matt pulls onto the road, and the GPS recalculates. Just under an hour to go.

"I forget how much I've told you about my family—but I feel like when I talk about them, there's always the necessary backstory, so prepare to listen, even if you've heard it before, and not interrupt."

I smile, turn to face him, and lean into the headrest.

"My parents met in 1985 at Live Aid, a massive fundraising concert."

"Matt, I know about Live Aid. Everyone does."

"What did I say about interrupting?" he teases. "Anyway, they met there. My dad likes to say that he saw my mum on the shoulders of some other dude and immediately felt like she should be on his own instead. Very romantic stuff . . ."

I listen as Matt describes his family members one by one. His father, a Canadian in London to study, meets his mother, who was visiting from Upolu. Somewhere between Bowie and U2, they fell madly in love. They eloped, moved to Canada, bought some land with the money his dad got from selling his flat in London, and made a life for themselves.

They built a small cabin by hand with some help from the community that so lovingly accepted them. They had four children in six years, then Matt two years after that. His mother loves to say that Matt was such a good baby that they felt like they could have even more. So they built more rooms and did. The kids were all homeschooled and Matt's parents had gardens and greenhouses on their property that fed them all year long—with the help of trading with their neighbors for eggs and meat.

It sounds heavenly. Idyllic, even. I can almost smell the wet grass as Matt describes helping his mother tend the garden and feel the chill on my skin as he describes lazy winter days spent reading or chopping wood with his dad.

We don't get to the debates he settled, or much about his siblings, before we pull into the parking lot of a motel that, I have to say, looked a *hell* of a lot nicer online.

"I rambled, didn't I?" Matt pushes some hair out of his face.

"Yeah, but I still want more."

"Good thing we have the drive back," he says, peering out the windshield. "This is the place, right?"

"Yeah . . ." I bite my lip. "I, uh, think so."

"Nice," Matt says unconvincingly.

We grab our bags, the leftovers from dinner, and snacks from the vending machine from our last stop, then head inside to the front office.

"Welcome to Morph Motel, where *we* prioritize *you*," a very bored-looking teenager says from behind the desk. "Checking in?"

"Yes, we are." I start to open my phone to find the reservation number.

"Hourly or nightly?"

Matt laughs but turns away to hide it.

"Uh, for the night. It's under Elaine Rothsford."

The kid perks up. "Oh, you're the one who made the reservation." He puts down his phone. "I've never had one of those before."

I wince but attempt to turn it into a grin ineffectively. "Cool."

"Here's your key." He slides it across the desk. "I did give you the best room but . . . well, you'll see."

Sounds fantastic. I look at Matt with an apology, but he's just reaching into his pocket to tip the kid.

"Have a good one." He holds the door over my head, and I lead him toward the room up a rusting metal staircase outside.

"I *promise* it was nicer online."

"It's an adventure."

"It was painted blue in the photos—does it look blue to you?"

"It's hard to tell in the dark."

"It's just the closest one to Carl's garage and the rental place, and I figured after the long drive, we wouldn't want to go much farther." I stop in front of our door, number nine.

"Lane, it's one night."

"Okay." I nod, the key cutting into my hand as I hold tightly.

"You gonna open that?" Matt points to the door.

"Yeah . . . any second now."

"Allow me." He puts out his palm, and I give him the key. He jiggles the lock, but it won't budge. "Oh." He flicks the number nine with his finger, and it spins. "Missing a screw. This is room six."

We walk a few more doors down, and sure enough, there's number nine.

This time, the door does open, and it's pitch-black inside.

"Gentlemen first." I wave him in.

He switches on the lights, and they flicker for a while. But altogether, the room's not terrible. Two beds, both covered in yellow and orange floral comforters with white sheets. Brownish carpet, and nothing but a few hooks on the wall, a console table with an older TV, and a side table between the beds. There's a door to what is presumably the bathroom, which I will open once I have the courage to move.

"This is way nicer than I was thinking!" Matt hops onto the bed enthusiastically, and it groans under him, to the point where he stands to make sure he didn't break it. "My bad. Won't do that again."

I stare from the doorway, my feet unwilling to take me inside. "Maybe we sleep in the truck?"

"It's one night. We'll be fine. There's Wi-Fi!" He gestures to the sign on the wall. "We can watch *Sherlock*."

I nod, stepping inside so the door closes behind me. Trapping us in.

SEVEN

MATT BRAVELY ENTERED THE BATHROOM, DECLARED IT "workable," and took a shower, which he said alternated between jacuzzi hot and ice plunge. I went for a quick sink rinse with my washcloth and a bar of soap instead.

We've been sitting together on the bed farthest from the door, attempting to watch *Sherlock,* but the internet speed is about as fast as my great-aunt Ethel hiking with her two bad knees. So instead, we've passed the time by seeing how many stains we can spot without moving our necks.

A part of me is aware that I am sitting next to Matt on a bed, which people have probably used for sex at some point. The thoughts quickly lead to sex *with* Matt, but I push them away. I've been described as strong-willed most of my life, but the universe is unkind, and he's wearing gray sweatpants. Furthermore, we'd both have to be tested if we had sex here, and of course there's the matter of our friendship and *keeping* it.

The last eighteen months have been fairly dry for me in the intimacy department, to be honest. The last man I was with, probably over two years ago, was awful at sex. He couldn't find my clit if it was under a giant, flashing neon sign. He rubbed my body like a red wine stain on a white carpet, and when I left, he messaged almost *immediately* that he was getting back together with his girlfriend.

When I don't shut down the thoughts *right* away, I imagine Matt is good at sex. He's thoughtful and considerate outside the bedroom and has *those* lips. I liked kissing Matt the one time I did. It was awkward and fumbly and hesitant—but it was *good*.

A loud boom of thunder rattles the walls, and the lights flicker.

"Hey, uh, Lane?"

"Yeah?"

"I don't want to alarm you, but . . . there's a consistent stream coming in from under the window frame and drenching the headboard and top of my bed." Matt points to what *would* have been his bed.

"Awesome." I fall back with a thump against the stiff mattress, and the bed frame groans. "Well, I dragged you into the pits of hell, so you can choose your poison. Share with me, or I can sleep on the floor."

"I'll sleep on the floor."

"Nope, not an option. That's not fair."

"Okay, then we share." He lies on his back next to me, and the bed all but collapses.

We both break out into a fit of giggles so ferocious it almost distracts me from the drip that's begun falling onto the tile of the bathroom.

"This," Matt forces out through laughter, "is their *best* room?"

"You tipped that kid!" I laugh until tears are streaming down my cheeks, almost like the wall above the other bed. Matt's also wiping his face as the bed creaks and we both attempt to steady ourselves, bracing for the impact that doesn't come.

"We can't sleep here, babe."

Matt called me babe. "What's your plan?"

"There has to be another hotel."

Matt called me babe. "There really isn't. Not within an hour of here. We're in the middle of nowhere." I chew my lip.

Matt called me babe. I should say something, right? I'm going to say something.

Matt shifts onto his side, and the bed collapses, the mattress cushioning our short fall. Thunder cracks outside, and then the power goes out in quick succession. The room is lit by a streetlamp outside and the screen of my laptop that has fallen between us.

There's a silent, stunned moment as our laughter builds and builds, before I have to force myself to stop laughing or else see my brain deprived of oxygen.

"Matt?"

"Yeah?" He coughs, attempting to steady himself.

"I'm so sorry about all of this," I say, voice dejected.

"You can't control the weather, right?"

"Well, no."

"And you didn't build this bed?"

"No, it doesn't look like my signature style."

"Okay then." He sighs out the last of his laughter. "I mean, this is somehow *more* comfortable now." He lies down. "At least it's not squeaking."

I close my laptop, and the room falls pitch-black. After placing it on the floor, I lie down and smirk at the ceiling, feeling brave in the dark. "You called me babe, you know."

Four seconds of silence.

"Heh . . . yeah. I heard it, and hoped the moment passed," he says.

"I heard it, and I'll probably bring it up often," I tease.

"Goodnight, Lane," he says dryly.

"Night, babe," I return, but my eyes refuse to close. "Matt?"

"Yeah?" He yawns and sighs, curling into the mattress like an overgrown puppy.

"Could you tell me more stories?"

"Are you asking me to bore you to the point of sleep?"

I scoff. "Not bore, I find it . . . relaxing."

He shuffles against the mattress, then clears his throat. "All right, consider me your personal bedtime story connoisseur. Would you like to hear about the time my eldest brother, Aaron, got chased by a family of ducks, or when my sisters Ruth and Tabitha smuggled a goat into their bedroom?"

"Both, please," I mumble into the sleeve of my sweater.

.   *   .

WHEN I WAKE up, the lights are on, but it's still dark and raining outside. I'm also entirely on top of Matt. His arm is across the length of my back, pinning me against him, like I'm his blanket or favorite stuffed animal. His breath is warm on the crown of my head, and the rising and falling of his chest lulls me into closing my eyes again. I don't fight it.

The second time I wake up, I'm being gently placed down on the mattress. I only feel disappointed for a second before I fall back to sleep.

The third time, it's to an alarm in a room no longer lit by overhead lighting, but by the sun through broken blinds.

"Morning," Matt groans, reaching over me and smacking my phone until it's silent.

"Hey." I sniffle and comb my hair with my fingers.

"We survived."

"We did." My neck is sore, and I feel gross, but we *did*. "How'd you sleep?" I ask.

"Fine, yeah. I woke up, and the lights were on, so I got up to turn them off. Guess the power came back."

Matt's hair is down and passes his shoulders. It's not as unruly as mine is this morning, but it's definitely messy. "I have an extra hair tie if you need it." I offer him my limp wrist where I wear them like bracelets.

"Perfect, thanks." He makes quick work of tying up his hair into a bun.

"Thank you, again. For . . . doing this. I'm sure it's a lot worse than you expected."

"Nah, I usually account for power outages, rainstorms, and horror-film motels," he teases softly with a smile. "Seriously though, it's all good."

"Okay." But it isn't. It's far from okay.

"The company isn't half bad." He offers a sleepy smile, his eyes still adjusting to the light.

God, I could get used to waking up to that smile.

"No?" I scrunch up my face. "Even when I make myself your personal weighted blanket?" I bite my lip, squinting like he's the morning sun coming through the window. *Did I make him uncomfortable?*

"What?" He startles like that is the single most preposterous thing he's ever heard. "That was the best part. I was *cursing* those lights for making me move." He jumps to stand, as if he didn't say anything important at all. As if my heart didn't just perform a triple back handspring. "You know, people would pay for that service. Like a deep tissue relaxation massage." He offers a hand to pull me up.

Once I stand, I look down at the bed and press my palm to my cheek. "Wow. It's really wrecked."

Matt chuckles. "When we get back, we can tell Chloe and Warren we both shared *and* wrecked a bed." Matt places both hands on his hips while he studies the broken bed frame.

"Oh my god. Do they bug you too?" I ask reactively, my voice pitching up, as if to say *Ugh! As if!*

"You mean about us?" He blows out through tight lips. "Yeah. Tons."

Why did I like the way he said *us* so much? I'm clearly still half asleep.

"They're the worst." I look out of the corner of my eye to see if he agrees. Not because I want him to disagree, *obviously*. Just curious.

Matt shrugs nonchalantly before he begins gathering his things and shoving them into his backpack. "I'll be out in a few." He shuts the bathroom door to get changed.

I begin packing up my things while lecturing myself.

Don't think about him being naked in there. Stop thinking about it. Stop it right now!

Something moves. Scurries.

A blood-curdling scream comes out of me as I leap onto the only bed left standing. Rat! Rat! Rat!

"What?" Matt comes rushing out in nothing but his boxers.

"No, no, no," I whine. "Ew!" I shake out my limbs as I resist the urge to gag.

"Lane! What?"

"Rat!"

"Where?"

"It ran!"

"Where?"

"Back to hell? I don't know!"

"Point," he commands.

I gesture toward the console table on the opposite wall from the water-drenched headboard. "It was the size of a toddler, Matt." I roll my shoulders as my spine begins to curl in on itself in disgust.

He fights it but fails to suppress a smile. "It's probably gone now. I'm going to grab your stuff, and then you can go wait outside, okay?"

"Oh my god, what if there's more outside waiting for me?"

"What? Like a rat-mobster hit?"

"Maybe."

"Do you think they have an SUV out front? Is the boss a rat too, or are the rats just his minions?"

"I hate you!"

"Well, I won't help you with that attitude." He puts his hand on his hip, popping it.

"Please help me. I'm sorry. I'll be nice, I swear. Get me out of here."

Matt gathers my things one by one and places them gingerly into my backpack. Honestly I'd rather he just chuck it all out the window and get me the fuck out of here.

I suppose I'm not *too* terrified of the rodent lurking in the shadows, because I'm still able to admire Matt's tree-trunk thighs. His body is thick all over, soft in the best places and solid in others where labor has toned him. I'm a little obsessed with the broadness of his chest and the swell of his stomach. I can't even rationalize his shoulders and the effect they have on my brain. All I know is that I'm suddenly wanting to attend a concert with him, just to take a seat. I notice a bulge at the front of his black boxers— because I'm human—and lift my eyes to the ceiling to avoid staring at *it*.

"That everything?" he asks, holding up my bag.

"Think so." I have *no* clue and I do *not* care.

"Okay, I'll open the door, and you make a run for it."

"Nope." I shake my head fiercely. "Floor is lava. Rat territory. Death Valley."

"Lane, it's way more scared of you than—"

I interrupt. "If the rat was more afraid of us, then why did it decide to run around in broad daylight like it owns the place? *No.* He's clearly got no fear. Which makes him unpredictable."

"Fine." Matt walks over to me, shaking his head. "Come 'ere." He holds my backpack in one hand and opens his opposite arm toward me. I step into the space between his chest and bicep, and then it's curled around my upper thighs.

He's carrying me. Like I'm an overgrown baby . . . but still. The short distance between the edge of the bed and the door seems to last an eternity.

I consider myself a feminist. Not always a *perfect* one—but I do my best. However, right now, I'd let this man take me back to his cave and have his way with me. I'd put on a fifties housewife dress, make him his favorite meatloaf, and sit with an empty plate in front of me, adoringly watching him eat. I consider the complications that may arise if I attempt to carry his giant babies between my narrow hips and decide it's worth it.

"There." He opens the door and places me outside, quickly handing me my backpack and the keys to the truck. "I'm going to get clothes on now."

"Wait." *What? He needs clothes, you pervert.* "Uh, thank you."

"Yeah . . . okay." He laughs in confusion. "Five minutes, tops."

The door shuts, and my brain turns back on, leaving the magnetic force field of his half-naked body. Note to self: Do not go to the beach with Matt this summer. You may drown.

He dresses, and we return the key to the front office attendant, who couldn't care less about the bed, leak, or rat situation. We then drop the truck off at the nearby rental place and walk a few blocks from there to Carl's yard, which is mostly scrap and commercial vehicles with one big, beautiful, golden bus in the center of the lot. My bus.

"There she is." Matt bumps his shoulder with mine as we stand on the other side of the chain-link fence. "Your soon-to-be home."

The sudden reality that I actually did buy a full-ass school bus hits me like . . . well . . . a bus. My throat feels a little tighter, my hands a tad sweaty. But I can't shake off the smile on my face. My gut says this is a good idea.

Although, my gut has been wrong before.

We walk around the fenced yard to the trailer office and find Carl inside on the phone. He's an older man, probably in his late sixties, and dressed like an off-duty cowboy.

"I gotta go. Customers." He promptly hangs up the phone and opens his arms wide. "You must be Lane." He claps. "That's an awfully big bus for such a little girl."

Matt clears his throat, and it sounds an *awful* lot like a warning.

"Ha, well . . ." *How the fuck does one reply to that?* "It's going to be relatively small once it's my home . . . ya know, comparatively."

Carl just smiles wider, and I get the impression I could have said almost anything and his expression would remain the same. He's not entirely listening. He's selling. "You gotta point there, honey."

Matt's arms cross, and I almost wonder if gentle misogyny has joined the ranks of his other pet peeves. It's nothing I'm not used to, so I keep my body relaxed—trying to show Matt that there's no real threat here.

Carl opens a desk drawer with a grunt. "Let me get you the ownership papers, and after a few signatures, we'll be all set. Will your beau here be taking care of the remaining balance?"

With a sigh, I pull out a check from my floral purse—which feels right for this moment—and hand it over. It's the most money I've ever spent, and I sort of wish it wasn't going to this guy. I glance quickly at Matt, who is performing a convincing bodyguard stance and glowering at Carl.

"I'll be paying. My *beau* is here to drive the bus back." I tilt my head in challenge.

Carl's smile falters to a more sincere one with a long breath. "Boy, am I glad to hear that."

"Why?" Matt asks sternly before I can get the same question out.

"Pardon, son?" Carl pulls out a manila envelope and starts flipping carelessly through the papers.

"Why are you glad to hear that I'm driving?" Matt smiles like a predator. It's strangely doing *things* to me. Like, *turned on* things.

Yes, protect my honor, dear knight!

Carl squares off with Matt, clearly hearing the frustration in his tone. "Didn't mean anything by it, son."

"All right." Matt nods, his arms flexing across his broad chest, the ropes of muscle along his forearms bulging.

Oh my god.

"Where do I sign?" I take a seat in the chair closest to me, opening my legs wide in an attempted power move.

A few awkward minutes later, Carl makes a show of handing me the keys with a nod at Matt as if to say, *let's let her have this moment.* Matt's jaw tics, and I fight a laugh at his expense.

"Take good care of her, son!" he calls after us as we take the side door out to the yard toward the bus.

"Is he talking about me or the bus?" I ask, disgruntled.

"Fuck that guy," Matt grumbles.

"Oh, but Matty," I say in a sickeningly sweet baby voice. "He's right! My wittle hands can't drive da big bus!" I hold up two limp wrists.

"Please, dear god, never do that again." Matt looks disgusted, even as he fights a laugh.

We're close enough to the bus that the light reflecting off its sides turns the air around us yellow. "Wow." I gawk at its sheer size and feel my heart begin to flutter. It's here. It's cool and it's real and it's huge and it's *mine*. "Think this thing has a speaker for *Jane Eyre*?" I ask.

"I love that that's where your mind went." Matt opens the door and gestures for me to go inside. "After you."

EIGHT

THE BUS DOES HAVE AN AUDIO SYSTEM—THANK GOODNESS—
but before we jumped right back into *poor* and *obscure* Jane's life, I
had something important to do.

"With the Frizz? No way!" a chorus of children shout through
the speakers.

We dance up and down the aisle to the *Magic School Bus* theme
song. Even though Matt has most likely never watched it, he joins
in all the same. As stiff and awkward as he is when he dances, at
least he gives it his all. We're both out of breath when we stop, and
now the bus feels christened appropriately.

"Lily Tomlin was the original voice of Ms. Frizzle. Did you
know that?" I say through panting breaths.

"Who was what now?" Matt is flipping switches on the dashboard, and I peer over his shoulder from the row behind like a
naughty schoolgirl. Hey, this would be an excellent place for some
student-teacher role—*nope. Bad brain.*

"Whatcha doing?" I rest my chin on his shoulder.

He turns an inch to see me, eye to eye, and I reel back. *That* was weird of me.

"Just making sure she's ready to go." He smiles over his shoulder. "Or he. Or they. Does the bus have a name yet?"

"No . . . not yet." I look around for inspiration but come up empty. "It'll come to me."

Matt turns the ignition, and the engine roars. Damn, this thing is loud.

"All right kids—settle down back there!" I shout to the imaginary group of children behind us. "All set, driver." I pat his shoulder.

Matt laughs as he adjusts a mirror. He begins driving off the lot as Carl waves us through the open gate. My bus is going home.

*   *   *

"*AS IF I had a string somewhere under my left ribs, tightly knotted to a similar string in you. And if you were to leave, I'm afraid that cord of communion would snap. And I have a notion that I'd take to bleeding inwardly. As for you, you'd forget me.*"

The British narrator of the book does a lower, husky voice when representing the male lead of Jane Eyre, Edward Rochester.

I hit the pause button forcefully.

Matt looks over at me with concern as he bounces in the driver's seat.

"Need a minute with that one," I say.

He blows out a breath. "Fair."

"Imagine loving someone that much"—I bring my knees to my chest—"that you worry you'd literally die if they left you." I plant my chin on my knees. "It's a tragic sort of beautiful."

"And yet you also think *they'd* move on. . . ." Matt checks over his shoulder as we switch lanes. "Brutal."

"Surely he knows Jane loves him too, right? He doesn't *actually* think that she'd forget him."

"It's hard to know. Maybe it's not that he thinks she doesn't love him, but he thinks she doesn't love him as much as he loves her," Matt says.

"Thank you for choosing this book. I actually really like it."

He smiles at me in the mirror on the windshield above him. "I'm glad." He laughs under his breath. "Things *are* about to get weird though."

I hover my finger above the play button. "Even better."

We drive for another two hours before the end of the audiobook lines up with our stop for lunch almost perfectly.

"And *that*"—Matt puts the bus into park and shuts off the engine—"was *Jane Eyre*."

"I'm going to buy a physical copy." I open my phone to search online. "Like a trophy for my shelf."

Matt stands, stretches, and cracks his knuckles. "Driving this thing is fun, but it shakes *a lot*. I feel like I'm on a roller coaster up here."

"I wish I could trade off with you. I'm sorry," I say as we exit the bus.

"I really don't mind." He brings an arm around my shoulder, then squeezes me into his side. Sometimes, very rarely, it's like Matt is touching me because he just *wants* to. Like maybe his body is begging to be nearer too.

"Lunch is on me." I smile up at him, and as we stop a fair distance from the door while a family leaves, we hold eye contact. His arm around my shoulders, our smiles matching, the sides of our bodies touching. It's familiar and yet new. Comforting and yet exhilarating.

I feel my smile fade as his expression turns contemplative. The door shuts, and we're both made aware that we let a moment last longer than necessary. But Matt just smoothly removes his arm as I grab the door and hold it open with a flourish.

"After you, my liege," I say in a silly accent.

"Thank you." He bows as he steps through.

We get a medium pizza to split and carrots and celery on the side because Matt insisted that he hasn't seen me eat a vegetable this whole trip—or ever.

"Rabbit food," I mumble, taking a bite.

"Speaking of, where's Simone right now?" He wipes his beard with a napkin.

I swallow a bite and talk through chewing. "Oh, she's staying with Chloe and Warren. Willow adores her."

"How many pictures has Chloe sent you of them?"

"Willow and Simone? About a hundred." I smile. "In her defense, toddler with a bunny is a *very* cute combo." Matt nods with a warm grin as I open my phone and show him the one I've made my background. "I'm so obsessed with her."

He picks up another slice and holds it above his face, bending it into his mouth. "Do you think you'll ever have one of those?" He grins mischievously.

"A kid?"

He nods, chewing. "People presume I want a bunch because I have so many siblings, but honestly, I'm not so sure. What about you?"

"Uh, I don't know. I've never given it much thought, to be honest. Plus, I'll probably die alone." I smile exaggeratedly, showing all my teeth like a kid.

"Lane." He rolls his eyes.

"Seriously, though." I gesture to myself and, with a frown, notice a drip of pizza sauce on my shirt. "Nobody wants *all* of this. Let alone a miniature version." I scoff. "Don't see it happening. And kids usually come from commitment. I don't do commitment."

"Someone will try to make you a mother—you'll see."

I huff a laugh. "Dude, they're not interested. I told you, I'm on apps now! No bites!"

Matt shakes his head. "Let me see."

"The app?"

"Well, your profile."

I consider saying no, but curiosity gets the better of me. "Fine." I unlock my phone, open the app, and slide it across the table. "Judge away. I can take it."

Matt wipes his fingers, then picks up my phone. One brow raises as he scrolls and reads diligently. He blows out some air through his nose in an *almost* laugh, then he places the phone face down on the table between us.

"Well?" I ask. "Is it terminal?"

"I mean, it's very *you*." He bites his lip, his beard folding over to disguise his smile.

"Oh god, what does *that* mean?"

"Your answers are all great—funny—and your photos are hot, obviously." He picks the phone back up. "This one especially." He shows me the screen for half a second. It's a candid shot of me at Warren and Chloe's wedding on the beach in Barcelona. I'm coming out of the water in my bridesmaid's dress after we all ran into the ocean. I almost considered not including it because my laughter caused me to have a crazed sort of expression, but it made me smile.

"This one, I'd delete." He shows me my first photo, which is the photo any prospective suitors would see before swiping right or left.

"What? But I look like I almost have a hint of cleavage in that one!"

I study the photo from a fresh pair of eyes. Matt's eyes. I'm posed in a selfie, the camera above my head. My lips pushed out and my eyes dead. I look hot but deadly. I don't look like the girl you bring home to your family.

Why that even crosses my mind is beyond me. I'm looking to get laid—not meet someone's mother.

"You look great. It's just . . . It gives off a *vibe*."

"Slutty?"

"No." Matt's eyes go wide.

"You can say slutty. We're taking back the word."

"I cannot, and no. It's . . . you don't look happy."

"What if I'm *not* happy, Matt?" The words fly out of my mouth as a joke, but they don't land that way.

He stills, studying me with sincerity but no trace of pity. I find it unusually settling. "Well, then I think we've got a bigger issue than getting you laid." He smiles softly.

"We?" I ask.

"Oh, yeah. I'm in this now."

I smile and let my eyes close to play back the sound of him saying *we,* then immediately feel the urge to create distance between us through teasing. "This is basically practice for me." I point to the pizza between us. "We've pretty much been on a date all weekend. We even *slept* together." I waggle my eyebrows suggestively.

Matt laughs and shakes his head. "No. This is not even close."

Okay, jeez. Ouch.

"You'd know if this was a date." He looks up at me through his brows as he bends forward across the table.

My body stiffens, and I'm not completely sure I'm breathing. A nervous, breathy laugh escapes me.

"Well, then." I clear my throat. "Enlighten me." I sit straighter in challenge and lower my voice to a sultry pitch. "What is a date with Mattheus Tilo-Jones like?" I cross my legs under the table to stop from fidgeting.

Matt's eyes trace down my face to the rest of my body that's

visible above the table. "First of all, you wouldn't be so far away."
He stands and casually walks over to the back of my chair, lifts it
effortlessly with me in it, and places me down next to him across
the table. He falls back into his seat, and I watch him swallow as
his eyes duck to my mouth. "Then I'd probably tell you how beautiful you look today." His confident stare burns through me, and I
decide to push back.

"Hmm, yes. If I had taken time to get ready for this date instead of waking up in yesterday's clothes in a rat-infested motel."

"No. I said *today*." His voice is stern, making my throat tighten.
"Then I'd ask you why you're not happy, and probably ruin the
mood." He relaxes into his chair, but I can't just yet.

"Bit of a mood-killer, yeah," I say softly.

"Is that why . . . is that what the bus is about? Trying to find
some happiness?"

I cross my arms in front of my chest. "A little. It's more like I'm
trying to find out what life is going to look like for me. Ya know?"

Matt tilts his head, waiting for me to go on.

"I sort of thought that by the time I got this far into adulthood,
I'd have a clearer vision for my life." I shrug. "The bus is sort of me
grasping at straws. Maybe if I slot myself into a lifestyle or a way
of life, then it'll just become what I'm supposed to do."

"Why do you think there is something you're *supposed* to do?"

"Isn't there?" I laugh pathetically. "Sometimes it feels like
everyone else has a script, and I'm doing improv."

"My parents always taught us that life is what you do between
what you *have* to do." He places a hand on my knee. "What do you
have to do?"

"Make money to pay my bills?"

"Okay, and what do you do when you're *not* doing that?"

"Not a lot."

"Sounds like you need a hobby." I shove his shoulder, and he laughs.

"Or a partner," I say, knowing that's not the *right* answer.

"You don't need anyone else, Lane. You've got everything you need." Matt's hand leaves my leg, and I fight a groan.

"What about you?" I ask.

"Hmm?" Matt starts clearing the table.

"What do you want?"

His eyes shift side to side as he thinks. "I want what I have now, and maybe a person to share it with. I'd like to be married some-day. Call me old-fashioned, but that's important to me." He adds the last part hesitantly.

"But?"

"But the timing has to be right." He shrugs one shoulder, pout-ing his lips in a look that says "who knows?"

"You're not ready?" I ask.

He gives me a polite smile. He's done with the interrogation now. "Let's get back on the road."

NINE

AN HOUR FROM HOME, MY PHONE RINGS.

"Is it okay if I take this? It's my sister."

"Course." Matt reaches for the volume dial and turns the music off.

"Hey, Liz. How are you?"

"Hey, you okay? I couldn't get a hold of you last night."

"Oh, I was driving. Forgot to call back, sorry."

"Driving? Did you finally get a car?"

"Oh . . . er . . . no. A rental."

"You're going on a trip?"

"I was picking something up a few towns over," I say, and Matt scoffs. *Nosy.* I flip him off in the mirror. "Actually, Liz, I have something sort of exciting to tell you. . . ." I swallow. "I—"

"One second, Phillip's on the other line, and he gets pretty upset when I don't answer."

"Oh, okay. Did you want—" The line goes dead. "Me to call you back?" I whisper, lowering the phone to my lap. "Guess not." I lock the screen.

"Did she have to go?"

"Apparently."

Matt signals his exit off the highway, then looks over at me in the mirror. "You two close?"

"Hmm?"

"You and your sister?"

"Sort of?" My arms cross over my chest. "We're twins, right, so . . ."

"My younger siblings, Ian and Ruth, are twins."

"Yeah?"

"They fought like cats and dogs as kids." He tilts his neck into a stretch, his eyes on the road ahead.

"Well, they had other siblings to choose from."

Matt laughs. "Yeah, maybe."

I pick at the scab on my elbow with my thumb. Are Liz and I close? *Truly?*

"We aren't really," I admit. I focus on the head of a rusty bolt on the floor. "When we were kids, my dad would have to read us two different sets of bedtime stories." I smile to myself wistfully, remembering the hours he spent reading me stories of pirates and knights.

I can see it so clearly. My dad's black hair that he insisted on cutting himself—which often meant buzzing it off entirely— falling into his eyes, and him swatting it away as he lunged forward like a swordsman. The dimple in his chin when he shouted battle cries, and the wild hand motions he'd make when the good guys took victory.

"Liz would ask for these books about *real* people or important events. . . ." I shake my head. "She wanted to know *everything*. I've always admired that about her. She was born with this insatiable hunger to understand things. She'd sit with Legos for hours, meticulously figuring out how to build solid structures at like . . . five."

I take a deep breath in through my nose, chewing my lip. "I think I sort of put her on this pedestal. She was older by just ten minutes, but in every way, she felt years ahead of me. Her A grades to my Bs, her long silky hair to my messy waves." I subconsciously twirl a piece of hair around my finger. "Liz has always been perfect." I shrug. "And she loves me, but I know she doesn't *get* me."

"Do you think that bothers her?" Matt asks.

I blink at him, not sure what he means.

"You said she wants to understand everything, right? She likes knowing, figuring stuff out? Do you think she's frustrated that she can't figure you out?"

I take a deep breath in, my eyes widening. "Maybe." I rub my lips together. "I've never really considered that before."

"I bet she feels the same way about you as you do about her. She's probably jealous too."

"No way." I laugh, almost. "Like I said, she's—"

"Nobody's perfect, Lane," Matt says definitively.

You are, my lips beg to say. I resist.

"As an older sibling and middle sibling and younger sibling—"

"I get it, you're the people's voice," I tease, waving him on.

"She's definitely jealous."

I scoff. "She's getting married soon. I doubt she has the time for jealousy."

"But you're not so sure about the guy, right?"

"I haven't met him yet. I just have a sense." I've known *of* him for years. The way that you know small tidbits of information about a neighbor or a D-list celebrity—our grandparents and his parents travel in the same circles.

"Twin senses—I've seen those in action."

"I don't know. Maybe he's great. I hope I'm wrong." I look out the window. "I still need to find a date to bring to her wedding. And it seems like drastic changes are needed on my dating profile if—"

"You should take me," Matt says, our eyes catching in the mirror. "Bet his *conservative* parents would *love* to see a giant brown guy with longer hair than you show up as your date."

I laugh nervously. Us? Traveling alone *again*? To an event that should hypothetically be romantic? Is he trying to kill me? *And why do I want him to come so badly?* "I can't ask you to do that."

"What? I love weddings."

"Matt, you can't keep doing me favors. What about work? What about—"

"When are you going to understand that I *like* being around you?" Matt's voice is tougher than usual, as if he's trying to stop an argument before it happens. "This isn't a favor, and that wouldn't be either."

I start to protest, but Matt stops me with a warning glance in the mirror. An expression that says, *try me,* with a raised brow and stern frown.

"You really want to?" I ask softly, my voice barely audible over the sounds of the bus's engine.

"I do." He smiles until his eyes become half-moons, and I have to look away so I don't get lost in the crinkled lines next to them.

"Well, then I'm buying your plane ticket."

"Plane ticket? Where is it?"

"What?" I scoff. "No way . . . I've told you this."

"Lane, you don't talk about your family," Matt says bluntly.

My stomach drops.

"Sorry, I didn't mean that to sound—"

"Vancouver," I interrupt. "They're in Vancouver," I repeat, loud enough for him to hear.

"You mean this whole time I've been telling you stories about growing up on the island, and you didn't mention that? Do I *ever* shut up?" Matt laughs, shaking his head as he switches lanes.

"I was told not to interrupt!" I defend myself. "Plus, you have *stories*. I have memories. There's a difference."

The difference is perhaps not in the childhoods we had, but more so Matt's natural ability to find the joy in everything. My memories, even the happy ones, are shrouded by the loss of my dad. How are you supposed to look back fondly when you wish you had more to look forward to?

"When is it?" Matt asks.

"Eight weeks from now. It's a Sunday brunch thing . . . there'll be a rehearsal dinner the night before too."

"Okay. Do you think we could go up a few days early? Visit my family too?"

"Oh, yeah—I said I'd cover the flight, not decide *when* you fly."

"I mean . . . would you want to come?"

"What?" I ask, turning back to him from the view out the window.

"Seems fair. You show me yours, and I show you mine." Matt's body flinches. "Ignore that I just said that."

I laugh until I snort.

"Offer rescinded," Matt deadpans.

"No! Hey! I'd love to meet your family. How many of your siblings are still at home?"

"The three youngest and my eldest brother." Matt smiles. "Everyone else is spread out."

"Tell me about them." I snuggle into my seat, preparing to listen. Then my phone vibrates loudly. "It's Liz."

"Tell her I say hi," Matt says quickly as I answer.

"Hey."

"Sorry." Liz is out of breath. "I had to take that, and then I was running a bit late to my workout."

"Are you working out right now?"

"Yes, why?"

"That's efficient."

"I'm trying to fit into my wedding dress."

I could *puke* at that statement. "Clothes are meant to fit you, Liz. Not the other way around."

"You don't understand. You've always been thin."

Fair but . . . "Phillip okay?"

I hear her sniff, like she's catching her breath. "Oh, yeah . . . he's fine."

"Okay." I hesitate. "Good."

"What did you want to tell me?" she asks, groaning between words—presumably lifting or pulling something.

Not the *best* time to tell her my big yellow news. "Uh, I have a date! For the wedding."

"Really? That's why I was calling. Who is it?"

"Matt."

"The guy you kissed on New Year's a few years ago? The mechanic? The one you—"

"Yep!" I cut her off. "He says hi!"

"Oh, can he hear me?" She *almost* giggles, and it makes me feel warm.

"No, don't worry."

"Is it a *date* or more of a friend thing?"

I look at Matt in the mirror. He's got his lips pulled into his mouth, a concentrated look on his face as he nods along to the quieted song playing from the radio. A piece of his bun has fallen out on the back of his neck, and it has a soft curl to it. He taps the steering wheel, his rhythm totally off, and I feel a smile spread across my face. The feeling in my chest is similar to a too-tight hug. Comforting but also a little painful. It's a familiar ache that is present whenever I'm around him but has only grown heavier these past two days. And I fear I know what it may be.

"I don't know," I reply honestly before letting Liz get back to her workout. What I *do* know is . . . I'm screwed either way.

TEN

THIS MORNING I'M MEETING WITH MATT AND WARREN
to discuss what they want for the shop's branding. Thankfully, as a
contractor for my nine to five, I can take time off by turning down
projects when presented to me, so I've planned to take the next
two months off to work on the bus and for Matt and Warren exclusively. I'm here early, waiting outside the locked chain-link
fence, enjoying the brisk morning air.

I haven't seen my bus since we got back four days ago. My anxiety spiked and stayed high for two whole days after getting home.
I stayed in bed for nearly eighteen hours before I felt brave
enough to venture out to my bathroom. I had severely underesti-
mated how difficult it would be to be away from all my comforts
and routine for the weekend, and it caught up to me.

It's a blessing and a curse that I'm now able to forget the de-
bilitating anxiety that can so easily keep me locked away. The
more time it's been since beginning my medication, the more I
struggle to remember how hard it was before. Then days like that

sneak up on me, and I'm reminded why I need to keep doing the work to ensure I *never* go back to how it was.

Affirmations, medication, daily walks, and basic hygiene. Nothing that *should* be work, but for me, it is.

Today, I'm feeling okay. I can work with okay.

I check my phone as a text from my sister comes through. She's mailed three dresses that are set to arrive at my place today. I'm supposed to list them from most to least acceptable so she can gather the data from all three bridesmaids and make a fair decision about which one we will all wear. I'm also under strict instructions to get it altered to fit as soon as possible.

I have asked her if I can design their invitations, seating chart, or anything else—and she said she'd let me know. Which is a no. There's no way she's not got it planned out already since it's less than eight weeks away.

Warren's black car shows up at the gate to the yard with a polite series of honks. He gets out to unlock it and smiles at me. "Morning."

"Hey!" I check the passenger side and see Luke, Warren's younger brother, who I haven't seen since Christmas when he was briefly home from traveling. The moment Luke finished high school and turned eighteen, he took off to see the world—much to his brother's chagrin. "Hey! What are you doing here?" I sign to him, wearing a wide smile.

Emily and I took sign language classes the summer before last, partially because we wanted to stop relying on our friends as translators with Luke, and also a little bit because we can use it to talk shit about strangers in crowded bars like Chloe and Warren do.

"Hey, Lane." He points to his brother, wearing a brotherly, teasing gleam. "Warren begged me to come home for a week. Think he wanted to make sure I hadn't sold any organs to pay for room and board." Luke climbs into the driver's seat.

Warren glares at his brother playfully as he secures the gate into place and Luke drives the car through to the yard.

"He looks so much older," I say to Warren as we start walking toward the shop. "Like a *full* adult."

"I know." He rubs the back of his head. "It's freaking me out."

"Is he okay?" I ask. "He looks okay." I try to sound reassuring.

"I think so." He nods, and a half smile appears. "He seems happy."

"But you miss him and wish he was miserable so he'd move back," I tease.

Warren laughs just once before it fades to a sigh. "He's actually decided to attend the University of Barcelona. . . . He's gonna live with Chloe's parents in the fall."

"Oh . . ."

"Yeah."

"You okay?"

"If Luke's okay, I'm okay." He turns to walk backward so he can face me with a mischievous grin. "Anyway . . ." I *immediately* know what's coming next. "I heard you and Matt had *quite* the weekend."

"We had a very enjoyable, very *platonic* trip." I raise my brows in a challenge.

"That's not what I heard," he singsongs, turning to walk beside me again.

"Oh, and what *did* you hear?" I ask with a roll of my eyes, pushing the eagerness in my voice away.

"That Matt woke up under you on a broken bed."

I laugh, because when you say it like that—it doesn't sound so innocent. "Not sure why Matt would tell you that." I shake my head. "He's just encouraging you and Chloe's incessant need to play matchmaker." I swat at his arm as he enters the garage door's key code, and we step inside.

Warren flicks a panel of switches. The lights turn on, and the shop buzzes with the sound of fans and machines beeping to life.

"Oh, right, you have *no* idea why he'd perhaps want us to tease the two of you about getting together." He couldn't speak with more sarcasm if he tried.

"I'm not sure I know what you're implying."

"Careful, Lane. . . ." Warren walks over to the far side of the garage and hits a button that opens the hangar door. It starts with a loud hum. "Your poker face isn't as strong as it was *before* your little weekend getaway."

"Oh, shut it." I look at the table closest to me, pick up a welding glove, and throw it at him as he walks back toward me.

He catches the glove in front of his face and throws it right back. I don't catch it so easily, and it bounces off my shoulder.

"I also heard he's your date to your sister's wedding." He raises an eyebrow suggestively.

"I think he volunteered out of guilt." I laugh, but it fades to a whine. "Am I that pathetic?"

"No comment. I *do* think you two just need to talk some stuff out."

"I've told you. Nothing will *ever* happen between Matt and me. There's nothing to talk about."

"What you haven't said is why that is." He crosses his arms.

"Because we're friends."

"Chloe is my friend," Warren counters far too quickly.

"Right, but you two were barely friends when something else started. It's important to me to keep Matt as a friend and that our whole group gets along. What if we dated and then broke up and hated each other? You'd all have to pick sides." I sigh, putting on my best *you poor thing* sympathetic smile. "You only have one friend, Warren. I'd hate to get between you."

He smiles at my quip. "I think you'd have us all on the week-ends, and Matt would get us during the week."

"Ha." I roll my eyes.

"What if . . ."—he flashes two palms—"bizarre thought . . . it actually *didn't* end terribly?" he asks.

I feel my stomach sink, making me shift on my feet nervously. I look at my shoe as I twist my toes into the grit of the concrete floor.

No, it goes one of two ways. We break up, and our friends have to hang out with us separately, which sucks. I don't have Matt's calming presence in my life anymore, and he won't watch any good movies. Eventually, I get a call from Chloe where she gently tells me Matt's engaged. They all go to the wedding, and I'm not invited.

The second option is worse. We work. We work *well*. He likes the way I can't seem to chew with my mouth closed even though it's gross, and I brush his hair every night before bed. We fall madly, deeply in love. We get married. Maybe we even have kids.

Then one day—maybe not for a while, but certainly someday—I lose him. And it's as if the world splits open beneath me. I fall into an existence where I'm forced to live without the person who made it worth living. All my favorite things are ruined, because they were all his favorites too. All the places we liked to go for din-ner that I won't visit again. All the people who knew us both who can only see me as the one left behind—a walking tragedy.

How could I open myself up to that? Wouldn't that just make me a fool? I am a lot of things, but I hope a fool is not one of them.

"It will. One way or another," I mumble.

"You sure of that?" Warren's sincere tone drags my attention back to him. He sighs, his eyes narrowing on me. "Do you mean"—he wipes a hand over his head—"like your parents? Are the two options *really* only heartbreak or death?"

I shrug. It's morbid when you put it like *that*.

"I get it," Warren says plainly. "I do."

I know he does. He lost his mom. In different circumstances and a lot younger than me, but loss is loss. "I don't know if . . ." My voice softens to nonexistent.

"If you could do it again." Warren finishes for me, scratching his chin.

I sniffle, fighting back tears. "How did you get over it? The fear of losing your people."

Warren blows out a long stream of air. "Honestly?" he asks.

I nod desperately.

"I haven't. I'm still terrified. Probably more. I watch Willow sleep sometimes as if she'll disappear at any moment. I was a wreck when Chloe went to visit her parents solo—I read everything I could about the type of airplane she was on . . . filled my head with worst-case scenarios."

I huff a sad sort of laugh. "Great."

"Talking about it in therapy helps," Warren says.

"I'm just not sure I want to open up that whole can of worms with a stranger."

"Seems like the can is open." He grimaces playfully, then crosses the room, stopping to lean on a concrete pillar next to me. "There's this quote that I like about grief . . . about how it's really just all the love you want to give to the person you lost, building up until it hurts." He stiffly puts a hand on my shoulder, his arm outstretched in front of him. "You gotta find somewhere to put the love, Lane—or it's gonna keep hurting." He lowers his hand and shoves it into his pocket.

"Damn." I snap my fingers like Warren just performed spoken word poem.

"Not just a pretty face." He winks. "Listen, maybe Matt isn't *the one*. But I think he feels like a real possibility to you. And *if* that scares you—in my experience—that means there's shit you have to work through. The good stuff shouldn't feel scary."

"Do I have to pay for this session, doc?"

Warren holds up his hands. "Take it or leave it."

"So, hypothetically, *if* I did like Matt, *and* if I worked through this shit I've got going on . . . would he be interested?"

"He's never told me how he feels about you in exact words, and if he had, I probably wouldn't tell you." He kicks some gravel that's made its way onto the shop floor back outside before straightening. "But if I had to guess?" He holds up his palms, miming weighing the two possibilities. "I'd say he's waiting for the go-ahead from you."

I remember what Matt said on Sunday when we stopped for dinner. . . . *The timing has to be right.* Did he mean that about me?

Just then, the sound of tires against gravel alerts us to Matt's arrival.

Warren waves to him while speaking to me. "And if you *could* figure this all out sooner rather than later, I'm trying to win the bet I have with Chloe."

"She bet against Matt and me?" I don't hide the offense in my tone and regret it when I see Warren's smirk grow.

"Neither of us bet *against* you. Chloe said it would take another year for you two idiots to figure it out."

My friends are assholes. But I love them.

"Hey, you two," Matt chimes from the entrance, hanging up his backpack and leather jacket. He's wearing dark blue jeans and a gray long-sleeve shirt that hugs his arms tightly. "Morning." He wraps his arm around my shoulder. "What's up, man?" He tilts his chin toward Warren.

Warren's fighting back whatever he wants to say so badly his mouth is practically twitching. "Tour?" He turns to me, and I nod abruptly.

He points over his shoulder. "Coffee first, though. I have a feeling this is going to be a long day." He shakes his head, looking between Matt and me.

Matt's expression hasn't faltered once from a content, casual smile. I pat his back as we step away from each other and follow Warren to the break room.

AN HOUR LATER, we end up back in the front office, which has yet to open to customers for the day. It's the only area with a desk, and I need somewhere to put my laptop to show them some of the ideas I've drawn up. Luke is laid out over three of the chairs in the waiting area holding a book above him.

"So, before I start, I always like to say that these are suggestions, they're not the only options. If none of these are close to what you had in mind, that's perfectly okay. Consider it a jumping-off point."

I pull up the first mood board, complete with several shades of blues, greens, and grays that complement one another well, a main and subheading font. They both cross their arms and nod at the *exact* same moment, concentrated on the screen. I pull up option numbers two and three, and their expressions don't give much away.

"So between the three—which feels closest?" I ask.

They look at each other and Warren shrugs. "They're all fine . . . yeah, any of those."

"Well, great, but remember, this is just the first consultation. Which do you like the most?"

Warren nods to Matt to give his opinion. "Uh . . . I liked the second one?"

"The one with the dark blue," Warren clarifies.

"Okay." I open the second one. "So this palette?" They both nod. "Right, okay, but the font?"

"It's . . . readable," Warren offers.

"Yeah, it's a nice . . . shape?" Matt gestures to the screen.

I swallow my laughter. "Okay." I look between them as Matt rubs his beard and Warren picks lint off his sleeve. "So take this board and run with it is what I'm hearing?"

"Run with it. Run like Usain Bolt." Warren throws a thumbs-up my way. "We just want it to be approachable. We trust you to just go for it."

Total creative control? I love it here. "That I can do." They begin walking around to the other side of the desk before I stop them. "Wait!"

"Hmm?" Warren looks over his shoulder, then at Matt, in confusion.

"You need a name."

They both look cluelessly at each other. Matt shrugs one shoulder, then pushes both hands into the pockets of his jeans. "Warren and Matt's Auto?"

"WM Auto?" Warren asks *me* for approval.

"Uh . . ." I hesitate.

"Oh yeah, I like that. WM Auto." Matt nods enthusiastically.

"All right. . . . Cool, settled."

Matt puts out a hand for a high five, and Warren meets it. "We're pretty good at this branding thing."

"I'll go home and get started on this. I'll keep you posted." I shut my laptop and slide it into my bag.

"I've got a customer. See ya later, Lane!" Warren knocks his brother's feet off the chair as he passes by and motions to him to follow him to the garage area, where a red minivan has just pulled in. I shuffle my bag up over my shoulder.

"Hey." Matt smiles.

A soft laugh escapes my nose. "Uh, hi."

"You okay?"

I push out my lips and fold them to my nose. "Mostly. You?"

He watches me thoughtfully. "Yeah. It's been quiet."

"Here?"

"No, without you."

I feel my cheeks warm. "I do talk a lot."

"Wanna say bye to the bus before you head out?" he asks, taking one hand out of his pocket to point to my bus.

I smile brightly because that's *exactly* what I wanted but probably wouldn't have asked for. We planned to start working on it on Friday afternoon, and I was sad I wouldn't see it for the next few days. "Yes, please."

ELEVEN

I'VE BEEN WORKING ON THE SHOP'S DESIGNS SINCE OUR meeting, but I haven't been back until today. The shop closes early on Fridays, and I'm meeting Warren, Luke, and Matt, who've all agreed to stay late and help tear out the bench seating on the bus.

I brought my new pair of pink steel-toe boots and got my own pair of gray coveralls that match the boys. I'd never felt cooler. That was, until Matt fastened a tool belt around my waist.

He had to adjust the buckle against my hip, tightening it to fit. Each tug pulled me closer to him, each fastening had his fingers pressed into my skin in the most tantalizing way. I was so dazed afterward that I had to chug an entire bottle of water before I was fit to work.

He walked me through which socket wrench to use on which bolt, and we got to work. Warren and I removed the nuts and bolts, and Matt carried the benches off the bus and worked on the back rows, while Luke ground down the floor joists.

We had over half of the benches pulled out and thrown into

the rented dumpster before Chloe and Willow showed up with our dinner of pizza and beer. We all ate on the floor of the bus, and Willow got a kick out of all the buttons and the big wheel on the dashboard.

"I think I've got two more hours in me. What do you three think?" Warren signs and speaks to Matt, Luke, and me.

"We can call it. I don't want to take up your Friday evenings," I sign back to the group.

"I don't mind." Luke shrugs.

"Yeah, I think we'd finish on the left side too, if we keep going." Matt's newer to signing, having been taught slowly by Warren, but his practice is paying off.

"Well, okay. Thank you." I reach up to Matt as he extends a hand to pull me up. My foot rolls over the top of a removed bolt, and I fall into his chest. His solid, broad, *sexy* chest. I don't move away for a second too long, and I've made it weird . . . again.

I clear my throat and step away. "Back to work, lads!" I call out in a British accent. Because *that's* a normal thing to do.

Almost three hours later, Warren and I high-five while wiping sweat off our foreheads with our opposite arms. Matt picks up the bench effortlessly and carries it out, and Luke grinds the final two floor joists and then gives me a big thumbs-up.

"Thank you," I sign to him. He smiles sweetly, and for a moment, the sixteen-year-old kid I knew is back. I pat Warren's back when Luke gets up to pack away the tools. "He's the best."

Warren nods, his proud smile infectious. "He's all right."

Matt sits on the back of the bus where the double doors are open, and I watch as his shoulders rise and tense with a big breath of air. His back is drenched with sweat down the middle of his spine, and the hair that's fallen out of his bun is sticking to his neck.

"We're gonna go." Warren pats my shoulder. "Be good." He

points to me before wrapping his arm around Luke and walking off with him.

I turn back around and watch as Matt rubs his dirty palm over his forehead. None of these things should be hot, right? It's gross. He's dirty. *Filthy*.

I swallow audibly. "I'm gonna head out." My voice pitches higher.

Matt turns over his shoulder and gives me a beaming smile that shoots into me, spreading warmth throughout my chest. "Okay, I'll probably just hang back for a minute and watch the stars." He points up, as if I was confused about where they were. But when I duck my head to admire what he's looking at, I realize it's because the stars are particularly beautiful tonight against the deep purple-hued sky. "Wow," I say softly, lowering to sit next to him.

His legs dangle off the back of the bus, but I sit cross-legged on the edge. He passes me an opened beer from the cooler next to him and we clink bottles without taking our eyes off the sky.

"Is it warm for early spring, or am I just learning what hard work is and my body is angry with me?" I break the silence.

"It's not just you. Coveralls are like personal saunas."

"Do you think we look like two prison escapees who took a school bus hostage?" I gesture to our matching uniforms.

Matt laughs, his lips curling into a bemused smile. "No, I think we look like two mechanics fixing up a bus."

I shove his shoulder playfully. "Thank you for helping me today."

"Thank *you* for the brand stuff. We both really like what you've done so far."

"Yeah? Not too . . . soft?"

"We're trying to become approachable, right?" Matt shrugs. "I like it. Warren likes it. I think it'll help with our image."

I nod silently, going back to admire the night sky.

Matt sighs longingly. "When I was a kid, my mom would tell us stories about the stars. It was like she could tell tales that would repaint them in the sky. It never feels the same looking at them now."

"What kind of stories?" I ask.

"Mostly stuff that had been passed down through generations. The first Samoans were seafarers—they used the stars to guide them—so a lot of sea monster shit, mostly." He chuckles. "Her name, Fetu, means star."

"Fetu . . . That's really cool." I stretch my neck side to side, aware of the day's labor building an ache in my back. "My dad was Irish. All we really got were stories of famine and drinking songs."

Matt snorts. "That sounds fun though." He tilts his head to look up again. "Would you tell me about him? Maybe not now . . . but sometime?"

I lift my knees to my chest and wrap my arms around them. "Yeah . . . I'd like that." I clear my throat and admire the moon. "His name was Dominic, but everyone called him Nick or Nicky." I smile at the memories suddenly flooding in that I usually keep at bay. "He was a musician. He loved to play guitar and piano, but what I remember most was his singing voice. He had a *beautiful* voice. Like, haunting, you know?" I swallow, looking toward Matt, who is intently focused on my every word.

"He had a lot of siblings, like you, but they weren't close. He was freshly eighteen when he came here to work at a ski resort. Just so happens that was the one my mom's family owned and frequented." I bite down on my smile, which threatens to take over my whole face. "She says he was this scruffy, lanky, funny boy, and she didn't pay him much mind. The whole season, her family would go up to the resort every weekend. She was just about to leave home and go to university and was driven as hell. She was going into business, like her father and her grandfather, and just took life *so* seriously. He took nothing seriously. He made her laugh."

I breathe in slowly as my eyes close, remembering when my parents told us this story on their anniversary one year. My mother clasped her hand over my father's mouth when he was getting into the more *lewd* parts, where he convinced her to sneak out of the lodge late one night. She was giggling as she forced him to be quiet and rolled her eyes when she fell back into her chair.

They were *so* happy.

"His job ended when the season did, but he just couldn't get enough of my mom. He said she reminded him of the lighthouse back home that guided all the fishermen. Nothing was clear without her. He called her his *guiding light*. Once the season was over, my dad went back to Ireland, determined to make enough money on the boats with his brothers and use it to earn her hand. Then one day, out of the blue, he got a letter from her. My mom was engaged."

Matt gasps, and I laugh. "Right?" I sniff, keeping the tears at bay. "He was having *none* of that. He got on the first flight he could. But turns out, my mother made it up. She wanted to see what he'd do about it. My grandfather was *not* pleased about the match, but she just kept saying that she had her own money; she didn't need his. She just needed someone who would show up."

"Lane, that might be the most beautiful story I've ever heard." Matt clutches his chest.

"Yeah, well . . ." I sigh, wiping a single tear away. "Look how it ended."

Matt turns his body to face me, his spine in line with the door's opening. "You must miss him."

"Every day."

"How old were you when he passed?"

"Seventeen."

Matt does the math, and his shoulders fall. *"Oh."*

"This summer." I wince. "A decade."

Moments pass where neither of us speaks. The crickets make music, and the road sounds grow louder without our voices covering them up. We just sit, letting the past linger a moment longer. Like we have all the time in the world.

"To Dominic." Matt raises his bottle. "For being a good man and raising a fine daughter."

I choke over a sob but raise my beer to meet his. "To both of our fathers, their stars, and guiding lights," I add before we cheers gently.

I finish my beer and toss it into the dumpster with surprising accuracy. With no drink left, my sudden descent into vulnerability makes my stomach feel like it's in a tumble dryer. I decide to call it a night. "I should get home."

"Want a ride?" Matt asks.

I shake my head. "No, I want to walk." I hop off the bus and toss him the keys from my pocket. "Lock up for me?"

"You got it." He holds my keys in a tight fist. "Night, Lane."

"Night." I smile softly before disappearing around the side of the bus and calling for a ride to meet me down the street, out of view.

TWELVE

OVER THE PAST TWO WEEKS, WARREN HAS STARTED throwing objects at me when I zone out and stare at Matt for too long. It started as a gum wrapper to the forehead, and it's escalated to pencils or balled-up pieces of paper. Thankfully, this week has been a cooling-off period from working in such close proximity.

Today the solar panel guy came to install the four panels and inside systems. Yesterday, it was the water tank guy, and the day before that the propane guy. If we stay on plan, the bus should be ready just before my sister's wedding in four weeks.

I know from my hours of research and forum-hopping that I'm really lucky to have friends willing to help me out but also the funds to pay professionals to do the bigger tasks. Having the money to speed the process along and make it exactly what I want it to be makes it feel as if my dad is here, spoiling me just like he used to.

After another day of branding from a lawn chair in the shop's parking lot as the tradesmen come and go, I take today's progress photos and lock up.

"Heading out?" Matt asks from behind me, both of his hands in his pockets and a line of smudged oil across his forehead.

"Yeah, they're all finished. We've got power now!"

He looks up to the roof at the solar panels, covering his eyes from the sun. "Look at those bad boys." He smiles. "It's coming along so fast; you're going to need to start packing soon."

"I have to find a place to park it first."

"Well, you can always keep it here. I like having you around." He smiles and wraps his arm around me, keeping his grease-covered hand in a tight fist to avoid dirtying my shoulder. We start walking toward the shop to gather my things—a now familiar routine at the end of my workdays here.

"I've not started annoying you all yet?" I ask.

"What? No." Matt whistles toward the shop as we pass by the open garage door. "War!"

Warren rolls out from under a truck and sits up, looking over his shoulder.

"We've got power!" He points over his shoulder to the bus.

"Nice. Great job." Warren gives a thumbs-up before going back to work.

Matt nods thoughtfully, like he just remembered something, and speaks just for me. "Now that the solar panels and batteries are installed, I can get the miter saw in there and start framing."

"Ooh! I've always wanted to use one of those."

"I've only got a tire rotation booked tomorrow morning. Want to take a break from branding stuff and frame out the bathroom after that?"

I grab my stuff from the hook on the wall of the front office. "Yeah, that'd be great!" I stop, admiring him. "Thank you again for all your help. I really appreciate it."

"Course. Anytime."

The cool thing about Matt is that he really means *any* time.

"Just make sure you're getting some downtime too, okay? Do something fun." I've definitely stopped inviting him over for movie nights at my place.

Not only because he's most likely sick of me by the end of our workdays, but also because lately, I've been struggling to imagine sitting on opposite ends of the couch like we used to. I've actually been imagining a wholly different activity we could partake in together, on my couch. Which I'm not proud of.

"Right, you mean like you?" he teases. "Finally found a hobby?"

"No hobby just yet, but *actually* . . ." I waggle my eyebrows. "Yes, like me." I poke his chest and do a small spin. "*I* have a date tonight. And I'm hoping it will be *a lot* of fun."

Matt nods slowly. "A date," he clarifies, as if I've misspoken.

"Yeah?" *Is it so unbelievable?*

"With?" He crosses his arms.

Oh. I cross mine and tilt my chin up. "A guy from a dating app."

"Well, I hope you know his name." He's teasing with his expression, but his voice remains slow and concentrated.

"I do. It's Jake."

"Okay, and Jake is . . . ?"

This is jealousy, right? Or is it just protectiveness? Big brother habits die hard. Or maybe . . .

"Hot?" I answer, shrugging one shoulder. "A guy who I matched with and whose bio was relatively funny. He has no pictures of him hunting, fishing, half-naked at a club, or holding up money."

"The bar for men is in hell." Matt shakes his head and moves his hands to his hips. "Who goes on a first date on a Wednesday?"

"Everyone. Wednesday is the first-date day. Thursday is for second dates, and Friday is for the third." I push open the office's door to wait outside.

"And Saturdays?" Matt asks.

"That's when long-term couples go out, I think."

"I assume you have, like . . . a safety plan? Chloe or Emily on speed dial?"

"Uh . . ." Damn, it's been a long time since I dated guys. "Yes?" I lie.

He rolls his eyes. "Text me if you need to be rescued."

"Rescued? Yikes. He seems harmless."

"Fine, then text me regardless," Matt says, running a hand through his hair. He's flustered. And annoyed?

"Why?" I ask, near a whisper. *Tell me why,* I plead with my eyes. *Tell me not to go.*

My ride pulls up with a polite honk. The eager driver rolls down his window. "Lane?" he calls out.

"Yes, one second!" I wave over my shoulder, studying Matt's stern expression.

"Have a nice time, Lane." He swings the door open and goes back inside.

Fine. I will.

TWENTY MINUTES AFTER I get to the sports bar on time for our date, I'm wondering if I've been stood up. Jake chose this place, saying it was his favorite hidden gem in the city. I'd never heard of it, and I can see why. It's a dingy bar with more televisions than light fixtures. Everything feels sticky and crowded.

There is some sort of sports game on. Blue jersey and red jersey wearers are scattered around the room, shouting in intervals that appear to be *totally* random. I know that if I got a good look at the television, I could identify which sport it is—I'm not a total idiot—but the crowds are blocking them. Still, I whoop and boo whenever the rest of my new friends do.

A chorus of chanting starts from the far side of the wrap-around bar, and I join in by clapping over my head while simultaneously trying to get the straw from my drink into my mouth. If I finish this one before Jake arrives, I'll leave.

I write and delete a variety of *still on?* messages and then look up to see him walking in, wearing a blue jersey. We're team blue, I guess. Jake's just like his photos—lanky, blond—but I feel disappointed all the same, as if he's not who I expected. He's not smiling.

Matt's always smiling, my inner voice decides to point out. *Shut the fuck up,* I reply.

Jake makes his way straight to our table. "Hey, sorry. My roommate was locked out, and I had to run over with a spare key."

"No worries." I stand and hug him briefly before we fall back into the seats around the bar-height square table I was grateful to find away from the bar.

Jake points to my drink. "Want another one? I'm going to go grab a b—" The crowd erupts in loud applause, and Jake raises up to peer over the top of their heads. "Dammit." He spits out. "Fucking—" He stops, falling into his chair. "Sorry, it's a big game."

I just purse my lips and nod.

"Oh, sweet." He points to the bar. "Two spots just opened up. C'mon." He dashes over, just beating out another couple, who look at him with annoyance. He hops up onto the seat and places his hand down to save a seat for me. *Such a gentleman.*

"I'll take a light beer—whatever's cheapest—and she'll have?" He looks at me.

"Just a Coke, please." I smile politely, lowering gingerly onto the sticky barstool.

"Tons of sugar in that. You sure?" He looks between me and the bartender.

I blink my eyelashes like I'm not seeing—*or hearing*—correctly. "Yeah, I'm sure." I force a smile, but I know my gaze would signal to any other women in the near vicinity that I'm contemplating spilling my Coke over his excessively gelled hair.

"Suit yourself." He shrugs.

I will, Jake. I squint at him in disbelief as he looks back to the television, the opposite direction from me.

"So, what do you do for—" I'm interrupted by an echoing of boos.

"Red card? For that? You've got to be joking!" Jake shouts.

I swallow my pride. "So, what do you do for work?" I ask his shoulder.

"I work for my dad's company." He tilts his chin to answer me, his eyes locked on the screen.

"Doing what?"

"This and that." He looks at me for maybe the first time, and his eyes fall right to my cleavage. Don't get me wrong, that's what this top and push-up bra were chosen for, but suddenly I don't want *his* eyes there. When he turns back around, I grimace at the bartender and place a five-dollar bill on the counter. She winks and takes it.

"I'm just going to run to the washroom," I say loud enough for them both to hear.

"C'mon!" he yells, standing with such force his stool falls behind him. I jump away from it, and he turns to me. "Yeah, okay, I'll save your seat."

My teeth grind against one another as I push through the crowds toward the inevitably nasty bathroom that awaits me. I close the lid and sit on the toilet, pulling out my phone to order a ride home, when I notice Warren has texted me for perhaps the first time *ever.*

I open it to see an image of the shop's security cameras, Matt's body blurry like those photos you see of the Sasquatch online, holding some of the lumber I've purchased for the bus.

WARREN: Somebody's doing overtime. Thought you'd want to know.

LANE: Is he always like this??

WARREN: Not for me. He doesn't want to get in my pants.

LANE: You kiss my best friend with that mouth?

I open Matt's contact information and hit call. He answers on the third ring. "Everything okay?" he asks urgently, catching me off guard. "Lane?"

"Sorry, sorry, yes. Fine," I stutter. "Well, safe but not fine. He sucks. Can you come get me?"

I hear a door shut. "Yeah, of course. Where are you?"

"This seedy bar on the corner of Fourth and Longview. There's parking out back."

"The place with the giant football on the roof?" he asks, the sound of a turning ignition in the background. Damn, he's wasting *no* time.

"Yeah . . ." I pinch my nose. "That should have been my first clue."

I can *hear* his smirk. "What do you mean? That's *totally* your scene."

"Mm-hmm. I'm one of the jersey-folk now. Team blue."

"What sport?"

"One that gives out red cards and requires yelling."

He laughs just once. "Okay, I'll be there in less than five minutes. Want me to wait in the parking lot or come in?"

"Definitely parking lot."

He tsks. "That's no fun."

"Mattheus," I warn.

"Fine. See you soon. Tell the guy the Maple Leafs suck on your way out."

"Will do." I hang up and leave the washroom after sitting for a while, trying to time Matt's arrival with my exit.

Jake's waiting back at our original table with a shareable plate of nachos. He sees me and gives me an upturned nod, so sneaking out is no longer an option. "Hey." I lean into the chair, but don't sit. "So, I actually think I might head out. Sports are just not really my thing and—"

The crowd erupts; a goal or a touchdown occurs. It feels like *ages* before they settle down and I can continue. "And it's a little too loud to get to know each other." I tuck my purse over my shoulder.

"Wait, you're leaving?" He scoffs. "I just got nachos." His tongue pushes against his cheek as he shakes his head. "Unbelievable," he mutters under his breath.

"Well, I didn't order them or ask for them, so . . ."

"That's *rude*."

"This is rude?" I ask, eyes widening. "Me? *I'm* being rude?" I cross my arms. "You were twenty minutes late. No real explanation, no text. You didn't ask me a single question about myself or answer when I tried to ask you one, you impolitely tried to correct my drink order, and you've spent more time looking at the television than me, and less time looking at my face than my tits."

He shakes his head, speechless apparently.

"Enjoy the game, *Jake*." I spit out his name as I turn on my heel and nearly walk right into Matt.

"Everything okay?" he asks, looking between Jake and me. His hand falls to my elbow, which is bent at my side. "When you didn't answer your phone, I got worried."

"Fine." I pat his chest, telling him silently to turn around and walk out with me.

"This your boyfriend?" Jake laughs, pointing. "What kind of

whore has her boyfriend pick her up from a date with another dude?"

"What the fuck did you just call her?" Matt's shoulders hunch forward as he takes two steps around me and grabs hold of what *was* my chair.

I step between them and open my mouth to unleash hellfire on Jake, but I stop myself seconds before the litany of curses falls out of my mouth.

Instead, I reach into my purse and pull out a ten-dollar bill, slamming it onto the table. "Nachos are on me. Hope you have a *great* life." I can't hold back the obvious disdain in my tone, but the words are at least kind.

I tug Matt away, pulling him like a stubborn dog on a leash all the way out to the parking lot. Once outside, it takes a minute for my eyes to adjust to the moonlight after being under the horrendous fluorescent lights inside. Matt's standing unusually still, hands clenched into fists at his sides.

"I did it," I tell him quietly.

He turns to me, his expression softening only a little, but appearing more curious than murderous, as it had been.

"You've got to act like everyone's having the worst day of their life, right?"

His hands untighten, and his shoulders relax as he nods.

"I like this more." I nod to myself. "The high road feels pretty damn good." I smile up at Matt.

"I'd like to throw him *off* the high road. A bridge, preferably," he says, voice eerily relaxed.

"Meh, not worth it." I shrug. "Now . . ." I raise a brow and cross my arms. "What were *you* doing at the shop after hours?"

"What? How did you . . . ?"

"Warren." We answer in unison.

He rubs his neck before shoving his hand deep inside his jeans pocket. "I was hoping it'd be a surprise . . . but I have to go back after dropping you off anyway. I left in a rush."

"I'll come with," I say as Matt starts walking toward his car. "To make sure we *both* go home."

We get in and set off down the road, putting distance between us and the giant football.

When we arrive back at the shop, I appreciate that Matt at least took the time to lock up all the important doors before bolting to get me. He unlocks the gate, then drives into the parking lot. Closer in, I can see a ladder leaned up on the side of the bus and a couple of working lamps set up.

When we walk over, I notice paint cans too.

"I was going to try and get it all primed tonight and come back early and paint it tomorrow."

My jaw goes slack as I look at the sky-blue color dotted on top of the paint cans. "But . . . I didn't get the paint," I say softly. "It was out of budget."

"No, but you told Chloe what color you wanted before you priced it out and . . . we all chipped in."

Oh, no. Tears. Making their way up. Burning nose. Wobbly lips. "You guys shouldn't have done that."

"Chloe said they owed you. Free babysitting, the flight to Barcelona for their wedding, bridesmaid duties. Emily, I think, was more inspired to help out of a deep distaste for yellow." He shrugs. "I have an auto paint guy, so it wasn't that expensive."

"But . . ." I shake my head. "This is too much. It's completely too much—"

"We know how special this is for you, Lane. We wanted to be a part of it."

My eyes fill with tears of gratitude, and I don't fight them off. "Thank you." I reach up, my arms over his shoulders, and pull him into a hug. "My bus is going to be blue," I mumble into his shoulder.

He breathes in against the side of my hair, a deep inhale. Of me? That's new. The butterflies in my stomach are not.

Matt steps back first. "I'll just tidy up, then we can head out," he says as we part. "Or . . . we could paint? If you're not too tired?"

"Yes! I just need to find something to change into. Can we order pizza? I didn't eat before my date."

"Pizza and painting. Perfect."

"Sweet alliteration." I look between the paint cans and the bus again. "I'm so excited."

Matt smiles at his feet, then the bus, then me. He lingers. His eyes are warm and soft and full of something daring to be spoken.

THIRTEEN

MATT ORDERED THE PIZZA WHILE I CHANGED INSIDE the office. He had a spare shirt in his car that he suggested I wear under coveralls instead of my blouse. It fits like a dress on me, so I'm just wearing it with the bike shorts I had under my skirt and forgoing the coveralls entirely. And it smells like him. *He's never getting it back—covered in blue paint or not.*

I finish taping off the lights and metal accents as Matt starts priming the roof. He suggested I leave the roof white to reflect heat, and I think the two-tone look will be great. We get the back and left side primed before our pizza arrives and we pack up the paint supplies. Then we take a couple of tarps and a lantern inside and set up a picnic of sorts.

"Matt?" I ask, looking at the *very* new wood framing around where the bathroom will be. "Did you not go home today?"

"I . . . I got a little carried away."

I shove his shoulder. "You once told *me* to get some hobbies."

"I read and help you with the bus." He laughs, eyes glancing at me mischievously as he reaches for a slice. "Those are my hobbies."

"Does that mean I have a hobby now? The bus?" I take a bite.

"No. You can't count it because you'll be living in it."

"Okay, and the shop's branding?" I ask through a full mouth of food.

"Nah, that's a barter for the bus, which we established is a necessity."

"Fine." I wipe the crumbs off my hands. "I'll think of something."

Matt chews, a smile forming on one half of his face as he stares at me.

"What?" I ask him, narrowing my eyes.

"You could always get into sports."

"Fuck off." I laugh. "No." I pretend to shudder. "Definitely *not* that."

He sucks some sauce off his finger, and I feel my chest flip. I blink to reset. "It's cozier in here now, with the slats overhead." I give myself a reason to look away from him. His gravitational pull is strong, however, so when he doesn't respond, I find myself looking back.

He's admiring the ceiling, his *gorgeous* neck on full display as he tilts his head up. I long to lick up the column of his throat. "I like the birch. That was a good choice."

"Mmm." I agree. *Fucking weirdo—he's talking about design choices, and you're thinking about licking him.*

"Sorry your date sucked." He takes a bite, humming his approval and shimmying in satisfaction.

I shrug. "*This* is fun, at least."

"So, who's next?"

I must have misheard him. Surely he said *what,* not *who.* "Hmm?" I mumble, mouth full.

"Jake didn't work out, so who's next?" he asks, casual and mouth nearly full.

I swallow a lump in my throat as he swallows pizza.

"I don't have a roster." I laugh. "I only had like *three* matches to start with."

Matt droops his bottom lip and nods as he leans back on his palms. "Right."

"Why?" I ask. The word felt harmless until it left my lips. Now it feels like a challenge.

Matt smiles knowingly. His head tilts as his eyes narrow in on mine. "Why?" he asks, as if he's never heard the word before.

I clear my throat. I swear I feel a cold sweat forming on my forehead. "Why do you . . . care?"

He smiles that predatory smile I've only seen from him once. The one at Carl's office when he wanted to rip his head off. Is he angry? With me? No, that doesn't make sense. He's just . . . faking it, probably. While the rest of us have well-practiced, over-thought, polite smiles, Matt has no need for one. So his forced smile is slightly scary.

Or maybe he's seeing me as prey. *Maybe.*

My pulse beats against my neck like everything—including my skin—is suddenly too tight.

"No reason." He shrugs and tilts his head farther. He's toying with me, grabbing another piece of pizza like a strange moment didn't pass between us.

Fine. Two people can play this game.

"It's just a shame he didn't work out." I elongate a mournful sigh. "It's been *so* long since"—I pick at my food—"you know," I say, faking shy.

The corner of his lip twitches ever so slightly. "Has it?"

"Yeah. I mean, it's not like the guy had to impress me. He just had to be nice enough to go home with, you know?" I pop a pep-peroni into my mouth.

Matt studies me. "Because it's been *so* long."

"Yeah, just about *anyone* would work at this point." I freeze under his confident stare, my confidence shrinking.

"Anyone," Matt repeats, licking his lips.

When did I start leaning in?

"Anyone," I answer, straightening.

Matt claps his hands just once, startling me. "Well, we better get back to work. The night is young." He hops onto his feet, then offers a hand to pull me up.

I was kidding myself. Matt's not interested in doing *that* with me. He wasn't jealous. I'm so horny it's affecting my judgment.

I grab on to his forearm begrudgingly as he pulls me upright. But . . . he doesn't let go. We're in the center of the bus, just a tight grip around my wrist and not a single sound other than my heartbeat in my ears.

"Or . . ." He leans in, just the smallest amount, and yet my lips part. "We could call it a night and get you home?"

I'm misreading him. Again. I have to be. "We'd have to clean up first." I look at his lips and can't help but lick my own.

"Mmm." He nods slowly. "We would."

"And lock up," I croak out as Matt tugs me even closer.

Maybe my judgment isn't so terrible.

He leans in, his chin at my jaw, and inhales deeply *again*. "You wear perfume for him tonight?"

"I wore it for me." I correct him, my voice breathless.

"I like it."

"You do?"

"A lot." He brushes his nose against my jaw, and my eyes roll back in my head.

"Are you flirting with me?" I ask. Or at least I *think* I do.

His soft, single laugh surprises me. "For over a year now. Thanks for noticing." He kisses next to my ear.

"You shouldn't."

"Okay, tell me to stop." He kisses my cheek.

"What?" I ask, struggling to speak while he occupies all of my focus.

"Tell me why I should stop." He curls his arm around my lower back, pressing me into him.

"Because you're my friend," I say with little conviction.

"That doesn't need to change." His beard brushes my jaw, and I *fight* not to whine for more.

"Because I'm not interested in anything more than just sex," I say, eyes fluttering closed as his warm breath travels across my cheek.

"I can do that." He kisses just below the brush of my eyelashes.

"It might complicate things." I'm arguing for fun now, not to win. I want his reasons, his defense. I want him to want me.

"I thought it could be *anyone*," he says, his tone mocking lightly.

One thought breaks through the thick fog of indulgence. "Why now?" I ask. "Why now and not on our road trip? Why now and not before that?" He pulls away, not straightening fully but enough that I can see his eyes and the desperation within them. It shocks me.

It *thrills* me.

"I don't know if you've noticed, but we seem to have this dynamic where you ask for something, and I take care of it." He licks his lips as my eyes fight to close and give in yet again. "You need me to drive cross-country with you?" He kisses my cheek. "Done." He ducks lower. "Need me to work on your bus?" He kisses my chin. "Done." He moves to the left. "Need a ride home from a shitty date?" He kisses the opposite cheek. "Done."

I gasp as his hand curls around my jaw and he tilts me to look at him, his rough fingers in my hair. "You need someone to take care of you in bed?" He kisses my lips, so brief and teasing, regret washes over me, having missed it. "Done. It doesn't have to be complicated."

"I wouldn't want anyone else to know," I stammer. "They just . . . they wouldn't get it."

"Done."

"And I mean it. I'm not looking for more. You can't fall in—"

"Would you *please* stop talking?" he asks half a second before *making* me. When our lips meet again, I do not hold back. My hands are in his hair and around his shoulders with *urgent* need. Months and months of secret longing pour from my lips to his.

Matt reaches down and lifts me, hooking my legs around him.

If I knew, if I even suspected it would feel *half* this good, we'd have been doing this a *long* time ago. He kisses like sparks—flickering and fast—but I want more. I swipe my tongue across his lip like a matchstick, and he ignites, opening to me.

His hand, spread in the middle of my back, keeps me pressed to him as I let my own wander. I find his biceps and squeeze, cling to his chest and commit it to memory, massage his scalp as I grip his hair in tight fists.

He swears under his breath as I nibble his lip.

"God, Lane, you're going to eat me alive." His hazy, flustered laugh is the sexiest thing I've ever heard.

"Problem?" I ask, tugging his lip between my teeth.

"No. Destroy me if you must." He pushes my back to the wall, jarring my head away from his neck, where I'm attempting to leave marks. "But I'd like to do something before I go." He looks at my bike shorts with steady focus, then back to my face through thick lashes. "Can I take these off?" His fingertips brush under the hem of my shorts.

I nod, panting.

If I wasn't experiencing it, I'd think it impossible to be *this* turned on. I'm *almost* embarrassed at what he'll find when he touches me.

He turns sideways just enough that my legs loosen around his hips. I stand on wobbly feet as he bends down to one knee in front of me. My upper back remains against the wall of the bus, providing me the balance I'd lack otherwise.

After he helps me step out of my shorts, Matt grabs a hold of my calf, stopping me from placing my foot back down. He massages it in his hand and presses a few delicate kisses on the side of my knee before hooking it over his shoulder. He does the same with the other leg as he sinks down to both knees and presses my lower half against the wall, his head between my thighs.

"Damn . . ." I hear him say as he presses his nose against my thin, soaked cotton underwear. "This all for me?"

"Yes," I say.

He licks the entire strip of fabric between my legs. A raspy *fuck, Lane* escapes his lips.

It sends a chill up my spine that fills my whole body with greedy, incessant need. More than need, actually. A ferocious hunger.

He tilts his mouth, hooking his teeth under my panties. I curse and fist his shirt, feeling like I'm going to explode from anticipation. I'm desperate, and he knows it, so what's the use in pretending? "Please," I beg, winding my hips.

He bites down on the fabric and pulls it aside, tucking it away so I'm fully exposed to him. "Perfect," he whispers solemnly, right before devouring me like he, *too,* is starving.

Almost instantly, I'm yelping and gasping and pulling so tightly on his hair that I may actually tear it from the root.

"So responsive." He licks up my center, cooling me off.

"Please don't—don't stop."

"When someone offers you help, Lane, you don't tell them how to do it. That's rude." He sucks on my clit to the point of pain, making me hiss. "I'm going to take my time."

"Matt, please."

"You're not very good at taking compliments, you know that?" He flicks me with his tongue. "Look at me."

When I do, it's a shocking and heady force that greets me.

Matt, *my gentle, friendly Matt,* eager between my thighs. His beard wet and glistening from the pleasure he's already awarded me.

I wish I could take a picture—he's so pretty like this.

"I'm going to make you come on my tongue tonight, but next time we do this . . ." I open my mouth to protest, and he raises a brow in warning. "*Next time* we do this, I'm going to ask you to compliment yourself while you finish. I might have you in front of a mirror too. You're perfect, manamea. And I won't rush perfection. Hear me?"

I'm speechless and whimpering and experiencing a headspace that I can only describe as carnal. It's nothing I've felt before. Most guys don't even want to talk during sex, let alone get you *off* with their words. I should have known Matt would be different.

"Please," I whine.

"Please what?" He licks my inner thigh, curling his tongue.

"Please, Matt."

"Not my name, Lane. Tell me what to do. You wanted *anyone,* right? Use me."

"Your tongue."

"Better," he teases, massaging my hip in his hand, rubbing his thumb under the hem of my shirt.

"Please . . ." I groan. I don't fucking know what he wants, and I can't take it. "Tell me what to say."

"What do you want?" he asks, his tone short tempered.

"I want you to make me come, Matt. Hard."

"Done," he says, diving at me.

I writhe against his mouth, pulling at his hair until I'm most definitely hurting him. But I can't seem to stop.

I squeeze my thighs around his ears so tightly I may bruise us both. But when the orgasm comes like a bullet out of a gun, my body melts around him and collapses. He catches and steadies me, holding me upright with two strong hands.

When I feel strong enough to support my own head, I look up to the ceiling and attempt to catch my breath. A laugh of disbelief escapes my lips as a bead of sweat drips down past my ear.

Matt. Mattheus Tilo-Jones. My friend, Matt. Is the best I've *ever* had.

FOURTEEN

MATT HELPS ME BACK INTO MY BIKE SHORTS AND HAS me sit in the driver's seat before he begins cleaning up. He moves quickly around the bus, storing the paint and supplies away, cleaning up our leftovers and throwing out the garbage outside. A few minutes later, it's as if we were never here. As if *nothing* happened.

I bite my lip and try to force all my nervous energy into my feet as they tap against the edge of the seat's base. *What do I do now?* Do I go back to talking with him about movies? Do we keep working on the bus together? Are we going to do that again? More? I check my phone, and it's barely past eleven. Which is strange because it feels like *days* since my terrible date.

"Ready?" Matt asks from the door.

I nod and follow silently. When we get into his car, I beg silently for him to turn the radio on. But he doesn't.

We drive in a *painful* quiet all the way to my apartment's parking lot. I fidget in my seat.

"Talk to me," he says, turning off the ignition.

"About?" I ask.

Matt shakes his head. "Whatever is going on in there." He taps my temple. "You freaking out?"

Am I freaking out? Is he serious? "Uh, yeah!" I scoff. "We just . . . *you* just . . . I just—"

He interrupts. "Do you regret it?"

I consider the question, but the answer is instantly obvious. It felt good. *So good.* "No."

"All right, so you don't have any regrets." He smiles softly. "But did you enjoy it?"

"Yes." I laugh, because I thought *that* was obvious, based on the way I screamed his name and soaked his beard.

"Me too." He nods. "So, what's wrong?"

I groan. "I don't know . . . I guess I'm still worried we're going to mess up our friendship over this."

"I think we can avoid that, but we're going to have to talk." He raises a brow. "Not just shut down in panic."

"Fair," I mumble. "I think I'm also feeling a little insecure."

He sits up straighter, his brow furrowing, and concern tugs down on his full lips.

"I don't want . . ." I take a deep breath. "I don't want it to feel like you're doing me a favor. Like it's fixing the bus or a ride home. I want it to be for both of us. Otherwise I'll just feel pathetic."

Matt's nostrils flare as a smile grows, his lips shaking with restraint—trying not to laugh.

"Matt . . ." I whine.

"No, I hear you." His laughter bursts out. "If you want to return the favor, I guess I'd be fine with that," he says, biting his lip. "If I *must.*"

"I hate you."

"That's not what you were saying thirty minutes ago," he mutters. I smack his chest with the back of my hand. He catches it and winds his fingers through mine. My pulse races against his.

"Listen, Lane." He kisses my intertwined hand before turning to face me. "I know you're not looking for anything more. But . . . you should know something. I've been waiting for this chance for a while. If this is what you can give me, I'll take it."

"*That* feels complicated." I look at him, and a swirl of emotions races between us. It's both invigorating to be wanted and terrifying to know just how much. I almost wish he'd let me believe it *was* just for me.

"Yeah, probably. But you let me worry about that." He smiles.

"I don't know. I don't think I'm cool with that. I mean, if your feelings are involved . . ."

He sighs. "Okay, yeah. You just let me know."

"No!" I look up to the ceiling and pull my hand from his, winding both my hands through my hair. "Don't. Don't be so understanding and nice. Then it's just going to keep feeling like I'm being selfish."

"Why is that such a bad thing?" Matt asks, laughing in confusion.

"Being selfish?" I ask incredulously. "Not caring about my friend's feelings?"

"You obviously *do* care. You're more worried than I am."

"Right, but . . ."

"Try being selfish. Just for a little bit. Just with me." He grabs the back of my neck and pulls me toward him over the center console. "I want it like that." His voice is *deathly* low.

"Why?" I ask softly, but if I'm being totally honest, I'm having a hard time caring why. His hold on my neck is shattering my better judgment.

"Because I want it," he says, as if it's just that simple.

"Okay." I nod, my nose rubbing against his cheek. "Okay." I nuzzle into his profile.

"Can I come up?" he asks quietly, tilting his lips to mine.

My smile presses into his mouth. "Yes, please."

A chaste, soft kiss.

"I like kissing you," I say, doing it again.

"Me too," Matt answers, brushing his lips against mine delicately. He kisses down my jaw to my neck. My eyes roll to the back of my head, and I quickly decide I have to be certain before pleasure overrides my senses further.

"You're sure? You're absolutely sure you want this, no strings attached?" I just need one more reassurance. One more, and then I think I'll feel okay.

"Hmm . . ." He hums against my throat. "No, actually." He bites, soliciting a gasp from me. "I don't think I want this at all." He takes my hand and puts it in his lap—showing me *exactly* how much he wants this.

"Oh." My hand involuntarily twitches with eagerness. "Let's go take care of that." I kiss him, my tongue grazing his upper lip.

"Mmm. I'd appreciate that." He kisses me back, our mouths crashing and opening for each other. It's never been my favorite part of hooking up before, but kissing Matt feels like true foreplay. A preview of what's to come, mimicking future movements his body will make against me. He listens so intently to every sound, gasp, moan from me, as if he's trying to perfect his craft.

His hands find the waistband of my shorts, and my eyes shoot open, looking at the parking lot around us. "Mattheus," I gasp. "Parking lot."

"See anyone?" he asks, panting softly next to my ear.

I don't check again. "No."

"*So*"—he elongates the word—"open your legs."

"I thought we were evening the score upstairs." I lean into the headrest as he kisses up my neck.

"I thought we agreed you'd be selfish." He slips his hand into my underwear, and I instinctively grab a hold of his wrist. His forehead presses above my ear as he leans across the front seat.

"There?" he asks.

"Little to the left," I answer.

"Here?"

I nod with a moan.

"Yes?"

I nod, gasping.

"There?"

"*Yes,*" I cry out.

He leans back, keeping his hand in the exact spot. "Open your eyes. Look at me."

I turn to him, his gorgeous face lit by the moonlight. We hold eye contact as he gets me closer to release, and it feels shockingly erotic to watch the determination in his eyes.

"You're incredible," he says fervently.

"You're . . ." I try to speak, but as soon as I open my mouth, he begins moving faster against me, forcing my jaw to close tight with a keening whine.

"No, just listen," he says.

I grab a hold of the door's handle, needing something to grip on to as my body tightens to an unbelievable point.

"You're incredible, Lane. I've been wanting this—my name on your lips, my fingers getting you off, my mouth all over you—for over a year. You're scared, I get it. You don't want more?"

I shake my head, even as I approach what I suspect will be an earth-shattering orgasm.

"Yeah . . ." He licks his lips. "We'll see about that," he says, capturing my lips in a kiss and pushing two fingers into me.

I come undone, grinding my teeth together at the sheer intensity overtaking my body.

Matt doesn't stop until I'm slapping his wrist, silent and heaving for air. When he does remove his hand, he uses his other to turn my head. I watch through drooping eyelids as he puts two fingers into his mouth and sucks.

"I don't think I'll get enough of that taste."

I fall back into the headrest, allowing bliss to overtake me.

Before my body's even stopped shaking, he's out of the car and opening my door. He scoops my lifeless body up and carries me toward the lobby of my building.

I sincerely hope none of my neighbors see me, because they'll think I'm shit-faced on a Wednesday night.

But I feel so safe. I feel so *good*.

I think Matt's a sex expert. A *sexpert*, if you will. I once heard that to be an expert at something, you had to practice it for ten thousand hours. I feel like it's impossible for one human to have *that* much sex unless they're a paid professional. But he at least has his PhD in sex or something. There's a dick joke there somewhere—but I'm too worn out to find it. Oh . . . wait. Pretty Huge Dick. Found it.

"Keys?" Matt says against my temple.

"Under the mat." I snort. "Under the Matt, under the mat."

"Wow." Matt draws out the word, bending down to lift the mat and get the keys. "Please tell me you don't leave your keys here every day."

Attention: New kink unlocked. People who can carry you and squat while doing it.

"Okay, if that's what you want to hear . . . I don't keep my keys here," I say dryly.

"Lane." He chastises me with my name alone.

"Put me down if you're going to be grumpy," I mumble.

"No, I have plans for you." He unlocks the door and tucks the keys away in his pocket.

"In the interest of being selfish, I'm saying now that we're not doing anything else tonight. My body feels like it just ran a marathon."

"Not those kinds of plans but glad to hear it." He winks, turning to walk us backward through my door.

He lays me on the couch, and Simone comes into the open area of her cage, investigating the sudden interruption of whatever she was doing in there. I like to imagine she has an extensive beauty regimen she does before bed and is now angry at us for barging in.

"Hey, Simone," Matt greets her, walking past the cage to the bathroom. I let my eyes close briefly before I hear running water.

"A bath?" I ask loud enough for him to hear.

"Where's your bath stuff?"

"Um, under the sink." Is he drawing me a bath? Like I'm a sickly Victorian child? I stand and walk to the bathroom, proving I still have *some* capabilities during post-orgasm bliss. "Hey."

He startles, knocking his head on the underside of my sink. "Fuck, you scared me."

"What's going on here?"

"Aha." He pulls out a tiny bottle of bubble bath my mother sent as a part of a care package.

"Are you having a bath?" I ask him.

"Well, it's not big enough for two. So, no."

"It's not big enough for one, if that *one* is you." I look between him and my small, apartment-sized tub.

He places a hand under the faucet, sitting on the bath's edge, and then adjusts the taps. He smiles at me kindly, and it makes me all sorts of shy.

"I don't know if I like *this*," I say, though the pink blush spreading up my neck tells a different story.

"What?"

"This." I gesture to the tub. "This feels like a *boyfriend* thing."

"Your words, not mine." He stands and approaches me, stopping at a respectable distance.

"We should talk about what you said in the car." I tap his chest.

He puts his hands up, feigning innocence. "Just caught up in the moment."

I circle him with one eyebrow raised before pulling off my shirt and shorts and lowering into the warm lavender water, moaning my approval.

Matt wets his lips, and his eyes widen as if he's trying to take in my body all at once. "Why do you *ever* wear clothes?" he asks, running a hand through his hair. "It should be a crime."

I push down a giddy smile—it's much safer to deflect. "It is a crime to be naked, dude."

"Do me a favor and lose the *dude.*"

"You call me *kid.* That is way worse!"

"Fine. No more platonic pet names." He finds a lighter and lights a candle at my feet. "But for the record, I was calling you *kid* in a Frank Sinatra, suave type of way."

"It certainly did not come across that way." I point to the candle. "And no more *boyfriend* shenanigans either. This bath is nice, but it's a one-time thing."

"I don't have to be your boyfriend to want to take care of you, Lane." He bends down next to the tub, collects my hair, and ties it into a loose bun on top of my head with ease. It matches his, and I like that.

I sink farther into the water. God, this *is* nice. Is it bad to like being spoiled? Just a little bit? "Fine, but it can't just be one-sided."

"What do you have in mind?" he asks, sitting on the closed toilet seat.

"Well, for starters, your hair. I want to wash it, brush it, braid it, you name it."

"So, you have a hair fetish," Matt teases.

"Maybe," I answer plainly. *"Yours,"* I mumble.

"Okay, I like a little pampering." He playfully crosses a leg over his knee.

I look at him in this increasingly vulnerable, intimate environment and wonder why I feel so unencumbered. This should be weird. It *is* weird. Why does it feel like we've done this a hundred times? "If someone had told me twelve hours ago that you'd be sitting in my bathroom while I take a bath after getting me off in the front seat of your car, I'd have . . ." My voice falls off.

"You'd have?" he asks, leading.

"Well, maybe I wouldn't have been *completely* shocked. Surprised, though, for sure."

Matt laughs. "It felt like a long time . . . coming?" He pushes his lips together.

"Did you just make an orgasm joke?"

"*No.*" He pretends to be offended. "Get your mind out of the gutter."

"I hate you."

"You keep saying that. Deflecting much?"

Shut up. "Shut up." I splash him. "Let me enjoy my bath."

"Do you have a washer here?" he asks, looking at a pizza stain on his shirt.

"Yeah, in the front closet."

"Happen to have any spare men's double-XL shirts laying around?"

"Maybe. Check the bottom drawer of my husband's dresser. Don't worry, he's away for work." I smile up at him coldly.

"Well, I guess I'll be sleeping shirtless then." He starts to strip off.

"Uh, no sir!" I sit up, the water's surface tickling below my breasts. "You are *not* sleeping here."

He scoffs, and his eyes drift down, up, down, up, down, up.

Huh, a triple-take—nice work, boobies. "You're joking," he says, finally focused.

"That is *definitely* against the rules."

"What? Whose rules?" he asks. "Not mine." He slides off his boxers, and *whoa.*

I lower into the water until I must look like an alligator peeking out of a swamp—just two hungry eyes.

He laughs at my reaction to his naked frame, his Adam's apple bobbing. He brushes his beard down before holding his arms up and doing a slow spin for my benefit. His body. *His fucking body.* It's *cruel* in its beauty. I'm envious of his curves.

His wide frame isn't particularly muscular, but he's built strong. But most of this I knew from the rat-half-naked-carrying incident. The new surprise is his dick. Which I'm a big fan of. *Big* fan. *Big.* Fan. You get it.

His ass, however, is the star of the show. My god. There may be no words. What I *do* know is that I'm going to take a bite out of it if I can. It should be cast and hung on a wall at a museum. The plaque will read: *World's Best Ass, belonging to Mattheus Tilo-Jones, as discovered by Elaine Rothsford on the eve of her demise.*

"Can I stay now?" he asks, toying with me.

I come back up for air. "You're clever, I'll give you that. You knew *exactly* what you were doing." I wet my lips.

"I *could* put my clothes back on." He pops his butt out as he bends to pick them up.

I stretch a hand out and smack his ass, which is met with a hearty laugh. "Just for tonight"—I reach down between my feet and pull out the bath's plug—"you may stay."

"Are you talking to me or my butt?"

"Shut up and pass me a towel."

He holds the towel with both hands outstretched. When I stand, he wraps me in a giant hug, tucking it into place at my back.

"I can do *some* things for myself." He holds my hand as I step out of the tub.

"You can, but this way, maybe you'll keep me around." He licks his front teeth as he smiles roguishly.

I glare at him as he moves around me, turns the shower on, and pulls back the curtain before stepping inside.

As soon as he gets in, he's humming under his breath. Over the course of me pulling out my toothbrush, wetting it, and beginning to brush my teeth, he's belting out "Bennie and the Jets." I giggle and roll my eyes as I spit into the sink. I'm not sure if I'm blushing because of how ridiculous his attempts at the lyrics are, or because of how embarrassing it is to like having him here *this* much already.

"Bennie!" He screams in a falsetto that I'm sure my neighbors will assume is a cat being murdered in a nearby alley. I shush him and use it as an opportunity to take a peek around the shower curtain. It's the most obscene thing I've ever seen. Sudsy, wet Matt. Inky hair dripping, his naked body so . . . available to me. Casually so. *Natural.*

"May I help you?" His tongue darts between his lips.

This is a bad idea. It will end horribly, my brain informs me.

You don't know that, I argue. *He told me to be selfish. Let's try it.*

"Nope. Going to bed." I turn on my heels and already miss the view.

"Meet you there."

"To sleep," I call back over my shoulder.

I fall asleep cocooned in my own blanket-turned-shield, facing away from him, long after he falls asleep. Hours later, I wake up to an alarm far earlier than any I've ever set and with my body draped across him like a starfish stuck to an aquarium's glass wall.

FIFTEEN

"OKAY, DROP ME OFF THERE, AND I'LL WALK IN SEPA-rately." I point to the gas station around the corner from the shop.

"Or we could just say—if Warren is even there early *and* notices us arrive together—that I picked you up."

"Why would you suddenly decide to pick me up?" I roll my eyes.

"I think you're being paranoid." He pulls into the gas station regardless.

"See you in ten minutes."

"What?" He laughs, locking the door to stop me from bolting.

"I'm going to sit on that bench for a while; let time pass be-tween our arrivals."

"You've lost it." He smiles. "Co-workers typically arrive at the same time. That's not suspicious."

"Fair point, but we're here early. So it would be strange if we arrived *early* together."

"Even if you walk in and I'm driving?" He sighs, apparently ex-asperated.

"See you in ten." I unlock the door, but he's faster.

"Or, instead of being early," Matt waggles his eyebrows, wearing a smirk, "we could park over there and make out."

I lean in, one hand still on the door, offering a sultry smile. The moment his lips touch mine, I unlock the door and open it in one swoop. I flip him off as I shut it. He drives away, shaking his head and smiling.

And because I have ten minutes to kill, I call Liz. Normally I wouldn't call her this early, but I know for a fact she's up because she's already posted on Instagram for Phillip's birthday. He is apparently forty-five today.

I knew he was older than her, but not almost twenty years older. I know they're both consenting adults and they didn't meet until she was twenty-six . . . but it gets added to the list of concerns brewing in my gut. Has he been married before? If not, why? Do the women his age find him intolerable? God, I wish I could *actually* talk to her.

"Morning," I say cheerily into the phone.

"Hey," Liz replies quietly.

My stomach drops. "What's wrong?"

"What?" She clears her throat away from the phone. "Nothing. Why?"

"You always greet me the exact same way. I find your consistency comforting."

"Sorry, guess I'm still waking up."

"Okay."

"You sound different though. Peppier than usual . . ."

"I'm just walking to work."

"You work from home, don't you?"

"Oh, right. I forgot to tell you. I'm working on a new project!" *She's your sister; just tell her.* "I, um, bought a bus, and I'm renovating it into a home."

Silence.

"Liz?"

"You're joking, right?" she says in a tone that tells me she knows I'm not.

"Not kidding." I hold my breath.

She laughs just once, snarky and heavy with sarcasm. I can practically hear her roll her eyes as she does it. "That's ridiculous."

"Well, it's half done, and it's actually very nice. I'm really proud of it, and I think you could ease up a little bit."

"*Half done?* Then what?" She laughs more, and it's like a knife twisting in my stomach. "You're not *actually* going to live on a bus . . . surely?"

"Why?"

"What's next, a trailer park?"

"Maybe! I'm going to need somewhere to park it. And that's *in* the name." I take a deep breath. "You don't have to *understand* it, Liz, but you could be less of a dick about it."

"*Wow.*" She tuts. "Nice. Real mature. You know, Lane, if you wanted to be homeless, you could at least not waste money doing it."

I knew she wouldn't get it. Fuck her for ruining my good mood and hating on the bus. Rage sizzles out of me, like vapor off hot concrete. "Yeah, you're *so* mature," I mock. "That's probably why you have a hundred-year-old boyfriend. Tell me, can he get it up, or are you saving yourself for marriage like they all did when he was young?"

"Maybe you should consider closing *your* legs once in a while— a bus isn't a suitable place to raise a baby."

Classic Liz. Still convinced I'm the same girl everyone in high school called *Loose Lane*. She was so embarrassed. I couldn't care less. They were all assholes—and they got real quiet when it was them in the back of my car getting off.

"I'm sure Phillip can't *wait* to get you pregnant—otherwise he'll be in the retirement home before your kid is in high school."

"Grow up, Lane."

"Grow a personality, Liz."

Neither of us hangs up. We should, but we don't.

Shit.

I sigh, pinching the bridge of my nose. If Liz wanted the conversation to be over, she'd hang up—but she *never* breaks first. In all of our many sisterly disputes over the years, she's not once apologized first. I can't stand the silence, but she's immune.

"Did you . . . did you get my email yesterday?" I ask quietly.

She makes a hum in the back of her throat. "About the dresses?"

"Yeah," I mutter.

"Yeah, I'm going to go with the one you chose."

"Oh, nice . . . I'll go get it tailored, then." I grind my back teeth.

"The other two bridesmaids liked the second one more."

"Oh then . . . ?"

"But *you're* my sister," she says pointedly. "So."

"That was *almost* a nice comment."

"Don't push it."

"Do I sense an apology next?" I ask, knowing she never will.

A heavy breath down the line. "Yeah, I'm sorry."

I'll be damned.

"I'm just—wedding planning isn't what I thought it would be. I had a weird day yesterday, and . . . it feels like we're just in really different places, and I guess I wish I had some of your . . . freedom."

"You mean because you're an adult and I'm not?"

"I mean you're living, and I'm going through the motions."

"I want the motions." I shrug. "Or I want *to want* to go through the motions."

She huffs a laugh. "If we were identical, we could pull a *Parent Trap.*"

I'd never marry Phillip, I think—but don't say it. We're done fighting . . . for now. "Damn you for being taller," I tease. "I'm sorry too. Phillip's not *that* old."

"He kind of *is.*" She laughs quietly. "But I like it."

"That's our daddy issues talking," I say, voice smug.

"Ew, don't use that phrase. It's gross."

"I'm serious. Someone gave me a bath last night, and it unlocked a whole new thing in me."

Liz grumbles. "Stop, I do *not* want to know about your sex life!"

Fine. I check the time, and *now* I'm late. "I've got to go. I love you, Liz."

"I love you too, Lane. Call me tomorrow?"

"Yeah."

"Bye," she says before hanging up.

WARREN KNOWS. I'M not sure how, but he knows. Which means Chloe will find out. Which means we may as well put it in the local paper.

"Why do you keep looking over your shoulder?" Matt asks, checking behind us as we put the second layer of blue paint on. "You're freaking me out."

"Warren's watching us and . . . smiling."

"So?"

"So? So he *never* smiles."

"Maybe he likes the color you chose."

"Or maybe he knows he's about to win a bet with Chloe." I glance back. He's cleaning a tool, eyes still on us.

"What? What bet?"

"He didn't tell you?" I ask, and Matt shakes his head, his brows furrowed. "He and Chloe have a bet about when we'd hook up. He said this year; Chloe said next."

"Those assholes . . ."

"Those are our best friends you're talking about."

"Are Amos and Em in on it?" he asks.

"Emily pleaded the fifth when I asked her."

"Okay . . . and you don't want them to know?"

"Obviously." If they know, then it's not just between Matt and me. If it's not just between us, then it's not private. If it's not private, it's subject to opinion. Opinions that I'm not interested in hearing. Because I know my best friends, and they will think that this is the start of a fantastical love story instead of just a series of very hot hookups.

"So don't act any differently." He shrugs nonchalantly.

"How? How does one act normal after they—" I stop myself from saying *had the best sex of their life.* Because we haven't even had sex—not really. Matt hasn't received a single orgasm, whereas I've had multiple. *Is this the glass ceiling I've heard so much about? Did I smash it?*

Matt's tongue darts out, licking his bottom lip. "After what?" He crowds me, and I check over my shoulder to see no sign of Warren, thankfully. "After . . ."

"Stop it." I flash my eyes at him, rolling more paint onto the side of the bus.

He leans in close to whisper. "After the best sex of your life? Is that what you were going to say?"

"No. Actually, the opposite." I frown mockingly. "After such a disappointment. Not even really worth their bet."

He throws his brush onto the nearby tarp. "Oh really?"

I squeal as he makes a dash for me, going under his reach. He chases me around to the other side of the bus and captures me in his grip, tugging me to his chest. "The worst?" he asks, gruff in my ear.

"Just terrible." I laugh at him, swatting his grip around me.

"Then you are an *excellent* actress." He nips at my earlobe before releasing me.

"I was in the drama club throughout high school." I stand proudly. "My teacher said I had potential."

He rolls his eyes. "Back to work, trouble."

"I think this is an excellent time for me to take my break." I look around the side of the bus to see if we've been spotted. "You stay—"

"Yes, yes. No one will suspect a thing." He waves me on, backing away slowly. "Look, I'm nowhere near you."

I blow him a kiss off my middle finger, and he mimes catching it and putting it in his pocket.

When I get to the staff room, Warren is halfway through a sandwich and coffee. I politely nod and go about getting my food out of the fridge.

"Hey." I sink into the chair across from him.

"Hey," he says, not looking up from his phone.

"How's your day going?"

"Fine, yeah. You?" He speaks with a mouthful of food.

"Good . . . good." I bite down on a forkful of pasta salad.

"How was your night?"

I choke a little. "Hmm? What?"

"Chloe said you went on a date?" He looks up and narrows his eyes.

"*Yeah*. Yeah, I did!" *Why am I shouting?* "Went fine."

"Did it?" His smile is downturned—cocky. "Huh." He goes back to his phone. "Interesting."

He knows. He knows I know he knows. But how do I find out what he knows and to what extent?

"Interesting?" I ask.

He turns his phone around. Blurry video of security camera footage plays at six-times speed. Us painting, us going inside, vague shadowy movements, but nothing explicit—thank god. Then Matt leaves the bus to gather supplies and tidy up. He's got nothing. I relax into my chair.

"Wait—I missed my favorite part." He pauses it, rewinds it slightly, then hits play at regular speed.

I watch, my face burning, as Matt exits the bus after we'd *finished,* and he began tidying up. The moment he's outside, he spins on his heel and mimes scoring a touchdown. I'm mortified, and yet I can't find the strength to not laugh at such a dorky show of emotion. How does he go from *I'm going to fuck you in front of a mirror* to doing a silly victory dance?

"This proves nothing." I push the phone back toward him like evidence in an interrogation room.

"I'm not sure Chloe will see it that way." He lifts a brow in challenge.

"We're not . . . we aren't together," I explain unconvincingly. "It's just a casual thing."

"Yeah, that's the dance of a *casually invested* man."

I wince.

"What's happened since our talk?" he asks, sighing.

"Matt and I came to an understanding." I take another bite.

"Did you find a grief therapist?"

"Was that the assignment? Missed that part," I say with a shrug. I'm *so* unbothered. Not worried about his or anyone else's opinion . . . *obviously*.

"So your commitment issues went away overnight?"

Fucking hell. Can't a girl eat in peace? "No." I glare at him. "There's no commitment to take issue with."

"And your concern about ruining your friendship?"

I scrunch up my face. "Like I said, Matt and I have an under-standing. We're adults."

Warren mimes repeatedly smacking his forehead against the table.

"Different types of relationships exist. We can be good friends and take care of each other's . . . needs."

"Right." He studies me. "But are you exclusive?"

"No? Maybe?" *Shit, did we talk about that?* "Yes."

"And it's . . . indefinite?"

I wag my finger at him. "I see where you're going with this but—"

Warren interrupts. "*And* the two of you will continue to hang out as friends."

"You've made your point."

"You're dating, Lane."

"No, we're not," I reply sternly.

Warren shakes his head, laughing. "Take care of yourself, okay?"

"I'm a grown woman, Warren." I glare at him. "Don't patronize me."

"Okay, sorry." He leans back in his chair. "You're right."

We finish our lunches in silence. When Warren goes to stand, I stop him at the door. "Show me the security camera feed."

He looks at me with humor dancing in his eyes as he opens the security app on his phone. I screenshot the main feed of the six different camera angles and hit share with text.

"Really?" I ask, voice cold as ice.

"What?" He chuckles at the back of his throat.

"I'm saved as *Lame* in your phone."

"A happy accident."

"You're the worst," I mumble, hitting send on the photo.

"Why do I feel like I'm giving you all the secret make-out spots?"

"Because you are." I grin like the devil, but it fades when I see his phone's lock screen—his beautiful wife, my friend. "Let me tell Chloe, okay? I want her to hear it from me."

"Two days . . . that's the longest I can keep a secret from my wife."

"A week," I counter.

"Fine, but only if you tell her in front of me." We shake on it.

SIXTEEN

AFTER A LONG AFTERNOON OF PAINTING, I FIND MATT locking up, the shop otherwise empty. "Hey, you . . . Can I get a ride home?"

"Is that not suspicious?" he teases softly, wrapping his arm around me.

I sigh exaggeratedly. "Yeah, so, I was right. Warren knows."

"What?" He stops and turns me by the shoulders to face him. "I swear I didn't tell him a single thing."

I smile to help ease him. "The security cameras."

His mouth parts as his eyes flare. "Oh god."

"*No*. No. He didn't see *anything*. It's all blurry, and you can't see inside the bus."

He releases a puff of air. "I almost had a heart attack." We start walking back toward the office in unison. "Wait. Then how did he know?"

I giggle, looking up at him. "Your victory dance."

Without a word, Matt takes his arm off my shoulders and begins walking in the opposite direction, across the parking lot.

"Where are you going?" I call after him.

"Looking for a hole to crawl into." He kicks at the gravel under his feet, committing to the bit. "It was fun while it lasted, but I'm going to go die now."

"It was endearing!" I walk over to him and grab his arm with both hands, pulling him back toward the office and our things.

"I've lost any edge of cool I might have had."

"We've been friends for too long for me to think you're cool, babe."

"I guess I wasn't going to be able to keep that up anyway." He opens the door for us, and we grab our gear before going back to his car.

"You're funny, handsome, and probably good in bed . . . so"— I tilt my head back and forth—"cool is overrated."

"Probably?" He scoffs, clutching his chest as I bend into the front seat. *"Probably?"* he asks again, turning the ignition.

"That's what you took from that?"

"Probably?" he asks again, voice pitching up.

I roll my eyes. "Fine—you're a fantastic lover, Matt. Happy now? But technically, we haven't been *in* bed. . . ."

"That can be arranged." He tilts his head, wearing a mischievous smirk.

"It can, huh?"

"Do you have plans tonight?"

"Nope." I smile into my lap. "You?"

"I was going to drop you off and then come back to do a final coat on the bus. . . ." He places his palm across my leg, his fingers digging into my inner thigh. "But if you want to do something else, I'm free."

"Cool." I buckle in.

He doesn't move or take the car out of park. "You okay?"

"Yeah, why?"

"Well, this morning you were very adamant that no one could find out about . . . us."

The truth is that I thought about it all afternoon while painting, and I've yet to decide how I feel about it. On one hand, getting to talk about my sex life with my friends is a pastime I quite miss. On the other hand, it could mean more pesky opinions like those Warren so freely expressed. But why do I care what they think? Their goals—the marriages, babies, and lifetime-together packaged deals—aren't mine. So why would my happiness look like theirs?

"I mean, it doesn't have to change anything, right? If they're all concerned about our sex lives, then that's their issue. We know the arrangement. It works for us." Self-confidence flies out the window when I see Matt's lips twitch downward ever so slightly. "Right? Is it still okay for you?" I ask, my voice far more intense than I'd have liked.

"Of course. Nothing has changed." He starts the car. "In fact . . . I think when we get back to your place, we can solidify this agreement," he says in a slightly over-the-top serious manner.

"Mmm. I concur."

*　　*　　*

THE MOMENT MY front door shuts, Matt has me pinned up against it. I fiddle with the lock and drop the keys carelessly onto the floor.

Matt hoists me up, wrapping my legs around his hips. One palm spread against my lower back, supporting my weight, the other in a ferocious grip on the back of my head. He pulls my hair out of its bun, and without thinking, I do the same to him. When we finally get to my bedroom, he kicks off his shoes and drops me onto the bed with a bounce.

"Off." He points to my clothes as he rips his shirt off over his head.

Instead of complying, I lie back and admire the view of him undressing like he's never been in such a hurry. It makes me feel desirable. Alive. I'd forgotten what it's like in the newness of wanting. When everything feels electric and exciting and desperate. It's an addictive feeling.

He shakes his head as he approaches me. "Fine, have it your way." Then the sound of ripping.

"Did you just?" I look down at my tattered shirt, still in his grasp. He's torn it right down the middle, turning it into a button-up without the buttons. "I liked that shirt, you dick!"

"I asked nicely first."

"You *did not*."

He tugs at the buttons of my jeans, grumbling under his breath.

"Those don't rip, you oaf." A raised brow is my only warning before he grabs a tight hold of my hips and flips me over. "Stop manhandling me!"

He knows I'm full of shit. I'm practically beaming with approval. He pulls my jeans clean off, and I desperately cling to my sheets so I don't go flying across the room with them.

Matt's large palms find my ass and massage both cheeks. I attempt to go on all fours to climb up the bed, but he pulls my legs out from under me. "Quit it," he says, laughing.

"Please," I scoff, "it's not like I have a butt to admire."

He smacks my ass, and not in a watch-it way, but a that'll-shut-you-up way. It stings and shocks me silent, but I *like* it. Maybe I even love it. I turn over my shoulder and feign shock with a slack jaw. "How dare you!"

He stares me down. "Let's get one thing straight. You're my friend, and I don't take kindly to people talking shit about my friends. Expect me to react."

A huff escapes through my nose—so turned on, I'm embarrassed enough to laugh. "Do your worst." I prop my butt up in the air.

"I've got something else I'd much rather do." He flips me onto my back and moves between my legs so we're chest to chest. His hair falls, curtaining us both. I reach up to tuck it behind his ears so I can see his beautiful face and tug him down to my mouth.

This time, unlike all our other kisses so far, we take our time.

A kiss like a slow, rolling tide. Languid movements melting two bodies into one. I sigh contentedly against his lips, giddy like a teenager. "You're a great kisser," I whisper to him.

"I was just thinking the same thing about you." He nips my chin. He slowly makes his way down my throat, making me writhe from the soft brush of his lips that *almost* tickles.

I wait for him to pause for a breath, pull him up by a hold on his hair, and whisper, "I want you," against his mouth.

He slides his tongue between my lips.

"I want you so badly," I breathe into him. He inhales like he's taking the message inward to his very soul.

Twisting a hand between us, I try to take off my underwear.

"Let me." He says it like a request before he begins kissing his way down my torso.

"If you rip more of my clothing, I'll put them *all* back on," I tease, looking up at the ceiling as he kisses over each rib. "I'll put *more* on. A parka," I threaten.

"Please . . . you liked it." He bites my hip, and I yelp.

"You're going to pay for that," I growl, laughing.

He studies me with a face that screams *you sure about that?* "Don't threaten me with a good time." He tugs my panties down, and I bend my legs to assist him, my feet in front of his chest.

"I could kick you off the bed right now." I press my toes into him.

"You could try." He takes both of my ankles in his hands.

With purposeful, tender movements, he massages from heels to calves, trailing kisses along the inside of one leg and back down the other before lowering both of my feet to the mattress. The bastard disarmed me with lulling touches. Clever man. Worthy opponent.

While I'm laid back, annoyingly relaxed into a stupor, he reaches beside the bed and into his jeans for a condom.

I hear a wrapper tear before he hums in pleasure, stroking it onto himself.

I expect him to just go for it, but instead, he kisses the moth tattoo just above my knee. I go mindless under him as he follows the path of patch-like tattoos up my body.

I've never felt as wanted as I do with Matt. He gives equal attention to every part of my body, marvels at it with his eyes, hands, and tongue, as if he cannot believe I'm real. Like if he's not looking or touching me, I might just disappear.

I want to ask him what he likes about my body so much—or *me*, for that matter—but it feels like a trap of my own making. For me, not him.

I play with his hair, massaging his scalp, and combing his hair through my fingers as he takes his time coming back to me.

"Your skin is so soft." He nuzzles his cheek against the fleshiest part of my stomach. "I love it."

"You're killing me," I whine, arching my hips up, hoping gravity brings him toward me.

"I really want to taste you again. Can I?" He rests his chin on my hip, digging in slightly.

"Can I have you first?" I ask.

"Should we flip a coin?" He licks across my lower belly, looking up at me through heavy brows. My breathing is suddenly ragged. I'm unable to concentrate on the simple task of filling and emptying lungs.

"I've never had to ask a dude *not* to go down on me," I whisper, half serious.

"They're clearly all idiots." He kisses my pubic bone, and I fall back to the mattress in silent permission. "Because you've got heaven between your legs." Then his tongue finds my clit with shocking precision as he curls his mouth down.

"Whoa." My head tilts farther back, raising me off the mattress. "Oh." I grab a hold of his hair, like a leash in my hand—but it feels more like an anchor keeping me in my body.

He hums, producing a long, guttural moan from me.

He does it again.

This fucking guy.

"Yes!" I cry out as he lifts up to bring a finger inside me. He hooks it, tapping against the exact right spot, and between waves of cresting pleasure, I wonder if *this* is how sex was always supposed to be.

Matt doesn't need a how-to guide or a step-by-step manual, though I'd gladly have given it to anyone in the past if their pride could've handled it. He just intuitively knows my body. He hears me, takes notes, and does as he's told.

Perhaps this is the upside of sleeping with a friend. There are risks, sure, but they *know* you.

I whimper as he removes his mouth and hand before lifting himself up my body, shifting until his stomach rests on my hips. I reach out and pull at the curves on the side of him and lick my lips as he pushes into me.

"Fuck," we say in unison.

"Okay, maybe I should have gotten you off first." Matt presses his forehead into my shoulder. "This feels way too good."

"I want to be on top." I kiss him just once. "Can I?"

He nods, smiling against my lips as he rolls us.

Once I've adjusted to this new angle and how deep it feels,

I begin to carve out figure eights against him. I feel myself tighten as a quick jolt of pleasure, a sign of what's to come, shoots through me.

His eyes are hooded, watching me writhe on him, darkened with pure lust. His lips mutter praises and prayers of thanks, switching between English and Samoan—calling me by the word he used during our first time together. Manamea.

It took me a while to find it online later that night because I had to spell it out phonetically.

Manamea translates to: favorite person, dear, darling, sweet-heart, lover.

An all-encompassing sort of word. Perfect for us.

I whimper as I feel my orgasm come within reach, desperate for it.

"You're riding me so well, Lane," Matt groans out. "Fuck . . . look at you." He rubs his hands up and down my sides like he's shaping clay on a pottery wheel. His thumbs push into my sharp hip bones, the rest of his fingers hook around my lower back. He begins assisting my movements, dragging me against him in the most fantastic way.

I gasp as he tilts his hips up and hits *just* the right spot, deep inside me.

He does it again. And again. And again. Gasps escape each time, louder moans escaping between. "More . . . please. Yes . . . I'm so close!"

Matt sits up with a ravenous fever. His mouth burrows into my neck like he wants to draw blood, his hands pressing in tightly as he lifts and drops me onto him rapidly. It sets me off almost instantly, the sensation overcoming my senses as I feel him tense and twitch inside me.

We come together, tense and breathless, our kisses mostly teeth and panting.

"That was amazing," I say, pressing my forehead against his—feeling his sweat mix with mine. "We should have done this *months* ago."

Matt struggles to catch his breath, a sign of a job well done.

"The anticipation probably helped," he says, kissing my cheek. "But you're even better in real life than you were in my guilty fantasies."

I lift off and lie down next to him, and he immediately tucks a blanket over me. "Guilty?" I ask.

"Friends aren't supposed to fantasize about friends naked and moaning. But then again, you've dreamed about me too."

"Ha! You wish." I tuck the blanket up to my chest, rolling onto my back.

"You talk in your sleep, remember?"

My cheeks heat, and I close my eyes tight. "Oh my god, you have to tell me what I said."

He disappears to the bathroom, then comes back wearing an arrogant smile. "Something about my fingers going up your legs and under a dress." He laughs. "Oh, *Matt*," he mimics me. "Don't stop," he whispers in a feminine, mocking voice.

"I hate you."

"You keep saying that to me, and I'm going to develop some sort of strange need for it." Matt laughs, falling beside me.

I curl my leg over the top of him and plant my head on his chest. I take a deep inhale of his comforting scent—woodsy and salty like an ocean breeze. "You're all right, I guess."

"Yeah, you'll do." He palms my butt.

SEVENTEEN

"WHAT ABOUT THIS ONE?" MATT POINTS TO THE ORANGE-slice tattoo next to the crook of my arm. For the past few hours, between fetching us snacks and water, he's been inquiring about each of my tattoos. Which has led to several lovely but entirely mindless conversations. So far, our list of topics, the memorable ones at least, includes rabbit caretaking, which Disney villains are hot (out of the films Matt *has* seen), and what animal we would be if we got to choose at reincarnation (if such a thing exists).

I picked a rabbit that belonged to Matt following my excellent tutorial. He chose an otter because physical touch is his love language, and they're apparently cuddly.

That led to a discussion about love languages. I learned that mine could perhaps be receiving gifts—which made me feel a little shallow. Matt was adamant it was just as valid as the other options.

Then the topic of exes, which was brief. Matt had a girlfriend for almost a year while he was in trade school. She was also training to be a mechanic—which caused my mind to flash to Megan

Fox in *Transformers,* spiking mass amounts of jealousy—but Matt said there weren't strong feelings involved on his part. He'd never say it, but I get the sense he sort of fell into a relationship when she expressed feelings, and he was too shy to say no.

"That one." I tap his thumb, gently brushing the orange-slice tattoo. "I just thought it was cute."

He sighs, pouting like a kid.

"Sorry, most of the answers will be that."

"No, no. It *does* look cute. They all do. I guess I'm just hoping for some secrets or deeper meanings. Like they're some sort of window into your inner workings."

"Well, the little heart on my butt is a secret to most people."

"I *really* like that one."

"And this one"—I point to my thigh—"has a special meaning."

He traces the lighthouse tattoo with his fingers, delicately, like he's worried he could rub it off. "Guiding light?"

"Guiding light," I answer. I'm not surprised he remembered the story about my parents. He's thoughtful like that, but hearing him clarify in two words makes me feel warm and fuzzy.

"I *love* this one," he says, circling it.

"Yeah?"

"Yeah. They're all great. How many do you think you have now?"

"About thirty. They're all great? Even the little ghost-sheet guy?"

"Especially the ghost. It's got gothic-book vibes."

"Would you ever get a tattoo?"

"They're pretty common in Samoan culture, so I've considered getting one. My mother's brothers and father all had the same tattoo on their forearm, a tribal mark. I've thought a lot about getting that."

Had. "Had?" I ask softly.

"There was a fire. When my mom was nineteen. She was out at a friend's. The rest of her family didn't make it."

"Her entire family?" I sit up, wide-eyed. "All of them?"

Matt sits up too. "Well, not her grandmother. She was in England getting an experimental treatment for this rare type of cancer."

"Fucking hell."

Matt nods before rubbing down his beard. "My mom is the strongest person I know."

"I don't want to pry but . . . what did she do after the fire?"

"She went to be with my grandmother. Because her mother was too ill to travel back home, my mom stayed with her until the end. After she passed, my mom decided to travel around England for a few weeks before returning to the island. The last day she was in London, she went to the concert and met my dad."

My heart drops. How could she have been sound of mind enough to make the decision to fly off into the sunset with a stranger? Surely her heart was trampled on the floor. What awful timing.

"She never hid her pain from us. I'm sure some people might think she should have. I know other families don't really talk about death and stuff until later on, but . . . she always did." Matt smiles to himself. It's a subtle, aching smile. Gratefulness mixed with pain. "She wasn't worried about us not getting it or being frightened. She was just telling us how she felt. What she'd overcome. And, also, about our family—our history."

I nod thoughtfully before Matt continues.

"My mom's a reader—I guess that's where I got it from—and she had this line from *The Count of Monte Cristo* she'd quote often." He clears his throat with one small cough. " 'Happiness is like one of those palaces on an enchanted island, its gates guarded by dragons. One must fight to gain it.'"

I breathe in the words, letting them fill me. "She fought," I say, barely above a whisper.

"Yeah, she did." He curls his arm tighter around me. "And she won."

"She's happy? Even after everything she's been through?"

"She's the happiest person I know." Matt sighs. "Honestly, it would be easy to forget it happened to her if she didn't talk about them so much."

"She sounds wonderful. I can't wait to meet her. Your dad too."

"They're pretty great." He nods, and silence settles between us. He takes a few minutes to trace some of my tattoos down my arm before stopping at my wrist. "What about this one?"

I study the rose tattoo and suddenly want to transcribe a deeper meaning to it. I feel so vapid in my vanity, but I give him the truth. "I like flowers."

"Are roses your favorite?"

"No." I shake my head as if that's preposterous—like he should know better, which is silly.

"Are you going to make me guess? That could take a while," Matt teases gently.

"Tulips."

"Huh . . . I wouldn't have guessed that one."

"No?"

"Well, they're . . . cheery."

"I'm not cheery?" I ask pointedly, raising one brow at his growing smile.

"You're all black ensembles, wry wit, and tattoos . . . which I happen to really enjoy." He kisses the rose on my wrist. "But no, not really *cheery*." He fights back a yawn.

I swallow, nodding. "Tulips come back every year at the same time. No replanting. No gardening necessary. They're colorful, and they're a sign of spring." I shrug. "Everyone likes tulips."

"You like their hopefulness," Matt says, looking at me intently.

"Something like that."

Matt nods. "They keep coming back. . . ."

"They make it through the cold of winter," I say, feeling a little embarrassed at how clear it is that I've equated my love for a flower with some deeper meaning.

"Tulips . . . It's so obvious now." Matt kisses my cheek, then lowers himself down to lie flat against the pillow. "I shouldn't have doubted you." He smiles sweetly, his eyes closing.

I turn off the light and remain sitting up against the headboard. "Goodnight, Matt." I look down at him as his smile fades to a contented line, almost asleep. I brush my knuckle over his beard, down one side and up the other.

"Mmm. That's nice," he says, half awake.

"Physical touch," I remind him. *See, I listen too.*

"I'll get you a present tomorrow," he quips back, mumbling.

I flick his nose gently. "Do not."

"Fine. I won't."

I pout privately in the darkened room.

"You changed your mind, didn't you?" he says, his smile almost audible.

"*One* gift couldn't hurt." I laugh quietly.

"Are you not tired?" He tilts his chin up and tries to see me in the darkened room. He takes a moment to adjust, blinking like a newborn.

"Not really. I have a hard time falling asleep. Most nights, it takes hours."

"Come here." He opens his arm out toward me, and I shuffle down the mattress, curling myself into him.

I tell myself that it's simply a friend giving another friend comfort. Nothing more. A sleep aid, like melatonin in human form.

"Did I tell you about the time my brother Ian jumped into an old well on a dare?" he asks.

I huff a laugh. "No."

"Well, then brace yourself."

I fall asleep before they get him out.

EIGHTEEN

MATT AND I HAVE GOTTEN INTO A PRETTY GOOD RHYTHM the last four weeks—and I don't just mean in bed. There were a few hiccups with the bus's renovation—I would not recommend trying to install a joint air and heating unit on your own—but we're still on track to finish this week, a few days before we need to leave for Vancouver.

WM Motors is now officially rebranded. Their website is up and running, and their new sign is being delivered this week, complete with logo. It's not an *inspiring* name choice, but seeing that it was the only suggestion either of the men had, I wasn't going to fight them on it.

I've held up my end of our bargain, and both of them are happy. Now I just need to convince them to paint and spruce up the place a bit. A few coats of bright white, an updated sign or two, maybe even some new waiting room chairs that match. But convincing them may be a task for Chloe, who has more sway.

Under the guise of being busy at work, I've navigated not having to tell Chloe or Emily what's going on between Matt and me.

Warren's either forgotten—not likely—or he's dropped the ultimatum. And I'm silently grateful. I don't want to have to justify or rationalize it. Because I'm barely convincing myself it's a good idea. I can feel every little glance, touch, kiss, or joke shared between us tearing down my proverbial wall, brick by brick. If I'm not careful, the whole thing will come tumbling down.

When I'm not overthinking what's to come, the days are easy and repetitive. Matt does shop work in the mornings while I work on my bus. When he has breaks, he comes to find me—sometimes for a quickie on the driver's seat, but most often to just hang out or lend a hand. After the shop closes, we either stay late to work on the bus some more, or he takes me back home and, inevitably, gets invited up.

I've still yet to go to his apartment, but I've decided to worm my way into seeing it before we leave for our trip on Thursday. Because after our trip, we have to be done.

We haven't explicitly talked about it, but I think Matt senses the end is near too. His hugs are a little longer, his glances held steadier, his hands hold more admiration. Like he's memorizing me.

It just makes sense. When we get back, I'll be moving onto the bus and driving it off the shop's property—this phase will be over. The lust and constant company bubble *will* pop. We'll become friends who've seen each other naked, and nothing more.

Sure, I'll miss it. I'll miss the orgasms, the feeling of being pinned under him, the sound of him reading me to sleep or singing along badly to the shop's radio as he works. But this is a natural end, the most painless option. This was never going to be more than a blip. A sex blip. A great, blissful blip.

And it *is* for the best.

"Can we go back to your place tonight? Instead of mine?" I say, interrupting our otherwise silent ride to work.

Matt grimaces. "But your place is so much nicer, and Simone will miss me." He's right. Simone has gotten rather attached to Matt. I keep telling her it's not permanent, but she doesn't listen—rabbits have very small brains.

"I wouldn't know if it's nicer or not. I've never seen it."

"Tomorrow? Give me some time to . . . tidy?"

"There's no way it's dirty—you've been making *my* bed every morning. I haven't done that since the eighth grade."

"I'm stalling."

"Why?" I ask.

"I don't know." He looks genuinely nervous. "I guess I'm feeling private?"

"You're the least private person I know." I laugh. "I know everything about you. How you grew up, what you like, what makes you tick . . . what books you love . . . that sexy birthmark on your—"

"Okay, I get it." He laughs, pulling into his spot. He puts the car into park and turns to me with a loaded expression.

I've gotten a handful of these looks over the past few weeks, and each time, I can feel my heart harden in resistance. His eyes turn sincere and focused, his smile light and wistful. Then he says something that makes me look for an emergency exit.

"I *am* private, Lane. You're the only one who knows half that stuff."

I wave my hand flippantly. "Oh, please. I'm sure Warren knows this stuff too. You see each other every day. You're best—"

Matt interrupts me. "*You're* my best friend, Lane." He runs a hand through his hair, smiling to himself. "Do you really think Warren would say I'm his best friend? If he would use such a term . . ."

No. He'd say Chloe. She's his person. *His* manamea.

But I'm not Matt's person . . . or I can't be much longer. Someday, when this sexcapade is long over and we're back to movie marathons on opposite ends of the couch, he'll tell me about her. The woman who will be his forever.

She'll have a big heart and hopeful eyes. Equipped with a biting sense of humor but always willing to lend a hand to a friend in need. She'll be sweeter than me, easier than me, sexier than me. She will have read all his favorite books and be able to talk about authors—the old British and Russian ones too. He'll sweep her off her feet. They'll have chubby babies and dance in the kitchen. She will be the luckiest woman in the world. If she's brave enough to let love in.

And I'll watch.

"Manamea . . ." he says *too* softly. Too sweetly. "You have to know that. We've been together every single day for over a month, and I'm not the least bit sick of you." He forces a laugh. "Of course you're my best friend."

"For now," I respond coldly in an unprovoked jealous rage, thinking of *her*.

I only see his face fall out of the corner of my eye as I get out of the car and cross the yard toward my bus. Normally I stop in to say hi to Warren or grab a coffee, but I need some space. I need to get to work and stop thinking so much. Because that's what I'm best at—distracting myself. From the tightness in my jaw that makes my molars grind together. From the stiffness in my neck that reminds me I've been sleeping in Matt's arms—forgoing comfort for his nearness. From the feeling in my gut that reminds me I don't deserve the label of best friend—that he deserves so much better than me in friendship *or* more.

In a parallel universe, one where grief hadn't broken me, I could be with Matt. Easily.

It would be beautiful and simple and mundane. He'd want marriage, and I'd go to the courthouse the next day. We'd sit across the kitchen table to write grocery lists. We'd shower together without a happy ending. We'd fold each other's laundry and bandage each other's wounds and life would be easy. Easy and content and calm and the opposite of lonely. But that won't happen. Because of me. And I hate myself for it.

I'M FASTENING A handle to what will be the pantry cabinet, humming along to the radio, when I hear a cheerful voice from outside the bus's open window. Peering out, I see my sunshiny friend and the world's cutest toddler crossing the yard toward the bus, hand in hand.

"Knock, knock," Chloe calls.

"Knock, knock," Willow's little voice repeats.

"Hi!" I drop the screwdriver and run to open the door, immediately snapping my niece up from off the ground. "Simba!" I exclaim, kissing her cheek.

"I no Simba. I Willow!" She giggles at just how *ridiculous* adults are.

"What? Then what's this mane doing on your head?" I ruffle her wild curls.

"You so siy-y Auntie Yane."

"Did you come to see Auntie's bus?" I ask, looking toward Chloe.

"Warren said it was probably kid-proof enough by now, and we were nearby. . . . I hope this is okay." She smiles warmly, curling her arm around my shoulders for a side hug.

"Of course. I needed a break anyway." I walk up the steps and sit with Willow in the driver's seat. She immediately starts pretending to drive and pushing buttons.

"I feel like I haven't seen you in ages. How are you?" Chloe's eyes go wide as she looks around. "Wow!" She covers her mouth, her smile poking out on either side of her palm. "This is so much more gorgeous than I was expecting. Bigger too!"

I look around at the bus, trying to see it through her eyes. It's really coming together. The walls are all a soft sage, with bright white window trim. The floors and ceiling are both a light birch wood. There's a little dining nook with two wide benches and a table that can stow away to make way for the benches to become a single bed for a guest.

The kitchen cabinets are a darker green with a butcher countertop. I went with a deep, square, porcelain sink with gold accents to match the drawer pulls. Toward the back of the bus is a bathroom, complete with a compostable toilet, alley sink, and sunroof above the shower surrounded by white subway tile.

At the very back is my bedroom, separated by a sliding door that doubles as a mirror. Custom built by Matt is my queen bed. It's on hinges so I can store my clothes or other items underneath. I've installed a projector that connects to my laptop or phone and a drop-down screen for watching movies in bed. Above the bed is the other sunroof for stargazing.

It's perfect. My vision came alive. I feel pride swell in my chest and gratefulness for Matt right there with it.

"Lane . . ." Chloe breathes out. "Look at this place!" She sits at the nook, which I still need to cut cushions for, and touches everything within reach. "It's incredible."

"It's getting there. I'm just waiting on the hitch and outside storage to arrive, then once that's welded on and a few final details are fixed, it's just a matter of moving in."

"This week?"

"Should be." I smile.

"But then you're going to leave it to fly to Vancouver? Crappy timing."

"I know. If we hadn't booked flights already, I'd want to drive it."

"Oh, right." Chloe waggles her eyebrows. "*We*. Flights. Plural."

"Beep." Willow pushes the steering wheel. "Beep. Beep," she yells.

"Inside voice, Will," Chloe says sweetly. "So, how are you? Obviously you've been so busy because you were building this masterpiece, but"—she clears her throat suggestively—"anything else going on? Perhaps with a certain handsome mechanic?"

I turn over my shoulder, one brow raised. "What do you know?" I ask plainly.

"Warren may have told me to ask *you* for myself."

"What did Warren tell you to ask about?" I roll my eyes, laughing.

"Why you and Matt arrive at work together every morning." She shimmies side to side. "Is he picking you up, or is he *picking you up*?"

My brain goes straight to him *picking me up* and pinning me against the shower wall last night. Apparently my poker face is not what it once was because Chloe starts giggling.

"Oh my goodness. When did *this* happen?"

"Okay, breathe." I catch her eye and shake my head at her obvious joy. "It's not what you're thinking."

"I'm thinking that"—she smiles at Willow and chooses her next words carefully—"Uncle Matt and Auntie Lane are having some *private* play dates."

I bury my face in my hands, peeking between fingers. "They are."

She bites down on her smile, her eyes growing wide.

"But . . . we're playing *just* for fun. We're not committed to playing together long term."

"Playing feels like a dirty word now." Chloe grimaces. "But wait . . . you're not *together* together?"

"No, not dating."

"But you've been . . ." She winks twice, soliciting a laugh from me.

"Yes."

"How is it?"

I blow out a long breath and flare my eyes. "Incredible."

She claps her excitement, but then I watch as her smile slowly fades. "Isn't that complicated? I mean, you guys were—are—really close."

"Honestly, our closeness makes it more enjoyable. It's comfortable. We get each other. It's *very* good." Maybe, *I think,* if I keep trying to bring it back to sex-focused girl talk, she won't pry about the emotional side of things.

"You don't want more?" she asks.

My jaw clenches. Want? That's a tricky word right now. Obviously, I want more. More time, more orgasms, more shared jokes and comfortable nights. But I can't do more. Can't and won't. But if I explain that to Chloe, the leader of all optimists, she'll hear hope. False hope. "No, I don't."

"But Matt—"

I interrupt. "Matt is the best. It's me." I shrug. "I'm just not . . . looking for that right now."

"And he knows that?"

That question lands like a sharp blow to the gut. Does she really think I'd be capable of leading Matt on? Sweet, kind Matt? "*Yes,*" I say defensively.

"Sorry, I just . . . It's not making sense to me."

"Then maybe you're overthinking it."

"Maybe." Chloe gathers her long brunette hair and bunches it over one shoulder. "It's just . . ." *God, she's relentless.* "I think Matt might be in love with—"

I interrupt. "Whoa, there." I force a flippant sort of laugh. "We have feelings, yeah . . . chemistry, for sure, but"—Chloe nods like I'm speaking a different language—"I certainly don't think he's in *love* with me. He *definitely* loves my—"

"Toys!" Chloe interrupts me, giggling nervously. "Uncle Matt loves your toys." She flashes her eyes to Willow. "Look, if you're having fun and you're happy, that's all I care about." She smiles, but her eyes remain wary. "But . . ."

"Can we leave that *but* locked away?" I ask, officially exhausted. "We're not going to be *playing* together after our Vancouver trip anyway."

"No?"

"Nope. Our playing days are numbered."

"Speak of the devil." Chloe points out the window as Matt comes bounding across the yard.

"Do I see a wild Willow driving the bus?" he bellows from outside. I flick the doors open. "I *did*." He claps.

"Matty!" Willow hops off my lap like I'm old news and bounds toward him. I turn to Chloe with an offended expression, and she rolls her eyes. This little girl has so many grown men wrapped around her tiny finger.

Willow jumps from the last step and into Matt's arms outside the bus. He spins her around as she giggles above his head. "Hiya, baby girl." He tosses her, and she goes flying. I watch Chloe's body go rigid until he catches her again.

"Careful," she whispers to herself, mostly.

"Hey, Chlo," Matt says warmly, stepping inside. "I was about to go on my break when I saw your van out front. Does Warren know you're here yet?"

"No, we're surprising him," Chloe says, beaming like a woman still very much in love.

"Matty?" Willow pats his shoulder as he leans on the countertop, holding her to his hip.

"Yeah, baby?"

"Why you yove Auntie Yane's toys?"

I choke on air. Matt turns to me and then to Chloe, who is suddenly occupied with the wood stain on the table and the feel of it under her hand. Her lips twitching to laugh gives us away, though.

"Is *that* what you've heard?" he asks Willow, grinning ear to ear.

"Yup! You pyay with her toys and you yove them."

"Oh my god," I mutter under my breath.

Matt fights a laugh so hard I think his jaw might snap. "Well, she's got *great* toys. Probably the best toys I've ever played with."

"Mattheus!" Chloe chastises in a higher pitch than I thought possible for humans.

"Let the man talk!" I add, my laugh breaking through.

"Auntie and I are friends, baby."

"Like you and Dada?"

I bite down on my fist and just decide to cover my entire reddening face.

"Err . . . yeah, kind of like Dada . . . but *not*. Speaking of, wanna go find him?" He looks to Chloe for permission, and she nods. "Let's give these two a chance to talk about Uncle Matt's toys and *their* superior quality."

"Yeah!" Willow says excitedly.

The minute they're outside, I turn to Chloe, and we both burst into laughter.

She covers her face with both hands. "You two are *never* baby-sitting."

NINETEEN

CHLOE LEFT THE BUS TO FIND HER HUSBAND SHORTLY after Matt took Willow but not before arranging a time for her and Emily to help me pack up my place tonight. I told her I'm in no rush, given that I'll still have my apartment for an extra month—but she insisted. I have the startling feeling it may be an intervention of sorts she's organizing since she is still unconvinced about mine and Matt's situation.

Less than an hour later, I hear the familiar sounds of the shop's garage door closing—early for a Monday afternoon. I tighten the last screw for the curtain rail above the sink and decide to go investigate, locking up and taking my bag with me.

"Hey," I call toward Matt as he rolls some tires into the storage room out back.

He lifts a hand to me in greeting. "I was just going to come find you." As soon as I'm within arm's reach, he pulls me against his hip and keeps me there. "No bookings for the rest of the day, and Warren wanted to spend the afternoon with his girls. I told him to take off and I'd close up early. Thought we could work on the bus."

"The bus is"—I smile softly, not quite believing these words are about to come out of my mouth—"done." I shrug, looking at the sky. "Nothing else to do. I'm waiting on a few deliveries, and I have to actually move in, but . . . yeah. Finished."

Matt's eyes flood with admiration. "You did it," he says softly.

"We did it," I correct him, bopping his nose with the tip of my finger.

"I was just the help." He releases me and turns to push a tire half his size into the back storage unit. His grip showcases the muscles of his forearms, and I squirm, looking at him. With one final push, he grunts, sending illicit images running through my head. As he locks the door, an idea strikes.

"You know . . . I don't think I've thanked you properly." I take a tie off my wrist and put my hair up into a ponytail.

Matt's back is turned toward me as he checks the door. "No?"

"No." I walk until my front is pressed against his back. He lowers his keys to his pocket and turns within my hold.

I look up at him, doe-eyed, puckering my lips as I bat my eyelashes at him. "And unfortunately, *sir,* I have no way to pay you for all of your *hard* work."

It takes him a beat, his face disgruntled in amused confusion before where I'm going with this clicks. Matt bites his lip and clears his throat. God, he's an adorably terrible actor. "Well, that's no issue, ma'am. I'm sure we can come to a *different* arrangement." He fights a smile, and I can't help but roll my eyes.

"Well," I unbutton his jeans. "I can think of *one* way to pay you."

"Outside, in the daylight? Someone could see us," he says, unable to hide the excitement in his tone.

"I sure hope your boss doesn't come looking for you." I sink to my knees on the hard earth.

"I own this place," he says defensively. "Well, co-owners but—"

I tug his jeans to his knees roughly and give him a stare that says *really?* He nods and shuts up. "I've never done *anything* like this." I curl my fingertips over his boxers. "But I'm just *so* grateful you helped me."

Matt's lips part as he sucks in a breath. I think he's no longer cognizant enough to keep improvising. I carefully pull his boxers down and wrap my hands around his waist to his ass—my favorite part of his body—grabbing hold as I slide my mouth over his hardness.

He swears under his breath as his hand finds the back of my head. He pumps his hips a few times, making me relax my throat to take him deeper. I hollow out my cheeks as I suck him back, enjoying the salty taste on my tongue and the tension in his body *begging* to be released.

My bare knees scrape against the ground, and I'm sure they'll be marked. I hope they are. I want this memory carved into my skin.

I try to capture the moment, looking up at him. A beautiful man watching me like he's never seen anything sexier in his entire life, the sun beaming down on us, and my shorts riding farther up my thighs as I kneel before him. It'll be the visual I replay in my fantasies for years to come.

"Stop," Matt groans, fisting my hair and pulling my eager lips off him. "Need you." He tugs me up by my hair. I grip his wrist so it doesn't hurt as much, but god, I *love* it. Seeing Matt become more forceful over the past few weeks as he learns what we *both* like—it's sexy as hell.

His mouth meets mine in a commanding kiss, and he spins us so my back is against the shed's door. I unbutton my shorts and slide them down my legs. They'll be covered in dirt, but I couldn't care less.

As soon as they're off, he lifts me straight up, his entire body pressing into me, so I can't wrap my legs around him. "I just need to run to my car and get—"

"No, can't wait." I buck my hips, attempting to hoist myself up around him.

"Babe, we've never talked about that. Slow down."

How can he be so practical at a time like this? My body is on fire, and he's the only relief.

"I have an IUD, and I haven't been with anyone else in so long. *Please.*"

"Are you sure?" He hooks my legs around him, bringing his hands to my ass and kneading it in his giant palms.

"God, yes." I reach between us and shove my panties to one side. "Please."

"Keep saying please," Matt says darkly.

"You're evil." I press into him, trying to guide him inside me. He resists, tilting away, a teasing smile mocking me.

"Manners, Lane," he corrects.

"You're evil. *Please* fuck me." I reach between us to lead him.

He grabs my wrist, forcing me to let go of his erection. When he drops it, I move my hold to the neck of his shirt, pulling him as forcefully as I can. He doesn't budge.

"How?" he asks, standing straighter to torture me, apparently.

"Hard," I reply, practically jumping to reach his lips. He leans down a little, and I capture his mouth with mine. "So hard we break through this door," I whisper as he kisses my neck.

"Can you handle that, manamea?"

That word in my ear sends a shiver up my spine. Enough teasing. "I can. If you can't, I can go see who else is around."

Matt's jaw hardens, his nostrils flare. He's furious, like I knew he would be.

He's inside me with such an intense jolt, I lose my breath.

"Don't you *ever* fucking say that again," he says with his teeth at my neck.

I gasp for air as his thrusts become unrelenting. My arms and legs are wrapped around him as his hands pin my hips to the door. "Damn, remind me to get you angry more often," I tease, breathless, before he grips my jaw and pulls me to him.

He kisses me slowly and passionately as his body does the complete opposite. I'm going to be sore after this, but I don't even care. He'll look after me, he always does.

I break our kiss with a sharp breath as pleasure overtakes me.

"You're *mine*." He makes eye contact so intense I might run if I could. "Hear me?"

The world around us goes blurry, like a camera struggling to focus. I nod without thought—because I'm incapable of it.

"Tell me." He pushes into me, and my eyes roll back from the sheer bliss of it all.

"Yours," I reply breathlessly.

"And what am I?" he asks between grunts. He's close. We both are.

"Mine."

"Say it." His voice is low, like the words are burning their way out of his throat.

"You're *mine*!" I yell, desperate for reprieve.

"Atta girl."

My orgasm shatters against our kiss. He swallows each sound greedily until his hand hits the wall next to my head and he curls into himself, filling me for the first time. I've never had unprotected sex before, and the sensation of his climax is new and surprisingly erotic.

I've never felt so grounded and yet unbound from the earth. My head tilts up to the sky. Matt catches his breath as a beam of sunlight finds my face and I sigh contentedly.

"You okay? Was that too much?" Matt wraps his arms around my back and lifts me as he removes himself.

I smile, shaking my head. "No. No, that was great."

"Can you stand for a second?"

I nod. He lowers me to shaky legs as he pulls his pants back up, checking around, as if it's not too late to see if we had a surprise audience. When he turns back to me, he does a double-take and stills.

I tilt my head in curiosity as he stares back at me, eyes soft and hesitant.

It could be a few seconds, or it could be minutes, but neither of us speaks. We just look at each other. I look at his hair blowing in the wind that comes through the alley between the two buildings. His neck as he swallows. The love bite I left there last weekend that has yet to fade.

He steps to me, kisses me once, briefly, then lowers to one knee, taking off his shirt to wipe me clean from his release. He's thorough and gentle, and I feel grateful and shy all at once as he helps me into my shorts. "C'mon, gorgeous. Let's get you home."

He smacks my ass once before curling his arm under it to lift me over his shoulder.

"*Matt,*" I squeal. "Matt, my butt's hanging out!" I attempt to cover my backside with both hands.

"*Now* she's concerned about modesty," he mumbles to himself, bending to pick his dirty shirt off the ground. He balls it up in one hand.

"It's so hot when you do that," I say, admiring his shoulders from this strange, new angle.

"What?"

"Squatting like that when you're carrying me. Like I weigh nothing." I giggle over his shoulder as he begins doing lunges across the yard to his car. "You're a maniac. Put me down!"

"What?" he yells, spinning on his heel, trying to find the voice speaking to him. "Who said that?" He spins in the opposite direction.

"I'm going to puke!" I'm laughing so hard I'm shaking. "Put me down!"

He lowers me in front of the passenger door of his truck. "*Now* he's a gentleman." I raise my brow, mimicking his words as he opens my door.

"I'm a multifaceted man," he calls, walking around the front of the car. I shut my door as he opens his.

"You're a pain in my ass is what you are."

He pretends to be deep in thought, recounting something with his finger against his chin. "No, I don't think we've done *that* yet."

My jaw hits the floor. "Mattheus! What has gotten into you today?"

He smiles like a schoolboy. "I don't know. I think I'm just really happy."

And my heart balloons and deflates in the same breath. Happiness isn't a bad thing, of course, but it's dangerous territory. If his brain tells him I provide him with dopamine, serotonin, whatever the other ones are, then he'll get attached. *More* attached. Clinically, it's bad news.

I smile sweetly before turning to face my window, trying to choose my next words as carefully as I can, but they don't come. I have to tell him that this is coming to an end. It's selfish not to.

I turn to him, ready to say whatever I *can* get out when he looks at me, wearing the biggest smile I've ever seen. He reaches out and takes my hand from my lap.

"Since we're off early," he kisses my knuckles, "want to go home, change, then grab dinner out?"

"Um, actually . . . Chloe and Emily are coming over tonight."

"Oh, nice. I can pick up pizza."

I wince. "I think maybe I'll just have you drop me off."

"Oh." Matt nods. "Okay, sure."

He can't mask his disappointment, but I'm grateful he doesn't name it. He's been in my bed every night for over a month now.

"I haven't hung out with them in a while."

"That's true." He smiles and nods once.

"Plus, we leave for Vancouver soon . . ." I clear my throat. "Speaking of our trip, I was thinking that when we get back—"

"Shit!" Matt honks and swerves. The tires squeal and then bump onto the sidewalk before coming to an abrupt stop.

My heart lurches in my chest, and I fight the sensation that prickles my skin and begs for me to crawl out of it. The airbags didn't go off. We didn't hit anything. I open my eyes and see that Matt narrowly avoided hitting the car in front of us that went into the side of the truck turning in front of them. I catch my breath, swallowing air like water.

"Are you okay?" he asks, voice strained. His eyes scan my body with urgency, his arm braced in front of me, as if he instinctively reached out to protect me.

I nod, slowly. "Yeah." I pat his arm, because it seems like he doesn't know he's still in a crash position, stretched across me. Though this is the opposite of a crash position, isn't it? They teach you to protect your head and brace yourself. But that isn't what Matt did. He reached for me. His instinct was to protect *me*.

Be selfish, he told me. And clearly, suddenly, I realize that I never should have been. He's protected me all along, and who's looking out for him? Bracing him for impact?

I'm a bad fucking friend.

Eventually, wordlessly, he lowers his arm.

Once we're sure everyone involved is okay, we drive home in silence. We pull up outside my apartment building.

Matt clears his throat. "I'm so sorry. Are you okay? I—"

I interrupt. "No, what? Don't be sorry . . . it's not your fault." And I'm honestly not sure which "it" I'm referring to.

He smiles unconvincingly and goes to speak, but I watch it fade from him as he closes his mouth. He exhales, his body curving inward.

Everything in me wants to find and dismiss all the insecurities flashing across his face and elongating his breath. Have him name them, one by one, and comfort him. But that's just not possible. Not right now.

"I'll see you tomorrow," I say.

He nods, his eyes on the floor. "Yeah. Have a good night."

When I reach the lobby, he still hasn't driven away. I wave goodbye, and he does too—but it's not until I'm inside, out of his sight, that he leaves.

TWENTY

I CANCELED ON CHLOE AND EMILY TONIGHT. ANXIETY brain demanded bed and distraction if possible. I told myself I don't deserve the company. Matt's going home to an empty apartment, and that's what I deserve too.

To offset further guilt from canceling, I tell myself that it's for their benefit. That they wouldn't want to hang out with me while I threw myself a pity party. That they were only coming over to sort me out and fix the mess I've made with Matt.

They'd have known the truth. They're smart and intuitive. If they came here, it would be to call bullshit on my hesitancy. They'd want to protect Matt *from* me. Because even though I'm their best friend, Matt is the *best* of us.

I'll never be like them. Strong like them. Selfless like them. Brave like them.

I can't grow past my traumas, fears, or reservations and open myself up to a world of hurt for the sake of love like they both have. They've faced hardship after hardship, and instead of it making them fearful, it's made them powerful. Chloe's strength and determination to provide her sister with a better life than she had, her ability to bring out the best in those around her because she *sees* the good in them—it's a gift born from suffering.

Emily's bravery to become who she was always supposed to be—coming out to her family as transgender and giving them grace as they stumbled through the process of grief to tolerance to acceptance to joyous appreciation—she's learned to be bold yet kind, a fierce protector for herself and others.

The only trauma I've experienced was the result of my own actions. An otherwise spotless childhood—complete with silver spoon—made me soft, weak, and prone to stupid decisions. I derailed my own life with a selfish choice that tore my father away from an anniversary dinner with my mother and then from our family forever. I don't deserve the happily ever after. I don't deserve what Emily and Chloe have worked so hard for. Earned.

And while I'm admitting that to myself for the first time, it's not disturbing. It's almost comforting. It can't bring my father back, but surely grief in the form of self-sacrifice is better than nothing at all. A life of atonement.

Perhaps this is what drove me to Matt. A classic self-sabotage. He's the good I will deny myself. The light at the end of the tunnel while I clutch on to a stick of dynamite and a match. So even in these last days of being together, of feeling *whole* while with him—I have to know that it won't last. I have to know I'm going to hurt one of the best people I've ever known *and* myself.

I've been such an idiot.

*   *   *

TWO HOURS LATER, I'm still uneasy. Tossing in my bed, I finally make the decision to get up and do something with all this pent-up energy.

I haven't been alone with my thoughts in so long it's like they're all playing catch up. A near-perfect loop of dread, one piling on top of the last. Liz's wedding, staying with my mom, seeing our extended family, traveling with Matt, meeting Matt's family, Matt. Then Matt again. Then Matt some more. The look on his face when he told me he was so happy, then the look on his face when I told him to drop me off.

His charger is on my bedside table. His toothbrush is above the sink.

I push off my couch and pace around my floor in a fury. Anxiety storms through my body and begs to be released, exerted. I channel it into building box after box.

Fold, fold, fold, fold, tape, cut, tape, cut, flip.

Fold, fold, fold, fold, tape, cut, tape, cut, flip.

Over and over and over again, until twenty boxes are built and splayed across my apartment, stacked on one another or carelessly tossed aside.

I mark one for donations and chuck things in it with a manic clarity. Suddenly sentimental items don't hold such value. Nothing does.

Because what *is* the point? I drift from one stage of life to the next. Not happy, not clear about what to do, not sure who to be. A bad daughter, a worse sister, a shitty friend. It's all just stuff. Stuff that moves from one place to the next.

I've felt this ache before when I packed for university. It felt overwhelming to leave until it was overwhelmingly necessary to get out. Panic turned to concentrated focus that led to impulsive and flippant decisions as I packed away my childhood. I threw so many memories away that day, as if I could make them all hurt less by causing them to disappear.

But I was wrong.

Nothing hurts less.

I've been running for ten years.

And I'm fucking tired.

TWENTY-ONE

I DIDN'T GO INTO THE SHOP TODAY; I STAYED IN BED.
Sometimes crying. Most of the time, just staring at the wall.

I text Matt and tell him I'm sick when he calls for the tenth
time. He offers to bring me soup. I say I have lots. I don't eat anything.

TWENTY-TWO

CHLOE AND EMILY BOTH CALLED TODAY. I DIDN'T ANSWER.

I just watched shitty reality TV and cried when I spilled popcorn on my sheets.

It's like I can feel time moving around me, but it's not happening *to* me.

I'm supposed to be packing. I'm supposed to be leaving to go to my sister's wedding in two days. I'm supposed to be fine.

TWENTY-THREE

I SHOWERED THIS MORNING, THEN MADE TEA AND toast. I chewed slowly, like I was fresh off a dental surgery. Everything feels slow, but steadier. I packed a suitcase for Vancouver. I put my bridesmaid's dress by the door. I fed Simone and apologized for being a horrible mother. I let her scamper around my room and shit on the laundry accumulating on the floor.

When Matt called, I said I was feeling better.

He asked if he could come over.

I asked to go to his house instead.

He agreed.

I'm going to end it. I have to.

TWENTY-FOUR

I TOLD MATT I HAD ERRANDS TO RUN BEFORE GOING TO his place because I needed time to think on my walk over and didn't want a ride.

I've never broken up with anyone before, but that's not *technically* what this is, right? We agreed to be casual, and it doesn't feel casual, so it has to end. Simple. We'll go back to normal.

It's more fair to tell him now. To give him the choice to bail as my wedding date and not have me meet his family. Though I hope those things don't change. When we agreed to them, we were just friends and nothing more.

We can go back to that. Like nothing ever happened. Like I don't know how he tastes or the way his eyes flutter before he comes or the droop of his bottom lip as he sleeps.

I walk down the narrow path at the side of the house Matt rents. The basement entrance is toward the back of the old brick home. I knock three times and hear a bellow from below. "Coming!"

My stupid heart does a stupid spin, momentarily forgetful as the organ often is at the sound of his voice. Three days apart, and I miss him. Exactly why *this* is necessary.

"Hey." He swoops me up off my feet and curls into me. "There you are."

"Hi." I breathe him in. It could be our last embrace.

"Come in." He gestures to his door.

I follow him down some very steep steps. There's a damp smell, and he has to duck to get down the last few steps before a basement straight out of the seventies comes into view. Linoleum floors, and beige and brown brick walls with more bookshelves than your local bookshop. It's all one big room with a kitchenette off to the side and a bathroom through a half-open pocket door.

I brush my hand along his bookshelves, admiring his vast collection of antique books and colorful spines. "Have you read *all* of these?"

"Not that shelf." He points to the smallest of six bookshelves next to a green wingback chair. "Once I read them, they get put into their permanent home." He sits on the end of his bed.

"How do you sort them?"

"Genre, then by author."

I nod mindlessly, reading a few of the spines. I trip over a chair leg and bump into the shelf. Something falls off the top and onto the floor in front of me.

"Hey," I say affectionately. "It's your worry doll." I hold it up for Matt to see. "Mine's nicer." I wink.

"I felt so embarrassed after your birthday."

"What? Why?"

He shrugs and sticks out an arm for me to come over to him. I step between his legs, and he burrows his chin into the middle of my chest. I wrap my arms around the back of his head. If I had boobs, I'd be smothering him.

"Can I show you something?" he asks softly.

I nod, releasing him slightly so he can look up at me. "It's not a knife collection, right?"

"What?" Matt laughs.

"Or teeth? A collection of taxidermy?"

"What sort of vibe do I give off?" He laughs in disbelief.

"No one can be *this* perfect," I say, and he rolls his eyes in such a way that they might strain. "All right, show me."

"Here." He pats my thigh, so I step back, and he reaches under his bed and pulls out an antique red toolbox by the side handle. He opens it, revealing a top section filled with tools that I assume are for wood carving. He takes out the top, and under it is at least a dozen other worry dolls. "I wanted it to be perfect." He scratches his beard.

I sink to the floor, sitting cross-legged. I pull one out and rub it between my hands. It's nearly identical to the one he gave me. They're all similar, actually—at least to an untrained eye. *This is not good. This is just my point.*

"Told you I was cool," he says self-deprecatingly.

"It's kind of ironic you were *worried* about which one to give me," I jest half-heartedly.

His eyebrows shoot up before he nods. "True."

"You really like me, Matt," I say plainly. My tone is more concerned than joyous—as it ought to be.

He sighs, and his face falls. "I *really* like you, Lane."

I curl my legs up to my chest, my knees pressed to me and my arms wrapped around them. "It's starting to feel messy."

"Life's messy." Matt moves to sit across from me on the floor.

"I wish I could . . . I wish I could give in to it."

He tilts his head, his eyes calm, but his expression confused.

"But I'm scared." I smile weakly. "Really fucking scared."

"Of what? Of me?"

I press my tongue into the side of my cheek and roll it under my lip, back and forth. A few tears break free, but I don't worry about them being seen anymore. Not by him. "The night my dad died, I went out to a party." I tuck my chin between my knees. "It was my parents' anniversary, and they told us to stay home when they went out for dinner—which was no problem for Liz. She had studying to do or something . . . but I was stubborn. It was an end-of-year thing for the seniors at my school, and *everyone* was going." I could almost laugh at my teenage stupidity if it didn't hold such consequence.

"I had too much to drink and got into an argument with this other girl and her boyfriend. I don't even remember what about, honestly. I just remember crying and calling my dad. I gave him the address to come get me. He picked me up, and I awaited a lecture that never came. The last thing I remember was the sound of tires screeching."

I pull my sleeve over my fingers and wipe my cheek. "When I woke up, everything hurt. I was in a hospital bed, and I ached all over, like I was one giant bruise." I swallow. "My sister pressed a straw to my lips for water because my mouth was so dry I could barely talk. When I asked what happened, she went white. So pale that I just instantly knew."

Matt brings his thumb to his mouth and tugs his lip, his eyes falling to the floor.

"The other driver was texting and went straight through a red light, way over the speed limit. She had just gotten off a night shift and was trying to let her babysitter know she was on her way to get her kids, I guess. She hit the driver's side." My voice pitches up, shaking. "My dad died on impact."

I inhale a long breath that does nothing to soothe me.

"My mom, she just never looked the same." The tears sting my nose until it's twitching. "She wailed at night. So loud the neighbor's dog across the street would howl back at her. I heard her one morning on the phone with a friend . . . she said she wished it was her driving—that she'd rather die than live without *her* Nicky."

I look up to the ceiling, willing my thoughts to clear. "If I ever loved someone like that . . . If I ever lost someone like that . . ." My breathing becomes rapid. "Losing my dad was horrible, but it took the *life* out of my mom." I can't catch my breath, and my hands begin to shake. "I couldn't . . . I can't." Panic overtakes me, and I rock back and forth, sobbing. One second, I'm on the floor, the next, I'm in Matt's arms.

"Breathe, manamea, breathe." He grips the side of my head, rocking me into him like an infant. "It's okay. It's okay. It's okay," he chants, over and over and over.

My mouth opens, and a sob comes out of me that feels like it's lived in my chest for *so* long, cracking me in two.

"I've got you." He kisses the top of my head. It's worse. It's worse to hear that.

"No." I fight him off me, push up, and walk to the far side of his room. "No, because"—my jaw trembles with such force my teeth chatter—"I'm on my own, Matt."

"You aren't. Not if you don't want to be." He stands, squaring off with me.

We look at each other for a full, strained minute. As my body calms, he only seems to grow more tense. As my breaths slow, his eyes become more fixated on me. "I *have* to be."

"Nobody does." He shakes his head. "Nobody has to be alone."

"You're too good, Matt." I wipe my face. "Too close to the real thing."

"You *really* like me, Lane." He crowds me but puts his palms out, facing upward, like an offering. When I don't shy away, he places both hands on my elbows, steadying me.

"Of course I do. You're *you*." I laugh at my frustration. "You make it really hard not to."

"Just be here with me, Lane. At this moment. What do you want? Right now?"

To yell, to kick, to scream. To call my mom, to let myself love Matt the way he deserves to be loved. To run away. To stay here forever. To kiss him. That's the issue. I have no idea.

I want all of it and none of it at all.

"I wish I knew," I answer. "But it's not this. It's not me and you. Not now. Maybe never."

He blinks in surprise but then bounces back. "All right," he says matter-of-factly. "I understand."

"You do?"

"Well, not entirely but Lane . . . I have *eight* siblings. I know how to wait my turn. If it's time you need, I can give it to you. If it's space you need, it'll hurt, but you can have that too. I can wait."

"I don't want you to wait, Matt. Waiting feels like pressure. To fix myself. To be better."

And this, I think, *is how I know both halves of my brain work.*

Because I'm divided in two. The more thoughtful, logical part of me spoke—*Don't wait.* Matt *deserves* the best version of me, a version that might not or could never exist—so making him wait is cruel. But the greedy, selfish part of me is desperate for him to wait forever. The thought of him being with someone else, the idea that he could *want* someone else, *destroys* me.

"You should want to do that for *you,* Lane. You deserve to feel better."

"What if I can't?"

"Can't what?"

"Be better. What if I'm stuck like this? What if I'm not brave enough to fight those dragons?"

"You are." He takes my hand. "You're going to kick dragon ass."

"I think I could live a hundred lifetimes and never deserve you, Matt."

"I think that's bullshit, and you're the best person I know."

"It might not end the way we want it to."

"That's okay. At least you said *we*."

"We might just be friends from now on."

Matt takes a sharp breath in, his weary eyes falling between us. He nods to himself, and I can almost *hear* him thinking. "Then I'm a very lucky guy." He looks up tentatively.

"Do you have an answer for everything?" I ask, half joking.

"Maybe." He shrugs, wearing a sad sort of smile. "Let's keep going."

That *almost* makes me smile. "I *want* to love you Matt."

"I know."

"Did you just Han Solo me?" I ask.

"*Star Wars*—I know that one." Matt rubs his neck, laughing without sound. He looks like he wants to say something, but instead, he moves quickly, wrapping his arms around me and squeezing me tight. I hear him sigh over the top of my head. His shoulders tense then relax, as if he was fighting something and has resigned himself to lose. "I love you, Lane. I want you to know that, even if it changes nothing. It should change nothing. But it matters to me that you know. I know you don't *want* me to wait—but I can't imagine a world in which this feeling just goes away."

I rest my forehead on his chest, and tears come with a slow burn. I leave his embrace and wipe snot and tears on my sleeve. "Can we please be friends again?" I ask with a weak laugh.

"We never stopped." He noogies me, the universal sign of friendship, before he goes and tucks the box of worry dolls away under his bed. If it wasn't for the red tip to his nose and the dampness in his beard, I wouldn't have noticed he'd been crying at all. "Want to hang out for a bit? Watch a movie?"

"I need to pack for our trip and get Simone to Chloe's . . ." I walk over to his bookshelf. "Which one of these should I bring with me?"

Matt stands and joins me—at a platonic distance. I hate it, and yet am so grateful for his easy acceptance of what needs to be our new normal. Or, rather, our old normal. "This one."

He hands me the thickest book I've ever held, and I momentarily wonder if he's joking. Then I flip it over and read the title. *The Count of Monte Cristo.*

"Ah." I nod thoughtfully. "Okay."

"I'll see you tomorrow morning?" he asks as I slip it under my arm and make my way to the stairs.

"Of course."

"Good." He moves toward me, then steps back, swallowing thickly. "Bye." He covers his mouth with his hand, as if he's forcibly trying to not say more.

He's holding back. For me. And that creates an ache in my stomach. Gratefulness mixed with guilt.

"Bye." I turn and leave without looking back.

TWENTY-FIVE

MATT HAD THOUGHTFULLY DOWNLOADED *THE COUNT of Monte Cristo* audiobook for the early drive to the airport. He picked me up just after six with a coffee in the cup holder next to the passenger seat and a box of donut holes.

We chewed and drank and listened for ninety minutes, and while it wasn't the most comfortable silence, it wasn't intolerable. I was grateful for that. I answered a flurry of text messages from my mom and sister—last-minute details that needed a second, or third, set of opinions. We won't see them until a few hours before the rehearsal dinner in two days, but they know we're flying in early to visit Matt's family on the island—which is about a five-hour drive from them in Vancouver.

Last night, when I dropped off Simone and her things, Chloe and I sat for a few hours, talking about Matt and me. Warren even joined in at one point between fetching us water and wine. I didn't get any more clarity about what comes next, but I do know that I have to figure myself out before I bring Matt back into my stratosphere.

I don't know what else this weekend is going to hold. I'm too nervous to ask what sort of accommodations we're looking at once we arrive at Matt's parents' place. Will we be in one room? Two? Do they know about *us*? Do they know about yesterday?

I'm so preoccupied with these thoughts and questions that getting through baggage and to our terminal feels like it takes no time at all. With only two hours until our flight, Matt wanders around the airport stores, and I sit, curled up against the window with my book.

A family of four sit at the end of my row. Young kids climb all over their parents, hyper and excited. An elderly couple sits across the way and periodically sneaks them treats. The mom has noticed but smiles into her magazine as if she's going to let it be their little secret.

Announcements ring out for flights that aren't ours; a group of college-age kids takes selfies in the far corner of the room. I've read three pages, preferring to take in all the life around me. Traveling has always made me feel closer to my dad. The flights he took from Ireland to Vancouver all those years ago, his poor attempts to get his piloting license, the way he'd insist on being five hours early for any flight we took.

Growing up, I saw my parents fight only three times. The first was after my mother's fortieth birthday, when he had obviously forgotten who he was married to and threw her a surprise party. The second wasn't for any significant reason at all. Something about a broken dish and who chipped it. The third was when we traveled to Disney for our tenth birthday.

That was also a surprise. My sister had absolutely no interest in Disney World—other than Epcot—but I, on the other hand, had been begging to go for most of my life. My mother whispered something that sounded an awful lot like *playing favorites,* under her breath, and that set him off.

They took a walk and came back on the same page. I remember thinking that I wish they had let us in on the fight. Both so I could know if he was playing favorites and if I *was* his favorite, but also because I didn't like not knowing every facet of them. I was always trying to figure them out. Who were they when Liz and I weren't around? I hated the idea of them being married before we were born. I hated each time they left the house for Friday date nights and we stayed with a sitter. I hated that they had a love beyond us.

But now, as an adult, I recognize how special that was. They always had each other. Before us, during us, what would've been after us—*they* were the team. That's why their marriage worked when so many of my friends' parents' marriages didn't. Because they prioritized each other every day.

"Look at all of this!" Matt falls into the chair next to me with a bounce and I remove my headphones that were silenced for people-watching.

His arms are filled with an assortment of things I can't quite make sense of. There's a stuffed animal, a few bags of candy, an unopened box of playing cards, a few different teeny bottles of liquor.

I laugh, confusion arching my brow as I take it all in. He drops it onto the floor and begins rifling through it like a little kid. "Where did you get this?" I ask him.

"I won all of it!" He looks up to me, beaming.

I can't help but smile in response to his joy. "What? Where?"

"There's an arcade in the other terminal, next to the bathroom. I went in because curiosity got the better of me and well, I think I'm good at it."

I scoff. "Clearly. What game was it?"

"Pac-Man."

"You got all of this from Pac-Man?"

"Yeah, apparently I got their new high score. I basically emptied them out."

He holds up a bag of candy.

"The arcade had alcohol as prizes?" I ask, pointing to the little bottles.

"What? Oh, no. I got those at the store down that way." He places a few items on the seat next to me, a notebook, a flamingo pencil, a plastic ring, and a slap bracelet. "For you, darling," he says in a silly voice.

"Why, thank you." I hit the bracelet around my wrist and slide the ring onto my pinkie, where it fits snugly. Then I flip the notebook open. "What shall I write?"

"Hmm . . ." Matt says, zipping up the outer pocket of his backpack after putting all his other *treasures* away. "Your speech?"

"Don't need one, I'm not the maid of honor—remember?"

"Right, shit, sorry. Um . . ." He licks his lips and I flash to the night we "met" when his lips were all I could think about. The night of our first kiss, which makes me think of our last less than a week ago, which makes me remember how *strange* this all is.

I can feel his concern as I zone out over his shoulder.

"Maybe whatever's making you feel like that." He tilts my chin in his hand, acting as if he's trying to get a better view. A shy smile replaces my pout. "Ah, that's better." He lowers his hand. "Candy?"

I nod and take a gumball from his backpack as he holds it out to me like he's sneaking contraband aboard the plane. He zips it up when the overhead announcement calls our flight to begin boarding.

"Are you a nervous flyer?" he asks me when the engines turn on with a high-pitched hum.

"Not really, you?"

"Never done it before."

"What?" I gawk. "This is your first flight?"

"Yep!" His leg is bouncing next to me in our row of two seats.

"You okay?"

"Going to have to be. I hear there's no getting out once you're in the sky."

I nod. "Well, it's very safe."

"Is it?" he asks me, his eyes holding mine. A desperation behind them. He's looking to *me* for reassurance. That's new.

"Very." I pat the back of his hand, white-knuckle gripped on the armrest between us.

"Want to talk about something? Keep our minds off take-off? That tends to be the worst part." I reach into my purse and grab some mints. "Suck on these—so your ears don't pop."

He nods, takes some, and presses himself into the seat like he wants to disappear from view. The plane begins reversing to turn down the runway and he grabs my hand. "Sorry. Shit." He grips the seat instead.

"No, it's okay." I pull his hand back. We'd have done that as friends, I think to myself. I'd comfort him.

"Can you talk to me about something?" he asks, as the plane's front wheels lift off the tarmac. "Oh, god." He closes his eyes.

"Hey. It's okay. Um, a story . . . okay, got one."

"Good, good," he says tensely, the plane tilts farther up and he swears under his breath and crosses himself with his free hand.

I fight a laugh—Matt isn't the tiniest bit religious. "Have I ever told you about the time my sister and I switched places in class so she could take my math exam?"

He shakes his head, shoulders clenched.

I go into the story, in every minuscule, boring detail. How my sister and I aren't identical but could pass better as kids—how I had to sit in on her art class and pretend I wasn't very good—and sit straighter like she would. I talk and talk and talk about this seemingly pointless story until we're no longer pointed up to the sky and the seat belt signs turn off.

"Did you get caught?" he asks, his shoulders lowering slightly as he unbuckles himself, letting go of my hand.

"Yeah—Liz couldn't hack it. She cried after handing in the paper to the teacher and had to go home early from guilt. They couldn't console her."

"Oh." Matt huffs a laugh. "Did you get in trouble?"

"Not really, because she confessed. I did have to retake the test, but I actually did pretty well on it."

"So you didn't need to pretend."

"Guess not," I say, shrugging.

Matt opens the book in his lap, and I put my headphones on to watch an in-flight movie.

FIVE HOURS LATER, we land on the island. We wait in our seats at the back of the plane while everyone else stands and crams themselves into the aisle as if that's *ever* made deboarding faster. We get our bags—well, *my* bag because Matt didn't check one— and make our way toward the airport's exit.

"I figured we'd rent a car. Apparently near exit 4B there's a rental—"

Matt lifts a hand up in a wave and turns to me with an apologetic smile. "I think we might have a ride." He gestures with his chin toward a group of four Matt look-alikes and one white man who's smiling alongside them.

"*Matty!*" a beautiful young woman calls out, probably one of his younger sisters.

She runs up the ramp at full speed and leaps at him. He twirls her around, laughing. "Good to see you too, Tabby-Cat."

"Tabitha?" I ask softly.

He nods.

"You told her about me?" Her eyes light up at her big brother as he sets her down and fixes his backpack. Tabitha has dark, tight curls half up in a ponytail. The rest fall below her collarbone. Her eyes aren't brown like Matt's, but a soft green—and wider than his. She's taller than me, but not by much. Her nose is wide, and her chin is rounded, making her face a perfect heart. She's simply adorable.

"Of course." Matt hooks an arm around his sister. "Lane, this is my youngest sister, Tabs."

"Lane!" She frees herself from his hold and grabs my shoulders, looks me over affectionately, then pulls me into the tightest hug of my life. "It's so nice to meet you."

I'm aware my arms are pinned at my sides, but I can't move, nor has my brain caught up to what's happening. "You too!" I try to match her enthusiasm. "Hi!"

"Hi." She stands back, smiling wide. "C'mon, everyone's dying to meet you." She grabs my suitcase and wheels it away at top speed. Running is apparently her go-to state.

"The rest of them are much calmer." Matt laughs quietly, leaning into my ear. I get goose bumps from his lips at my neck but internally tell them to shove off.

At the end of the ramp, in a neat row, waits the rest of Matt's family. His mother first, who greets her son with a warm smile and a hand to the cheek. "Missed you, darling." She pats his beard. "This suits you." She turns to me, her smile not faltering at all. "And this must be Lane."

"Hello, Mrs. Tilo-Jones, it's—"

She interrupts. "Oh, my love, you're far too old and I'm far too young to be *Mrs.* anything to you." She winks, and her face for a split moment is *all* Matt's same levity. "Call me Fetu, or Mama—that's what I hear most often anyway."

Matt and his father embrace, part, and embrace again, and I turn my attention toward them. "I insist on being called Mr. Jones, *however,*" he says to me, wearing a stern expression, his hand still on Matt's shoulder in a tight grip. Fetu slaps his chest with an eye roll, and he gives in, laughing warmly. "Just kidding." He extends his hand. "Simon."

"Lane." I shake his hand. "Good to meet you."

"These are some of Matt's many siblings—Aaron here is, of course, my favorite as the eldest son."

I watch out of the corner of my eye as Matt shakes his head and pinches the bridge of his nose, laughing softly—confirming that his dad *is* joking.

Aaron is sitting in a wheelchair, and yet still manages to shove his father with a force that nearly knocks him over. "He's only saying that because he still feels bad for running me over with his car," Aaron says to me with a mischievous smile.

Matt mutters an expletive under his breath.

I look between him and Aaron and feel myself turn red. Tabitha steps in to save me. "He's lying. He doesn't get out much and has decided to torture you."

I laugh at the absurdity. Matt's family dynamic is becoming so very clear all at once.

"Yeah, I'm lying. It was actually a shark attack."

"Hey, Aaron." Matt leans down and hugs him with one arm. "Be nice," he whispers loud enough for us all to hear.

"I'm sure you're tired, so let me take over. I'm Tabitha; we met already. I already *love* you." She points to herself, then to the girl next to her. "Ruth, we call her Ru—she's nice but prefers animals to people." She steps behind her sister and grabs the last in line, a young man, by his shoulders. He shrugs her off with an annoyed affection. "This is Ian. He's a poet, so he's also a bit of a dick." She pats his arm.

"*Tabitha.*" Fetu sighs. "We're very excited to have you, Lane. Please don't mind my children—they're not all as lovely as Mattheus." She reaches out for him again, and he takes her hand briefly.

"And if you haven't noticed, he's *her* favorite."

"The bookworms," Ru adds, near whispering.

"I do not have a favorite." Fetu turns to me. "Except *you* will be this weekend." She wraps her arm around me and leads us toward the exit. "Let's get away from these people." She shoos her family back with a flick of her wrist.

I turn over my shoulder and look at Matt as he greets his siblings and follows behind. He nods at me, wearing a hopeful smile, and I feel it settle in my chest.

TWENTY-SIX

LESS THAN AN HOUR LATER, WE CROSS A SINGLE-LANE bridge among thick greenery. I'd forgotten how beautiful the island is, and the farther we get from the airport, the more overgrown and wild it's become.

In the last ten minutes, we've passed only a handful of properties, and Tabitha has had stories about them all. Which siblings got with which neighbor kids, who shoved her brother's shoulder back into place after he jumped—incorrectly—off a cliff, who keeps chickens and drops eggs off to everyone once a week. It's so quaint and small and lovely it nearly makes me emotional. What an incredible way to grow up.

Every few minutes, when there's a brief pause in his conversation, Matt will turn over his shoulder and check on me. It's a quick glance, a tilt of the head and a smile with a nod—then back to his father.

When the twelve-passenger van is parked at the bottom of a hill, I look up through the trees and can just about make out the front of a cabin-like home. Wood slats like floorboards across the front, a black metal roof, stones expertly laid as a foundation. A dog comes bounding down the hill to greet us, then another, then another follows behind—the last missing one leg.

Matt opens the sliding door and helps both of his sisters out with their hands in his as they jump down. I do the same and feel a twitch of his palm under mine. These are physical reminders of what has happened between us and what may never go away. He helps me down, and we all go to the back of the van where our luggage is stored and where the ramp for Aaron's chair is being lowered.

Matt bends at the waist as Aaron wraps his arms around his shoulders and hoists him up. "Thank god you're here. Tabitha keeps dropping me."

"You're bigger than I am," Tabitha grumbles, pushing the empty wheelchair after them.

I reach for my luggage, but Simon is faster. "Allow me."

Ru grabs Matt's bag, and Fetu shuts the trunk after Ian lifts the ramp away. For so many people, they seem to work around one another seamlessly. It's effortless in its chaos and fascinating to watch.

By the time we reach the top of the hill and I can see the full house—I've decided I may never leave.

The front of the home is covered in a large wooden porch with no fencing but several supporting joists throughout, with an overhanging roof and a few scattered rocking chairs. The door is the only thing with its original stained wood painted over—a bright yellow. The windows are all mismatched in shape and size, but mostly light-colored pine. You can tell which parts of the house are extensions, based on the state of the siding—and a few spots without any siding at all.

It's like an unfinished puzzle, and I *love* it.

There's a fenced-in garden to the right that is probably the same square footage as the house, an old treehouse that looks fairly abandoned, and a wide-open field of tall, fluffy grass beyond that. A row of apple trees off to the right, flowered but no apples in sight, and a clothesline filled to the brim.

It feels magical. Untouched and otherworldly, almost.

I've yet to move as I take it all in, my feet stapled to the grassy earth below me.

"It's something, isn't it?" Simon asks, pulling my focus.

I turn toward him, nodding. "It's . . . beautiful."

"We're very lucky." He looks at his feet, smiling.

Behind Simon, Matt is sitting on the edge of the porch next to Aaron, who's showing him some sort of pocketknife or wood-carving tool. Tabitha and Ru have run off inside, and Fetu has Ian helping her take the laundry down. He holds the basket begrudgingly, and she tosses each item at him, landing over his shoulder or face, until he lightens up.

"Matt makes so much sense now." The words tumble out of me. "He's so certain. So secure."

"He wasn't always." Simon pushes his hands into his pockets and blows out a long breath. "No, he was our worrier. In his own head a lot, or his head in a book. Matt's always struggled with feeling his feelings instead of analyzing them. As you may have noticed." He raises a brow.

"He tends to . . . ." I choose my next words carefully. "He tends to prioritize the other people in his life above himself."

"He'll probably always be that way, like his mother. She'd give you the coat off her back before you even asked." He crosses his arms. "Matt tell you about how we met?"

"Yeah." I nod, smiling.

"Ever since that day, she's been reminding me to slow down, give more, be kinder, all the while building me up, and I need that, of course—we all do. But what she and Matt both need is someone who's willing to do the same. Natural caregivers like that, they burn out. They give and give until they're emptied and have nothing left for themselves."

"How do you . . . how do you do that?"

"She doesn't make it easy, hence the reason we have *nine* children." He laughs. "But it's the little things. I tell her every day how grateful I am for her. I do my fair share, I *make* her rest, I remind her that her worth isn't what she's giving away—but who she is."

I've never gone from meeting someone to having this level of depth with them so quickly, but Matt's dad has the same calming quality Matt has that puts me at ease. The setting, the swaying of the grass in the field, the happy muttering of family—it's all so soothing that it doesn't feel strange at all.

"I'm never sure if I'm asking too much of Matt. I'm not sure if he mentioned my bus?"

Simon smiles wide and nods. "He did, yeah."

"He's done way more than I could have ever asked of him. He never hesitates to help or do more than asked, but I wish he would."

"That'll come with time. When he feels more secure, he'll work less hard. You have to remember that they see it as guaranteeing that we need them around. But, and correct me if I'm wrong, that's not why we keep them around—is it?"

"No." I look at Matt, who's now holding the three-legged dog under Ru's watchful eye. "But, um . . ." I don't want to contradict whatever Matt's told his parents, but I also think we're crossing into *relationship advice* territory. "It isn't."

Simon pauses, his eyes squinting ever so slightly as his smile becomes softer. "So, keep telling him that—eventually he'll believe you." He points toward the door. "In the meantime, let's get you some food. If I don't offer to feed you soon, Fetu will summon lightning to strike me down."

I notice Fetu standing in the kitchen window and wave to her.

"Do you think I could change first? I feel like I'm covered in airport and plane."

"Course. Ask Matt to show you his old room." He walks off toward the back of the house, and I go to the porch, where Matt and Ru sit together.

"Who's this little guy?" I scratch under the dog's chin.

"Humphrey," Ru answers shyly, avoiding eye contact.

Matt smiles up at me as he brushes along the dog's back. "Ru was just telling me she's going to be leaving for veterinary school in a few months." He pats Humphrey, and the dog lifts off his lap to waddle off.

"That's really cool. I have a rabbit, Simone, who frequents her vet. She's accident prone, and I'm worry prone."

Ru laughs sweetly. "I love rabbits—that's the one pet we *don't* have." Then she hops up to follow after Humphrey, tossing him a stick she picks up off the ground.

"Your dad said I'd be staying in your old room?" I ask.

"Oh, yeah. I'll show you."

Matt opens the creaky storm door, and we're instantly in a mudroom with cubbies and coat racks and closets with doors that don't quite shut. Every wall, every surface, is wooden. It smells divine, the mixture of sunshine hitting pine and whatever heavenly meal is baking in the kitchen. A cat hisses as we step over it on the welcome mat, and Matt weaves his way through each room.

There's overhead lighting, but none of it's on—the many windows doing the task. The floors squeak under us, but they're covered in colorful rugs—some look handmade with almost a quilted appearance. The kitchen is the center of the home, with a wall of windows on one side, a dining nook on the other, and two hallways in either corner. Fetu is feeding Simon something off a spoon, and he grabs her hips with lust at the taste. It almost feels like we're invading their privacy, but when I look at Matt, he seems relatively unbothered as he continues down the hall.

There are two doors on the right, two on the left. One door is painted bright purple, with a sign that reads TABITHA AND RUTH surrounded by green vines. An open door shows a room filled to the brim with books. Another has a missing handle that's been stuffed with a rag. There is a closed door, and one more where Matt stops.

"Here," he says, over his shoulder, halfway through the doorway. "It's been a while. I bunked with Ian before I left, but I guess he took Rae's old room when she moved out."

My god, how am I going to keep track of all these people and their whereabouts? How do his parents do it?

"Rae is your eldest sister, right?" I ask, stepping in behind him. There are two twin beds across from each other with a beautiful old dresser between. Two shelves above each bed, one filled with books and one entirely empty. I sit on the edge of the red quilt on top of the one with the empty shelf.

"Yeah, Rae is thirty-six. She lives in Nova Scotia with her wife—they run a small convenience store. Aaron is thirty-three. He's engaged to Natasha, who you might meet—she's great. He's been staying here with my parents while she's been deployed, but she's done for now, and they're going to get a place in the city."

Matt sits on the edge of the bed, his tongue pressing against his lips as he recounts all the information.

"Then it's Joanna, she's just turned thirty-one. She's in New Zealand doing *something* with the Canadian embassy—don't ask me what." He laughs, crossing his leg over his knee. "Oliver is twenty-nine. He's a few hours away finishing his law degree."

"Then me, Matt, twenty-seven, we've met." He smiles mischievously, uncrossing his legs and leaning forward. "Then we've got a bit of a jump—when my parents thought five kids was enough. But alas, it wasn't. Emma, twenty-one, she's in university out East, staying with Rae. Then the twins—Ian and Ru, they're nineteen, and Tabitha who's seventeen. My mom was thirty-eight when she had her, and there were some complications—so they called it at nine kids."

"I'm going to need to write that all down."

Matt laughs. "No one will expect you to remember. Just focus on the ones here in the house."

"Aaron, Ian, Tabs, and Ru." I nod. "Got it."

"I'm going to see if I can help with dinner—you okay?" Matt walks to the door.

"Yeah, going to change, then I'll meet you out there." He nods and steps out before I remember something. *"Oh,"* I exclaim.

"Yep?" He pops back around the doorway.

"Thank you. For bringing me here." I smile and try not to let the butterflies in my stomach escape through my mouth when he studies me and gives me the most sincere smile I've ever seen.

"You fit here nicely." He tilts his head, brings an invisible camera to his face, and "takes" my photo, then looks at his feet, as if he's suddenly shy. "Bathroom is the one with the rag for a handle."

He's gone down the hall before I can thank him again. I throw myself back onto the bed to capture a moment of stillness as thoughts and emotions continue to rush through me at lightning speed. Normally my anxiety would be sky-high right now, being in a new place—totally out of my control and miles from the nearest *anything.* But I feel fine, mostly. My anxiety—if you can even call the swirling in my stomach that—is mostly fixated on what comes *after* the wedding and this trip. Once obligations are aside, what comes next?

I've never wanted to jump forward in time before, but I'm desperate to take a glance six months into the future. Then maybe I could figure out what my next step should be.

TWENTY-SEVEN

THE HOUSE IS SMALL, BUT THE CENTER OF THE HOME IS the kitchen and dining room, with a large twelve-seater table that's used for both preparing and eating. Fetu has made a stew that smells heavenly, and when we sit to eat, fresh bread is passed around in a soft basket. I'm sitting between Tabitha and Ruth, across from Matt, Simon, Ian, and Aaron, and Fetu sits at the head of the table. Behind Fetu is a large window that shows some of the gorgeous views of the back of the property.

Throughout the meal, they've told story after charming story. Aaron recalled when a three-year-old Matt decided to leave honey outside for the bears to find because he was worried that they were hungry. But he ended up creating a swarm of fruit flies thicker than a storm cloud. Simon laughed about Matt taking apart and rebuilding the lawn mower's engine in a day when he was only nine.

It's so comfortable here. I genuinely feel like I've known all these people for years. And I guess I sort of have, through all of Matt's stories.

"I wish all your siblings were here so I could meet them," I say between laughter.

Aaron wipes his mouth with a cloth napkin. "Really? We were told not to overwhelm you."

Shit—were they warned about me? Matt's not filtering his family, right? That feels embarrassing. I feel a lump in my throat and look anxiously toward Matt—who's glaring at his brother. If he's asked his family to not overwhelm me, what do they think of me? Some privileged city girl? They wouldn't want that for their son, would they? Some overwrought, demanding priss?

I hear a clunk under the table.

"Nice going, asshole. Can't feel my legs, remember?" Aaron smiles into his spoon.

"I just wanted it to be a relaxing weekend for you before the wedding—that's all." Matt catches my eye.

"Don't worry. This family is incapable of being anything but genuine—we're all too mad." Simon slurps his stew obnoxiously loud, staring at Matt with a teasing gleam as he does.

I smile and take another bite of homemade bread. "I'm going to dream of this food," I say wistfully, changing the subject.

"I made that!" Tabitha beams. "I'm not a good cook—but I can bake."

"Tabitha is a renaissance woman," Simon adds. "Very skilled at lots of things. Languages especially."

"Well, when you grow up in a family where everyone kind of has a *thing*, you gotta try to find your own. Baking *could* be mine." Tabitha shrugs.

"It really is good, Tabs." Matt takes a large bite.

"What about you, Lane? What's your *thing*?" Tabitha asks me, wide-eyed.

"Uh . . ." I blow a breath out, trilling my lips. "Well . . ."

"She's fantastic at graphic design. She rebranded the shop, our new website, everything," Matt adds. I open my mouth to speak, but he continues for me. "She designed all of her own tattoos too—she's like a walking gallery of her own art." I smile politely, nodding, and then just as I open to say—

"Lane's also incredible at making playlists, suggesting movies. Oh, and she is fluent in sign language."

"How is she at answering her own questions?" Fetu asks, raising a brow at her son.

He relaxes into his chair, smiling to himself. "Probably good at that too," he mumbles.

I look between Fetu and Matt before turning back to Tabitha. "I don't really have a *thing*—I'm sort of just figuring that out," I answer, taking another bite.

"And what about this bus I've heard so much about?" Fetu asks me.

"It's done now. All there is to do is fill it with my junk and find somewhere to park it."

"That's very impressive," Simon says.

"It is," Matt says under his breath, like he's not supposed to talk anymore.

"And your sister is getting married. That's very exciting!" Fetu places both palms on the table. "You're twins, right?"

"Yeah, her name is Liz."

"Are you close?" Tabitha asks, slurping back the stew.

"Um, yes and no."

"Why?" Tabitha asks.

"Tabs, cool it," Ian says.

Simon begins gathering everyone's empty dishes with a clatter at the end of the table. I stand to pass him mine. "Can I help clean up?" I ask.

"No, no. You should go enjoy the outdoors before sunset—it's beautiful this time of day."

"If you don't mind the company, I was hoping to get some fresh air," Fetu says, standing.

"Of course," I answer.

Matt rises, and Fetu sticks her hand out to stop him. "Sit. Your siblings miss you."

"You don't?" he asks, feigning offense.

"Your father does!" Simon adds from the sink.

"Yes, spend time with your *old man*!" she calls back toward him, emphasizing the last two words with a cheeky grin.

Simon scampers over, flinging a cloth onto his shoulder, and pulls his wife to him with a devious grin. "You never minded me being older before, manamea. You going to trade me in for a younger man?"

She giggles and quips back in response, but my attention turns to Matt, who's staring up at me—wondering the same thing I am.

Do I mind that my pet name is what his father calls his mother?

The answer is that my heart skipped a beat, but my brain doesn't know. As usual, my body is ten steps ahead of my logic.

Matt mouths, "You want me to come?" Signaling to the back porch.

I shake my head, smiling softly.

"Let's go before we lose daylight," Fetu says, shrugging free of her husband's hold. I follow her to the back door through a sunroom.

"Don't keep her too long! I want to show Lane my albums!" Tabitha shouts after us as the door shuts.

As it does, it's like the world goes back to regular speed. Less color, less chaos, less conversation. Stillness. The stream sparkling, reflecting the orange sun, the long grass in the field moving in time with the warm wind.

"You get used to it." Fetu loops her arm through mine and pats my wrist. "Going from crazy to calm in an instant." She leads us down toward the stream. A gravel walkway turns into a wide dirt path carved by activity over time. When the trail narrows, she unhooks our arms and walks in front of me.

"My house was pretty quiet growing up. This is a really nice change. You all clearly love one another very much."

"Mmm, quiet sounds nice." She laughs slowly. "But yes, we're very lucky."

"Simon said that too . . . earlier."

"He better. He's married to me." She winks over her shoulder before ducking under a low-hanging branch.

We walk for fifteen minutes, the only sounds the birds above us and the rippling water next to us. The sun is setting lower, but we have lots of time to get back before nightfall when we arrive at two cut tree stumps carved into chairs. I notice a pattern carved into the wood, and it takes me a moment to realize they're constellations.

"These are beautiful." I press my thumb against the wood.

"Aaron. He's incredible with a knife . . . a sentence no mother ever thought she'd be proud to say."

I laugh, lowering into the seat across from her.

"They were a Mother's Day gift about fifteen years ago. This is the constellation that would have been above my home when my parents married. That one is when they passed." She points with a limp wrist to my chair, then rubs her hands over her knees as she rests back.

"Oh." I sit up, not wanting to rest on the memory of her family.

"My family all died when I was rather young," she says plainly, but not without emotion. There's a sturdiness about Fetu, despite her soft and billowy exterior—and her eyes are piercing, like she can *see* into you. "Did Matt mention that?"

I nod and fidget in my seat.

"He told me you lost your father when you were young as well."

I nod again.

"I'm sorry," she says.

"Me too." I clear my throat quietly. "For you—for *your* family. That's just terrible."

She takes a long breath in, her lips turned upward but not quite in a smile. "There's a term for Samoan beliefs and practices that my family has followed for generations. *Fa`a Samoa*. This also means we view death differently than other cultures under this nature of beliefs." Fetu looks up at the sky.

She might be letting me off easy, not forcing her beliefs or conversation on me . . . but I want to know more. "Differently how?" I ask.

Fetu straightens, smiling. "We do not believe that their spirit is gone, just out of view. I still speak with my family as if they're walking beside me every day. I can't see them, but I believe they are all around us." She looks from left to right, as if for a moment she *can* see them, and smiles fondly. "That's why the kids made this spot special for me. I take these walks, speak with my parents, siblings, and grandmother. I seek their guidance or just rest with them."

I curl my legs up to my chest and nod, looking around. I wonder if my dad's here too. I wonder if he's watching me sit here, talking with Fetu's family—meeting them. That thought makes me laugh softly.

"I think my dad would be a very entertaining spirit." I smile and wipe a stray tear off my cheek. "He'd get a kick out of no one being able to see him."

"He's welcome to join us." Fetu stands and comes to kneel at my side. I look down at her in confusion as she reaches up and wipes a tear from my chin. "You must miss him very much."

"Yeah." I sniffle and roll my eyes upward, embarrassed to be crying to a near-perfect stranger. To someone who knows so much more loss than me. Someone I want to impress.

"Hmm." She pats my knee. "How about I go back on my own, and you can borrow my spot for a little while? Let your dad rest with you here."

I nod a thousand times. "Yeah. I'd like that."

"Okay, hon." She stands, straightening with a small groan. "Don't stay out too late. It gets very dark in the woods, and I'm not interested in seeing my son become some *alpha-male rescue hero*." She laughs softly, her eyes holding mine.

"Thank you, Fetu."

She rubs my shoulder before turning and walking back down the path. Once I no longer hear her footsteps on dried sticks and leaves, I lean back and let my eyes close.

The wind rushes through the thick pine trees all around me, whistling between the needles. I can't explain it, and I know it's not logical, but with every gust of wind, it feels like my father's spirit is flying toward me. I open my eyes in time with another gust, and when I do, it's like I just *know* he's sitting across from me.

My heart pounds in my ears, and I smile wide as a sob escapes me. Both overjoyed and overcome. "Hi, Dad," I whisper, blinking back tears. "Thanks for coming." I laugh, looking up to the sky and then back toward the other seat. "I really miss you," I choke out.

Tears come, and I let them. I don't look up; I don't blink; I don't wipe or take deep breaths. I let them run free, just like the water next to the path.

"I'm sorry," I cry out. "I'm so sorry." I flick my hair off my neck, where it feels like it's sticking to me. "I never should have gone out that night and—"

A ferocious wind blows around me, leaves fly up and drop at my feet, and the atmosphere changes—like rain is near. I look around me. "Did you do that?" I ask, almost laughing.

I feel a single raindrop fall on my leg, then another, and another.

"What do I *do*, Dad?" I ask, catching the rain in my palms. "I don't know what I'm doing. I'm lonely and scared, and I have no idea what I'm supposed to do." I tilt up, letting the rain fall slowly on my face, mixing with my tears.

"I wish it was me," I whisper. A confession that's been on the tip of my tongue for nearly a decade. "It shouldn't have been you. I wish she would've hit my side of the car."

Lightning cracks in the distance, and I shudder. "Okay, got *that* one loud and clear." I laugh softly. Now that he's giving clear answers, I think of the questions I want answered most.

"Do you forgive me?" I ask.

Instantly, I feel warmth settle in my chest—like taking a long sip of hot tea.

I spend the next ten minutes asking silent questions with silent answers. Are you okay? Are you with us? Do you forgive me? I ask that last one a few times, just to be sure.

Each question is met with a rush of love.

Eventually, the space under my ribs that has felt weighted for so long feels void. I wrap my hands around my middle, reveling in the feeling—not realizing how much it ached before.

There's a lot of work left to be done. I'm not magically healed by one forest spirit encounter—*what a sentence*—but now I know what I need.

Forgiveness, from not just what may have been my dad (but could have just been the wind), but my mom and sister too, for leaving them. More than that, I think I have to give *myself* forgiveness too, for calling my dad that night. That'll be the hardest part. But I'm willing to try.

Because being *here* with Matt—with his family—I feel like I belong somewhere for the first time in a very long time. And I want this. I want him.

I stand up, take a deep breath, and shut my eyes tightly. I imagine my dad kissing my cheek and waving me off back down the path toward the house before sitting back down in Fetu's chair, crossing his legs and watching the birds fly overhead with a contented smile.

I wave to him over my shoulder—feeling a little silly—and make my way back toward the cabin.

TWENTY-EIGHT

"SHE'S BACK!" TABITHA SHOUTS, WAVING TO ME FROM the porch.

I wave back, looking between her and Matt, who's placing wood down strategically inside a fire pit. Tabitha runs over and loops her arm through mine. "He's building us a campfire. I think he wants an excuse to cozy up to you." She giggles. "Because he won't tell me *anything,* I *have* to ask—are you two dating? Do you love him? He's never brought anyone home before. He told us you were just his friend, but *friends* don't look at each other the way you two do, you know?"

I blink, adjusting to Tabitha-speed. "We're friends."

"But do you *want* more?"

"What did Matt say when you asked him that?" She guides me to a bench across the fire from Matt.

"It was complicated. What makes it complicated?"

Ian curls into a lawn chair next to us and nods once as a form of greeting.

"Because complicated could mean *so* many things," Tabitha says.

"Uh . . ." I stutter. "Well, it's . . . you know."

Ian turns toward us, glaring skeptically. "Tabs, are you freaking Lane out?"

"No!" She scoffs.

"Don't be nosy." He sighs.

"Oh, like *you're* not curious." She crosses her arms against her chest. "I read your poetry, Ian—you're a hopeless romantic like the rest of us."

I look at Matt, who's watching the three of us carefully, a fond look in his eye but with tense shoulders. Like he's not sure if he should help or watch or whether he wants to hear the answer. I choose to be brave.

"I've got some things I need to work through. Some family stuff . . . that has made it difficult for me to open up. Matt's been very patient with me, and he's truly one of my best friends."

Tabitha clutches her chest and kicks her legs out. "How romantic!"

"Oy vey." Ian sighs, opening a book in his lap.

Matt lights the fire, and I watch as sparks turn to flame. Once the rest of the family joins, Simon begins playing guitar. Quietly at first, then louder once a few of his children begin to sing along.

Matt is directly across from me, and every few minutes, we catch each other's eye over and through the tip of the fire. The glow casts brilliant shadows and shades of oranges and reds against his skin. His lips twitch into a smile, his eyes crease into half-moons, and he checks in each time with a different type of reassuring look. A wink, a nod, a head tilt. He waits for my smile in return, then he settles—knowing I'm okay.

And I realize that I haven't felt anxious for a moment since we arrived. That loud hum in the back of my mind that plays constantly like elevator music has ceased. Because Matt is my own personal comfort. A walking hot-water bottle. A favorite blanket. A cozy hoodie. A cup of tea delivered with a kiss on the forehead. Warmth builds and builds inside my chest, and I realize suddenly, clearly, and certainly—I've never felt like this about *anyone* else. I think I'm in love with Matt.

I know I could let this blissful realization turn to dread if I'm not careful, so I actively decide to just let it be. While we're here, with his family, in the woods, in a cabin, around a campfire—I can love him and not worry about what comes next. I can enjoy the feeling, the knowledge that I'm capable of such a feeling. That I'm not *entirely* broken.

Hours later, the fire is burning out, and I can hardly see Matt on the other side. Crackling wood under what's left of a flame, the soft finger-plucking of a guitar, and whispering between sisters down the bench from me are met with the sound of Matt's footsteps as he approaches. He crouches down to a knee in front of me and ties my shoelace.

When he's done, he looks up, smiling. "How you doing?"

"Fine." *Fantastic.*

"Ready for bed?"

I nod, yawning at the mere mention.

He tucks a stray hair that's broken free of my low ponytail behind my ear, then freezes like he's done the wrong thing. I watch him shake his head swiftly, as if he's chastising himself. So I reach out and do the same to him—except I can't seem to make my hand leave his cheek when I'm done.

"You sure you're okay?" He cups my hand with his.

"I've honestly, truthfully, never been better," I whisper.

He breathes like a man on death row who's just been spared his

life. A heavy, quick inhale with a long blown out breath. "Okay."
He nods.

"Okay." I swallow as he stands, and I follow suit.

"Night, ladies." I turn to his sisters. "Good night," I say as we
pass his parents, cuddled up as Simon continues to play. "See you
in the morning," I say to Aaron, who's leaned back, admiring the
stars.

When the back door closes behind us, Matt leads me through
the dark house to his bedroom with the hint of his hand hovering
over my hip. We're not touching, but I can *feel* his hold.

"I'll be back in a few." He opens the bedroom door, switches on
a lantern, then steps around me toward the bathroom.

The bedroom is only lit by the soft light of the lantern and the
pale white moonlight coming from the window.

I pull out my pajamas and get changed quickly into a crewneck
sweater and black bike shorts. When I pull them on, the memory
of Matt taking them *off* rushes through my system—making my
body hyperaware of *every* sensation. I'm still calming my breaths
when I hear a soft knock.

"Yeah," I answer.

Matt steps inside, sees me, then turns his whole body to shut
the door, pressing his forehead into it. I hear a soft groan, then he
stands straight. "Good night," he says curtly before practically
throwing himself into bed and under the covers, facing the wall.

I tuck myself in, my movements small and intentional to avoid
making too much noise. But the bed is old, creaky, and not subtle.

"Matt?" I whisper after a few moments, curling a hand under
my pillow.

"Yes?" His voice is scratchy, like his throat is dry.

"Is it the bike shorts, or were you just *angry* to see me?" I joke
poorly.

Matt's laugh is pained. "*Cruel* woman."

"Not intentionally."

"Subconsciously," he fires back.

"I don't *want* to torture you, Matt."

"Are you sure about that?" He turns to face me, the bed under him sounding an awful lot like the motel bed all those weeks ago. "Because I can't imagine being actually tortured feels worse than this."

"The shorts are *that* powerful, huh?" I tease.

"No, Lane. Not the shorts. Laughing with my family, taking walks arm in arm with my mother toward her place of solitude, singing along to my father's old folk music, the looks—" He stops himself. "The looks across the campfire that almost made me walk straight through it." I hear him rub his face and breathe through his palms. "Sorry. I'll stop. I'm sorry."

"No, I'm sorry, Matt. I didn't think it would be this hard."

"I didn't either," he says, almost whimpering.

"If you want, I can leave tomorrow. You can drive me to the closest car rental place, and I can go to the wedding. You can stay and visit—"

"I do *not* want that. Trust me, I thought about it. I've thought about *every* possible option here. And the only thing that's worse than being around you and not being *with* you—is the idea of not being near you."

I fight the urge to tell him what became abundantly clear at the campfire—because I know it's not right. I'm still so frightened. Like a scared animal, I could bolt or attack. He deserves my certainty. I can't toy with him; I shouldn't.

But every part of me wants to make sure he's still willing to wait—despite my having told him not to. Because the idea of our timelines not overlapping—of our love not aligning—is terrifying. I could just ask him point-blank, but—

"This is my fault," he says, interrupting my thoughts.

"What? No—"

"I wasn't honest with you, and I feel horrible about that."

"What? Honest about what?"

"It wasn't ever going to be casual for me, Lane." His breath is long and full of despair. "You told me not to fall for you. Do you remember that?"

"Yeah, of course but—"

He interrupts again. "I was already in love with you. I convinced myself that I was letting you be selfish, letting you take what you needed without getting caught up, but it was wrong of me. It was short-sighted. It was weak. I didn't take you at your word, I thought I could convince you to love me back . . . and now . . ." He pauses, and I know he's trying to avoid hurting me by whatever he says next. "I don't know if I can go back to being just friends. That's my fault."

I nod, not that he can see me. Because he's right—this *thing* between us is far too big to be contained in a label like *just friends*. We aren't *just* anything.

"Maybe we don't have to go back," I say softly.

The longest minute of my life passes in silence.

"What are you saying, Lane?" It's not that he sounds mad—just that he might be on the brink of losing his mind. As if he's remaining tight-lipped to keep the rest of his questions buried. And I can see why.

Two days ago, I was telling him that all we could be is friends, and now I'm practically speaking in riddles. It's not fair, but—false hope is only false if it's a lie, right? I *do* want this. I have the startings of a plan now. Start with forgiveness, and the rest will follow.

"I . . . God." I press my palms into my eye sockets. "I'm not sure. I still need time, but if I'm going to love anyone, if I'm going to face my fears, if I'm going to give my heart away, as worn and hardened as it may be . . . it's going to be you. It could only be you."

Dreadful silence again.

"Time?" he asks mercifully.

"Time."

"Any approximations on *how* long?" He laughs, just once, and uneasy.

"None whatsoever. Do you think you can handle that?" I hate myself a little for even asking, but I *need* him to wait for me like I need my next breath.

A deep inhale accompanies his pondering moment from across the room.

"Done," he says, as if he's signing his name on a contract. "But . . ." *Shit.* "I can give you all the time you need, so long as we're together, in whatever way. Just . . . stay close." And I hear him. What he said *and* what he means. *Don't close up on me. Don't leave me behind while you go fight those dragons. Let me fight next to you.*

"I'm not going anywhere." *I'd like to be a lot closer, actually.* "Think I can be your blanket tonight?" I ask hesitantly.

"I don't know if this old bed will take it."

I'm disappointed for exactly half a second before he stands, and I hear him pick up his mattress and place it on the floor between our beds. "There. Just like old times," he says, as he lies down and extends a hand toward me. "C'mon."

I curl into his side, but he rolls me on top of him, spread out like a human shield. His arms curve around my hips, holding me to him with glorious pressure.

"You take all the time you need, manamea," he whispers into my smoke-scented hair.

"You sure?" I ask.

"I'm sure."

The same familiar doubts rise up, but they're easier to dismiss now. Not entirely, but mostly.

"I was doing some thinking. The night after you left my place."
He sighs. "I stayed up all night thinking, if I'm being honest. . . ."

"Dangerous," I tease, nuzzling into him.

"Maybe, as scary as it is, time running out is a gift." He drags a
lazy hand down my back. "If we were infinite beings, I wouldn't
worry about holding you like this every second I could. I'd know
I'd get to do it again. The love I have for you is urgent. It's a needy
thing. Maybe it wouldn't be if we had eternity. I'd get lazy with it."

I groan, furious with myself. "Fuck you," I whisper, tears breaking free. "Let me have the better words *once*." I joke through
ragged breaths.

He laughs against my neck. "Goodnight, manamea."

"Good night, Matt." I wipe my tears on his chest and don't feel
the least bit bad about it.

I spend the next few hours feeling him rise and fall underneath
me, unable to sleep. It's not that I *love* the idea of my dad lingering
around all the time—for instance, if Matt and I were doing this
without clothes—but I sort of hope he can see me right now. Safe,
comforted, loved.

I think he'd really like Matt.

TWENTY-NINE

AS WE DRIVE AWAY FROM MATT'S PARENTS' HOUSE, TWO things occur:

1. My anxiety increases.
2. My phone gets more service.

Two feeds back into one as an onslaught of messages pile in from my mother and sister. The florist is sick; the caterer is down a server; they didn't get the asparagus delivery (my god!); it's calling for rain—then it's calling for sweltering sun—which is worse?

Yesterday, I immersed myself fully in Matt's family life. They had several ideas about activities we could do or more interesting things to try, but I requested that they change absolutely nothing. I just wanted to exist in their bubble. So we hung laundry, tended to the garden, walked a basket of vegetables over to the neighbors—who were *delighted* to see Matt—and helped cook a delicious meal. After dinner, Fetu and I walked to her spot again. This time, we let Matt and Tabitha tag along. It was noisier—but just as peaceful.

At night, Matt and I lay down together again. Nothing other than a chaste kiss on the forehead and hands curled above clothing. I loved *every* moment of it.

It's a five-hour drive to my mom's place from the island, but we've got an audiobook and experience on our side. We switch off halfway—less than one *Titanic*—and in what feels like hardly any time at all, arrive at the gated community in which my childhood existed. In total contrast to Matt's welcoming rustic cabin—my mother lives in a prison of the rich variety.

"Lane?"

"Mm-hmm?"

"Quick question . . . are you *rich*?"

"My mother is, yes. Very."

"Okay . . ."

"Is that . . . is that bad?"

"What? No. I just would have laid on the charm a little thicker if I knew I could end up wealthy."

I roll my eyes. "The bus ate up all my inheritance." The gate opens after my license is checked and okayed by the security.

Matt ducks to look out the window as we pass mansion after mansion. "Dude."

"Don't *dude* me."

"You're right, my apologies; how unbefitting. Ma'am," he says in a dry British accent.

"I honestly feel embarrassed."

"About being loaded? What? I'm the one who just took you to my parents' make-shift cabin. They have a rag for a bathroom door handle, Lane."

"We don't have handles on our bathrooms here either," I tease. "The servants just open them for us."

"See, I *know* you're joking, but I don't think it's massively far off."

When I pull into my mother's long driveway lined with precisely cut shrubs and circle around a small fountain to the front steps, Matt's laughing almost hysterically.

"Are you okay?"

"I'm Cinderella!"

"Oh my god." I press my head to the steering wheel.

"I'm Elizabeth arriving at Pemberley!"

"Huh?" I ask.

"Pride and Prejudice?"

"Nope."

"Okay, well . . . we'll work on that." He opens his door, gawking at the house.

"Be cool."

"Be cool? Lane, you *be* rich!"

"This is going to be a shit—Hey!" I wave at my mom as she comes bounding outside, squealing.

"Lane! My baby!" She grabs me in a tight squeeze and rocks me from side to side. She pulls back, checks me over, holds my face, then goes back in for another long hug. "I missed you, darling."

"Mom. Air," I choke out. When she releases me, I catch my breath and gesture to Matt, who's suddenly standing straighter and laying on the charm *thick*—he takes my mother's hand and kisses her knuckle.

"So good to meet you, Ms. Rothsford." He nods once, letting her hand drift back to her side.

"You too, Matt. Please, call me Katherine or Kathy." She turns on her heel to me, wearing an exasperated smile. "Your sister is on the phone with Phillip's aunt—who apparently has developed a serious allergy to both chicken and fish and is requesting a steak option." She widens her eyes. "She's about twelve seconds from a mental breakdown. Think you can work some magic?"

"Yes, if anything, my number one skill is calming Liz down," I say with more sarcasm than a human should be able to wield.

My mother raises her brow.

"I'll try!" I put my hands up. "C'mon," I wave at Matt to follow. "You may as well bear witness."

"So, Matt . . ." I hear my mother say behind me as Matt grabs our luggage from the trunk. "Where are you from?"

"Dear lord in heaven," I mutter under my breath. "Mom," I yell.

"My mother is Samoan." He nods politely, wearing an unforced smile, then catches up to my side. "Friendly reminder, you once asked me why I was so tan," he whispers.

"I was drunk and didn't remember you being so tan the first time we met."

Matt snickers.

"What?" I ask snidely.

"Nothing, just—you also asked my name and introduced yourself to me."

"Why's that funny?"

"Because I only went to that party to see *you*."

I stop. Liz's meltdown can wait. "Shut up."

"We met at Willow's first birthday party six months earlier. You were taking photos and waltzing around the room with such ease that I couldn't believe it when Chloe said you were taking off early and didn't love socializing all that much. When she later told me you'd agreed to go to their New Year's party, I suddenly became available. I got there early to help set up, just in case. I waited for hours to work up the courage to talk to you. When I thought you were speaking to me, you were mumbling to yourself."

"Oh my god . . . then I introduced myself."

"Yep." He pops the *P.*

"I'm such an asshole," I whine.

"I like that that's your takeaway and not that I'm some stalker."

"Well, now that you mention it . . ." I tease.

We round the corner to the kitchen, and Matt looks *amused* by the sight of it, like this is some elaborate prank. However, I'm focused on the sound of my sister's heels pacing on the tile.

"Liz?" I call out.

She turns the corner and charges at me. "Thank god you're here." She drags me to her, and I'm not sure if she's about to hug me or murder me. Neither. She just holds me with a talon grip, like she's steadying herself.

"How ya doing, pal?" I ask, voice hesitant.

"Is this Matt?" She points to the man who is either my date or an intruder with a hell of a lot of ease.

"Yes."

"Hi, Matt."

"Hi, Liz." He matches her crisp delivery.

She bites her fingernails with the hand that isn't gripping me to the point of searing pain. "It is so *you* to bring a hot date to *my* wedding."

Matt nods and runs a hand through his hair as I check my sister's temperature with the back of my hand. "Are you okay? You're sweating."

"I'm hosting an event for two hundred people with little-to-no help, and the goddamn weather app can't decide if it's going to rain or be blazing hot."

"Umbrellas?" I offer. "A universal solution?"

"Why didn't I think of that?" She almost stomps her foot. "Hi, Matt," she says again, as if she's suffering from short-term memory loss.

"Uh, hi, Liz."

"Sorry for calling you hot."

"Don't be." He shrugs.

"You seem nice." She turns to me. "Is he nice?"

"The nicest," I clarify, leading her to a stool at the counter. "Let's sit." I pet her hair. "What needs to be done? You've got brains and brawn here. Put us to work." I look at Matt, who's nodding his agreement.

"And beauty, apparently," he says with a cheeky grin.

"Well, the rehearsal dinner is in . . ." She taps her phone so many times I think she may chip a nail. "Three hours." She withers.

"Okay. Is there anything we can do to help?"

"No. Just . . . I need to get my hair and makeup done."

"Right. Where is the dinner?"

"Lane."

"Sorry." I wince. "I forget."

"Phillip's grandmother's house."

"She's still alive?" The question slips out, and Liz gives me a gracious warning stare.

"Got it . . . To grandmother's house we go!"

WE PULL UP in a town car exactly two hours and fifty-five minutes later. Phillip, who I recognize from pictures, is waiting out front for us.

Matt is wearing a white button-down with a few open buttons and a black blazer over it, so I'm essentially in heat. However, I'm choosing to ignore said feelings because my sister looks like she is about to pass out.

"You're going to be great," I say, like she's going into a school talent show and not the party to celebrate the night before her wedding. This *should* be fun, right?

"Let's get this over with." She takes a flask out of her white purse that looks like it costs more than my rent, throws back a swig, then gets out. She greets Phillip with a kiss on the cheek, and I watch as he wraps his arm around her waist and leads her inside.

"Guess he's not sticking around to meet *me*," I say to my mother.

She sighs but looks resigned. "Let's just go inside. Try to have a nice time."

"Aw . . . but Mom!" I do my best interpretation of teenage me. "I *love* actively trying to have a bad time!"

She waves me off and scoots out of the car.

Matt, our handsome escort, walks us in with both arms out at his sides for my mother and me. I'm too busy sizing up the joint to listen, but they're making conversation back and forth—at one point I even see my mother pat his forearm, and my heart swells with pride. I don't know what Matt and I are to each other just yet—but I know I love that he's making a good impression.

When we find our table, it almost feels like we've skipped right to the reception—the room is large and glistening white, with chandeliers in neat rows. Twelve round tables with ten guests apiece, and I'm wondering who is footing the bill.

"Fancy," Matt mouths, pulling out my mother's chair.

"Right?" I mouth back.

He sits next to me and pushes on my knee as it begins to bounce frantically under the table. "Groom or bride?" an older woman asks my mother bluntly from across the table.

"Bride," my mother answers softly. "Her mother."

The lady looks bemused, as if she *too* is wondering why we're sitting in the back corner at *my* sister's rehearsal dinner. "Well, such an honor," she says, bit out with the old-timey bitchiness that you can't quite call someone on.

My mother, the elegant lady she is, chooses to say nothing at all. The sound of cutlery tapping against glasses sounds from the front of the hall, and we all turn our attention to the groom and the woman who *vaguely* resembles my sister at his side, pale and wide-eyed.

"We are so delighted you could all be here this evening." He nudges my sister, who apparently missed her cue—but her mouth appears glued shut.

"Elizabeth and I," *I hate the way he said her name—like a pet or a plaything,* "are thrilled to have you all here at my grandmother's *humble* estate."

Matt covers a laugh with a cough, then reaches for his water glass. I bite my lip and do the same. Taking sips of water, I glance around the room.

I don't recognize a single person. None of Liz's university friends, not even Sam—who she's been best friends with since kindergarten.

"Is Aunt Ethel coming?" I whisper to my mom.

She shakes her head. "Didn't get an invite."

"There are a million people here. Your *one* living relative didn't get invited?" I say incredulously.

My mother reaches for her wine, sighing.

"Dad's family was invited, right? They just declined?"

"I didn't ask."

"What? Why?"

"Because your sister has been under a *lot* of stress, Lane."

"Who are all these people?" I whisper-yell.

"Lane, leave it." My mother scowls.

I fall back into my seat, catching the last of Phillip's drawn-out speech. He's not what I'd describe as . . . attractive. He's dressed well, groomed well, but he's got a long face, teeny lips, and an overbite.

My sister is pulled behind him with her hand in his from table to table during the entire meal. It isn't until we're served dessert that they make it to our table. I stand to greet my soon-to-be brother-in-law. "Phillip, this is—"

"Elaine," Phillip sings out, like I'm a small child. "So good to finally meet you."

We could have met outside. "Hi, Phillip. You can just call me Lane." I raise my arm up for a hug, but he just stares blankly. Matt comes to stand behind me, still chewing and attempting to swallow what I presume was the world's largest bite of cake. I lower my arms.

"And this is?" Phillip looks to my sister.

"Matt, Lane's date."

"Ah." He nods curtly. "Pleasure."

He sticks out his pale, bony hand, and it looks almost ridiculous inside Matt's. "Good to meet you, man," Matt says, his mouth finally empty. "Beautiful home."

"Thank you." He looks between Matt and me like he can't quite place how we'd be together, and his eye lands behind us to the rest of the table. "Excuse us." He nods politely. "Elizabeth, I'd like to introduce you to my father's secretary, Gladys."

The crotchety old woman stands up, and I look at my mother—who's uncharacteristically on her third glass of wine. "We're seated with his father's secretary, Mom."

"I heard."

Matt excuses himself to use the washroom, and my sister takes his seat as Phillip makes conversation with a table of men in suits who are far too rowdy for such an event.

I watch as my sister rubs her wrist, her eyes zoned out onto the plate in front of her.

"Liz . . . are you okay?"

"I didn't get to eat."

"What?"

"I spent weeks picking out the menu, and we didn't sit. We didn't eat."

"Oh . . . sorry."

"I just met over one hundred people for the first time."

"Right."

"They're coming to *my* wedding."

"Yeah?"

"I have three people here, and they're shoved into a corner. That's not normal, is it?"

"Jean-Paul had to work—it would have been four," my mother slurs.

"Who *the fuck* is *Jean-Paul*?" I ask.

Liz turns all her attention to me, then to my mother, then back to me.

"Who is Jean-Paul, Mom?" I raise a brow.

"My lover."

I choke on air. "Dear god," I sputter.

"You really could have just said *boyfriend,* Mom." Liz grimaces.

"*Boyfriend* is a term for young people," she argues.

"*Lover* is a term for perverts," Liz says with a shudder.

"Or Taylor Swift," I add distractedly, then shake myself. "Wait. Mom, you have a boyfriend?"

"Yes." She takes *another* sip of wine.

"Why did no one tell me?"

"Can we do this later? *I'm* the one having a crisis right now," Liz whispers across my mother.

"Fine." I throw my hands up. "Liz . . . are you happy?"

"What?" She switches my mom's glasses as she reaches for them, giving Mom water instead of wine, like a reverse Jesus.

"Are you *happy*?" I ask. "Simple question."

"It's far from simple," she argues.

"Does Phillip *make* you happy?"

"Often."

"How often?"

She winces softly. Her eyes land somewhere between Matt's plate and my mother's. "It doesn't matter."

"It does," my mother says. "It really, really does," she adds, more slurred.

Liz sighs, and I think it's for a thousand reasons—but also because my mother may need to be air-lifted out of here. Matt does a second lap around the room, waiting for his seat but unwilling to interrupt. I catch his eye and wave him over.

"Okay, here's the plan." I look at my family. "Matt and I are going to get Mom home, and when tonight is over—I want you to come find me. We have a lot to talk about, and we have to do it *tonight*."

Liz nods softly.

I feel the rush of being the eldest sister for half a second as she takes my hand and gives it one squeeze before walking toward Phillip's entourage circled around him.

"Hey—everything okay? That looked intense." Matt falls into his chair.

"I want you to remember how much you like me, okay? Because this is quickly becoming a shit show of red flags for my family."

"Red's my favorite color," Matt muses, laughing softly.

"Can you help me get my drunk mother to the door without anyone suspecting anything?"

He looks at my mom, who's turning a pale green.

"We better hurry." He nods, and on a silent count of three, we hook my mother's arms through both of ours like she's simply being escorted by two gentle-folk and not being kicked out of a dive bar.

I don't bother with goodbyes to the rest of the table. Fuck all these old bitches.

Once outside, my ordinarily couth mother vomits into an empty urn.

I hold her hair back. "Mom, I know this isn't a good time, but you're getting cooler as you get older—look at you, vomiting after a party, and you have a boyfriend. . . ."

"I'm regressing."

"But if you're good at it . . . you're *pro*-gressing," Matt says.

I stare at him like he's lost his mind, because maybe he has. And he shrugs, mouthing, "I don't know."

"Just help me get her over there." I gesture to the black town car where our driver waits.

"Hold on, he just sits out here? Waiting for you?"

"Yes." I groan, lifting my mother less delicately than we did inside.

"How the other half live," he mumbles, winking at me.

Matt opens the back door, and I assist my mother in settling inside. She puts her head between her knees. "Is she . . . um . . . does your mom struggle with alcohol—"

"No. She's probably never been drunk before. This is her after two and a half glasses of wine. She chose *tonight* as her debut into chaos."

"She *was* seated at the back of the hall at her daughter's rehearsal dinner."

"I can hear you both," my mother growls. "I'm not drunk. It was probably the fish—it smelled *weird*."

"We had the fish too." I scowl at her and shut the door. Matt and I walk around the car, and I sit across from her, rubbing her back the entire drive home as Matt pretends to be fascinated with whatever we pass.

When we get back to the house, I help my mother undress and get settled into bed. My private high school education was mostly wasted on me, but I *do* know how to expertly lay a drunk person down, padded and rolled onto their side as to avoid choking on vomit. She's not blackout drunk, so I doubt it's necessary, but it means I don't feel so bad leaving her to find Matt and wait for Liz.

THIRTY

MATT AND I TOOK TURNS PACING AND KEEPING WATCH for Liz to arrive. I filled him in as soon as he came downstairs in his regular clothes—a moment of silence for my loss—and then we switched so I could change out of my dress too.

Hours pass with no sign of Liz. No text. No answer when I called. Nothing.

We finally gave up at three A.M., knowing I was supposed to be awake, bright-eyed, and on bridesmaid duty at seven. I slept in the guest room with Matt—who swears he's going to steal the mattress. We were so tired that we both passed out, but I loved waking up in his arms—even if I had to quickly leave them to throw my shit in a bag and rush out the door.

The car promptly came to pick up Mom and me to meet Liz and the other bridesmaids at the hotel. My mother hid her hangover well, with dark sunglasses being the only clue. I keep thinking that at some point today, I'm going to meet my mother's boyfriend. More than that, I'm going to have to process my mother *having* a boyfriend. But one battle at a time. And I do have a distinct feeling this morning will be a battle—if not the whole war.

"Good morning!" I say, waltzing into the hotel suite. I was expecting to walk into a scene buzzing with action. Girls everywhere, hair and makeup artists strewn about—instead, it's quiet. Liz nowhere to be seen.

"She's left!" my mother exclaims—surprisingly elated.

"I'm in here, Mom," Liz's voice bellows from the bathroom. She opens the door and storms past us toward the center of the suite, falling back onto a chaise lounge dramatically.

"Where is everyone?" I ask.

"They're coming at nine."

"Oh, okay . . . so this *is* happening, then?"

"What choice do I have?" Liz asks, her usual confident voice shrunk to a near whisper.

"Liz . . ." I go to my knees next to her chair. "Do you want to get married today?"

"Yes."

"To Phillip?" my mother asks, resting on the end of the bed across from us.

She hesitates for enough seconds that the answer no longer matters.

"Honey . . ." My mom's tone is familiar. She's making an internal pros and cons list. Would she rather see her daughter unhappily marry and divorce, or run away from her wedding like a country song? She sighs and straightens. "You need to decide what the plan is." My mom checks her watch. "And I suggest you do it in the next forty-seven minutes."

Liz looks at me. "What would you do?"

"Well, I'd probably not be getting married to *anybody*."

"Okay, if you were me."

"I'd never have gotten bangs in eighth grade."

"Lane."

"Okay, sorry. I'd get the hell out of here, dude. Where's Sam? Why isn't he here? Did you guys get into a fight?"

"Sam and Phillip don't get along . . . so . . ."

"Liz." I sigh. How can someone so capable, so smart, so logical, be *so* stupid? "You and Sam have been friends since kindergarten. He should be here."

"Tell her." My mother crosses her arms. I look between them, confusion growing as I watch my sister resist my mother's stare.

"Is this going to keep happening? God, Liz. We talk on the phone every day, and Mom's *lover* doesn't come up? Or this fight with Sam? What is going on?"

"What's going on, *Lane,* is that we're never sure what you can handle," she snaps.

I laugh without humor. "You want to treat me like *I'm* a mess? Right now? As you contemplate *leaving your wedding*?"

"Sam told her he loved her," my mother says calmly. "Six weeks ago."

"What?" I screech. "Pardon?" I look at my sister. "What?" Her face falls as I do the calculations. "Oh . . . the day of our fight."

She groans, covering her face with two hands. "What do I do?"

"Liz, this is *so* dramatic—I love it."

"You're insane!" she yells at me.

"Liz, you can't marry Phillip."

"I can."

"You don't love him."

"He's very calm, rational, and well-off. He'll be a good father."

"You do not *love* him, Liz. And he isn't very nice."

"He's just . . . a little self-involved."

"And controlling," I add.

"A touch."

"And old."

"He's not *that* old!"

"He's old because of his heart, not his actual age. He talks to you like you're a child. He sat Mom at the back table with his father's secretary."

"That was probably more his mother than him."

"He was raised by that woman. Who, by the way, is not *conservative,* she's homophobic."

"I'm sorry I told you that about your date. I hated doing that."

"But he wanted you to."

She nods a hundred times as tears start to pour.

My mom consoles her while I take the cue to begin getting us the *fuck* out of here and pull out my phone.

"Hey." Matt answers on the second ring. I knew he'd be on standby.

"Operation Alpha is a go," I say.

"I'm assuming that means you want me to come get you guys?"

"Just pretend we assigned the plan a name."

"Fine. Alpha. Code received. Niner-niner."

"Texted you the address."

"This wedding is so much more fun than I thought it'd be," Matt says, breathless, as he presumably jogs to our rental car. "Okay, address is in the GPS thing. Ten-ish minutes."

"See you in ten. Room 403."

"Affirmative."

I hang up and slap the phone against my palm as I take in the room, figuring out what needs to come with and what our next move is. "Okay, where is Phillip getting ready?"

"Room 311."

"He's here? In this building?" I ask.

"Not yet, but soon."

"All right. Do you want to tell him face-to-face?"

"No."

"Fine by me. Do you want to keep your dress?" I point to the white fluffy thing hanging on the wall.

"No, I hate that thing."

"Okay, we *are* taking this." I grab the champagne and the box of chocolates. "For later."

"Honey, are you *positive*?" my mom asks. "Did Sam just get in your head?"

"No . . . No. I mean, I don't know if it's Sam I want either, but I knew before then—Phillip is the safe choice. Bet small, lose small . . . you know?"

"You were scared," I mumble. "Of finding something *real.*"

"We've seen how that can end, right?" She curls in on herself.

"Right." I nod thoughtfully. God . . . we're more alike than I've ever realized.

"Liz?" I say softly.

"Yeah?"

"I'm really proud of you. It may be the most last-minute decision of all time . . . but I'm really proud of you."

"He's going to be *so* mad."

"He is." I nod, lowering into her lap and hooking my arms over her shoulders. "But *you* are going to be so happy."

*　　*　　*

THERE'S A KNOCK on the door precisely ten minutes later. We've gathered all our supplies and written out a note to be found by Phillip's sister and mother. Liz is on the phone with the airline, canceling her flight and refunding it to Phillip's card. We Rothsford women are *excellent* in a time pinch.

I answer the door, and Matt ducks inside. "You know, when you asked me to be your date—I really just imagined free food and dancing."

"But this is *so* much more fun?" I ask.

"Obviously. Fuck that guy. Nobody puts Kathy in a corner."

"Did you just quote *Dirty Dancing* at me?" I clutch my metaphorical pearls. "I'm so proud."

"I feel like we should be doing something else right now." Matt looks around the room.

"Right. Yes. Take this." I hand him the box holding the champagne, my sister's accessories, and the complimentary shit the hotel gives.

"Liz? Mom? Our getaway car is here."

"Hi." Matt balances the box in one hand and waves.

Liz swoops past us, takes the champagne from Matt, and pops it in one fluid motion.

"When the fuck did you get so cool?" I ask, mouth ajar.

She puts sunglasses on and turns over her shoulder, shrugging as she drinks straight from the bottle.

"Lord, have mercy . . ." my mother frets, following us toward the elevator.

We walk out of the lobby like three security guards in formation around a president. My mother gets in the front seat with Matt, and I climb into the back with Liz.

We drive off in silence. In movies, they never show this part. It's always a car pulling off at top speed with the windows down and tulle in the wind. It's an eighties song and a montage. But in reality, leaving your fiancé at the altar looks an awful lot like stop signs in a posh neighborhood.

Liz starts laughing under her breath, then a little louder, then hysterically.

"Mom?" I cry out anxiously. "She's broken."

"Elizabeth?" my mom asks, looking in the rearview mirror. "Are you okay?"

"I feel fantastic." She laughs harder. "I . . . I feel *free.*"

"Okay, well, hold on to that feeling, because Phillip is calling." I point to her phone between us.

Without hesitation, she picks up her phone, rolls down her window, and chucks it into a ditch. "Matt?" she says.

"Uh, yeah? Yep?" Matt answers.

"Can you please drive to McDonalds?"

"Course. Whatever the bride—er—whatever you want!" He laughs awkwardly.

"Phillip ordered my dress *two* sizes too small. Did I tell you that?" she whispers to me, a little tipsy and *very* smiley.

"I'm so glad you left, Pudge."

"Me too." She nods, then takes my hand in hers. "This is why I love you. You make everything *so* clear."

"Then why does *my* life feel like such a train wreck?" I lean onto her shoulder, and she lays her head on top of mine.

"I don't know, Lane. You're the conductor."

"Okay, dial it back." I take the bottle from her mid-swig, and it dribbles down her chin. My straightlaced, intimidating, stern sister is drinking and getting poetic before nine A.M. in the back of a getaway car. I *love* it. "So, what now?" I ask.

"A McMuffin," she answers.

"And after that?"

She smiles wider than I've *ever* seen from her. "Who knows."

THIRTY-ONE

MATT AND I WAIT IN THE CAR WHILE MY MOTHER AND LIZ run into what *was* her and Phillip's place to get emergency items.

"Hey." I lean forward and hold his shoulder. "Sorry and thank you."

He turns over his shoulder. "This will be a *great* story someday."

"You okay?" I ask.

"Fine." He reaches out and takes my hand off his shoulder and brushes his thumb over the top of my knuckles. "You?"

"Relieved. Worried about the shitstorm that follows Liz blowing up her life. She's tough, but Phillip's family is well connected. It'll be hard on her to stay."

"Doctors can work anywhere, right?"

"True."

"She'll be okay."

"Yeah."

"You will be too, you know."

"I find *that* harder to believe."

"But look . . . you also thought your sister was perfect. You thought she had *everything* together. But who rescued who today?"

Damn . . . he has a point. And this feeling is *good.* It's purpose. She needs me right now. I sit back and pull my seat belt into place as I see my mom and sister approach the car with a suitcase and a single box.

"You know what's sad?" Liz says after throwing her stuff in the trunk. "That's actually *all* of it. I emptied out all my belongings in less than ten minutes."

"Let me guess . . . Phillip had a particular *style.*"

"Damn. How was I so stupid?"

"It's refreshing, honestly," I tease. I look around, expecting to see Phillip any second. "Where to?" I ask urgently.

"Mom, can I stay with you?"

"Honey, of course." She reaches around to the backseat and takes both our hands. "You both can *always* stay with me."

"But what if our *new* stepdaddy doesn't want us?" I ask mockingly, pouting my bottom lip.

My mother glares and drops our hands. "You're a brat." She puts her sunglasses on as she turns over her shoulder. "Mattheus, darling, back to mine, please."

Darling, Liz mouths to me, giggling.

* * *

MY SISTER SOBERED up quickly when my mother's house phone wouldn't stop ringing. Eventually we unplugged it, and Liz went upstairs to lie down. My mother followed quickly after her, and I've been sitting at the kitchen island with Matt, silently eating the box of chocolates, courtesy of the hotel, since we arrived home.

"This one is coconut." He points to the round one with white flakes. "Beware."

"Oh, I'm not allergic."

"I know—they're my favorite. I don't want to share." Matt pops it into his mouth with a grin. "You okay?" he asks when I don't match his expression.

"Yeah, just worried about Liz."

"Come here." He turns on his stool so his body faces me. His legs widen so I can step between them. The instant I'm in his arms, things seem to melt away—as they always do. I lose my better judgment when I'm in his embrace, but I also lose the nerves I seem to constantly carry around.

"I needed this. Thank you," I mumble into his chest.

"Me too."

"Really?" I ask.

"I always need your hugs, manamea."

"Happy to give," I tease. "So . . ." I breathe him in.

"So," he says above my head, "I guess the wedding is over."

"Yeah." I sigh.

"I was thinking I might spend the rest of the weekend at my parents' place if you can get a ride to the airport. I don't think me being around will help Liz."

I'd never have asked, which is exactly why his offer means so much. Of course I want him here, selfishly, but he's right—this is a weird time for Liz, and she barely tolerates me after twenty-seven years, let alone a near-perfect stranger. She doesn't do vulnerable well, and today's been a crash course.

"Are you sure?"

"Yeah. I was thinking maybe we'd see if we could postpone our flights. I already checked with Warren—he and the interns got it covered. It's pretty slow this month. I could spend the week with my parents, and you could spend it here. I think it'll be good for both of us."

I stiffen. "A week, huh?" I blow out a breath. "I don't think my sister's problems, or mine, or my family's as a whole, will be solved in a week."

"When did that become the goal?" Matt looks down at me, confusion furrowing his brow. "Solving everyone's problems? None of these things have easy solutions, manamea."

"I know that," I say pointedly. "I just . . . I don't want to run again. I don't want to keep feeling like part of me is held up here because I leave my family when it's hard."

"Right, but it's not like you're thinking of being here . . . long term . . . right?"

"I don't know yet. Maybe. Depends on how long it takes to get closure."

"Closure," Matt repeats slowly. "Closure," he says again, his brows knitting even tighter.

"I'd like to—"

"What does that mean for us?" Matt interrupts.

I go still, looking up at a man who's more exhausted than perhaps anyone I've ever seen. The image makes me think of the Sunday school lessons at the Catholic church my father would sometimes make us go to—the good Irishman that he was. He's been wandering the desert for forty years and is just about done. He's perhaps lost all faith. It makes muscles I didn't even know I had tighten.

"I think my sister needs me," I say rapidly, forcing the words out. I think about what comes next, and for the first time in a *very* long time, it feels certain what my next move should be. "I think I'll keep my flight the same, go home, pack up, and then drive the bus back. Then I can stay here, work, whatever, while I take some time to fix things." I reach out to cup his cheek, and he stills.

Matt's jaw twitches under my hand as he tries—and fails—to remain stoic. "Okay," he says, voice gruff.

I tilt my head to catch his eyes, which he is attempting to point in every direction *except* toward mine. "Matt."

"Hmm?" He finally looks at me, and tears brim his eyes. "Yeah, I get it."

"Matt, I—"

"Sorry." He raises a hand, interrupting me. "Just . . ." He paces in a small circle. "Lane, I don't know how many more hoops I can jump through here." His jaw tenses, and a neck muscle I've never seen before jumps along his throat.

I scoff. "What?"

"How long?" he asks forcefully.

"How long what?"

"Will you be staying here?"

"I just said I don't know. I haven't thought *that* far ahead yet, but I think I should fly back, get the bus, and drive back."

"So you'll be living here," he states, rubbing his beard like he's going to pull it clean off.

"For a while. I—"

Matt laughs. And it's not his belly laugh when he's surprised. It's not his throaty laugh when he finds *himself* amusing. And it's not his soft laugh—when he's winding me up. He's laughing like he can't believe his luck—or lack thereof. Like someone who's giving up.

"I have done *everything* you've asked of me." He pauses, studying me like he's in disbelief. "I've been your friend; I've been in your bed; I've been your chauffeur; your helper . . . I've shown up. And what, now you're going to send me back home alone? Indefinitely?"

I open my mouth to speak, but nothing comes out.

"Lane, please. Please come home with me. We can figure this

out together. We'll do it on your terms—*always* on your terms—I won't even kiss you if that's what you'd prefer. But hell, do *not* make me be away from you." His arms flare out to the sides, exasperation pumping through his entire body. "If you do this, what was any of this for? What happened to being afraid of losing our friendship?"

I lift my chin in defiance. "Is that an ultimatum, Matt?"

"What?" He raises his arms above his head. "Is what an ultimatum? Me saying I have nothing left to give here without some damn reciprocity?"

"You said 'be selfish, Lane.' You said 'take your time, Lane.' You said 'I love you, Lane'! Why does it matter if I'm here or back home with you?"

"Because I'm scared too, dammit! Do you know what it's like to finally feel like what you want *most* in this world is within reach, but it could crumble at any damn moment? I've *barely* got you. If you're here, and I'm back home, I could lose you. We could lose *this*. What if you don't come back? How can I convince you that you need me if I'm a thousand miles away?"

I throw myself into his arms, and he almost falls out of surprise. "Matt, you don't have to convince me. You don't have to woo me. You don't have to spoil me. You don't have to *do* anything. You're enough for me. I was content to be miserable before. *You've* shown me what I can have, and I'm going to try, but—"

"Try back home. Try near me." He steps back, and I feel untethered from the earth.

A warm, thick tear makes its way down my cheek. "I can't, Matt. I'm needed here. I want to be here. I have a lot of shit to work through, and I need to do it here."

"Why?"

"Because I've been running from home for so long. Because my dad *haunts* this place. Because my mom has a boyfriend I've never met, and Liz is . . . blowing her life up! And I knew nothing! I'm terrified of letting myself fall for you—but when I'm near you, I forget that I have to think about anything at all, and that's not okay. I need to work on *this* first." I take a breath. "We will *never* happen if I don't figure my shit out on my own. It won't work."

He runs a hand through his hair and rocks back on his heels. He keeps starting to say something and stopping, stuttering and trying to grasp on to what he wants to say. So when he goes silent and his eyes fall to the floor, I know he's given up.

He nods to himself slowly and looks up with a hesitancy that splits me in two.

He briefly kisses my forehead with a hold on the back of my neck, and I feel his thumb rub my hairline. "Okay," he says softly. Then he turns and walks out of the kitchen.

"Matt?" I call after him.

"Tell your mom thank you from me." His voice is shaky, and he wipes his face with his sleeve. I know he's crying, and it *crushes* me.

"Matt . . ." I follow him out the front door. "Matt, wait."

He stops between the open car door and the seat. "I want this for you, Lane." He looks broken. *I broke him.* "I just wanted to be a part of it." He taps the roof of the car. His lips tremble, and I know he's giving me the chance to stop him, to say I've changed my mind. And I want to. I so desperately want to wipe that look off his face, to hold him, to tell him I love him. But that's not fair to either of us. Not yet.

His shoulders fall before he lowers himself into the driver's seat. Once he's inside, he doesn't hesitate to drive away. I hear my mom's footsteps on the stone steps behind me as I wipe snot and tears away and Matt disappears out of view.

"How much of that did you hear?" I ask her, not bothering to turn over my shoulder.

"Enough." She curls her arm around my waist, and I lean into her. "We're going to figure this out. All three of us have work to do, baby. But it *will* be okay." She pets my hair and rubs my back as I cry into her shoulder. "I know baby, I know."

"I just want to do the right thing," I say through tears.

"I know you do. You did. C'mon. Your sister's laid up in my bed. Let's go join her."

"I just need a minute." I straighten and step away. I need air. Several minutes of silence. Room to cry.

"Okay, hon. Take your time."

THIRTY-TWO

"ROOM FOR ONE MORE?" I SAY, STEPPING AROUND THE almost-shut door of my mother's bedroom. She and Liz are in the middle of the bed, Liz wrapped around my mother as she brushes long strokes down her back.

My mom opens her arm on the opposite side, and I curl into her as well.

"My girls." She whispers as we both press our heads into her chest. "I missed this. Having you both here." She kisses the top of Liz's head, then mine. "What a decade we've had, hmm?"

"Mom?" I ask, wiping my nose on my sleeve. I don't know if it's because I'm already this emotional, or because I'm desperate to get the ball rolling—but I can't quite seem to stop the next words from tumbling out of me. "I'm so sorry."

"Oh . . ." She pulls me in tighter. "Honey," she tuts, "whatever do you have to be sorry about?"

"Because . . . Dad would still be here if I'd just stayed home."

"Elaine Marie Rothsford, you take that back *this* instant." She uses her full chest, only heard-a-few-times-like-when-I-almost-stuck-a-fork-in-a-socket voice. "You are *not* responsible for what happened to your father, the accident, *or* anything else that we've done in lieu of grieving properly." She pats my arm like she wants to *slap* it, and I catch Liz's eye. She appears to be just as confused as I am.

I notice *she* isn't quick to tell me it's not my fault. But she's had a hard day. I'll talk to her another time.

"I have a confession to make," my mother says. "Jean-Paul, well, he's not only my lover . . ." *Gross.* "He was my grief counselor." *Worse.*

"Ew!" I whine. "Doesn't that break like a hundred rules?"

"You girls know that I can struggle to be . . . emotional. When you find someone who you can talk to, who you feel safe with—those lines can blur. It wasn't until our last session that I made my feelings known, and he took time to decide whether he was all right with it." She smiles to herself, a sultry one with the edges of her mouth turned down. "You could even say I pursued him."

Liz laughs, and we both look at her with skeptical glances.

"What's so funny?" I ask her.

"Nothing!" She's still trying not to laugh.

"*Liz.*"

"I was just going to say that this guy helped Mom get *over* Dad by getting *under* her." She covers her mouth like she's sworn in front of the Pope himself.

It takes my mother half a second to laugh, and then I let my laughter escape as well.

"What has gotten into you?" I ask. "You're making sex jokes!"

"I could ask you the same thing. We could hear your whole conversation downstairs—when did you become so mature?"

I gasp exaggeratedly, holding up my palm as if I want her to place hers against it. "We've swapped bodies!" I cry out.

My mother pushes my wrist down, and I curl my hand around her hip, tucking back against her.

"We're going to all go see a counselor." I open my mouth to interject, but she beats me to it. "Not Jean-Paul and not anyone else as handsome." I open my mouth again, but don't quite make it. "And yes, you have to. Both of you." She looks at Liz, wide-eyed and stern—a look usually reserved for me—and I feel a little burst of pride in my chest.

"Bossy." Liz scowls.

"It's time, girls. We've taken long enough to throw ourselves a pity party. Don't think I didn't hear what you said in the hotel today, missy." She taps Liz's shoulder. "Or what's going on with you." She pokes me. "No more holding back from the good in life because you could lose it. Nothing would make your father more upset than that. Plus, it can turn into very expensive mistakes, like renovating a bus or a canceled wedding."

We both begin protesting at the same time, but my voice carries louder. "The bus is actually a very good decision. It's given me a lot of clarity. And I'm pretty proud of it. You'll both be seeing it soon, then you'll know." I shuffle against the feather duvet on top of my mother's mattress to sit up and look down at them both. "I'm going to fly home on Tuesday, pack it up, and drive it back here. I'm going to stay here for a while. To sort myself out."

"Yeah, we heard, remember?" Liz says, and my mom tuts.

"Let her have her announcement." She glares at Liz. "We're very excited you'll be staying. This will be good. For all of us."

We fall asleep on my mother's bed together for the first time in almost ten years. Not since the night after the funeral. In some ways, it's as if a time-loop was created, and we're back in that moment. I'm still seventeen, terrified of an unsure future, desperate to crawl out of my own body, and yet the body I'm in is now twenty-seven and ready to try again.

*   *   *

I WAKE UP in an empty bed to the smell of eggs frying and coffee brewing. Being enveloped in the smell and familiarity of my mother's home after an *exhausting* day meant I slept like a baby. But waking up—getting up—feels challenging.

I already miss Matt. Like a soft, quiet nagging in the back of my memory—how he sounds when he wakes up, the soapy smell of his beard, the way he'd mumble compliments against my neck as I stretched and yawned.

It's no longer a question if I love him. I know I do. It's whether I can love myself as much as I love Matt that matters. If I can allow myself to love him in a way that he deserves, free from fear. So, I bury the pain of missing him down under a pile of well-wishes for his day. I think fondly of Fetu and Simon and hope they bring him some comfort. I imagine the sun rising over the creek, and a part of me feels calmer knowing he's where he's safest too.

Liz comes out of the bathroom in her robe and shuts me out of the bedroom so she can change. I walk down the hall toward the stairs and hear my mother in the kitchen, whistling along with music. Today's the first day of our healing journey—and apparently that starts with breakfast and show tunes.

"Morning!" my mother sings out, carrying a plate of scrambled eggs to the dining table. "Liz up yet?"

"Yeah, she just got out of the shower." I fall into the chair across from her. "I feel hungover, and I didn't even drink."

"That is called an *emotional* hangover, sweetheart. Plus, a little heartbreak." She lowers her mug. "Missing him already?"

"Are you?" I take a sip, raising a brow.

"I like Matt. Am I not supposed to like Matt?" she says defensively, her smile growing wide.

"You called him *darling*." I take a sip of coffee.

"He *is* darling." She narrows her eyes at me. "He seems it, anyway. But I liked Phillip at first, so perhaps it's best to ignore my judgment."

"Hmm. You're right this time. Matt's the best person in the world."

"Ah, step one. Get that man off the pedestal."

"What? Why?" I ask with a touch of anger in my voice I did not expect. I swallow it down along with my coffee. "He didn't do anything wrong. He asked me for one thing, to stay, and I let him down."

"Maybe not, but nobody's perfect, Lane. So long as you keep thinking he's *the best person in the world,* you're going to keep convincing yourself you're unworthy of him."

"Damn, therapy's already in session? I should have showered too."

"Joke all you want, but it's the truth. Loving yourself is only half the battle, hon. Seeing Matt as a full person will help too. He isn't some unachievable, perfect man, so quit acting like it." She wags her finger. "He's in love with you. All of you, warts and all. Do you think you can love the sides of him he'd rather not show you?"

"How much did you two hear last night?" I ask.

"The whole thing. Voices carry in this house. Why do you think I put you on birth control at fifteen?" She pauses. "For acne? Please . . . you've got perfect skin; always have."

"On that note, I'm going to go somewhere else now."

"Breakfast?" she asks as I stand.

"Not hungry." And I'm not anymore. The idea of my mother

hearing my teenage sex-capades has made my stomach tighten like a knot at the end of a balloon.

"Therapy is at half past ten! In the living room," she calls after me.

And though he's not here, I can *feel* Matt's reaction to hearing that my mother has a therapist who'd make a house call on hours' notice. *Rich people,* he'd mumble. His tone would be part judgment and part amazement. And he'd be right. It's ridiculous. However, it *is* efficient, so I won't complain.

I do, however, have some calls to make before then. Starting with Chloe, who answers eagerly.

"Hey! How was the wedding?"

I tell her in excruciating detail the entire happenings of the last forty-eight hours. Even Chloe can't seem to adapt to each new tidbit of information—and she's the *queen* of adapting. She went from single and childless to living with a stranger and fostering her baby sister within a week and a half, after all.

After some mumbling as she outwardly processes, she lands on, "Well, fuck Phillip!"

"Right?"

"And I'm sorry about you and Matt, but also glad? I'm not entirely sure."

"It's cliché, but it *is* for the best. For now. Just for now."

"So if I see him with another woman?" Chloe asks.

"Murder. Immediate murder."

"Gotcha. I'll let Warren know we may have to arrange conjugal visits."

"Okay, fine. Not murder. Maybe a stern look and a shake of the head. You don't think he will, right? Move on? I mean . . . it would be within his rights to, but . . ."

Chloe makes a noise like a whining, soft squeal in the back of her throat—like when something is so cute you can't put it to words. "No, Lane. I think he'll be waiting for you when you come back to us. He's going to stay another week, then?"

"Yeah, I just got the email confirmation from the airline delaying his flight. He's going to visit with his family a little longer. I'm coming back tomorrow to pack up and drive back."

"That's a long drive."

"Yeah."

"By yourself."

"Wanna come with?" I joke . . . mostly.

"I wish I could, babe."

"I know." I sigh. "I should go get ready. My mom has a family therapist coming soon."

"Efficient."

"That's what I said!" I laugh once. "Maybe she's desperate to have her house back to herself."

"Or to perhaps have her *lover* all to herself," Chloe teases. "Keep calling, okay? I'm always around. I'm going to miss you."

"Want to meet at the bus tomorrow? Em too?"

"Yeah, I'm already texting with her to make a plan."

"Love you."

"Love you too."

I hear a muffled laugh and the sound of Chloe squealing as the phone gets tossed around.

"Hey," Warren says.

"Hello?"

"Told you so."

"Warren!" Chloe shouts. "Not helpful!"

I laugh quietly. "You did."

"Take care of yourself, okay? Call if you need anything. We'll look after Matt—just worry about you."

I choke up because Warren would only say such a thing if he truly meant it.

"Okay. I will."

"Bye," he says. "War—" I hear Chloe start yelling, but the line goes dead.

"Bye," I say to no one, catching a glimpse of myself in the mirror of my childhood bedroom. I narrow my eyes, determination straightening my jaw.

Time to start kicking dragon ass.

THIRTY-THREE

HELLO, NEW JOURNAL. YOU'RE SO PRETTY I BARELY WANT
to write in you—but I'm under fairly strict instruction by Dr. Cope to
write after every session. (Yes, that's actually her name—I know it sounds
made up.)

Let's see . . .

It's been two weeks since I got back to Vancouver with my bus and
Simone. That drive was . . . hell. If I do decide to move back home, the bus
may have to stay here. (Kidding . . . mostly.) Living on it, however, has
been amazing. I've enjoyed spending more time with Mom, but it's nice to
have my own space at the end of the day. I get a sense of pride going to
sleep each night in a home I had a hand in creating. Simone certainly en-
joys her new burrow under my bench seating.

I also feel closer to Matt when I'm in here.

Sometimes it feels like I traded in one ghost for another. I feel nearer to
my dad than ever before, being here, talking about him, reliving so many
memories. But I feel farther from Matt each day. I realized yesterday
that even before we became a "we," there hadn't really been longer than a
two-week period in the last year or so where we didn't at least chat or run

into each other. I've resisted the urge to call him, my thumb held above the dial button several times. But I won't call. I'm not going to disrupt his life any more until I'm certain of what I want—and ready to make it happen.

Dr. Cope has encouraged me to write in this journal about where I'm at to help reflect my progress. She says I'm fixated on being healed when I need to view it more as a lifelong journey. Apparently (yay) I'll always carry this with me. She calls it PTSD, but I'm not sure I'm ready to agree with her just yet.

When she told me that I may be as "fixed" as I'll ever feel, I asked if that meant I was ready to go home. She sighed. I took that as a no.

According to the good doctor, you can't graduate or pass therapy. So, here I am—journaling, which does feel like homework. So, maybe I can?

Anyway . . .

Today I'm feeling okay. I've had some really excellent sessions with my mom about the guilt I have for how Dad passed. She apologized for not telling me sooner that she wasn't upset or angry with me. I apologized for running away before she had the chance to.

She's had some revelations that have led to several late-night cry sessions in each other's beds, though she refuses to sleep on the bus. "Not once," she said. "Not a single time have I blamed you for that accident. Not even for a moment."

That relief is indescribable.

But . . . Liz and I have been on less great terms, again. When the calls from Phillip stopped about a week after I got back, she sort of fell into her old routine and patterns. She's been short-tempered and snippy and refuses to answer any questions about Sam or what comes next. She's thrown herself into work, and the shifts at the hospital are long and arduous, so when she's not there, she's in her room resting.

Mom tells me not to worry about her—that I can only do my part. But I can't help but feel like our healing is tied up in each other.

But that's me setting a goal again instead of "letting it be." What I *have learned—and agreed with—is that moving on from grief is impossible. No one really can. We just learn skills to handle it better. Like the affirmations I've prescribed myself for years to deal with my agoraphobia. Dr. Cope has suggested some other strategies to implement. Journaling is just one of them.*

Overall, I'm okay. I can talk about my dad without crying, which is new. I've talked to Chloe and Emily a few times on the phone to make sure I'm not a friendless loser by the time I re-emerge into society.

They didn't mention Matt, or bring him up, so I didn't either. I don't know why—I know I could just ask, but I think it would hurt more to get secondhand information. I do wonder if Chloe's heard from him. Or, rather, what Warren's told her of him. I hope he's okay. I hope he misses me the same way I miss him, but maybe a little less painfully. Not much less, though.

Well, that's all from me. I'm not entirely sure if I found this helpful—but hey, Dr. Cope hasn't let me down so far.

Stay classy, journal.

—Lane

THIRTY-FOUR

SIX WEEKS IN, AND I'VE DECIDED I DON'T LIKE THERAPY anymore.

Have you ever gone to a fair and been in a room of prank mirrors? Because being in therapy feels like going into that room, looking at every warped version of yourself—shorter, wider, stretched out, squiggly, and squashed—then finding out the mirrors weren't prank mirrors at all. That's just what you look like. Every weird, awkward, gross part of you is on display, suddenly so obvious.

I also really love therapy. I could take or leave Dr. Cope. (God, will she request to read this journal? FUTURE LANE, TAKE THIS PAGE OUT) She's keeping her cards close, probably because she knows how desperately I want her to like me. She's only laughed at one of my jokes—and it wasn't even my best one.

Still, the woman is good at her job. I've had several "breakthroughs" about different areas in my life in which I've sabotaged myself. I knew, on a superficial level, that I was punishing myself because of the guilt I felt for what happened to my dad, but I didn't actually get how it's impacted my life.

I truly think that if I hadn't found Chloe and Emily as roommates, I wouldn't have graduated—but thank god they made me want to stick around, which meant I had to actually pass my classes. Other than that, I've given up a lot of potential to the idea that I don't deserve a future in which my father isn't present.

That has to stop.

Because it won't bring him back.

And no one wins.

Today's session was mostly focused on what I do want moving forward. We talked about the idea of me starting my own business, as I'm better at accomplishing tasks and goals when I'm able to set my own work and choose projects I'm passionate about, but ensuring I rent an office space to make sure I'm not isolating myself. I'm going to visit home at least twice a year—to help me feel grounded. I'm going to live on the bus for the foreseeable future—but where I want the bus parked is the one question left standing.

Most of me thinks of home as wherever Matt is, but when I'm falling asleep at night, I worry that with each passing day he'll no longer feel the same. Does distance really make the heart grow fonder? Or has he realized in my absence how much work it is to keep me around? Maybe he's come out of a daze. The fog of lust has lifted, and he's finally able to rest without me demanding so much from him.

I don't think I expected to, but each time I leave therapy now, I feel a little more certain and a little less weighed down. I think my newfound confidence is overpowering my guilt, and I'm loving the feeling of wanting to make the most of my days.

I don't dread waking up, checking in with work, or even going out. I'm not singing to animals to help me get dressed like a fairy tale just yet, but I do feel fine. Better than fine. Good, even.

My mom's boyfriend is sweet, if a little therapist-y. He's got long pauses and agreeing sounds from the back of his throat down to an art. But he seems harmless, and he looks at my mom like she lights up the room. Like she's his guiding light.

And while I think there will always be a part of me that will be sad that it isn't my dad doing so, it's nice to see her looked at like that. She deserves it. And, in part, seeing that she deserves it has helped me remember that I do too.

Also, I finished The Count of Monte Cristo . . . finally. I liked it a lot. I can see why it is Fetu's favorite after all she's been through, and why Matt recommended it to me.

I really liked this part:

"He who has felt the deepest grief is best able to experience supreme happiness. Live, then, and be happy, beloved children of my heart, and never forget, that until the day that God will deign to reveal the future to man, all human wisdom is contained in these two words, 'Wait and Hope.'"

So that is what I will keep doing, waiting and hoping.

—Lane xox

THIRTY-FIVE

"LANE!" I SHOOT UP IN BED TO THE SOUND OF POUND-
ing on the side of my bus.

"Yeah?" I call back.

"Can I come in?" Liz asks, already prying the door open.

"Uh, sure?" I say as she comes into view and sits on the edge of
my bed before adjusting her scrubs. She must have just gotten
home from her night shift in the emergency room—but I rarely
see her in the uniform—she's fairly strict about changing to prevent contamination. Actually, her scrubs look barely worn.

"Hey, you okay?" I ask as she picks at the skin around her
thumbnail.

"Hi." Her voice waivers, and two realizations hit me at once.

1. I have never seen my sister cry before.
2. She's coming to *me* for comfort.

"Hi, Pudge." I sit up more, curl my arms around her shoulders,
and drag her stiff body toward my mattress until she's awkwardly
in my arms.

She clears her throat. "I, um, just wanted to check on you."

"I was asleep, Liz. You pounded on my door."

She sniffles and rubs her nose.

"How was work?" I ask.

"I didn't go."

"No?"

"Well, I did. I went, and I walked in. Then I just walked out. I don't know what came over me."

"How did it feel?"

"Like my chest was going to tighten until it snapped."

I nod, then tuck my chin over the top of her head. "I really don't know how you do that. See emergencies all the time—see people on the worst days of their lives."

She relaxes into me, her muscles softening, and it's oddly comfortable—like we've done this hundreds of times. "I hated seeing you in a hospital bed, all beat up," she whispers. "I felt so helpless when I saw nurses take your blood and the needle that stitched up your cheek . . . I decided I'd be the person doing the fixing. I never wanted to feel that way again."

"Did it work?" I ask quietly. "Do you feel better?"

Her laugh is hollow. "What do you think?" Another sniffle, and she brushes her cheek.

"Well, you walked out for no reason, and you're crying in my bed right now, so . . . no?"

"I don't like medicine, Lane."

"No?"

"No. I actually think I kinda hate it."

I snort, not because I'm cruel—but because Liz does, and her laugh is so genuine and self-pitying it's almost rude not to.

"I think I've been sleeping for ten years," she says, sitting up and folding her legs across from me on the bed.

"Like autopilot?" I ask.

"Yeah. Whatever the next move was, the simplest move or the most strategic—I did it. I didn't think about what I wanted. I don't even know if I want *anything*. I can't seem to turn that back on. How do I figure out what I want?"

"You know, this is *exactly* what Dr. Cope and I have been doing."

"I don't need therapy." Liz went to *two* sessions before she got "busy" with work.

"Why not?" I ask, trying to not sound offended.

"I don't want someone else telling me what to do, telling me what I'm thinking—it's strange."

I scoff. "Oh, she doesn't tell you what to do. In fact, I wish she would. I've asked her to tell me."

"Why would you want that?"

"Because I hate making decisions."

"Why?" Her lips press together until they're tight and pale.

"Because it feels selfish—to decide what I want for myself."

"How on earth is that selfish?" Her eyebrows create a heavy line down the center of her forehead.

"I never said it *is* selfish. I said it *feels* selfish. Either way, I'm working on that." I widen my eyes for emphasis with a *touch* of sass. "In therapy."

"Well, if therapy was working, you'd have left by now."

"I may never leave," I say plainly.

"Why?"

"God, that's your favorite question today."

She doesn't blink, waiting for me to answer.

"Fine. It's not that I'm not . . . better. I mean, better is a relative term. I'm feeling better than I was two months ago. I feel less on edge; I feel less fearful of what's to come; I feel way less guilt. I don't feel like an open nerve waiting for a hit of pain anymore, distracting myself to avoid thinking and causing hurt. . . ."

"But . . ." Liz waves me on.

"But," I sigh, "I've had to confront a lot of really ugly parts of myself. And, while I feel more confident in who I am moving forward—I think I've realized how shitty I *have* been."

"In what way?"

"It's not that Matt deserves more than me—I think I'm pretty okay—I just think I've not been a very good friend to him. I've been selfish and taken more than I've given. If I go back, I don't know what I'll be going back to. That's scary."

Liz clears her throat, and a strange expression washes across her face. "Would you say," her voice is robotic, like a lawyer leading their client in questioning, "that you're perhaps having doubts about his love for you?"

"Why are you acting like that?" I gesture at her face with an open palm.

"Like what?"

"Why are you talking to me like you need me to answer a certain way?"

"Because I'm under *annoyingly* strict instructions." She clenches her jaw, and her eyes shift in annoyance.

"From whom?" I ask.

"Just answer the question."

"Yes, no? Whatever gets me to the next clue."

"Would you agree that you're ready to get back with Matt, but feeling held back by uncertainty? That you've accomplished what you set out to, and any further information would not influence or pressure you—but could validate your decision?"

I push the back of my hand to her forehead. "Are you ill?"

She raises a brow as a warning.

"Yes. I agree. I love Matt but think these two months may have caused him to grow better judgment or gain perspective that he's better off unhitching himself from my loony-wagon."

She rolls her eyes. "Then I have something for you."

Without a word, she stands and runs off the bus like a damn lunatic. The last time she ran out of my room with the intention of coming back was when we were twelve years old and she was going to get her calendar to figure out if our cycles had lined up. For science, of course.

I almost wonder if she's not going to return when I finally hear her coming up the steps and around the corner toward the back of the bus. She's holding the same box she had when she packed up her ten belongings from Phillip's place and sits beside me.

"I don't even want to think what this man has spent on stamps." She dumps the box out, and dozens of envelopes fall onto the bed. "This is the letter that was addressed to me." She hands me the opened envelope.

Liz,

I'm not sure if Lane has mentioned it, but social media isn't my strong suit, and I didn't know how else to get in touch, so please forgive my penmanship.

This is Matt, by the way.

Anyway, off to a great start . . . I was hoping you could do me a favor. It took me about twelve hours after getting to my parents' place to realize I made a massive mistake in leaving the way I did.

But I think calling Lane would only make things worse. She needs time and space to do this on her own terms—in her own way. I need to back off. So, this is my solution. I'm going to write her letters. I do not want you to give them to her until she's ready. If she isn't ever, then so be it. But I couldn't live with myself if she mistook my silence for apathy and gave up on us.

*If you don't mind helping me, I've put my number below. Give
me the go ahead, and I'll begin mailing. The pile is quickly growing.*

Sincerely, Matt

*P.S. It was great to meet you, and I hope we can see each other
again soon.*

I spread my hand across the letters on my blanket in disbelief.

"They just kept coming." Liz lifts one, examines it, and tosses
it aside. "Really, so much postage."

"It's really romantic," I whisper mindlessly.

"Yeah, unless he changed his mind and broke up with you in
one of these."

"Liz! Shut up!"

"Read then." She throws a letter into my lap.

"Wait!" My mother bursts in, panting. "I want to hear this—it's
not every day your daughter gets this many declarations of love."
She falls onto the mattress, squishing Liz slightly.

"How the—?" I ask . . . sort of.

"I saw Liz running with the box and followed. I've been waiting
for this."

I shake my head; this is *quite* the wake-up. "I will read these in
private, thank you!" I snatch a letter out of my mom's hand.

My mother and sister share a devious look, and my mother
nods, saying silently that she'll take this one. "You know . . . your
father and I sent letters."

"Oh, my god." I gawk at her and look to Liz for support—but
she just plays along, nodding thoughtfully.

"He was so romantic like that. . . ." She sighs wistfully.

"Yeah, and," Liz adds, whispering, "since I called off the wedding, I've been kind of down. This could really help me"—she
bites down on a grin—"believe in love again."

"You two need to get an acting coach. I'm not buying this."

"Fine!" My mother stands and straightens her clothes before waving for Liz to follow. I watch Liz contemplate snatching one and raise a brow in challenge. *Don't even think about it.*

She huffs and follows after Mom.

There's no indication of any sort of order to them being sent, no number or delivery date on the stamp—so I just go for the one closest to me.

Manamea,

I haven't discovered religion since you left, but I can only describe what I've been doing in your absence as praying. You come into my thoughts so often that I had to do something productive to dismiss them. So whenever I think of you, I inhale for a long ten seconds, soaking in the moment, and then exhale all my love for you out into the ether, hoping you'll feel it somehow. I ask whoever is listening to keep you safe and bring you home when you're ready. I ask for patience. I ask for every day you're away to be added on to how long we will have together. Do you feel it?

I think of the string Rochester described to Jane, tethered to each other's rib. That he felt like he was going to bleed out by having it ripped off him if she went too far. I didn't understand that until you. Missing you is painful. Physical and real. Perhaps if I keep tugging on this invisible string, you'll follow it home.

Yours, Matt

Reading the rest of the letters suddenly seems both irrelevant and yet entirely necessary. I open another and another and another. Most are beautiful confessions of love—and the swelling relief in my chest is like a warm balloon.

I smile fondly while I read the notes where he just tells me about his day. He's completed the list of movies I gave him. He's even gotten a Netflix account and is grateful his television's remote has a speech feature. Ruth got into veterinary school, Aaron moved to the city, Tabitha has decided to travel for a year or two instead of university—she's teaching herself *another* language. He tells me about his family because that's what he's always done. Stories, but in present tense—because I know them. Because they're my family too. He tells me that he's going to visit them the week before Ruth moves away for college. Which is now, I realize. Matt is just six hours away.

The last letter, by total chance, is my favorite. No poetic prose or details. He's not trying to impress me, and he's not trying to *earn* me. It's only ten words on a full sheet of paper—not even signed.

Fuck, I miss you. You've ruined me. Do it again.

I throw on slippers and run across the driveway, up the front steps, and into the kitchen. I enter, panting, and find my mother and sister mid sips of coffee and eyes widened in surprise. "I'm going to Vancouver Island. Today."

"Matt's in B.C.?" Liz asks.

"Matt's in B.C.," I repeat.

"Matt's in B.C.!" my mother exclaims.

Call it impulsivity. Call it spontaneity. Call it insanity. But I've never made a decision so fast. Or been *so* certain. "Mom, I need something from you before I go."

THIRTY-SIX

THE JOURNEY TO GET TO MATT HAS BEEN A COMEDY OF errors.

I got two hours away in my bus before it dawned on me that there was no possible way I was getting that monstrosity across the harbor on a ferry. I turned around to get the car my mother hasn't driven in years. It had a flat.

So I changed a tire for the first time ever with the help of Liz and an online tutorial my mother read off to us as she sat in a lawn chair she found in the garage. I gave them both strict instructions to take care of Simone while I'm gone and then *finally* left.

When I actually got back on the highway, ready to repeat half the trip, it began pouring rain. I white-knuckled it for four hours, shaking by the end because I had to pee so badly. But I was booked on the five o'clock ferry—thanks to my mom—and I was *not* going to miss it.

I got to the harbor with twenty minutes to spare, found a bathroom, and drove the car on. As the rain got worse, I tried not to take it as an omen.

Once across, my phone's signal began fading in and out. I screenshotted the instructions to Matt's parents' place and prayed that I didn't take a wrong turn.

Which I did. Because the rain made it nearly impossible to see street signs and because I can't focus for the life of me. So far, I've run into a convenience store, a smoke shop, a gas station, and a police station to get directions.

So a drive that should have taken me six hours has now taken me ten. I'm exhausted, drenched, and beginning to laugh and cry in turn when I see the familiar bridge and a home at the top of the hill.

On a rainy day like today, the house has an ethereal feel to it. Other houses would look spooky, straight from one of Matt's gothic novels. But this home is nothing but warm. I drive cautiously across the wooden bridge, willing my eyes not to shut in terror. Once on the other side, I see Matt's car in the distance and aim to park next to it. The mud and my tires have other plans.

I spin out and begin drifting in a literal mudslide back down the hill from whence I came. *"Shit, shit, shit, shit!"* I cry out, trying to spin the steering wheel to turn. Eventually, I manage, and the car slows to a stop, crooked and not parked in any sense of the word. But on level enough ground that I don't think it'll flow off the road and into the creek, so I call it. I put it in park and use the emergency brake—because surely that can't hurt—and open my door to an absolute assault of rain.

Throughout the entire drive, I've had Matt's eyes in the forefront of my mind. If I can see him, if I can picture him, I can make it there in one piece.

I certainly don't feel like I'm in one piece after this harrowing journey, but I did it. I made it. And at the top of this muddy hill is my person.

Fuck.

Matt's inside.

Matt's family is inside.

What if it's too little too late? No . . . No.

But his parents could be furious with me. The woman who scorned their child.

I shake the thoughts away, noting their ridiculousness. Even if I let them win, what would I do? Go home? There are no other ferries tonight, and I can't imagine it'd help to sleep in a car at the bottom of their driveway—to be discovered in the morning anyway.

No, I'm doing this.

Matt deserves this.

Grand fucking gesture time.

Finally exiting the car, I lift the hood of my raincoat. After slamming the door, I briefly wonder if I've lost the element of surprise before thunder cracks, and everything feels muffled.

I assess the climb ahead of me and decide to take the path of least resistance, where gravel has soaked up some of the rain. Carefully choosing my steps, I feel the damp, cold rain begin seeping through my coat.

My shoe gets stuck in a particularly thick patch of mud. I cover my face from the rain as I try my best—and fail—to remove it. When I finally wriggle out of it, it's not my shoe that takes the next step—but my bare foot with a squelch into the wet earth.

Fuck it. I waddle up the rest of the driveway, my toes disappearing with every step. When I reach the steps of the porch, I can feel my heart beating in my throat, climbing like it's going to fall out of my mouth.

It's the feeling of the moment before a wave hits, before the roller coaster pushes past the edge or the swing falls back from a soaring height. Excitement and fear bundled in an excellent way that resembles anxiety—but doesn't have the same kick.

I take off my jacket and wrap it around my foot, using it as a towel—but it sort of just smudges it around. I notice a watering can collecting rain from the awning and pour it over my foot, getting most of the mud off. That'll do.

I contemplate how long I can stay on their porch—because I'm very out of breath and also *really* unprepared. Matt's the one with the good words and swoonworthy phrases. I'm here to say *what* exactly?

A crash of lightning hits so loud that I swear and cower to the ground. When I straighten, determination swells in my chest. I count to three and summon all the courage and strength I have and open the door without so much as a knock.

THIRTY-SEVEN

"LANE?" IAN STANDS IN THE FRONT ROOM OF THE HOUSE, a notepad under one arm and glasses low on his nose. He looks me up and down in a way that lets me know that I look about as rough as the journey has been. "Uh . . . Matt's—"

"Lane?" Tabitha comes bounding around the corner from the kitchen. "Oh my god, it is you! I thought Ian was seeing things!" She pulls me into a long, tight squeeze, despite my muddy and soaked *everything*.

"Hey, Tabs." I hug her back. "Your brother here?" Tabitha brushes a wet strand of hair away from my cheek.

"Lane?" Simon comes around the corner and leans on the door-frame, admiring me with a crooked smirk that is identical to his son's. "Welcome back."

"Hi, I'm so sorry to barge in like this but—"

"Lane?" Fetu calls urgently from the kitchen, the sound of her quickened footsteps follows. She beams when she sees me and comes to hug me over the top of Tabitha, who's yet to release me from her hold.

"Welcome back, honey." She pulls away and studies my face. "Caught in the rain?"

"Yeah, a little bit . . ." I hesitate a second, but can't wait another second to ask. "Is Matt here?"

"What's everyone do—" Matt rounds the corner to the now *extremely* cramped front hall and stops dead. He's wearing a gray hoodie and black basketball shorts and his hair is down, with parts of it braided—probably his sister's doing.

He looks so good, but I resist the urge to charge at him, because he also looks terrified.

"Hi." I wave pathetically. Suddenly I'm aware of the five sets of eyes pointed at me. Ruth pops her head around the corner. *Six* sets of eyes.

I feel my throat tighten as the tip of my nose stings. Thoughts turn and change over so quickly in my head that I'm not sure what is causing the potential flow of tears. Relief? Fear? Anxiety? Pressure? All of it combined? Yes. The last one.

I croak out a few sounds that I intended to be the start of sentences, but nothing seems to be working. I can't get my hand to move my wet hair out of my face. I can't make my feet step closer to him or my eyes blink.

"Lane . . ." Matt studies me, confusion creeping into the edges of his soft smile. "You okay?"

I nod—or at least I think I do.

"Let's give them some room," Simon says, clapping his hands and bending at the waist. The family follows Simon in a near-perfect line to the other room, but there isn't anywhere to go— and with the rain outside, they can't give us any privacy.

Nor should they. I was the one who let myself in.

Matt places an entire palm in front of his mouth, then brings it down over his beard.

I can do this. I can do this. I can do this.

Four blinks, one swift shake of his head, and a hearty laugh of disbelief from Matt gives me the courage I need.

"Matt . . ." I feel two hot tears roll down off my chin, and another falls into my smile, the taste of salt on my tongue.

His chest collapses inward as he remains dazed, his smile growing, but his eyes transfixed and narrow on me. He looks at me like I'm a hologram and he's trying to find the squiggly lines or imperfect features that would tell him I'm not real. That I'm not here. But I am. He needs to know that.

I take three steps, and then I'm in his arms.

It takes him a moment to wrap himself around me, as if he's stunned. But when he does, he pulls me in forcefully, his arms crushing me against him.

"Hey, *you,*" he whispers over my shoulder. Two firm hands grab my shoulders, push me away so he can see my face, and then bring me back flat to his chest. His hand splays out on the back of my head.

"It is so good to see you," he says earnestly.

I'm forcing myself to not close my eyes. To not curl into him and rest like I haven't been able to in the time since we parted.

He lets me go and takes a fumbling step back, rubbing his beard like he's seeking out comfort. I notice the shadow of a tattoo peeking out from under his sleeve on his forearm. The tribal markings he'd once described.

I wonder, what else did I miss?

"So." I clear my throat. "I've got some things to say."

Matt nods, looking over his shoulder to the narrow, open entrance that does nothing to separate his family from hearing our entire conversation. "Do you want to go to my room?"

I hear Tabitha's soft whine of disappointment and shake my head.

"No . . . being vulnerable is kinda my thing now." I fake a smile, nodding my head.

He laughs, uneasy. "All right." He swallows, and I notice a quick twitch of his lips as he focuses in. Like he's fighting back a thousand words. As if his letters didn't say enough. As if it's not *my* turn.

"I've been doing a lot of thinking," is for some reason the phrase that finds its way out of my mouth. Before "I love you." Before "I missed you so much." Before "my god, you're a beautiful man."

He nods, his eyes downcast and heavy. Like this could go in so many ways, as if he's no longer able to afford the hope he once had and thinks I might have traveled hours and interrupted his family's evening to say *anything* except . . . "I love you," I say timidly.

No, let him hear it. "I love you," I repeat with my whole chest.

Relief washes over him in such a visceral way that it takes *my* breath away.

Again.

"I love you. I love your generous heart and your kindness. I love your insane number of books and your strange hobbies. I love that you sing in the shower and use your toothbrush as a microphone. I love that you can't just sip drinks but chug them. I love your hair, your beard, and your whole face, *really*. The rest of your body too. All of it." I take a breath, realizing I'm about to spiral.

"And I'm *ready* now. I'm ready for this. Us. All of it. The morning breath and the bedtime stories and all the parts between. I want your clothes in laundry baskets with mine and your books to take over my shelves. I never want to be parted from you, ever again. I don't even want to think about that, actually. Because being far from you . . . it was like its own sort of grief. I missed you. Like Rochester missed Jane. Like my ribs were torn out. I felt it too."

"Lane . . ." Matt wipes a tear from his eye and laughs at himself for it. The purest of smiles spreads across his face, like joy is overtaking his entire spirit, bursting out from within.

But I can't stop.

"And I've been doing a lot of work in therapy. I'm not going to stop doing it. Because we *both* deserve it. It's hard and ugly but necessary. It's necessary, Matt. And I promise to keep doing it—so we never have to do this shit again because—"

"Lane," he interrupts, firmly this time.

"Wait," I say a little too forcefully. "Just—one second, sorry. One more thing." I laugh nervously. "Just, if I don't do this now—I'll never get the nerve." I take a step closer to him, reaching out to hold one of his hands. I marvel at the touch, rubbing my thumb over his knuckle.

I hadn't realized it, but I reached out to him to calm myself. Because that's what Matt does for me. Even a brief touch from him can make things so clear. A piece of quiet in my otherwise chaotic existence.

Letting him go, I bring both hands to the back of my neck and unclasp my necklace. "I have something for you." I lower the chain into my palm, and it coils like a snake. Then, once I've removed my father's wedding ring from it, I lower to one knee slowly.

Matt drops to his knees in front of me so quickly that, for a brief second, I think he tripped. But upon seeing the eagerness cross his face, it becomes clear it was intentional. "Yes," he says, voice filled with awe.

I roll my eyes despite the tears pouring from both of us and the smile I can't seem to shake off—I still long to tease him. "You don't even know what I'm going to say. I need to ask before you answer."

"I think we're supposed to date before we get engaged too. But here we are."

I push his left hand down, which he keeps attempting to present to me, with a silent laugh. "Hush." I narrow my eyes on him. "This is important."

He nods, biting down on his lip.

I lose my carefully chosen words with the look of desperation in his eyes. This man, this incredible, gentle, admirable man, wants to be mine so badly. The words fall out of me in a spluttering sob. "Mattheus Tilo-Jones, will you marry me?" I hold up the ring between my thumb and index finger.

"Obviously." His hand is on the back of my head, pulling my mouth to his before I even register his response.

Our kiss is a reunion. It's running into someone's arms at an airport. It's spotting an old friend across the room at a crowded party. It's relief and joy and gratefulness and surprise. And it's *perfect*.

When our lips part, we press our cheeks together. I breathe in his addictive scent and nuzzle against him.

Home, my brain hums. *Safe,* it speaks again. *Agreed,* I answer for once.

"Manamea . . ." he whispers reverently. "Lane."

"Mm-hmm?" I ask mindlessly, leaning back as I slip the ring on his finger—a near-perfect fit. I play with it, rubbing it under my thumb. The same familiar gold band that I'd spin and twist and seek out for comfort when walking with my dad in public, hand in hand. The same ring my father spent hours searching for at the bottom of the ocean on our holiday, because it meant so much to him.

"Was this . . . was this your dad's?"

I nod, looking up to the ceiling to avoid *another* rush of tears. But Matt's choked-out sob *ruins* that entirely.

"I asked my mom for it before I left," I croak. "I didn't want to come empty-handed, and it felt right."

I hear a soft mumbling from the other room, and I have a distinct sense that we're not the only two crying.

Matt wipes his face roughly and grinds his teeth. His brows push together, creating a deep line down the center of his forehead. When he looks at me, his expression is far more serious than I've ever seen from him. His eyes are still glistening wet, but the rest of him is so ferocious. "It is an *honor* to wear your father's ring. I'm—" He swallows, gathering himself. "I'm going to look after it. I'm going to look after you."

I believe him with *every* fiber of my being.

"I know you will. And I'm going to look after you too. This goes both ways. Give and take."

He takes both of my hands in his and kisses each one. "Elaine Marie Rothsford, will you marry me?"

I smile to myself. "Hmm . . ." I tsk before darting my tongue out to catch a tear unconsciously. "Well, you see, I'm actually *already* engaged."

"Lane . . ." Matt sighs with a tilted smirk.

"Yes. Yes, please. Yes."

With the sound of a cleared throat next to us, we both look up. Fetu smiles down, shy in her approach. I watch as she removes a ring from her right hand and passes it to her son delicately.

"Mama, no." Matt shakes his head, trying to give it back.

"Your grandmother will not be pleased if this gorgeous girl doesn't have a ring on the day of her engagement." She winks at me. "And it's wasted here. This ring should be shown off to the masses."

"I think you're severely overestimating how many people we know back home." Matt laughs, lowering the ring to his lap, admiring it thoughtfully. Fetu takes a step back, her arm wrapping around Simon, who's stepped inside the arched entryway.

"Lane?" Matt smiles and wipes the last of his tears off his face with a bent knuckle.

I'm caught. Staring at the most gorgeous ring I've ever seen. A simple gold band with a beautiful black pearl in the center. I'd never have thought to pick it, but now I couldn't imagine *anything* else.

He takes my wrist, kisses the rose tattoo, then turns it over so he can slide the ring over my finger. I nod, because words fail. How could I possibly express *how much* I want this? How afraid I was that I'd never experience a love like this? How often I've convinced myself I didn't deserve it . . .

"We're engaged, I think," Matt says alongside a shocked laugh.

"We are. So engaged." I wrap my arms around his back. "How ridiculous is that?" I laugh too, my voice muffled into his shoulder.

"I'm so fucking in love with you, Lane. You know that, right?"

"I sort of got that by the third letter." I pull away, sitting on my heels.

"I could have stopped at three?" He brushes a piece of still damp hair from my face.

"No, I needed *all* fifty-seven to do this."

"There were fifty-seven?" Matt laughs, his brows furrowing. "That's embarrassing."

"Matt?" I reach out and take his hand.

"Yeah?" He kisses mine again, quickly.

"We should probably get off the floor now." I glance up at his parents behind him.

"I'm not ready yet." His eyes are so creased on either side from the smile overtaking his face that I press my thumb against the corner of his lips, marveling at his physical joy.

"This will be *quite* the story," I whisper, leaning in close.

He breathes in, flaring his nostrils. "It will." Matt stands, his hand still in mine.

He pulls me up and lifts me into an embrace, my feet dangling. "Thank you for fighting," he whispers as he kisses my cheek and lowers me to stand.

Like a dam breaking, his family members all charge in, surrounding us in a tight embrace. I expected a whirlwind of sound and chaos, words of congratulations and exclamations of excitement, but what happens is even better. A silent, lingering embrace of five people circled around two in the center.

I look up to see Simon brushing Matt's hair with his palm, a look of pride in his eye that creates a familiar ache in my chest. Except now there's joy there, too, alongside it.

A soft hand cups my chin. "A perfect dozen." Fetu rubs her thumb along my cheekbone.

I lean into her hand, partially to seek out her touch but also tilting my head out of curiosity.

"Nine kids and three spouses," Simon clarifies. "We're really hoping for a perfect eighteen." He winks. "So far, so good."

THIRTY-EIGHT

IN A CLOUDY HAZE OF HAPPINESS THAT FEELS STRIK-
ingly like being drunk, I'm curled up against Matt in the hammock on the back porch. He's got one foot hanging out the side,
pushing us off the back wall so we rock gently. The rain pours
down all around us, but the tin roof keeps us dry and sounds
amazing.

Tabitha and Ruth are across from us on a small wooden bench
they dragged outside from the dining table. They're asking about
a wedding I've yet to imagine, let alone plan, but I don't mind because Matt fields most of the questions with polite nonanswers
and bemused smiles. Every few minutes, he tucks me in closer
and kisses my forehead, nose, or cheek. I have my hand on his
stomach, rubbing slow, lazy circles around his belly because it
makes him sigh while his eyes flutter closed.

Fetu stands behind her girls and weaves her fingers through
Tabitha's wild curls. They're longer than her mother's forearm
when all stretched out. Fetu braids, untangles, braids, and untan-

gles as her daughter asks too many questions, makes too many suggestions, and talks until there couldn't possibly be anything left to say. I watch Fetu nod, her smile warm and sincere, while her eyes somehow are all fire and wit. She'd let her children talk forever. She'd soak in every word.

Simon and Ian are baking in the kitchen. It smells like brownies. I don't ask why they're doing it because I have a distinct feeling it's for Matt and me and it would ruin a surprise.

I breathe in the rain, the pine wood of the back deck, the wet grass, and the chocolate wafting from inside. I hear the gentle creaking of wood and woven string as the hammock rocks, Matt's contented sighs, Tabitha's excited ramblings, and Ruth as she hums while petting the dog on her lap. I feel Matt next to me, his warmth inviting, and his body the perfect comfort.

And it's too much joy to be contained. I sniff, wiping a tear away, and Matt's eyes blink open, his brow furrows.

"Lane . . ." he says softly. "What's wrong?"

I shake my head, smiling as my tears continue to pour. "I've never been happier." I laugh again. "You make me so happy. All of this . . . your family, this place. I get to experience it because of you. I get to experience *you* because of them. I get to be a part of this. I'm just . . . grateful."

He leans forward, and I instinctively close my eyes, expecting a kiss. But instead, I feel Matt's lips press on my cheek, on a tear. Then another. Delicate kisses for every tear that remains.

Once he's kissed them all away, he presses his forehead to mine.

"I think this might be the best day of my life. I'm not convinced it's all real. That you're real. Here, in my arms, my grandmother's ring on your hand. It's too good to be true."

"I've missed you so much," I reply tenderly.

I can sense the tension pulling him all over, feel his chest muscle under my hand and the flex of his jaw that shifts his forehead against mine. I hear his audible swallow.

The energy in our small cocoon changes, and I open my eyes to glance around us. We're tucked away in our little corner, covered by the fabric of the hammock.

"I've missed you *that way* too," I whisper, so quiet I'm not even sure he'd hear me.

"How'd you know what I was thinking?" His smile is wicked, his voice lower than mine.

"Because it's what I'm thinking about too." I pull my bottom lip between my teeth and release it with a flick that has Matt's eyes darkening.

"Not here. Not tonight." He frowns.

"No?" I ask, pulling his shirt into my fist, confident I could change his mind.

He grits his teeth. "No. The plans I have for you . . . the ways I'm going to thank you for coming back to me." He groans from his throat, shaking his head. "No. I need you screaming like I've been hearing you every night in my head while I—"

"Happy engagement to you, happy engagement to you. Happy engagement Matt and La-ane. Happy engagement to you!" Simon sings out as Ian walks over holding a slice of cake, oozing steaming chocolate goodness from the middle.

Matt sits up, almost toppling the hammock, and I laugh, trying to regain my balance to sit up beside him, our feet dangling over the edge.

"Thank you!" I take a fork from Simon, who presents it with a flourish and bow.

"Yeah . . ." Matt mumbles around his first piece of cake. "Thank-yousomuch."

"So . . ." Simon hooks an arm around his wife, pulling her in by the hip. "What comes next?"

I look at Matt, and he looks back at me. Our eyes meet and squint—as if the other is the sun. Our smiles grow at such a similar, rapid rate that it makes laughter bubble out of me.

"Whatever Lane wants. I'm at her mercy," Matt says, eyes fixed on the curve at the corner of my lip.

"Smart man," Simon says pointedly, and Fetu elbows his side playfully.

"Home?" I ask him.

He nods. "Bus?" he asks me.

As he did with mine, I know what Matt's saying with one word. Will we be driving the bus home, and will we be living in it together?

I nod. "Think you can part with some books?"

"I think I can find somewhere to store them, if that's what you mean."

I roll my eyes and kiss his cheek before taking the plate from him and trying some of the best damn cake I've ever had.

"So, what did your mom have to say when you called her?" Fetu asks excitedly.

"Shit." I giggle, crumbs flying out of my mouth. "We should go do that."

*   *   *

THE NEXT DAY, we left for the ferry after breakfast. Once we started the drive back to my mother's, I made a game out of pointing out every hotel along the way. It started as a subtle, flirtatious teasing, but I've gotten more unhinged the longer we drive.

I point and open my mouth to speak.

"I see it," Matt drawls.

"Looks nice!" I turn over my shoulder as we pass it, reading off the sign. "Could fuck there . . . Oop! Look at that! Five kilometers up the road, another hotel." I point to the billboard. "Seems like a great place to—"

"Elaine."

He's never used my full name before. It stirs something in me that does *not* need further stirring right now.

"Do that then, too."

Matt pulls off, throws on the hazard lights, and glares at me. But I don't buy it—I see the twitch of the corner of his mouth, begging to laugh.

"Here?" I pretend to be skeptical, looking to the backseat. "I mean, if you really *want* to . . ."

"Here's how this is going to go down. We are going to go see your mom and sister. We are going to have a *nice* dinner. Then I'm going to help you pack up your things and get you onto that bus."

"Then?" I bite down on a cheeky grin.

"*Then,*" he says mockingly—leaning in so I feel his breath on my cheek—"I'm going to find a good place for us to park for the night—far away from *anything*—and fuck you on the bed *I* built."

An embarrassingly loud whine escapes my lips.

Matt rolls his eyes, checks his blind spot, and gets the car back onto the highway. "Remember this feeling the next time you think about being away from me." He raises an eyebrow at me, and I flip him off.

Matt laughs, turning on the radio to an oldies station. He performs every song he knows loudly and in a way meant to piss me off. Joke's on him; it has the opposite effect.

*   *   *

WHEN WE *FINALLY* get back to my mom's, they're standing on the front steps waiting for us, arms wrapped around each other and waving.

"Lane?" My mom does a double take when I run past her.

"She really has to pee," Matt shouts before greeting them, while I throw open the door and run inside to the nearest bathroom.

After relieving myself and counting it as a win that I didn't piss on the front seat of my mother's car, I wash up and make my way to the front hall, where pleasantries are still being exchanged.

I kiss my mother on the cheek while I wiggle my left hand at Liz next to her. A soft gasp from Liz catches me off guard, and I look at her. She's teary eyed. Instinctively I turn to ask Matt what's going on, but he smiles lovingly. An expression that says *don't mind me, just watching.*

"Liz?" I ask. Meaning, *you good?*

"It's perfect. Perfect for you." She sniffles, her cheeks reddening.

"What? Let me see." My mother snatches my hand. "Lane . . . it's stunning. Well done, Matt." She winks at him.

His hands find his pockets, and he rocks back on his heels. "Actually, it was my mother's. Well, my grandmother's."

"It's beautiful." She cups my cheek. "Dinner? Susannah came and prepared a lovely spread—I got champagne to celebrate." I nod but look back at Liz, who's still quietly looking at my ring and blinking back tears.

I signal to Matt with my eyes. A widened glance at my mother and one toward the kitchen. *You take her. I'm going to talk to Liz.*

"Can I help you open that champagne, Kathy?"

"Oh, yes, please. And you can call me Mom if you'd like."

He nods enthusiastically, following after her.

Liz is about to follow them when I grab her wrist. She stops, looks down at my grip between us, and then back to my face.

"I—" I open and close my mouth several times but come up short. So I do what feels right. I pull her into my arms and squeeze tight.

"I'm so happy for you, Lane." She rubs my back. "You did it."

"I didn't have to do much. Matt makes it easy."

We pull back, but our hold remains. Mine on her elbows, hers on my shoulders.

"You're so much braver than me." She kneads my shoulder between her thumb and her fingers—like she's distracting herself.

"I have a suggestion. . . ." I start. "What if we stop comparing ourselves? What if . . . what if we just celebrate the wins and sit with each other through the losses? We aren't doing ourselves any favors being jealous or feeling superior, and I've done both."

"Me too." Liz's lips twitch. "Yeah . . . no more comparison." She brings me back into a tight hug. "Because I need *you,* Lane. Your heart, your creativity, your wildness." She steps back, and we both reach out our hands, and our fingers intertwine.

"I love you, Pudge."

"I love you too."

We eat an outrageous amount of food, and Jean-Paul comes over with dessert. He and Matt talk about the Harley motorcycle he used to have, and I reason with my mother as to why I will not be having a big wedding and how I'm not going to plan it any time soon. The engagement was the commitment. I'd marry Matt tomorrow. I'm just not in it for the white dress or the three-course meal. That's not us.

Unless, of course, that's what Matt wants—because then I'll do it.

THIRTY-NINE

"THAT IS YOUR *THIRD* YAWN, SIR. I'M CALLING IT." I rub Matt's shoulders as he drives. "C'mon. Time to switch off or pull over."

We left my mom's at half past nine, and Matt insisted we try to drive at least two hours—but it's been three, and he's fading.

"Twenty more minutes. I found the perfect place to park."

"Fine." I kiss his shoulder. "You better be *inside* me in thirty."

He sputters a cough. "Oh my god."

"You know what? Maybe I'll just go back there and handle it myself." I stretch, pretending I'm going to stand.

Matt pushes on the pedal, and I fall back into the seat.

"So where is this *perfect* place?" I ask with a coy smile.

"Well, according to a website called Skoolie Canada, it's a free place to park with little traffic and amazing star watching."

"You learned to google!"

"Of course I did. You were gone for three months, and Warren stopped answering my questions."

"I'm proud. And a little sad."

"I'll throw out my phone. I'll do it."

I kiss the back of his neck, and he rolls into it, still keeping his eyes on the road ahead.

"Baby . . ." I whine.

"I never found the term *baby* particularly sexy."

"Okay, fine. What dirty talk or pet name will get you to pull over and abandon this plan?"

"I'm just as desperate for you," he says with zero humor. "We can make it fifteen more minutes. I want you to see stars through the skylight while I taste you."

"Now you're being mean."

He looks once, briefly, over his shoulder, wearing a dangerous smile. "God, I can't wait to be between your legs again."

"Seems like you can, in fact, wait," I say sweetly, my arms crossed in front of my chest.

"Aw, are we having our first fight as a couple?" he asks.

"Are there laws about consummating an engagement?" I reply.

"We're going to consummate the living hell out of this engagement, manamea."

"Stop teasing me."

"Why?" he purrs. "I bet you're wet already. So needy." He signals his lane change, cool and collected, while I feel my breath hitch.

"Stop it."

"Truly?" he asks.

"No."

"Tell me something. . . ." I watch as he shifts in his seat, adjusting himself. *Why is he denying us both?* "Did you touch yourself and think about me?"

I *almost* laugh because, *obviously*. "Yes."

"Was it good?"

I feel a rush of warmth rising up my neck and heating my cheeks. "Not as good as you."

"What did you imagine?" Matt gets off the highway, and I check the GPS over his shoulder. Ten minutes. Might as well be ten hours.

"Well, sometimes . . . sometimes you were behind me, like the time we fucked against the dresser. . . ."

"You mean when I bent you *over* the dresser," he clarifies.

"Mm-hmm." I mumble my agreement, crossing and uncrossing my legs. "Other times . . . I imagined you were in bed next to me. Honestly, I'd get off on the idea of you just watching me touch myself—because even when I was doing it and trying my best to imagine it was you, I knew it wasn't. It didn't come close to the real thing. But imagining you near me, calling me manamea or your good girl . . ." I don't finish the thought.

"I know. I . . ." He hesitates. "Me too. I got off thinking about you smiling at me across the room while you brushed your hair once."

"Are we pathetic?"

"Aren't we supposed to be?" Matt replies, and I catch him smiling in the rearview mirror as we pass under a streetlight. Then I hear gravel under the bus's tires and look all around. A perfect spot. There's a view from the front of the bus of a beautiful river, the moonlight reflected—casting white light that flickers around. There are grasshoppers so loud we can hear them without a single window open. The stars *are* beautiful.

"Is this it?" The GPS still says nine minutes.

"This is it." Matt stands, and in one swift motion, I'm swept up into his arms. We're kissing feverishly as we tumble through the narrow path down the center of the bus. We bump into nearly everything, but Matt doesn't slow.

He drops me on my bed with a bounce, and the boisterous energy leaves through the skylight above us.

"I missed you, Lane," he says, seconds before he's on top of me.

"I missed you, Matt." I copy him affectionately, pushing his hair back as he crowds me.

He licks his lips, his eyes narrowing softly like he's capturing a moment.

I match his stare, fighting the urge to shy away from his intense focus. "What?" I laugh with only breath.

"You're the most beautiful person in the entire world." He says it so bluntly, so earnestly, I can't help but believe him. "You're everything," he whispers, shaking his head.

I lift to kiss him.

A slow sequence of kisses, like a swelling orchestra. Reverent, as if we're conscious of trespassing on holy ground, but gratifying all the same.

My hands wander slowly from his jaw to his neck to his shoulders to his chest. *No rush,* I think to myself. And damn does it feel good to not worry about an ending because you're so swept up in the beginning of something.

He's mine. For now *and* for as many days as we're given. And that's enough. That's winning the lottery. It's lightning striking three times in one spot. It's finding parking at a mall on Christmas Eve.

I'm allowed this. It's not about earning happiness. It's about never feeling like I have to earn it at all.

"Matt?" I ask as he kisses up my belly, lifting my T-shirt as he goes.

"Hmm?"

"I love you."

He pauses, swipes the side of my waist with his nose, and turns up to see me, his eyes reflecting the pale moonlight. "Keep saying that."

"Now?"

"Always." He abandons the shirt and takes his kisses lower, tugging my shorts down.

"Button."

"Weird time to try out a new nickname." He nips my hip bone, and I struggle to speak.

"No, the shorts—they have a button."

"Ah."

I watch as he brings shaking hands to the waistband of my shorts. "You okay?"

"Nervous, actually." He sits up, resting back on his heels, and rubs a hand over his face. "I wasn't going to admit that."

I sit up and join him, mirroring his position. "What's wrong?"

"It feels new again, doesn't it? It does to me. The first time I touched you—I'd been waiting a year, and yet these past months feel so much longer."

"Matt, in case you haven't noticed—you're *very* good at this."

"Confession?"

"Please."

"The first time . . . on the bus . . . when I tasted you—" He looks up to the skylight, his expression is as if he's hoping for aliens to abduct him from the midst of the night sky. "I finished in my shorts. Before you even touched me. Like a damn teenager. I was mortified."

Heat pools in my belly. "Mortified?" I nearly choke. "Matt, that's so hot."

"What?" He laughs incredulously.

"You're basically telling me that I'm sexy enough to get you off without touching you."

"That's *exactly* what I'm telling you."

"That's hot."

"Really?"

"Really. That's undeniable proof that all those pretty words and praises you threw my way are true. Physical evidence."

"Well, when you put it like that."

"I'm not worried about this . . . about us. I've missed you for *months,* and I'd happily lay here naked in your arms. Just feeling you near me will be enough. But if it doesn't happen, like, *now,* I might go insane."

"Okay . . ." He nods to himself, determination settling in among his features. "Fine. But you're getting off first."

"Ah, well . . . if I must." I bite my bottom lip and let it go with a pop as his eyes trace my mouth.

Before my next breath, his hand is firmly grasped on the back of my head, tugging me toward him. Knee to knee, we press all over. I lean backward to accommodate our height difference, and eventually, he's lifting me so I can uncurl my legs from under me and wrap them around his hips.

I decide to undress myself fully, impatient as ever, and Matt takes my cue, freeing himself of his jeans.

"Love the tattoo, by the way." I rub his forearm after he lifts off his shirt. "It suits you. Like it's always been there."

"I got two," he says.

"Really?"

"This one and one on my butt."

I crawl around him on all fours and realize he's winding me up. "Jerk! I—"

He stops me with a spank that stings *just* right. He massages it with a wide palm before he hits again. I let out a mewling sort of cry, and he laughs darkly.

"I'm never going to get over how much you enjoy being spanked, manamea." He does it again, with the back of his fingertips, then massages as I moan, lowering my chest to the bed. "I bet if I looked right now, you'd be dripping down your leg." *Hit.*

Well, *now* I am.

"Matt—" I gasp as he brings a hand between my legs and cups me in his palm.

He hisses through his teeth before his hand twitches around me. "Going to fuck my good little fiancée now."

I shake with anticipation as he licks up my spine, his body moving over me like a shield.

"I want to look at you," I attempt to say between panted breaths. He sits up on his knees, and I roll onto my back and open my legs wide for him, unabashedly.

His jaw works, and he pulls at the roots of his hair with both hands, his elbows out to either side.

"Like what you see?" I tease, bringing my knees together.

He reaches out and pushes them apart. "You're testing my will." He rubs his chin, his eyes fixated on me.

"Stop holding back." I lick my lips and tilt my head to catch his eyes, which are glazed over with pure lust. "Be selfish, Matt. With me. Please. That's what I want. Take me. Have me."

His smile is crooked and devious. "Done."

With a grip on himself, he guides himself to my entrance and thrusts deeply until my legs begin to shake. He brings my ankles to his shoulders, then pins my thighs against him as he drives home with a power so fierce I have to press my teeth together to stop them from chattering.

I snake a hand between my thighs and circle my clit.

Matt's grunting wildly with every thrust, and I'm getting drunk off the sound of him unburdened. He's giving in to what he wants, and that's enough to get me close to orgasm. That and the intense pressure of him filling and retreating from me with each push and pull.

"It's like you were made for me," he grits out.

He's nearly primal. Darkened eyes and bared teeth. The sounds of nothing but slapping skin and gruff praise. "Good girl . . . Take it . . . That's it . . . So tight . . . Give it to me . . ."

Being the person he feels safe enough with to be selfish for once? For maybe the first time? It's more rewarding than all his whispered praises combined.

I come around him, gritting my teeth and crying, animalistic, with one hand on my pleasure and one hand in a vise grip around his wrist, as he holds my thigh against him.

I feel him finish, the warm heat of his release filling me as his movements stutter.

It's a fast rush that overwhelms my senses before I feel hollowed out, gasping as I realize he's pulled out of me. I reach for him, unable to open my eyes, and don't find him.

But he finds me, or rather—his mouth does.

I grip on to his hair as he flattens his tongue against my entrance, humming his approval at my taste. *Our* taste. It's too much but somehow not enough. I'm writhing, like I'm being electrocuted, but begging him not to stop.

His thumbs and fingers press into the back of my knees, holding me still as he brings me to another climax. He draws it out, leisurely licking and kissing until everything is *too* good and my body is soft all over. Without opening my eyes to the skylight above us, I see stars.

Then delicate movements as he gently lays me flat and tucks me into him. His nose presses into my hairline, and I feel him whisper against my forehead. All sorts of calming, gentle praises. "I love you. I missed you. You're perfect. Thank you. I love you. I love you. I love you."

When I feel my soul re-enter my body, I tilt up to look at him. My man. My Matt. My best friend and my lover. My partner and my helper. My fiancé. My person. My safe place.

I trail a lazy hand up the center of his chest, brushing the faint hint of hair and feeling his pulse race on my fingertips. "All my heart is yours, sir. It belongs to you, and with you it would remain, were fate to exile the rest of me from your presence forever."

"*Jane Eyre?*" he asks, and I nod against him.

"I reread it. Actually, I read a few of your books."

"Which ones?" he asks, drawing circles on my back.

"*Jane Eyre, The Count of Monte Cristo,* and the one I saw on your bedside table the night before our trip—*The Hobbit*."

He tickles my shoulder in slow swipes. "You've been busy."

"I needed you with me somehow." I sigh, leaning my ear to his chest.

He pulls me on top of him fully. His personal weighted blanket.

"I didn't care for Tolkien," I confess, voice mumbled into his neck.

"I'm going to pretend you didn't say that."

Then we drift off to sleep.

FORTY

WHAT WAS SUPPOSED TO BE A FORTY-HOUR JOURNEY spread across four days turned into a week-long drive home.

Matt's concern for our safety and those on the road meant that he'd declined my urge to give him road head several times and insisted we pull over to do the nasty. We never made it longer than a few hours before one of us *needed* to stop. I think we've had sex in almost every major city between Vancouver and Toronto at this point. Like a sexy pushpin map where we made up for lost time and whispered dirty litanies to each other in emptied parking lots.

But now, almost home, I look in the mirror of the bathroom and fix my hair, humming to myself, unable to stop smiling—even if I wanted to. The glow I've seen on my friends is so utterly and perfectly present across my face that I want to photograph it. Show it off alongside my gorgeous ring.

I've texted Chloe and talked with Emily on the phone, letting them know of our reunion and return, but neither know about our engagement. I wanted to tell them in person—with Matt.

We're parking the bus back at the shop—for now—and all our friends are ready to meet us there for a welcome home slash told-you-so party, complete with beer, wine, and pizza.

"Lane?" Matt shouts from the front seat.

"Yeah, bear?" I've been trying out new pet names. So far, the only one that feels right is *gorgeous,* but it makes Matt blush—which I love, but he doesn't.

"Simone snuck out again. She's biting my shoelace," he calls back.

"God dammit, Simone," I mutter to myself, closing my mascara. "One second!"

I grab a treat from the counter and woo her away from Matt's feet as he tries not to squish her under the gas pedal. "You're a problem child." I pick her up. "But we still love you."

Matt reaches out, eyes on the road, and scratches under her chin. "You look beautiful," he says, letting his eyes flow down my frame and back up when we stop at a red light. "That color suits you."

"Reminds me of the drive to your parents' place." I twirl in my dark green dress, similar to the emerald of Vancouver Island.

"I love it."

"Nervous?" I ask, noticing his leg bouncing.

"No. Excited."

"To tell everyone, or to be home?"

"Both. Tell everyone and see you home. Have you back."

"You've had me back for a week now." I wind my fingers through his hair.

"Yes, but now real life begins. Regular routines, the mundane."

I laugh cautiously. "That won't be boring? You won't get tired of me?"

"You? No, I don't think that's possible." He points to the shop's open front gate as we round the corner. "Here we go."

As we pull in, I see our friends sitting at a picnic table that *definitely* wasn't there when I left. That, or the grass under it. Or the planted trees and flowers. Or the string of lights between two lampposts. "Matt . . ." I sigh, my eyes brimming.

"I needed to keep busy somehow, right?" He reaches out and takes my hand in one of his as he puts the bus in park with the other. "One last surprise." He smiles warmly.

I hear cheering as Matt opens the door. Our friends storm the bus, and in the middle of a series of hugs and squeals of joy, one large gasp breaks through the noise.

"Oh my god!" Chloe covers her mouth. "Oh my—" She squeals, grabbing my hand.

"What?" Emily turns to me, and Matt lifts his hand too.

"You got *married?*" Em covers her mouth with both hands.

"No, not yet." Matt laughs as Chloe tugs my hand around, trying to see the pearl in a better light. "Lane proposed, then I did," he clarifies.

Shrieking from Chloe, a giddy laugh from Emily, and a knowing smirk from Warren. All the exact reactions I expected.

"Congratulations, brother." Amos chuckles, bringing Matt into a hug.

"L-l-ane!" Chloe struggles through one syllable. "Lane!" She laughs, shuffling Willow on her hip.

"Yane?" Willow asks.

"Yes, Simba?" I turn my attention to my niece.

"Are you and Uncle Matt getting married?"

"Yes, we are, baby," Matt answers while taking her from Chloe—who looks close to passing out from excitement.

"Dat's nice." Willow pats Matt's beard, and he laughs, leaning in to her touch.

Warren places a firm hand on his shoulder and gives Matt a *nice work* look, accompanied by a wink.

"Pizza?" I ask weakly. What I mean is *I've been cramped on this bus for seven hours and need to see what Matt's done, because from here, it looks incredible.*

"Outside." Emily wraps her arms around my middle from behind. "But this first."

"Aw, friend sandwich," I mumble, pulling Chloe into a hug with her unrelenting hold on my hand.

"We missed you," Em says, her chin digging into my collarbone.

"So much," Chloe says over the opposite shoulder.

"I missed you too." I sigh. "But things are good now. I'm not going anywhere." *Not perfect, but good.* We stay like that for a minute before they both release me with heavy sighs and we follow our men off the bus.

I can finally take it all in. He's made us a backyard—in the middle of an industrial lot. Grass, green and not at all patchy, a garden bed with wildflowers, a few empty planters next to it. A bench under a tall lamppost with string lights going in either direction, a few newly planted trees behind it, casting shade. I notice a small plaque on the bench and bring my trembling hand to my cheek.

In memory of Dominic Rothsford.

"Welcome home," Matt says, kissing my cheek.

"Matt . . ." I choke out a sob, looking around at this oasis he's created for me. "It's perfect." He holds me tighter. "I'm never leaving."

He laughs, kissing the top of my head. "That worked as planned." He scratches his chin, like he's looking at an unfinished piece of art. "Those planters aren't empty. They've got tulips in them. I thought about putting fake ones in but—"

"We can wait for spring. There's no rush." I pull away, wiping at tears. My friends circle us, each with their arms wrapped around their person, and Willow walks along the edge of the garden bed, balancing with her arms outstretched. "This is all I want. To do life, as much as we'll get, next to you," I whisper.

"Even in a parking lot?" he teases, curling me into his side, hand on hip.

"Wherever you are is where I want to be." I look up at him.

And I *know* now that no one and nothing is perfect—but this feels awfully close.

EPILOGUE

WE ARE GOING TO BE SO LATE.

"One more round. C'mon." Matt licks his lips and fixes the fold of his crisp linen collar.

"No. Admit defeat." I smile proudly across the table.

"Best out of six."

"Mattheus," I warn, packing the Scrabble tiles into their designated felt bag.

"I've been practicing on my phone and everything." He gently tosses his tile rack across the table with a *hint* of a tantrum.

"Sore loser."

He flicks his watch into place on his wrist, and I bite my lip without thought.

"Pervert," he chastises, holding out the box for me to lay the board in. "We do *not* have time for *that*."

"Wow, so you'd make time for another round of Scrabble but not to bang your wife on this table?"

"Don't say *bang*." He laughs with a disgruntled face of distaste. "It's so violent."

I roll my eyes with a lofty sigh. "Sorry." I clear my throat sarcastically. "You'd make time for another round of Scrabble but not to *make love* to your wife on this table?"

He considers his options, looking side to side, and nods. "Yeah." He stands, leaning over the table so his face is inches from mine. "And you're not my wife . . . yet."

"Ah, right, that." I tsk. "We should probably go take care of that."

He kisses my cheek and offers me his hand. I slip my newly manicured hand into his and use the other to flatten my dress as I stand.

Neither of us wanted the big wedding. The tuxedo and fluffy white ball gown. The caterer tastings, floral arrangements, invitations, and RSVPs. It wasn't for us. But we didn't want the courthouse either. We wanted our people with us. Our families. And, admittedly, *part* of me wanted the fluffy white dress.

Emily made me the *perfect* one. It's actually in two parts. A white silk dress with a low back all the way down to the base of my spine and a gorgeous detachable tulle skirt. It falls just above my knee, and I look fucking incredible. The veil was my mother's, hideous in its true eighties form. But I wouldn't want it any other way.

Matt chose a plum-colored suit jacket, which he's paired nicely with black pants and a traditional white button-down shirt. He left two buttons open, revealing a smattering of dark chest hair, per *my* request.

Emily, Amos, Chloe, Warren, Luke, and Willow all arrived in Vancouver yesterday morning—after a delayed flight due to a snowstorm. Two of Matt's siblings cannot make it and are video calling in, but all in all, our people *will* be here.

We leave my dad's office hand in hand and make our way toward the back set of stairs that lead into the kitchen—where Chloe awaits our signal.

"Don't you look gorgeous!" I tell her as my kitten heels tap loudly against the kitchen's tiled floor.

"Oh, Lane . . ." Chloe's eyes well with tears. "You look incredible." She gestures wildly with her palm at both Matt and me. "You both do. This is *so* you guys. It's perfect."

"We clean up pretty good." Matt twirls me around.

Chloe sighs adoringly, then collects herself with a steady inhale. "Okay. So"—she walks to the kitchen island—"bouquet." She hands me a lovely bundle of white tulips—fake ones, because it's the dead of winter. "Check." She mimes checking a box in the air. "Guests." *Check.* "They're mingling, but I'll go in and let them know it's time to take their seats."

"And the music?" I ask.

"All set up."

"Thank you, Chlo." I pull her into a side hug. "And after? The food and—"

"Emily's on it. Liz too," she whispers before we step away.

"Thank you so much." I pull her in for another brief hug.

"Ready?" I turn to look up at Matt, taking his hand in mine.

"So unbelievably ready." He smiles down at me. "Want nothing more."

I suspect that a bride should feel nervous, if not anxious, on her wedding day. Especially seconds before walking down the aisle. But I feel no such thing. I'm giddy with excitement and filled with confidence—my shoulders pushed back, my posture straight, my smile genuine.

And it's not just that I'm marrying my best friend, who's walking in next to me, but it's that I know what awaits us in the next room too.

The front room of my mother's home has been transformed into our ideal wedding venue. What was a plain white room with cathedral ceilings and dark wooden floors has become a cozy nest.

Mismatched chairs, benches, and couches from around the house, all gathered to accommodate the twenty-two guests, fill the space. One of Fetu's handcrafted knotted carpets, which she's teaching me to make, laid down to mark where we'll exchange our vows. White bunting draped across the ceiling, with fairy lights expertly hung by my best friends and their spouses. It's already dark outside, and the moon is most likely coming in through the skylights, illuminating the room in a soft white glow.

Matt squeezes my hand three times. I squeeze his back twice. I hear the door open just out of view and a mumble from the officiant that has guests rising from their seats and "Ain't No Mountain High Enough" begins playing.

Before we make our way toward the doors, Matt picks me up and spins me, laughing against my neck. I slap his shoulder playfully. "We have to go!" He lowers me, smiling impossibly wide, and nearly pulls my arm off running into the front room.

I feel my smile grow as I take it all in. All my favorite people in one place. Willow waves enthusiastically at us as we pass by, shimmying to the music in her Uncle Luke's arms. Simon with his arm clasped around Fetu's waist, looking adoringly at his son and me as we make our way toward the front. Fetu, wiping her happy tears with a handkerchief.

When we reach my mother in the front row and I hand her my bouquet, she holds me a little too long. Liz rubs Mom's back and clears her throat, and I wink at her over Mom's shoulder as Mom finally lets me go.

The ceremony passes in a sublime blur. The officiant my mother hired—with a hilarious mustache that Matt and I will *defi-*

nitely talk about later—tells us it's time to exchange our vows, and I feel my jaw tremble.

Matt's eyes go straight to it, and he squeezes both of my hands. *I've got you.*

I squeeze him back. *I know.*

I slowly remove my hands from his and reach out to Liz, who has safeguarded my vows since we wrote them together last night.

I unfold the paper delicately and clear my throat. I can't look at him—not yet—because then I won't get any of this out.

"Matt . . ." Oh, shit. I'm going to cry straightaway apparently. Whatever, it's my wedding, and I'll cry if I want to . . . that's how the song goes, right?

"Three years ago tonight, we shared our first kiss, and I panicked." A few people laugh, and it gives me a chance to sniff back tears. "I panicked for a lot of reasons. One, because you're definitely the most gorgeous person I've ever kissed. And two, because you sat with me that evening and talked to me like you'd never stop listening. You saw me. And that was the last thing I wanted."

I look up to the ceiling to gather myself but fail miserably. Matt's thumb grazes my cheek and catches one tear—which makes them pour out more.

I blow out a forceful breath. I've got to keep going. "You've shown me patience, kindness, faithfulness, and generosity in spades. You're a *good* man. A kind and honorable man. Not only do you show this with words, but actions. The way you care for me and our families is so"—my voice breaks—"beautiful. And I *know* my dad would have *adored* you."

I look up when I hear Matt hum, and he covers his mouth, his face wet with tears. "Oh my god, we're never going to get through this," I say through a pitchy whisper.

"We're so bad at this." He laughs through tears.

"I promise to love you forever. Simple as that. My love will not always be perfect. I won't always be kind; I won't always be generous; I won't always be rational—but I will love you every single day I have on this earth. And I will tell you I love you with my words and with my actions."

I grip my vows tighter in one hand and reach the other toward him. "I will help you rest when you feel the weight of the world on your shoulders. I will remind you of your worth when you have nothing left to give. I will be your wife, your best friend, and your partner in all things. Wherever life takes us."

I *did* it. I fold up the paper and pass it back to Liz, who holds my stare, pride shining in her eyes.

Matt pulls his lips between his teeth and reaches to his dad, who hands him an entire notebook.

"We're going to be here a while." He slaps his palm with the book, laughing. "Just kidding." He turns to the guests. "Lane was very clear that I had to be concise."

"Time's ticking," I tease with a wink.

He tilts his head, and his chest rises and falls as his eyes lock on me. They crease, warm and familiar and so full of love I can't help but melt.

"Lane. My manamea. My best friend . . . Unfortunately there aren't many words I haven't already used over the past two years to describe you or the love I have for you." He smiles and rubs his chin as he keeps his eyes on his notebook. "So, I will just talk about what I hope comes next. I hope that tomorrow, when we wake up, it feels like the first of an infinite number of mornings. I hope our days together feel slow and our years long. I hope time passes mercifully."

His voice cracks, and instinctively, I reach out my hand, right as he lowers his toward me.

"I hope to make you proud of your husband. I hope to make you proud to be my wife. I hope we never lose our spark. I hope that if we do, we remember how to get it back. I hope that we are content to build a life of our own design, whatever or wherever that may be."

He straightens, projecting his voice louder. "I want to take a second to acknowledge my mother's family. Anaru, Kalea, Hemi, Melika, and Kimo—and all our ancestors who I believe are with us this evening in spirit. I also want to acknowledge and extend my gratitude to your mother, Kathy"—he looks toward my mom, who's barely holding it together—"for welcoming me into your family so kindly, as well as your father, Dominic." He swallows. "For raising you to be the courageous, spontaneous, and fierce woman you are."

I blink back tears and squeeze his hand so tightly that he may never get it back—it's conjoined with mine now.

"Lane, I love you. Endlessly. Completely and with every piece of me. You're funny and kind and smart and truly the best Scrabble player I've ever encountered." He laughs and wipes a tear from his cheek. "I cannot wait to begin *our* story. The best is yet to come." He closes the notebook tenderly and hands it to his father, who grabs his shoulder and kisses his cheek.

Returning to hold my hand, he leans in to whisper. "There were a few lines I cut out that I'll read to you later." He winks, standing back into position.

"Can I kiss him yet?" I ask the officiant, loud enough for the guests to get a good chuckle out of it.

"Almost." Mustache man answers with a kind smile.

More words are said, but I'm no longer listening. Matt and I are so ready to kiss by the end of the legal matters and nonsense that we're both practically marching on the spot, tilting forward toward each other.

2 YEARS LATER

MATTHEUS

WHEN WE ARRIVE AT EMILY AND AMOS'S PLACE, ARMS filled with decorations and pulling a wagon of food, the sounds of summer greet us. Kids giggling, barbecue sizzling, music playing from a speaker, all doused in sunshine and perfect August weather.

The little boys currently being fostered by Em and Amos greet us with giggles under sticky, cotton candy–covered faces peeking through the fence.

"Mama Em! Mattilane is here!" Joshua laughs, because combining our names is *prime* six-year-old humor.

"And they have balloons," Malachi, Joshua's younger brother, adds, looking at Lane with wonder. *Can't say I blame him.*

"Hey! Come around!" Emily shouts from the other side of their gate. When Amos and Em finished the work on their house, the backyard was the last to be fixed up. I personally think they saved the best for last. A new deck, overflowing garden beds of flowers, and a decent field of grass for their foster kiddos to play in. There's also a firepit where we've all let countless hours of conversation burn away alongside firewood.

Lane curses under her breath at the gate, fighting with the latch, and it tugs on a knot in my stomach I've been trying to ignore all morning. She's not doing well today. She hasn't told me, but I know. My wife is not a mystery to me anymore. Thank fuck for that.

"Hey." I lean in close, my arm reaching over her shoulder to help. She drops her hand from the fence, and I unhook it. "You say the word; we go." I pull her hair away from her cheek and over her shoulder and rub my thumb on the pulse point of her neck. It's beating hard and fast enough that I can feel it.

She pats my wrist. "I need to be here. We both do."

"Okay," is all I say. Partly because Lane's already waltzing into the backyard like she's not got a care in the world, but also because I need to trust my wife to tell me when she can fight her own battles.

Six weeks ago, Lane was over a week late for her period. We've been diligent all these years not to get pregnant. But we've taken turns introducing the idea of having kids. All the while, we've gone back and forth as to which one of us wants them and which one of us couldn't imagine altering our nearly perfect life as just the two of us, our rabbit, Simone, and our home, Benedict Cumberbus.

Regardless, we never settled on a decision one way or another. But with Chloe being pregnant and Emily having two kids at home, I think Lane was starting to come around to the idea more and more. I had felt the conversation brewing again. One with a resolution, finally. Because I was feeling ready too.

Then she was late, and we foolishly allowed ourselves to dream for the three days before our doctor's appointment. With every passing hour, our excitement grew at the possibility of our family growing.

I took the morning off work for her appointment. I had

planned to suggest we go out for brunch to celebrate afterward. I had a bouquet of flowers in the trunk and a *MILF* shirt I couldn't resist buying at the store the night before.

Instead, three words hit us like a brick through a window. Primary ovarian insufficiency. Otherwise known as primary ovarian *failure,* I've since learned.

In layman's terms, Lane may never be able to get pregnant. Her body doesn't produce the typical amounts of estrogen or release eggs regularly.

And while we hadn't fully made up our minds about whether we were set to be the cool, child-free aunt and uncle *or* have a bus full of mini-me's, we thought we had time to decide. Naively, we thought we'd *get* to decide.

So as I watch my wife place a box wrapped in cartoon baby-animal gift wrap on a sparse table and begin setting up a onesie-decorating station with Emily, my heart twists and begins to crack.

Before I excuse myself from my game of catch with the boys to go check on her, I get hit with a ball. Joshua smiles mischievously.

"Ow," I emphasize, rubbing my shoulder. The kid has a good arm.

"Eye on the ball." He hits his glove, ready for me to throw it back.

"All right, shortstop. Cool it." I throw it straight into his glove but get hit again when I distractedly turn to see my wife smiling with Emily, decorating and chatting all the while. *She's okay. She'll let you know if she needs you,* I tell myself over and over until my knees unbuckle and I relax into our game.

An hour later, the guests have begun arriving and I find Lane in the kitchen, stirring pitchers of punch.

"Nice jugs," I say, shutting the patio door.

She rolls her eyes, smiling.

"Can I do anything?" I ask. *Please,* I add inside my thoughts.

"No, all good. You did your job already. Em's just glad you tuckered the boys out." Lane grabs a cutting board and a bag of lemons from the counter behind her.

"They've got so much energy."

"Willow will be here to keep them in line soon." Lane winks before slicing a lemon in half.

"Can I cut those?"

"Then what would I do?" She raises a brow, the corner of her lip going with it. But something's wrong; it's the flatness in her tone.

"Watch me do it and look pretty." I walk around the counter, wrapping my arms around her middle and letting my chin hit her shoulder. "Please let me help," I whisper into her hair.

"I need to keep busy." She leans her head against mine, still slicing lemons. "Got to keep moving."

That's her way sometimes. Emotions can't hit a moving target, she jokes. I don't like it. "Okay." I kiss her cheek and tighten my hold around her waist.

"I need my arms, Matt." She elbows me playfully, demonstrating how she needs full range of motion, and I release her begrudgingly.

"Fine." But I can't help but feel I need a task too. Need to be doing something to help her, to help this day progress faster until I can take her home and pry these feelings out of her. And, just for thinking that, I get hit with a wave of guilt. Our friends have no idea what's going on with Lane and me, and I shouldn't want their special day to end for our sake.

Warren and Chloe are expecting their first child together, though they've raised Chloe's sister Willow as their own. They deserve this happiness, this new beginning. They *deserve* a kick-ass baby shower and friends who want to give it to them more than anything. But it's hard. And becoming harder by the minute.

Warren's been unnervingly pleasant at work for the past eight months. And while our interns and customers are glad for it, it was slightly unsettling for me to see my normally surly friend so peppy. He talks about his son any chance he gets, from weird pregnancy facts to details about the type of juice that makes the baby kick so hard he can feel it.

Truthfully, since our diagnosis, I haven't been as keen to hear what fruit or vegetable the baby currently resembles or what Chloe's cravings have been.

"You hungry?" I ask, wishing Lane had cravings I could satisfy.

"Nope. I snuck some crackers and cheese from the food table when Em was convincing the boys to put on sunscreen."

"Okay."

"You going to keep hovering?" she asks, not looking up.

"Probably," I answer, shoving my hands into the pockets of my jeans.

"If I promise I'm okay, will that help?"

"Maybe."

"I'm okay." I notice she doesn't promise. "Are you?" she asks me, setting down the knife and beginning to drop lemons inside the pitchers.

Not really. I want you to have every option in life available. I want you to never worry about anything and to feel in control. Plus, I'm starting to think I wanted a somehow-even-smaller version of you to hold, comfort, and raise with you. Maybe a few of them, actually. I'm wondering if I'd realized this earlier, we'd have been luckier with our timing. I'm wildly jealous of our friends and dreading seeing Chloe's giant bump and glowing smile. I wish it was your stomach everyone was reaching out to pet. Our baby being celebrated. I wish it was us. I don't know how to make it all okay, and I'm worried you won't let me try.

"Yeah, all good." I smile, then look over my shoulder toward the sound of cheering from the guests outside. Warren, Chloe, and Willow walk in, hand-in-hand-in-hand, and I feel my shoulders relax at the view of our friends beaming in their joy. I suddenly remember that what I was dreading was the arrival of our best friends, and I feel a little stupid for it.

"It's go-time," Lane says, picking up two pitchers and gesturing for me to do the same.

I allow myself to notice for the first time today that she's made an obvious effort in her appearance. She's wearing a black sundress with little birds on it, which seems quite fitting for "Baby Dove," as we've all been referring to the baby throughout Chloe's pregnancy. Her lilac-colored hair is curled, and her makeup is done with a bright pink lip.

"You look beautiful, manamea." I clear my throat. "Sorry I didn't say that earlier. You look stunning today."

She smiles proudly, tilting her chin up. "Thank you, bear." Then she walks to my side. "You look sexy, as usual." She kisses my bicep on her way out the door. "Come on," she calls over her shoulder from the deck. I grab the rest of the pitchers and follow her.

Hours later, I'm a sweating, heaving mess at the end of the garden with our niece and nephews. "No," I beg. "Please." The kids bounce around me on the trampoline.

"Get up!" Willow commands, bouncing over my stomach with such velocity I wince, bracing for impact. The boys are summoned by Amos, and they run off.

"I can't jump anymore. Uncle Matty is getting old," I tell Willow.

"Fine." She stops, does a singular bounce, then falls onto her back next to me with a jolt. "Then I'll lay down with you."

"Thank you." I sigh, laying my hands on my stomach. I should not have eaten two burgers and platefuls of various other snacks before jumping on here, but my body seemed to crave the comfort of food today. "Are you excited about having a baby brother?" I ask her.

"I mean, I guess? It's just a baby." Willow is never one to mince words, much like her father. "They're going to let me name him."

A seven-year-old naming a baby. This should be good. "Oh, yeah? What name were you thinking?"

"Rowan."

I pout my bottom lip, nodding. "Huh, that's actually pretty good."

"There was a Rowan in my class, but he might not be in my new class this year. Also! I can sing him "Row, Row, Row Your Boat," and he can sail away from me if he's got a poopy diaper." She giggles.

"Babies do tend to get poopy." *They also don't usually sail,* I think to myself.

"Are you and Auntie going to have a baby?" She puts her little hand on my stomach, and I wonder if I appear pregnant and laugh.

"I don't know." I pat her hand and gently remove it.

"Maybe don't. Then I can stay your favorite forever," she says before getting up in a series of unnecessary sporadic movements and running across the backyard right before I hear the words, "Willow! Cake!" shouted by Warren.

"She knew," I mumble to myself. "Kid has a sixth sense for cake."

"Bear?" I sit up at the sound of my wife's voice.

She fights a smile. "Without a kid in there with you, you're sort of the weird adult man on the trampoline, avoiding the party."

"It's peaceful in here." I lie back down.

The trampoline squeaks as Lane's body falls next to me. She shuffles her hip against mine, and I lay my arm under her head to use as a pillow. "Hmm. Yeah, this *is* nice."

"Willow told me what they're going to name the baby."

"Rowan?" Lane asks.

"Aw, I was hoping I had breaking news."

"Sorry, forgot to tell you. Chloe told Em and me last week." She sits up, placing her hand softly on my cheek. "Rowan Luke Dove."

I grumble.

"Be nice." She pats my cheek, but it's more of a very polite series of slaps. "You love Luke."

I loved Luke an awful lot more before I walked in on him and my baby sister in a position permanently scarred into my brain.

"Plus, Tabitha seems to have moved on," Lane adds, lying back down and curling into my side.

"We should invite her for Christmas again this year. I don't like her spending it alone in the city."

"She isn't alone. Tabs has never met a stranger."

"She should be with family."

"Okay, obviously we'll invite her. She just might not come if she knows Luke is coming home for winter break too."

"Does he have to?" I ask under my breath.

"Again, be nice."

I decide to let sleeping dogs lie and stare up at the clouds. We stay there quietly for a few minutes, wrapped up in each other in the private corner of the backyard. Lane rubs slow circles around my belly, almost in an unconscious, familiar pattern at this point. I rub at her hairline with my thumb as she sighs contentedly.

"So, I was thinking . . ." Lane says softly.

"Uh-oh."

"Ha-ha." She sits up, crossing her legs. That's how I know Lane means business, so I copy her, sitting up and leaning back on my palms. "Let's pull the goalie."

"What?" I ask.

"Let's tempt the fates."

I blink at her.

"Roll the dice."

"I'm really not following here." I wipe sweat off my forehead onto my sleeve.

The sound of her breathy laugh goes straight to my dick, as usual. I swallow in resistance. Unfortunately, even after all this time, it can never learn the proper time or place for *that* response where Lane is concerned.

"I'm saying"—she wiggles her eyebrows—"let's ditch the birth control—the pills, the condoms, all of it."

"Oh," is all I manage to say. "But—"

"I know what the doctor said. I know chances are slim regardless. I know there are more medical routes we could try, but that just doesn't feel right. I do think, though, that we should just . . . not prevent it." She shrugs, eyes searching for my reaction. "Let's give it the old college try. If it happens, it's supposed to happen, you know?"

"You're sure? Because it *could*."

"If this last month has taught me anything, it's that I'm not sure at all. But I'm also not sure about not being sure . . . does that make sense?"

"You want the universe to decide." My brows furrow, but I relax when Lane nods.

"Giving up control of it feels like controlling it." She bites her thumb and then presses it into her lap. "Leah seemed to think it was a healthy approach."

"You talked to your therapist before me?"

"Honey, if I didn't do that most of the time, we'd be divorced." I chuckle. "Fair."

"So?" she asks, eyes hopeful and wide.

I try to suppress a smile. "I mean . . ." I tsk. "Only if we *really* try. Like, we have to absolutely do our best to give it a fair shot. Really put in the work, you know? I'm talking no sleep, daily, diligent—"

Lane's smile bursts from her and hits me in the chest. If this is what she wants, I'll give it to her. I'd give her anything to keep her smiling.

"Oh, we are going to try *a lot*." Lane bites her lip after interrupting me. "A gross, filthy, *obscene* amount of trying." She giggles.

"How gross are we talking?" I fight back a laugh, leaning in.

"Babe, I'm gonna rock your world." She kisses me and nips my lip just enough that I'm now going to have to recover before returning to the party.

When she slides her tongue against mine, I break our kiss before we get too heated. There's something I need to say first. "Manamea . . ."

Lane whines, trying to press her lips against my rigid ones. "Lane . . ." I whisper against her, and she pulls back with a mischievous grin. "You know, either way, I'm so happy. Right?"

"I know." She presses her forehead into mine, nodding against me. "Me too."

"If it's *just* us, forever, that's still a dream come true."

I feel the smile crease her forehead and can't help but smile too. She hums from the back of her throat, her horny-tell, and I'm not sure I'm strong enough to fight off the kiss I think she's about to hit me with.

"Want to go fuck in Emily's new bathroom?" she whispers.

I think of the giant mirror above their vanity I helped install and nearly black out with the onslaught of lust-filled images— bending her over the sink; watching her come undone—rushing in.

"Most definitely," I answer. "For the sake of our efforts, of course."

"Of course." She giggles, attempting to pull me off the trampoline after her, despite being double her size.

And while we try to compose ourselves and walk through the crowd as if we're not about to defile a brand-new bathroom, one thought sticks and relaxes me for the first time all day. We're going to be okay. Either way.

ACKNOWLEDGMENTS

Thank you for reading *Next to You*! If you enjoyed it, please consider leaving a review.

I want to thank my incredible Beta readers, who helped polish this story with such helpful, diligent comments—Ray, Flic, Julia, Frankie, Kirsten, Laura, Sophie, Kristen, Nellie, Clare, and Marianne. My critique partner extraordinaire, Christina, and my *not-yet-manager* Tabitha who both workshopped this book and encouraged me away from many meltdowns with tender loving care. And, of course, my work wife, Tarah DeWitt, who cheers me on and writes books that inspire me.

I also want to thank all the ARC readers, members of the *Bookstagram* and TikTok's bookish community who welcomed me with open arms following my debut. I especially want to name the brilliant content creators Janni, Brittany, Lexi, Stacy, Elan, Amani, Ali, Megs, Crystal, Nikki, Kyla, Kelsey, Anna, Carlina, Jaci, and Jamie, who've been huge cheerleaders of my work online and in messages.

My husband, Ben, who provides more patience than one

human should possibly wield and talks about these characters like they're our friends and not people I made up. I promise I will soon read your favorite book, *The Count of Monte Cristo,* instead of just writing about it.

Our families for offering childcare, support, and encouragement throughout. Specifically my father-in-law, who retired and then immediately gave me days to write by watching my kids, and my mom, who loves to babysit and peddle my "sexy books" to all her friends (hello to you all). And Abi, who is always just one phone call away and really is my family too.

A massive thank-you to my editor, Beth, from VB edits, who is phenomenal at what she does and a joy to work with.

I also want to acknowledge myself this time around (bear with me). I wrote this book at the tail end of a pandemic, with two young kids home *constantly* over the summer, while promoting my first book. It was really freaking hard to be an author *and* mom full-time—and I'm proud that I tried my best to do both without having a *complete* breakdown.

Last, to anyone who has lost a loved one, suffered through trauma, dealt with anxiety, agoraphobia, depression, or any mental illness and keeps fighting through it, I'm proud of you. Keep kicking dragon ass—you'll get your happy ending, I promise.

* * *

ADDITION UPON RE-RELEASE:

Next to You was originally self-published in November of 2022 before Dell picked it up along with my other two novels, *Next of Kin* and *Out on a Limb*. So, I'd love to take this opportunity to thank the folks who made it possible for Matt and Lane to land on bookstores' shelves for the very first time. First, my agent, Jessica Alvarez, and the entire Bookends team. I am so grateful for your support, encouragement, hard work, and dedication. I'm immensely glad to have you in my corner. I'd also really like to thank the team at Penguin Random House (Dell) for all their kindness, passion, and excitement for these re-releases. My most wonderful editor, Shauna Summers, who by saying yes to my books, past and future, has made my dreams come true tenfold. Huge thank-you as well to Mae Martinez, Ada Yonenaka, Kathryn Jones, Taylor Noel, Brianna Kusilek, and Megan Whalen as well as everyone behind the scenes at Dell. I'd also like to thank Leni Kauffman for this stunning new cover and Lyla Sage and Hannah Grace for their generous words of support and friendship.

Keep reading for an excerpt of
Hannah Bonam-Young's

Out on a Limb

ONE

"DID YOU KNOW THIS SONG MIGHT BE ABOUT AN ORGY?"
I ask the witch standing next to the punch bowl, pointing toward
the speaker.

"What?" she shouts, using tar-black talons to pull her willowy
silver wig away from her ear.

"The song—'Monster Mash.'" I point toward the speaker
again.

"What about it?" she asks, louder.

"An orgy!" I yell just as the music comes to an abrupt stop—my
friend and host of the evening, Sarah, hopping onto a dining chair
to address her guests.

"No, thanks . . ." Witch woman sends daggers my way as she
slowly turns around and walks, funnily enough, toward the archway decorated in bloodied weapons.

"You should be so lucky," I mutter under my breath as I fill my
cup with an undisclosed neon-green substance, avoiding the
floating candied eyeballs successfully.

Sarah, my lifelong best friend, is giving her yearly *thank you so much for coming to my Halloween party; it's the only thing I care about* speech while I'm debating about whether anyone is secretly keeping track of how many hot-dog-mummies I've eaten thus far.

Nah. And so I reach for another.

"Aye aye, Captain Winnifred!"

Fuck, I've been spotted. I drop the mummy into my drink and cover the top of my cup with my hand.

"You okay?" Caleb, Sarah's husband, asks, eyeing my cup with suspicion.

"Never been better," I chime sweetly. "It's another successful year," I say, admiring their home, decorated with professional precision.

Caleb does the same, and when his expression turns to subtle pride and admiration for his wife's work, I place a bet to the universe that the next three words out of his mouth will be . . .

"Anything Sarah wants," we say in unison. He smiles into the top of his beer with a hint of guilty shyness, but mostly resolve. Sarah and Caleb met in the ninth grade. He's been carrying her textbooks, literally and metaphorically, since.

I love Caleb. He's like a brother to me. A brother-in-law if Sarah and I were *actually* sisters like we used to boldly claim (see: lie) in school. Turns out, according to a DNA test a few years back, we're fourth cousins once removed. Sarah simply says we're cousins now, when given the chance.

"You know, my friend Robbie is here. I thought I might introduce you," Caleb says after a long sip of his beer.

Yeah, absolutely not.

I've been successfully avoiding the guys Caleb wants to set me up with since my date with his buddy from work. Winston cried while describing his—*very much alive*—mother and the "beautiful bond" they shared. He also brought me an orchid, which could have been a sweet gesture—I do love plants. Unfortunately, it was in a large ceramic bowl with rocks and bark, and it weighed a ton. I couldn't just put it on the ground, lest a server trip over it and meet an untimely death, so it had to sit on the table between us—blocking our view of each other. Then, after a dull dinner, I had to carry it home with me, clinging to it in the back of the taxi as I wrote a kind but firm let's-not-do-this-again text.

If anything, that date only solidified my desire to remain casual and stick to dating apps where I could properly vet the men for myself.

"Maybe later," I answer Caleb. "I'm just waiting to talk to our hostess." I tilt my chin toward Sarah, who's dressed as the Princess Buttercup to Caleb's Westley.

"Okay, fine. This one is different, though. He even has a dead mom," Caleb adds far too excitedly.

"Oh, bonus!" I say, matching his energy. "I love when their mom is dead. It makes things so much easier around the holidays."

Caleb laughs, turning to fill a cup with lime punch. "Here." He holds it out to me before taking my mummified drink and tossing it into the trash can. "Eat however much you want, Win."

I take the drink, leaning toward him. "That might be the sexiest thing you have ever said to me, Caleb."

Just then, someone slaps my ass. "Is he flirting with you again? God, I've told you both so many times—if you're going to have an affair, at least be discreet."

"Buttercup! So nice of you to join us," I say, smiling broadly.

"Love the costume . . . again." Sarah sighs, pointing with a limp wrist to my elaborate pirate getup.

"Until I grow a hand, this will still be prime comedy." I jab her boob with my hook until she giggles, swatting me away.

"We have to go talk to a bunch of people, but do you want to sleep over tonight? I made up the spare bedroom and—"

"Yes, I will help clean up. I do it every year, babe," I interrupt. "Go! Entertain your masses."

Sarah jumbles the words *thank-you-you're-the-best* into one long sequence as she tugs Caleb away like an extremely willing puppy on a leash.

"Great costumes," an exceptionally drunk woman dressed as a red crayon slurs, walking toward me. The blue crayon next to her adds, "Think you might win the couples' contest," as they pass by.

Couples costume? Me? Single Winnie? Puh-lease.

They must have mistaken Caleb for a pirate and my betrothed. Westley was the Dread Pirate Roberts, after all. So it's not a far off presumption. But my pirate style is a lot more of your classic wench-whore. My boobs are practically earrings at this height, and my fishnet stockings are ripped from years of rewear, giving them the perfect *accidentally* slutty look. My waist is cinched with a wide pleather belt, and I've tied a red bandanna around my shoulder-length black hair. That's a new addition after my accompanying pirate's hat was lost during last year's debauchery. May she rest in peace.

I will keep wearing this costume until the joke gets old. That wasn't a lie. But it's also because—let's be real—I look hot in it. Additionally, I'm too broke to buy something new. But let's not talk about that.

There's another layer of Sarah's genius. Lock down the cutest computer geek as early as possible, make them fall madly in love with you, and then wait for them to become filthy rich. Now Sarah's the fun friend full time. Party hostess, event planner, voracious reader, a childless housewife with a maid. She's currently trying to decide between themes for *my* thirtieth birthday party, which still isn't for another eighteen months.

"Pardon me?" a low, sardonic voice calls from behind me, making me turn.

Oh, *there* he is. The other pirate I've been unknowingly paired with. Though this one, I would certainly not make walk the plank.

My first thought? He's tall. Really tall. As if his body was stretched out with a rolling pin before being placed into whatever magical golden boy oven he was baked in. He's got that tousled, nineties-boy-band, middle-parted hair that's suddenly back in style. It's dark blond, which I can choose to forgive. He has a crooked smile that says *get out while you can* under a not-crooked but rugged nose and soft eyes. The juxtaposition of which is strikingly adorable.

"I'm so sorry," he says without any sincerity, "but one of us has to change."

"Oh my god," I say, flattening my skirt before resting my hands on my waist. "This is so embarrassing . . . What are the odds?"

"Right? I mean there's no way either of us is winning the singles costume contest this way and"—he leans in to whisper by bending over at the waist, and he's *still* taller than me—"I'm not wearing anything under this."

I fight the laugh, not wanting this bit to end. I so rarely get a new sparring partner. Never one this cute.

"Well, that's unfortunate. You should have planned better. I have a few costumes under this one."

The corner of his lip twitches, but he seems to resist giving me any reaction beyond that. Challenge accepted.

"Such as?" he asks, crossing his arms over his chest.

"A Viking," I answer.

"Now that you mention it, I do see a horn peeking out just a little." He motions to the side of my head with a bent finger.

"That's actually standard issue for all of Satan's spawn, but I could see how you got confused."

"Concerning. What else?"

"A sexy maid, of course," I say, batting my lashes.

"Well, that I have to see," he quips back far too quickly.

Here, I think, is where I win the laugh-off we're pretending not to have. Shock value always wins.

"But I must insist on keeping the pirate costume, I'm afraid. You see"—I let go of the hook's inner handle and pull it away in my left hand, revealing my smaller, less-developed right hand underneath—"I am in need of a hook." I wave at him mockingly, my tiny, curled fingers, shorter than the first knuckle, waggling as best as they can.

He doesn't break like I want him to. But he *does* grin mischievously. His eyes crackle with humor, pulling me in at a concerning speed. I'd be frustrated if his expression wasn't so damn intriguing. Something about his amusement signals that, perhaps, he's one step ahead of me.

"Oh, I see. Well, then . . . maybe we can come to some sort of compromise." He sticks out his foot between us.

You've got to be joking.

TWO

HE'S GOT A PROSTHETIC LEG. IT'S COVERED, LOOSELY, in a vinyl sticker made to look like wood, the kind you'd use to line your kitchen shelves, giving the illusion of a pirate's peg-leg underneath black trousers he has tied up at the knee with thin, corded leather rope.

"God dammit!" I yell. Which finally gets him to laugh. And it's a great one too. A hearty, deep, boisterous sound from the back of his throat that makes his jaw tense and his neck jump. Uninhibited. And, dare I say, sexy.

"I really felt like I was going to win this round," I say, my voice unsteady.

He hasn't stopped laughing—harder than I am, actually. I'm not used to that, and it's honestly refreshing. I've been told I laugh obnoxiously loud. Some have even gone so far as to compare me to a baby seal calling for its mother. *Some* meaning more than one person—in two separate instances—have expressed that exact sentiment.

"This is a couple's costume. The crayons were right," I say through breathless fits of joy.

He clutches his chest as if to steady himself, his laughter finally beginning to die down. Then I'm treated to the view of a boyish, tilted smile and sincere eyes sweeping over me from head to toe and back again.

I wonder if he likes what he sees. Actually, I'm *hoping* he likes what he sees. Because I certainly like what he's got going on. The longer he looks me up and down, the more I consider him approving of my appearance.

My black not-quite-straight but not-quite-curly shoulder-length hair. My thin eyebrows from merciless plucking in my teenage years. My sharp-edged nose, with a simple gold piercing on the left nostril, set between glacier blue eyes. My body is shoved and tucked into this costume to prop up my tits and shrink my waist, but that's mostly illusion.

I would describe my frame as fairly average. I enjoy long walks, swimming, and dancing, but I equally love rainy days plastered to the couch, pastries, and overly sweetened coffees. My arms and back are strong and sculpted from years of training in butterfly and breast strokes, but my hips and stomach hold the shape of a well-fed, comfortable woman. I don't try to force my body to be something or deprive it of pleasures. It just *is*. And I like it, *enough*, as is.

But what does this seemingly perfect specimen before me look like on an average day? He strikes me as someone who grew up beautiful. Something in the small tilt of arrogance of his chin combined with the naive sweetness in his smile that I wish wasn't so disarming. He's probably a foot taller than me, and I can't help but wonder how hard I'd have to yank on his pleated pirate blouse to bring his lips down to mine.

"I'm Bo." He extends his left hand—which my body hears as *would you like me to fuck you?* Because there's nothing more awkward than shaking with my right hand and *nothing* more attractive than a man who could have anticipated that.

I shake his hand enthusiastically. "Win."

"Is that short for something?" he asks, dropping his hand and sliding it into his trouser pocket.

"Winnifred, but no one really calls me that. What about you?" I make a point to emphasize the stretch of my neck, staring up at him as if he's some sort of fairy-tale giant. "Are you tall for something?"

He can't *stop* laughing now. I can't stop wanting to make him.

"What?" he asks, eyes lit with enjoyment.

"Seriously, what are you? Nine feet tall?"

"Six."

"Six *what* though?"

"Six-five."

"Wildly unnecessary for daily life. Do you play basketball?"

"Eh, used to." His smile falters only a touch—but I notice. I notice, too, that he—perhaps subconsciously—moves to rub his knee, just above where his prosthesis begins.

I wince. "Sorry," I offer plainly. "I was born with my hand. So I stupidly forget other people—"

"No worries," he interrupts me, smiling with his chin pushed out.

"I ruined that. But this was nice before then, wasn't it?"

He looks away, smirking yet visibly shy, his eyes shifting and his body softly swaying. "It can still be nice. I could even the score? Make fun of your hand, if you'd like?" he offers, clearly unserious.

"Yes, please do. That would actually help a lot," I say, calling his bluff.

He turns to face me, staring me down with crescent eyes and an ever-growing smile that has the blood rushing to the surface of my skin. I raise a brow in challenge when he appears to be calculating his next steps, his head tilting to the side.

"All right." Bo holds out his palm, then crooks two fingers, gesturing for me to move closer. "Let me see it then."

I narrow my eyes on him playfully as I present my smaller hand to him, placing it in his open palm that is about double the size of mine. I swallow on impact, the brushing of our skin shooting sparks up my veins.

"Shit . . ." he whispers under his breath, turning it over with a grip on my wrist that I *love*. "It's adorable," he says, studying it intently. Then he tuts and lets go, practically tossing it aside. "What am I supposed to say?"

"Right?" I agree, throwing both arms up in the air. "It's impossible to make fun of. It's too damn cute. It's official. I've ruined the evening."

"The best I had was a sarcastic 'nice hand, *Finding Nemo*,' but that's sort of endearing, isn't it?"

"He's an icon," I agree.

"I loved that little fish." He rubs the back of his neck, looking past the archway and hallway to our left. "Want to sit?"

I nod, leading the way to the tufted yellow two-seater couch in Sarah's den. The walls are covered in Sarah's many books and maps of various lakes up in Northern Ontario. It's a cottage-inspired room. Because rich people have themed parties *and* rooms.

"So how do you know Sarah and Caleb?" I ask, curling my legs under me to face him. This close to Bo, I can see that his eyes are hazel with the smallest smattering of green. He's got more stubble than I originally noticed, but that's because it's fairer than his hair. He also smells *very* good. Like cinnamon and something else that's musky and warm and delicious. Like someone who could build a campfire and bake me a birthday cake too.

I keep studying him unabashedly. I can't help it, so I don't resist. And, eventually, when my eyes leave his *surprisingly* attractive collection of costume rings below his black painted nails, I realize he's looking straight down my blouse. He's doing some unabashed admiring of his own.

I smile to myself, pride lifting my shoulders and, in turn, my chest. I give him a few more seconds of leering before I clear my throat delicately.

"Sorry." He shakes himself. "What did you say?" He blinks like a caught, guilty man.

"Shameless!" I cry out, laughing. "You *ogled* me."

He chuckles nervously. "I know, fuck, sorry. I've never—well, I've never forgotten to pretend I'm not checking someone out before." He cringes bashfully, the corner of his lips still upturned.

"This costume has an intended purpose." I shrug, fiddling with the hem of my skirt.

"I really am sorry. I'm not—"

"How do they look?" I ask, interrupting him.

He looks up to the ceiling as if he's searching for some deity to help him handle me. I like that a lot.

I watch as a slow smile forms, the corner of his bottom lip tucked between his teeth. "They, like every other part of you, look great," he says slowly. Now it's his turn to clear his throat when I'm left blushing with my eyes stuck on his face. "But . . . what *did* you ask?"

I fumble, forgetting everything I said. But when I look around the room, blinking until I focus on my surroundings, I remember whose house I'm in and, therefore, what I asked. "How do you know Sarah and Caleb?"

Bo shuffles back against the couch, his hand playing mindlessly with the loose, ruffled collar of his shirt, tugging it away from his neck. "Caleb and I met through a mutual friend about six years ago. We reconnected earlier this year for a work thing. He's a good guy. What about you?"

"I've known Sarah my whole life. Our moms were best friends in high school and they both got knocked up accidentally during their senior year. They raised us together as pseudo-siblings."

"Damn, so you've known Caleb since—"

"Grade nine, yeah," I interrupt. "We all went to the same high school. I've been third wheelin' ever since."

"Third wheeling," he repeats. "So, you're not . . ." His smile quirks to one side. "I was going to ask if you were here with anyone, but let me rephrase. Is there someone who would deck me for checking you out the way I just did?"

"Nope." I cover my smile with a curled finger, tracing my knuckle along my lip before I gather my confidence once again. "No one. Here or in *any* room." That sounded a lot more suggestive than I intended, but it works in my favor when I notice his smile inching back up and his eyes darting to my lips for a second.

"Any room." He nods, chin tilted up. "Noted."

"What about you? Have a girlfriend I should know about?" I ask before swallowing.

He looks offended that I'd even suggest such a thing, his brows jolting upward. "No!"

"You'd not be the first unavailable guy to act totally available," I argue. My ex, for one, did that often.

"Fair." He settles down. "No, no girlfriend. Here or in *any* room," he taunts.

"Right." I get comfortable, leaning against the couch—pushing my breasts together, which Bo briefly makes note of. "Then . . . tell me about yourself. Who are you?"

"Why does that question always feel so intimidating?" He brushes his knuckles against his cheek, swiping his thumb along his jaw.

"Because human experience cannot be summed up in a few sentences," I offer, "but it's still polite to try."

He nods, side-eyeing me in a totally curious, stirring way that seems effortless to him despite the way it makes my heart pound. "Fair enough," he begins. "I'm twenty-nine. I'm a financial analyst." He puts up a hand, as if to stop me from interrupting—which I *was* going to do. "I know, it's a riveting career choice, but I actually love it." He scratches his nose with the back of his thumb, looking sideways across the room. "I'm an only child," he adds. "My father lives in France, so I don't see him all that often. But he's, rather pathetically, my best friend. My mother passed away when I was young." He laughs dryly, as if maybe he's unsure of whether he's oversharing.

"Uh . . . I worked as a barista through university, and it made me agonizingly pretentious about coffee. When I was a teenager, I read a book about healthy brain habits, and now I do a sudoku puzzle every day because I'm paranoid about my brain rotting. My favorite animals are dogs, but I've never had one as a pet. Um, my favorite color is purple?" he asks, as if he's unsure of where to stop.

"That was great, thank you," I say.

"Yeah? I pass?"

"Yes, very informative. Though I do have some follow-up questions."

"Don't you have to tell me about yourself first?" Bo asks, raising one brow.

"Oh, right, okay," I say, reaching for the cup that I placed on the table in front of us.

Bo waits for me to speak, his eyes intently focused as he leans farther against the back of the couch.

"I'm twenty-eight." I take a sip of my drink. "I work at a café, so I'm *also* a bit of a coffee snob. I work as a lifeguard seasonally, which I love. I'd spend my whole life outdoors if I could. My mother used to affectionately refer to me as her pet squirrel because of that *and* because I tend to hoard things. Currently, that's plants. My mom lives in Florida now with a string of boyfriends who are nice enough. . . . I try to visit her once a year, but we aren't exactly close. I never met my dad. And . . ." I try to think of one last thing. "Oh, *my* favorite color is green."

"Well, it's good to meet you, Fred."

"Please don't call me that," I say forcibly, half joking.

"What? Why not?" He looks comically offended.

"It's not a particularly sexy name," I say. "Winnifred is bad enough, but *Fred*? I sound like the creepy uncle you don't invite to Thanksgiving."

"Agree to disagree."

"Imagine crying out 'Fred' in the bedroom." His smirk grows, and I glare at him, deciding to make my point clear. "Oh, Fred." I moan. "Yes, Fred!" I cry, probably a bit too loudly, in fake passion. "It's awful." A few of the other party guests, confused and perhaps the tiniest bit offended, turn toward us. I salute them before they go back to their own conversations, my eyes held on Bo.

It's horribly cliché, but his smile is beaming—far brighter than the sun. I feel myself bloom with it, as if it's my own personal version of photosynthesis.

"Why are you looking at me like that?" I ask, feeling suddenly shy.

"You're funny," he says matter-of-factly, his expression remaining.

Huh.

I do my best to look around the room, pretending the other guests and their costumes are suddenly much more interesting to me. I'm hyperaware that I'm blushing at the compliment and wishing, desperately, that I could stop.

When I do finally look back, Bo's attention is focused on the back of the tufted couch. With his hand around the top of my seat, the tip of his thumb traces one of the fabric buttons in a small, circular motion over and over.

I shouldn't be affected by it, and I'll deny it if ever confronted, but there's something inherently sexual about the motion. I watch, feeling far too enraptured, as he circles the button tenderly. My throat tenses as my lips part, imagining his thumb working *me* over in a similar way. It's been months since a date went well enough that I allowed a man to touch me like that—not that it was all that great when he did. Still, judging by my quickened breaths, I think I'd let Bo give it a try.

"So," Bo says, dragging my gaze from the button toward his face, "you're not here with anyone. . . ."

"Is that a question?" I ask, regaining my voice with a noticeable rasp.

He rolls his eyes. I like that too.

"I suppose," he says, elongating the word, "the question is: Why?"

"Oh, so we've gotten to the *What are your faults?* part of the evening?" I ask.

"I was thinking more along the lines of *How is someone like you single?* but *sure*," he says.

"Ah, well, thanks." Despite my sarcasm, I feel my face heat again and curse myself for it. Three blushes in one evening? It has to be a record. One that I hope to never beat. "Honestly, the answer isn't all that interesting. I'm just not looking for anything permanent. I've been told by Sarah that I'm independent to a fault."

What I don't say is that I grew up watching my mom bring home loser after loser, knowing damn well we'd all be better off without them. It only took her boyfriends a few weeks into dating before they started acting like they had some sort of authority over her—*our*—life. They usually started off small, like my mom's favorite brand of coffee being switched out for their preference. Then it slowly escalated. Our soap-opera evening marathons became *well, sweetie, the game is on. Why don't you go finish up your homework in your room?* Or *no, we're not having tacos tonight. Insert-boyfriend's-name-here doesn't like them.* Then, eventually, they'd leave, and we'd reset. Sarah, her mom, and I would enjoy the brief interim before Mom's next man came through, and then we'd look after Mom when that inevitably went to shit again. Because of this, I learned quickly that in order to preserve the life I wanted, I had to avoid inviting a man in.

But, like most hopeless-romantic idiots, I forgot my self-appointed golden rule in my early twenties and moved in with my boyfriend Jack—who wanted *everything* his way and didn't care how he had to act to have it. That, of course, also ended terribly. I've been picking up the pieces since. My self-esteem and life plans are still, mostly, in shambles.

"What about you?" I ask. "In search of a wife?"

"No." Bo laughs out, his eyes flicking up to the ceiling momentarily. "I am not."

"Well, that's certainly . . . compatible." I chew my bottom lip, hoping he catches my not-so-subtle suggestion.

He catches it, all right, and stares at me a little *too* long. To the point where I start to feel my heartbeat pulsating in my neck. I wanted this response, sure, but for some reason, from Bo, it feels a little overwhelming. Perhaps it's the way his eyes search my face like he's trying to place me. Like we've met before. Or maybe as if he can't believe we haven't.

Whatever this *look* is, I need it to stop. It's causing too much blood to rush to my head—making me warm and flustered and dizzy.

"I like your pirate's leg," I say in a truly horrific attempt to take the attention off me. "I-I meant—your costume. Not just your leg, obviously. The whole thing," I say, floundering.

"Oh, well, good. I was worried you only wanted me for my leg for a second," he teases.

I choose to ignore his flippant use of the words *wanted me* and take a sharp turn away from my blunder. "Has that happened to you yet?" I ask, reaching for my drink, praying it can cool me off. "I got a doozy of a message last week on Instagram. Reese24 told me his dick would look huge in my *baby-hand*."

"Oh my god." Bo's face distorts as he laughs in horror.

"Yep."

"That's so many layers of fucked-up."

"Truly."

"But . . ." Bo lifts two palms, mimicking a tilting scale.

"No," I say, punctuated by a shocked laugh. "No. Don't you dare."

"I *mean*," his eyes turn teasing as he shrugs, "he's right. It probably would."

"Oh my god."

"It would do a great deal for the ego. Reese24 may be onto something."

"Awful," I sputter through a laugh. "You're both awful." I curl my lips up to my nose like the room stinks as Bo sits back comfortably, his arm once again resting behind me.

We continue to make small talk for enough time that Sarah's playlist has now replayed "Monster Mash" twice. Bo laughs at my theory around the song, unlike witch woman, and eventually decides he'll need to do his own research with a thoughtful analysis of the lyrics once he gets home. The party is starting to die down when our conversation does too. A slow fade to contented quiet and a third round of drinks fetched by me.

But, oddly enough, our lull in conversation isn't uncomfortable. I've been on plenty of dates where the banter stops flowing and it's easier to either call it quits or take things back to someone's apartment than it is to wait for the next quippy exchange to roll in. But tonight, there's no shortage of topics and no fear of some forced, humorless conversation.

These quiet reprieves feel more like intermissions. As if we're performing for each other. Taking turns being the entertainment and the entertained. Keeping each other laughing. Keeping each other guessing. It's *fun,* and part of me wishes we had more time before Sarah and Caleb decide to kick everyone out for the night. But *maybe* I could convince him to stay a little longer.

Given everything I've learned about Bo so far, I'll have to take the lead. He's so completely unaware of his own charm it's comical. He's shy, almost. I could see him asking for my number, but I doubt he'd be bold enough to ask me back to his place. Which, I've decided, is what I want to do.

"Is this a wig?"

I don't notice until I feel the back of Bo's finger brush my cheek, but he's holding a strand of my hair between his thumb and finger, twiddling it mindlessly.

"No, that's all me." I gulp as his thumb grazes the underside of my chin.

He continues twisting my hair through his fingers, curling it around the backs of his knuckles as if it's a snake he's charmed. I fight the urge to crawl into his lap and purr.

"Sorry," he whispers, wetting his lips. I notice that he doesn't let go, however.

"I don't mind," I answer softly. What I *should* say is: Keep touching me. Anywhere you'd like.

"It's beautiful," he tells me, looking at me with an unsteadying lack of humor. He releases my hair and leans back, taking a long breath that flares his nostrils. "I've had too much punch, probably."

"I really didn't mind." I lean in, trying to catch his gaze. Attempting to plead with him, silently, to ask for more. But it's no use. He's so gorgeous, yet clearly oblivious of that fact. It's as endearing as it is frustrating.

So I decide enough is enough. I can take charge. I'm a modern woman, dammit. I can go after what I want, even if I don't exactly practice that concept in my daily life. I can do this.

"Bo, would you like to go upstairs with me?" I ask, my voice a touch louder than intended after forcing myself to speak with confidence.

His eyes widen in surprise, and his head tilts. "Upstairs?"

I didn't count on having to repeat myself. Or clarify. I feel like covering my face with a couch cushion, but *screw* it. I'm in it now. "Would you, maybe, like to go have sex with me? I have a room here," I explain, trying my best to keep my spine straight in order to not shrink into myself. The illusion of confidence is key.

"Here?" His brow twists in confusion.

"Yes?"

"Do—do you live here?"

"No, I just stay here a lot." I wait a few seconds, hoping he'll put me out of my misery, but he appears far off and a little stunned. Was I truly misinterpreting all of this? I've been off before, but never *this* much. This seemed like a sure thing.

He laughs nervously, his head hanging. "Uh, actually, um—"

Blame the neon punch, I tell myself. "Sorry. Forget I said anything." I will lie to myself in order to move past this. Bo is a virgin. Celibate due to his solemn lifelong vow. I've been the most tempting offer he's ever had, but he must stay strong. It's not me. It's not me! It's not—

"No," he says a little too forcefully. "Don't—don't forget it. Uh, sorry, it's just"—he shakes his head—"I haven't since . . ." His eyes fall to where his hand rests on his knee, right above where his prosthesis begins.

Ah.

I should think. I should *absolutely* think before I speak. But I don't. I rarely do, unfortunately. "Did something happen to your . . . ?" I finish the sentence I never should have spoken by pointing to his lap.

Winnifred June McNulty, you cannot ask people if their junk is broken. What is wrong with you?

"Oh, no. Nothing. Top shape." He winces at his choice of words. Or perhaps just the conversation overall.

I have to fix this. I'm not this person—the one who pries and fumbles and makes someone feel uncomfortable about their body or its differences. I cannot be that person. That'd make me a *massive* hypocrite.

I approach gently, resting my hand on top of his. "Then I'm sure it's not all that different." I hesitate, waiting for him to make eye contact with me. "I'm willing to try, if you are. It could be a lot of fun."

He turns to face me, and his eyes are darkened, enlarged pupils and tight-knit brow. "Why was that so hot?" he asks, whispering, his voice near disbelief.

There it is, I think. A sliver of my pride returns.

"The moment you shook my hand with your left, I was ready to do this." I bite down on my smile. "I imagine it's something similar to that? Knowing I get the holdup, to some extent?"

His eyes dip down to my lips again as he nods, eyes entranced and glistening.

"So what will it be?" I ask, leaning close enough that I can count the exact number of freckles on his cheeks that spread across his nose like a bridge. "Because if I have to inquire again, I may attempt to drown myself in the punch bowl."

Without hesitation, Bo closes the distance between us and kisses me, tender and brief, with his hand across my jaw. His lips are plush and warm and damn near intoxicating. "Yes," he says, inhaling hungrily, his forehead pressed against mine. He laughs lowly, tucking a strand of my hair behind my ear before letting the same hand drag down my neck, shoulder, and arm. "C'mon," he says, taking my hand in his as he moves away to stand.

"Wait," I say, pulling him back. "I'm going to go upstairs first. I'll make sure no one else has gotten the same idea and is defiling the guest bedroom. You go to the kitchen and get us some water or something. It's the last door on the left."

"Okay." He nods eagerly, a few too many times for my liking. It reminds me of Caleb's puppy-dog willingness, causing a quick thrill of panic to course through me.

I can't handle one more guy being *too* nice in the bedroom. I need to know that all this chemistry between us won't fizzle out the moment we get upstairs.

"Bo, can you promise me something?" I ask.

His bottom lip pushes out as he nods again, less eagerly. "Sure?"

"I need you to promise me that we'll *both* enjoy tonight. I've had a string of lousy hookups this year, and if I have to fake another orgasm, I think I'll be legally required to become a nun or something." I bite my lip, anxious that I perhaps am asking too much from him, a near-perfect stranger.

He doesn't bat an eye, but his boyish grin comes back in full, brutal force. "Win, if you walk out of that room sturdier than me, I won't be happy."

A leg joke? Be still my beating heart.

I cover my mouth as I gasp, a singular laugh breaking through. "You did *not*."

"I did," he says, relaxing back on the couch. He raises his hand back to my hair again, playing with it as his eyes fall yet again to my lips with equal measures of desire and amusement. "Now . . . go upstairs and wait for me."

Hannah Bonam-Young is the author of *Next of Kin, Next to You,* and *Out on a Limb*. Hannah writes romances featuring a cast of diverse, disabled, marginalized, and LGBTQIA+ folks wherein swoonworthy storylines blend with the beautiful, messy, and challenging realities of life. When not reading or writing romance you can find her having living room dance parties with her kids or planning any occasion that warrants a cheese board. Originally from Ontario, Canada, she lives with her childhood-friend-turned-husband, Ben, two kids, and a bulldog near Niagara Falls on the traditional territory of the Haudenosaunee and Anishinaabe peoples.

hannahbywrites.com
Instagram: @authorhannahby
TikTok: @hannahby_writes